Chasing Happy

Laurene Bobb-Semple

ISBN-10: 1500857580
ISBN-13: 978-1500857585

DEDICATION

This book is dedicated to my family and friends; especially those who read the original drafts and believed in Chasing Happy before I did….

Thank you to those who both encouraged and lectured me…I literally couldn't have gotten to this point without you….you know who you are ☺

To my Grandparents who aren't here to share this with me, I hope I've made you proud.

To everyone chasing something, dreams, love, happiness… never give up, never lose faith, always believe….

PROLOGUE

Kieran examined her reflection in the mirror. Sparkling eyes and flushed cheeks expelled a glow that emphasised her growing excitement. It had been a long time since she looked so alive, so happy.

God I'm going to get myself into trouble. She thought and giggled like a schoolgirl.

If she gave in it would make everything Darren had accused her of true; she didn't want to give him that satisfaction. Did she really care what he thought anymore? He had accused her of cheating so many times that going through with it would be self-fulfilling prophecy on his part and maybe then he would let her go. She raised an eyebrow. Who was she kidding? Darren would never let her go. Not without a fight.

Sighing, she squirted toothpaste onto the toothbrush and began brushing her teeth, at the same time she heard her phone vibrating in her bag. Instinct told her it was one of her friends. She ignored it. What would she tell them? There was nothing to tell, at least not at that moment. She rinsed her mouth, grateful for the fresh feeling. There was nothing worse than a drunken furry mouth, especially after throwing up.

Kieran cringed as she remembered her embarrassment after vomiting in his presence. She covered her face with her hand wondering how he could still be interested in her after witnessing such an unladylike spectacle. If it was the other way round, Kieran would have made her excuses and run a mile. Still, there was something about him she couldn't resist, hence her standing in his hotel bathroom debating whether to cheat, or not to cheat on her boyfriend. It was obvious she wanted him. He knew it and so, too, did her friends. The question was would she be able to live with the guilt?

This scenario was new territory for her since she had never had a one-night-stand and she had no idea how to behave. All she knew was that there was something she couldn't explain going on between them and something she had never felt before. Was there any meaning to the something, or was it because she was intoxicated from consuming too much alcohol and now her senses were liquefied and she was incapable of being rational?

Kieran sighed. Her life was complicated. She should be strong and walk away. It was the best thing to do. With a steely look into the mirror she told her reflection;

You will behave yourself. Go out there and ask him to walk you to your hotel!

But the gleam in her eye and the heat she was feeling all over her body at the thought of the man waiting for her told her different. She was sure that all he wanted was a bit of meaningless fun. Who went on holiday to fall in love? A one night stand was all it would be, it was all it could be.

This sudden clarification cleared Kieran's mind and she felt empowered. Not only would she regret a one night stand, she knew a one night stand with him would torture her. Deep down she knew that she wouldn't want it to end there, no matter how many times she told herself it was just a bit of fun.

She needed to get back to her hotel, before she made a big mistake. Rummaging in her bag, she took out a hairbrush, brushed her hair, added a new coat of lip gloss and inspected her image in the mirror.

I still look happy, damn it!

He was asleep on the bed fully clothed and snoring lightly. Kieran's heart melted along with her resolve. She found herself being pulled towards him even though her conscience and sanity screamed at her to make her escape. She tip toed over to the bed and tentatively climbed in next to him. It wasn't her intention to wake him, Kieran just wanted to be close to the beautiful man who had come into her life hours before and made her feel emotions she didn't know existed, if only for a little while. Before she could settle, he opened his green eyes.

"Hi." he said

"Hey," Kieran replied with a grin.

"Are you getting into bed with me? I thought you wanted to go?" he asked raising an eyebrow.

"You looked so peaceful; I didn't want to wake you,"

"What happened to not being alone together because you weren't sure you trusted yourself?" he teased.

Kieran bit her lip, when she was drunk she had to make an effort to monitor what words came out of her mouth. Why would she admit that to him of all people? He was staring at her as if he was trying to figure out what was going through her mind. She didn't know herself. She knew she should have left but she just wanted to spend a little more time with him before they went their separate ways. Plus if they just slept how much trouble could she get into? They could behave – they were adults after all, they should be able to exercise some self-control.

Anything else would just complicate things. She didn't want to fall for him; she'd been through enough heartache. She looked down at Rome who was still staring at her.

"So do you want to go? You didn't answer my question," he asked sitting up and yawning.

"Do you want me to go?" she asked before she could stop herself.

He gazed at her for longer than necessary and Kieran felt as if a huge butterfly was fluttering in her stomach.

Breathe. She reminded herself.

"No, I don't. But the question is do you want to go?" he finally responded with a cheeky grin that emphasised his dimples.

Kieran shook her head, no. It was all she could manage.

Rome smiled. "Well that's settled then." He lay back down pulling her close to him and closed his eyes. She couldn't believe he wasn't going to try anything. Even though it was the smartest thing he could do, her ego was bruised.

"Are we really just going to sleep?" Her face flushed as she spoke aloud. Why couldn't she just go to sleep and shut up? It was like she had been struck down with a case of verbal diarrhea.

Clearly she was still drunk.

He opened one eye, a smile played on his perfect lips. "What else did you have in mind?"

The heat from her face flowed through her body. She wouldn't dare verbalise what she had in mind. She imagined she could fall big time for him if they took it any further. She'd heard a theory that when women slept with men, their bodies released certain chemicals that made them develop feelings. She guessed that was why friends with benefits relationships never worked. Someone would always develop feelings, usually the women, because men were good at turning off their feelings and generally being assholes.

Kieran frowned then heard him chuckle. He was teasing her. He reached out pulling her towards him. He smelled good. Kieran's heart pounded loud in her ears and she struggled to keep her breathing even. She closed her eyes as she lay against him. She tried to keep a handle on her errant thoughts, there was a lot she wanted to say but she kept it to herself. What good would it do to tell him how she was feeling? After some time had passed, she snuck a peek at him.

His jaw was clenched and Kieran could not deny that he was the most beautiful man she had ever laid eyes on. She rolled her eyes, aware how corny her thoughts were, but it was true. Her eyes were drawn to his lips again, full and inviting. Kieran wanted to kiss him so bad. It felt like hours since their first kiss. Her stomach danced at the thought of it. She leaned in to kiss him. Her face was inches away from his when he opened his eyes.

"You haven't answered my question, again." he said kissing the tip of her nose. Kieran couldn't answer. She was hot, too hot and she knew it was due to him, because the air conditioning was on full blast.

"I think I still have a lot of alcohol in my system, my head is spinning a little," she mumbled unable to look at him. He pulled her closer and ran his hand down her back. Kieran shivered involuntarily. He was torturing her. Was he doing it on purpose?

"You have goose bumps, are you cold?" he rubbed her bare arms. Kieran used the opportunity to snuggle against him. He made a sound of appreciation. "I could get used to this," he told her.

"Don't say things like that if I don't get to keep you," she whispered as she closed her eyes. He was intoxicating in more ways than one. How was her life ever going to be the same after this? How would she be able to look Darren in the eye when she got home? She didn't know or care if she was honest.

"Kieran?"

She looked directly into his eyes and was unprepared for the wanting that accosted her. Thankfully she was lying against him, since her legs had lost all feeling.

"I'm going to kiss you now, you can stop me if you want," he told her.

She could hear the laughter in her head; clearly he thought she was sensible where he was concerned - how wrong he was. His eyes burned into hers. Kieran felt like he could see into the very depths of her soul. She shivered again and he wrapped his arms around her. Kieran knew that she should stop him, that lying there together would lead to more than just kissing. She didn't want to stop him; she was already in too deep. The vibe between them, from the moment they met was just too strong. The possibility of intimacy lingered in the air; if he didn't make the first move, Kieran knew right then and there that she would. She wanted him more than she'd ever wanted anyone.

He cupped her face and tipped her chin up towards his mouth. Kieran closed her eyes as her heart rate picked up and her breathing changed. She welcomed his kiss, his touch and the feelings he sent through her body.

The last thing she was conscious of before their lips met was that what she was doing was wrong, very wrong. Strange enough though, it felt so right and she pushed all thoughts of Darren and their problems at home to the back of her mind. All she was certain of was that at that moment she was right where she wanted to be.

1 CHAPTER ONE

Two months earlier

Kieran clenched her teeth to control her shallow breathing and the erratic anger that pulsed through her body. She and Darren had been arguing for well over fifteen minutes, and neither of them showed any signs of backing down.

"I've never known anyone as selfish as you. You don't care how I feel about anything!" Darren continued to rant.

"I gave up a job in New York for you, what more do you want from me?!" Kieran screeched. She swallowed from the burning in her throat. The nonstop shouting was taking its toll, but she was outraged at her boyfriend's attitude and her stubbornness wouldn't allow her to back down. Who did he think he was?

Darren threw his PlayStation control across the room. A loud thud sounded as it hit the wooden floor. Kieran was familiar with this tactic. It was his way of trying to scare her into submission; she refused to give in.

"I didn't force you to stay!" he shouted.

"You didn't exactly give me a choice either!" she hissed as she stormed into the bedroom slamming the door behind her. Darren was right behind her. He threw the door open with such force, it swung back and would have hit him had he not sidestepped out of its way. Kieran wished it had. She wanted to smile at the image in her head but decided against it. Darren would only accuse her of something else ridiculous.

"I didn't give you a choice?" he repeated.

"No!" she snapped, "You didn't. Don't you remember?" she folded her arms across her chest in defiance and glared at him.

"Why didn't you just go?"

Kieran mulled over his query. It was a good question. Why hadn't she gone? Oh, yes. Maybe it had something to do with him threatening to hurt himself if she did. She wished she'd called his bluff. Before she could answer, he stomped over to the wardrobe and took out a jacket.

"I can't look at you right now. You are selfish, inconsiderate, and spiteful and I don't know why I bother sometimes," she said in a calm voice, as she sat on the bed. Reaching over to the nightstand, Kieran picked up a magazine and flicked through the pages displaying a lack of interest she knew would piss him off further.

"Fuck you!" Darren roared. He slammed the wardrobe door and stalked out of the room. Kieran heard the front door bang seconds later. She took a deep breath and fought the angry tears that threatened to flow she was livid. Who was he to tell her where she could go and who she could go with?

Darren, without shame, had told her she wasn't allowed to go on holiday after Kieran told him that she and her two best friends, Christina and Chantelle, had decided on a girl's trip for a week to Greece. The very thought that he felt she needed his permission incensed her. Kieran had left home a long time ago. She was an adult. She was tired of him trying to control her life. She had given in to him once too often. This time she refused to.

A few weeks before, Kieran had been offered a chance-of-a-lifetime to assist with setting up the New York office of the PR Company her mum's sister, Janet, owned and where she worked as Junior Publicist. It was not only an opportunity to showcase her expertise; Kieran wanted to experience living in a different country. Her dream was to travel across the world, go on adventures and meet new people. Her excitement came to a halt when she told Darren. He had not hidden his disgust at the idea, which led to a big argument and an even bigger ultimatum: her career, or their relationship.

Kieran chose the relationship and had been regretful ever since. The resentment she felt towards Darren for making her choose increased daily, more so when they argued. With a heavy sigh, she tossed the magazine aside and headed into the shower to cool down.

Over the following three days, Darren stayed at his parent's house and so Kieran didn't have to see his face. In a bitter-sweet way she enjoyed having her house and her bed to herself, until he returned and apologised for his behaviour. She gave in to him, not because she forgave him; it meant a quieter life for her – though she knew it would be short-lived.

Since the New York incident, his controlling behaviour had grown worse. After their shouting matches, he would apologise only to fly off the handle about something else a few days later. His apologies had since become redundant.

He held her tight as they lay in bed. Kieran eased herself away from him and sighed. She felt restless, claustrophobic and needed space in more ways than one.

At twenty-three, Kieran was a year younger than Darren. When she first moved into the flat, she loved the independence of her own space. The freedom to do what she wanted when she wanted without her parents moaning at her, she didn't have to answer to anyone. However, the novelty soon wore off and she felt lonely, so Kieran did the most adult thing she had ever done and asked Darren to move in with her.

He worked four days a week as an assistant manager for a well-known sports shop supervising the day-to-day running of the store, stocktaking and sorting through deliveries. His salary was average, allowing him to just about contribute to the household bills. He had been there since he was sixteen, appeared to be content, and showed no signs of wanting to leave.

The first eighteen months of their relationship were good, though tentative at times, like most relationships. His attentiveness and kind gestures made her feel wanted. She loved having him around; he prepared dinner for her after she returned home from work, surprised her by buying flowers and chocolate and took her out to dinner and the movies frequently, and they spent time making love, or just snuggling.

Since his ultimatum, maybe even before, he had stopped doing things for her. When he did anything nice, it was usually out of guilt for a past argument, which made the gesture less genuine. Kieran knew he loved her, but not the way she wanted to be loved, which led to her feeling irritated.

His faults that she tolerated in the past were now magnified and she grew frustrated with much of his behaviour for instance when he did not help to clean up around the house, or suddenly forgetting how to put the toilet seat back down. To add, Kieran hated when he invited his friends over. She was left to clean up crisps, chocolate packets and empty beer cans that they would leave lying around. Their untidy behaviour improved after Kieran returned home one day and saw the mess they had made while they played computer games. It hadn't helped that she had a serious case of PMT that month and in a premenstrual rage, she shouted at them to either clean up, or never come back. It worked.

Kieran sighed again. Maybe he'd change, Maybe he'd see with him was where she wanted to be and go back to normal. But did she really want to be with him? She rolled onto her side away from him.

It's not meant to be this hard or this twisted.

He was getting worse and showed no signs that he was going to change. She had to end it. She rubbed her eyes, looked at the clock and groaned. It was past midnight and she couldn't sleep. Perhaps it was the summer heat. For May it was unusually warm. Her flat was stifling.

Like my relationship with Darren.

Feeling aggravated, she got up. Darren didn't flinch. Kieran switched on the TV in the living room. The movie 'Waiting to exhale' flooded the screen. Though she had to get up early, she plunked her one-hundred-and-twelve-pounds body onto the sofa. Perhaps her eyes would get tired if she watched the movie. After a few minutes, Kieran lost interest; she had seen it umpteen times and she had enough man problems of her own. She thought about calling Christina or Chantelle to have a rant; neither of them would be amused if she called at such an ungodly hour.

She surfed the channels and smiled as Sex and the City, her favourite TV series lit up the screen; four women living and working in New York. Kieran felt a pang of envy and wondered why on earth she had given up her chance of emulating their lifestyle. She loved their independence and career aspirations.

Even though relationships were important to them, their true loves were their careers and the men in their lives had to accept that, or they weren't good enough to be with them. Kieran wished she could stand alone like them because she felt in her heart that staying with Darren would not make her happy the way progressing in her career and living in New York would have.

She smiled, as Miranda, Charlotte, Samantha and Carrie sat over a picnic lunch in Central Park sipping coffee, laughing and joking with each other in the bright New York sunshine.

Kieran's emotions suddenly got the better of her and the tears pricked at her eyes. Her life would have been different if she had been brave enough to make the move. She realised that she had made a huge mistake by staying. She should've gone, but she allowed fear to take over after Darren started his rubbish and she gave into him, because it made it easier for her not to have to do something so hard. She couldn't imagine being by herself, without her family and friends. She would've coped eventually wouldn't she? It had been her chance and she blew it.

Plus the shopping would have been amazing.....

Kieran changed the channel before she became more depressed. She cast her eyes towards the bedroom door. Darren was content with his life; Kieran wanted more. Her tired eyes surveyed her surroundings.

Two black leather sofas faced each other in the living room. They complemented the cream coloured walls. A rather large mirror was placed above one of the sofas giving the room a bigger feel. The flat screen TV and DVD player sat in front of the five-bayed windows. A bookshelf in one corner housed pictures of her family and friends, while a pine dining table and four chairs at the back end made up the dining area. Plants were strategically placed around the flat; Kieran especially liked the two tall yucca plants facing each other in the dining area. Kieran's friends found her plant obsession quite strange, and nicknamed the flat 'the greenhouse' which amused her.

Apart from her bedroom with its turquoise green walls that reminded her of Tiffany's, and pine furniture, the living room was her favourite room. The floors throughout the flat were laminated, which had a cooling effect in the summer. During the winter, she warmed the floor with rugs that she appropriately placed around;

all with hints of green. She fell in love with the first floor flat the first time she saw it. Sometimes she still couldn't believe she lived there. Kieran was proud of herself for working hard to make her flat her home. Until recently, Kieran hadn't thought about living anywhere else.

She headed into the stuffy kitchen. The yellow walls and blue tiled kitchen floor looked odd to her for the first time. She frowned. It was time for a change. The kitchen was the one room she hadn't decorated. Opening the window, Kieran allowed the light breeze to graze her face. It wasn't cool, but it felt good.

She reached into the fridge for a bottle of water, as Darren walked in. Kieran turned away and stared out of the window. She inhaled in an attempt to avoid erupting, as she felt anger bubbling inside her. She could never get a moment's peace with him around.

"Babe, why are you still up?" he asked yawning and squinting.

"I can't sleep. I'm surprised you noticed," she snapped unable to control her reaction.

"Of course, I noticed that's why I got up," he said taking a step towards her.

"Whatever Darren," she mumbled and walked past him. She sat back down on the sofa, picked up the remote and increased the volume on the TV hoping he would take the hint – she was in no mood to talk to him.

He followed her. "What's your problem?" he asked raising his voice.

"Go back to sleep," Kieran's voice was firm, but harsh. It was too late for them to start screaming at each other; the neighbours wouldn't be impressed.

Darren kissed his teeth and stomped off. After a few minutes, Kieran felt the guilt set in.

What was wrong with her? He hadn't done anything to annoy her. She was just being a bitch to him because of the New York situation, and it was only partly his fault. Kieran wanted their relationship to work, that had been the whole point of her not going to New York. She had to make an effort and she would attempt to make things better - but she was going to Greece whether he liked it or not. She entered the bedroom. Darren had turned on the bedside lamp. The faint light cast a warm glow around the room. He lay face down on the bed.

"Darren."

No response. "Are you going to ignore me now?" She asked through gritted teeth. She wanted to punch him. "Well?"

"No," he replied in an indifferent tone.

"So, then speak to me."

"I am speaking to you."

Kieran sighed; he was going to be difficult. She joined him in bed and kissed his shoulder. He turned and pulled her towards him. He was a sucker for any affection she showed him. Kieran had been avoiding any physical contact with him over the last few months. However, as she was planning on making an effort, she gave in. It was another conflict she let him win.

When Kieran awoke, she was in a surprisingly good mood, considering she only had three hours sleep; pleasing Darren had taken longer than she had expected. He was obviously sucking up, because normally he was a selfish lover. Maybe he wanted to make the most of it since she didn't stop him. It wasn't bad in hindsight. A refreshing difference compared to their usual lovemaking, which lacked any kind of spontaneity or excitement. Every move he had Kieran knew down to a T, and that made her unenthusiastic about having sex with him. She usually had her excuses ready when he approached her. Making love with Darren, however, wasn't why she felt happy about the day ahead.

Her good mood could only be testament to the fact that she was going to spend the day shopping with Corey, her older sister by two years. She was getting married in Jamaica in the next few weeks and Kieran agreed to go shopping with her as part of her maid of honour duties. Corey would take umbrage if she didn't take it seriously. Kieran, however, loved any excuse to shop, so she had no complaints about the day ahead. She dragged herself out of bed after snoozing the alarm clock twice, showered, got dressed – and then kissed the still sleeping Darren on his forehead before leaving.

Kieran poked her tongue out at her sister when she approached her outside Oxford Street station.

"Someone got some last night." Corey said with a grin.

"How would you know that?" Kieran asked as they linked arms and began walking, weaving in and out to avoid bumping into people. It amazed Kieran that Regent Street was teeming with crowds of people so early.

"I can see it in those big, light-brown eyes of yours; I've seen that glow before. Hell, I've experienced that glow," Corey added with a mischievous grin.

"Okay, where do you want to go first? I have stuff to do later," Kieran said ignoring her taunts.

"Darren?" Corey continued to tease her.

Kieran didn't want to discuss Darren. If she were to tell Corey about his behaviour, she would tell her to dump him. Corey didn't take shit from anyone, least of all men. She expected her little sister to be the same. She would kill Darren if she knew the truth about their relationship. Plus talking about him would ruin their shopping trip. "Corey, you're too damn nosey," she told her and watched as her mouth fell open in mock horror. Corey kissed her teeth and pretended to cut her eyes at her. They burst out laughing at their silliness.

At 5'4, and petite, they sported a strong resemblance to their father; the only distinct differences in their features being Corey's skin was a lighter complexion than Kieran's cinnamon skin tone. Her dark eyes were wise, knowing. Corey had a knack for reading people. She knew what was what.

Kieran often wore her shoulder length hair naturally curly and usually in a ponytail as she hated hair in her face. Whereas Corey's was cut into medium length bob that framed her face. Growing up, Corey was referred to as a tomboy by family and friends. She loved being outdoors, hated wearing dresses and as they grew into teenagers, she disliked makeup. As she matured, her outdoor activities escalated to rock climbing and sky diving. Corey loved all things related to sports. She had met her husband to be Jack, bungee jumping. Kieran had her tomboy moments; though she quickly grew out of it. She enjoyed watching football, tennis and sometimes rugby, although it was usually to ogle men in shorts as she preferred less strenuous activities than her sister. She was in her element visiting the theatre, eating out, travelling, and of course, shopping. She lived for clothes and make-up and loved being girly.

Kieran was well aware that she could be a drama queen at times and with her quick temper tantrums and stubborn nature, she was the most dramatic out of the two, which had been a constant annoyance to Corey when they were younger, as it meant Kieran usually got her own way. Their sisterly bond never wavered, however, and they made a pact that it was going to stay that way no matter what.

Kieran was grateful for her family and friends. It was comforting to know that there were certain areas of her life she wouldn't change for the world. She tightened her hold on her sister's arm and smiled as they entered one of her favourite shops, Zara.

2 CHAPTER TWO

The answering machine was flashing when Kieran got home. She placed her numerous shopping bags down, dialled her voicemail and heard Christina's voice.

"Where the hell are you?"

"Hello to you too, Christina," she said deleting the message before it finished then called her friend. They had met when they were two-years-old at nursery school. From then on, their academic lives were identical with both gaining ten GCSE's and three A' levels. Their friendship continued to go from strength to strength so that they were more like sisters rather than friends. Though she could sometimes be brash, Christina always had her back.

"You're home at last?" she said without saying hello.

"Yes clearly." Kieran teased.

"Yeah, well, we'll be around in five."

We, usually meant her and Chantelle, and in five meant they were probably at the bottom of Kieran's road. Chantelle, whom they met in secondary school, was the third of her four close friends.

"Melanie isn't with you is she?" Kieran asked as she spotted a beer can underneath the sofa. She blew out a deep breath and counted to five before prying out the offending can and feeling for any spillages. Lucky for Darren and his friends, the floor was as dry as a bone.

"No, Chantelle's ignoring her calls – we'll be there in a

minute." Christina hung up before Kieran could respond.

She smiled, glad that Chantelle was ignoring Melanie's calls. She wasn't being mean. Chantelle didn't have a mean bone in her body. Melanie was simply that annoying. When they had met her at college, she seemed friendly. Before long, however, Kieran grew wary of her shrill and obnoxious attitude, the most annoying being competing with the rest of the girls. Kieran avoided judging her and did her best to show her that females could be friends without competing against each other.

The problem was Melanie loved attention from the opposite sex, most of whom she slept with. At first, Kieran put it down to Melanie not knowing how to be herself around boys; perhaps she had insecurities, but in time it became transparent that she liked being the centre of attention. Kieran had told her many times that she didn't need to sleep with every man she met; Melanie didn't grasp the concept well, she took every opportunity to visit Kieran just to be around Darren's friends.

Kieran picked up the shopping bags as her landline rang. Melanie's number was flashing on the screen. Kieran kissed her teeth ignoring it, she wasn't in the mood for her company, she was glad her mobile had died.

"Melanie just called. She must know we're deliberately ignoring her. She isn't stupid," Kieran told Christina and Chantelle once they had arrived and were sat in the living room. Christina, who was a few inches taller than Kieran, picked up the TV remote and begun flicking through the TV channels.

"That's debatable. So, where did you go this morning?" Chantelle asked changing the subject.

"Oxford Street with Corey – wedding shopping."

"You must've been underground when I tried to call, so I phoned here, but didn't get much sense out of idiot boy," Christina added rolling her eyes.

Kieran laughed in spite of herself. Was it wrong that she didn't defend her boyfriend?

Nope. He deserves it.

"Did he change his mind about Greece?" Chantelle asked as she took her jacket off and laid it on the arm of the sofa. She was the second tallest, at five seven.

"I don't actually care whether he has or not. I'm going, and he has to accept it."

Chantelle applauded.

"It's a shame Amelia can't come. It would have been nice for all of us to get away," Christina added.

"I know. We hardly get to see her these days." Kieran said shaking her head.

Amelia completed Kieran's quartet of friends. She had gotten married when they finished college and had recently given birth to her second child. They had all shared the same loud personalities and during school the same sense of fashion, though Kieran tried her best not to remember that part. They disagreed over many things, but their individual opinions, however, did not interfere with their friendship. Kieran never took her friends for granted. She would be lost without them. They had been best friends for so many years, and had been through a lot on the road to womanhood. They still had a fair way to go and would get through whatever was in store for them together.

"That's what happens when your priorities change," Chantelle said. Kieran murmured in agreement

"So what are we doing tonight?" Christina asked changing the subject and the channel.

"Dunno, I'm up for anything," Kieran replied taking the remote control from her. She could never watch one channel and it drove Kieran mad.

"Give it back." Christina complained.

"No, I will find something for us to watch," Kieran said and selected a music channel.

"I don't want to listen to music." Christina whined trying to get the remote back from Kieran. She switched it to her other hand and screamed dramatically when Christina pinched her arm.

Chantelle cleared her throat. "How old are you two?" she asked raising her eyebrows.

Kieran laughed and pinched Christina back. She cried out in a high pitched screech.

"Shut up," Kieran giggled covering her ears; sometimes they were still so juvenile.

Their girlish giggles were interrupted when the front door opened. Darren entered, followed by two of his friends, Anthony and Jordan. Kieran rolled her eyes. Their fun was ruined.

"Hey baby," Darren said as he walked over and kissed Kieran on the lips.

"Hey," she replied.

They had all attended the same college, so no introductions were required. Sometimes they all socialised, depending on the girls' moods. It was evident the girls only tolerated the boys because Kieran and Darren were an item. The girls had outgrown them a long time ago. Darren had told her once that his friends believed the girls thought they were superior to them, because they seemed to like embarrassing them. Kieran didn't admit it to his face but it was true.

"What do you lot want?" Christina asked.

"Don't go on like you're not happy to see us," Anthony teased as he sat down next to her. He was possibly the cutest out of the boys, though he had his annoying moments.

"Okay Ant, whatever makes you happy," Kieran said rolling her eyes and joined her friends in sarcastic laughter.

"So what you lot on tonight?" Jordan asked as he sat down next to Chantelle.

"Would it hurt you to form a proper sentence? We aren't in college anymore. Try speaking English for a change," Chantelle told him as she flicked through a magazine clearly irritated by their presence.

Kieran wanted to laugh, but refrained, and watched as the boys exchanged glances. Darren kissed his teeth loudly from the back of the room where he was fiddling with the stereo.

"Kieran, what are you lot doing tonight?" Jordan asked.

"We don't know yet," she said stifling her laughter.

"Ben's having some rave, that we'll be reaching," Jordan offered speaking of his brother and ignoring their cackles.

"Are you inviting us?" Chantelle asked.

"I don't know if it will be suitable for you ladies," Anthony said in a posh accent.

"Yes, maybe you would prefer dinner with the Queen?" Jordan said, also in a posh accent. The boys laughed and touched fists, as if they had accomplished something worthy. Darren joined in guffawing.

Kieran, Chantelle and Christina exchanged glances; their expressions mirrored their thoughts; they were surrounded by idiots.

It was a twenty minute drive without traffic from Islington where Kieran lived to Hackney in East London, where the party was being held. The Girls had decided to join the boys since they had no previous plans and couldn't make any up quick enough; they decided to drive just in case they had to make a quick getaway.

Kieran got into Christina's car and developed an instant headache from the weird, no rhythm dance music bellowing from the CD player.

"What the hell is this?" she asked covering her ears and screwing up her face; Chantelle groaned and held her head.

"It's my car and my music," Christina told them. She had a point, but Kieran glowered at her all the same and cringed when Christina raised the volume and laughed wickedly at them before pulling out and following Darren and his friends in Jordan's car.

The house where the party was being held was situated in a cul-de-sac. Kieran heard the loud music and felt the vibrations when the car turned into the road. Christina parked the car and Kieran watched the boys get out of their car and stroll toward the house. They wore sunglasses even though it was late at night. It amused Kieran that the boys thought they were so hot.

"Seriously, why are we friends with them?" Christina asked.

"Friend is a strong word and I don't know," Kieran offered bewildered.

"They are boys masquerading as men," Chantelle offered.

Kieran studied Darren as he stood outside the house smoking. She wasn't sure she was attracted to him anymore. At 5'11, he was slim and muscular. His brown eyes complimented his chocolate complexion and his cheeky smile, which showed a gold tooth which matched his out-going personality.

They were friends for three years before they took their friendship to the next level, which was weird at first; soon it was almost as if they had always been a couple. He had made Kieran feel so lucky in the beginning. Now she felt they had grown apart, or maybe it was just that she had she grown up and he hadn't. Corey told her that emotionally and mentally men were a few years behind women regardless of their age. If she was right, Darren, at twenty four, had a mental age of around eighteen, which explained a lot.

"Look at them. They're so dumb," Chantelle mused and rolled her eyes.

Kieran watched as they bounced to the beat with animated hand gestures, and their mouths moved, which told Kieran that they were rapping along to the music – performing for anyone who cared enough to pay attention.

"Are you two ready to get this over with?" Kieran grumbled.

"Don't you want to go anymore?" Christina asked looking at her through the rear view mirror.

Kieran screwed up her face.

"We've been to so many parties recently. It would be nice if it was for a special occasion," Chantelle answered before Kieran could. Christina nodded in agreement.

"See, this is why we are friends. We are always on the same page," Kieran told them.

"Well, we're here now, if it's rubbish we'll leave," Christina suggested.

Kieran and Chantelle nodded in agreement before getting out of the car.

Surprisingly, the party was lively. The atmosphere was sociable with people dancing, or standing around in groups talking and laughing. Kieran quickly joined in. She was surprised to see acquaintances she hadn't seen in a while and not so surprised to see others - Melanie was there. She stood in the middle of a group of people recalling a story that interested none of them. The music changed to an old classic 'End of the Road' by Boyz To Men. The song filled the room and Kieran felt herself being whisked away by Darren. She was relieved to be away from Melanie, although she was sure she could still hear her voice over the music.

"Did I tell you how good you look tonight?" Darren said as he kissed her neck. "You are the most beautiful girl here. Everyone is looking at you," he continued.

Kieran tried not to roll her eyes. He always thought someone - some man, was looking at her. He'd put her on a pedestal when he must have known she wanted more than what he could offer her. She came to the conclusion that she just didn't love him anymore, and he must have seen it every time she looked at him, even the way she spoke to him was a giveaway. Kieran felt that was why he acted the way he did. He knew he was losing her; it was only a matter of time. He couldn't be as oblivious as he made out.

When she had needed someone in her life, he'd appeared like her knight in shining armour. At one time, Kieran worshipped the ground he walked on; that was a long time ago. So much had changed between them. She had changed.

"You're biased," she said craning her neck to look up at him.

"I'm not biased. My boys tell me every day how lucky I am and that we will get married," he gave her a wide grin.

Kieran looked at him and tried not to roll her eyes. He was delusional if he thought she was going to be around that long. "Really," she said trying to sound happy for his benefit, although she couldn't imagine anything worse.

"Yea man, they know we are meant to be," he said proudly.

She pressed her lips together in an effort not to make a smart comment. Sometimes her mouth got her into so much trouble. The song came to an end and an upbeat song replaced it. She let go of Darren. "I'm going outside for some air," she announced fanning herself with her hand. She felt trapped, claustrophobic and not just because she was in a house packed with people. She joined her friends who were huddled in a dark corner – probably hiding from Melanie.

"I'm going outside. It's hot in here," she told them.

"Want us to come with you?" Christina asked.

Kieran nodded and led the way. Chantelle and Christina followed her out into the front garden.

"What's up?" Chantelle asked.

"Nothing," Kieran lied sipping a drink.

"Hello! We've been your best friends for over ten years now we know when you're lying," Chantelle said nudging her playfully but harder than necessary due to her intoxication. If Kieran was drunk she would've gone flying.

"Oh, it's just something Darren said that bugged me," she conceded.

"What's he said now? I don't know why you don't end it," Christina added.

"I don't know either. He makes my skin crawl now," Kieran said cringing.

"Wow that is bad, how can you live with him? Just end it. He only takes the piss and tells you what to do. It doesn't work that way," Chantelle fumed.

"He said we will get married," Kieran said and screwed up her face at the thought.

Chantelle laughed. Christina looked mortified.

"It's not funny. Can I really marry someone who I am not attracted to, who tries to stop me from doing what I want or going where I want to go just to make himself feel secure?"

"Don't ask stupid questions. If you marry him, I will disown you and I'm not joking," Christina warned.

"Maybe it'll get better after our trip to Greece?" Kieran offered. She suddenly felt confused.

Her friends didn't respond, which Kieran took to mean that she was being stupid. Of course their situation wouldn't get better. Darren would be furious when he realised she was going and he would hold it against her for the foreseeable future.

Kieran sipped her Disaronno and Coke as his words swirled around her head. Usually she would brush off a comment like that, but it continued to bother her. Not long after, they left the party and it felt like no sooner was she asleep, the ringing of the doorbell interrupted her slumber.

Kieran groaned and got out of bed. The floor was cold, but she was too tired to fumble for her slippers. She stumbled to the door. Chantelle stood outside grinning at her.

"Are you mad?" Kieran asked her barely opening her eyes.

"It's one in the afternoon you should have been to church and back and have Sunday dinner ready," Chantelle said as she walked past her.

Kieran closed the door and followed her into the front room where she collapsed on the sofa next to her. She yawned.

"Don't sit around. Hurry up and get dressed. We are going shopping." Chantelle ordered.

Under normal circumstances, Kieran would not need to be told twice. However, she lacked sleep and she wanted to get back into her warm cosy bed. "Excuse me. We are doing no such thing," she said stretching.

"Yea we are. Summer sales, I need some bits for Jamaica," Chantelle said with excitement.

Kieran raised her eyebrows. She loved the summer sales and Chantelle knew that. "You are too damn sly," Kieran told her pretending to be annoyed. She folded her arms across her chest.

"How?" Chantelle asked in an attempt to look innocent.

"I'll give you how. Amuse yourself with the TV. I'll be back."

"See you in an hour then," Chantelle said rolling her eyes.

Kieran showed her the two finger salute before disappearing into her room.

"Why are we in here?" Kieran asked in a bored tone when Chantelle dragged her into Ann Summers a while later. She had no interest in spicing up her sex life especially her sex life with Darren.

"I want to check something out."

"Oh, we should get Corey something for her wedding night!" Kieran said brightening at the thought of her sister's wedding.

Chantelle ran her hands gingerly over a nurse's outfit complete with matching hat and crotch less knickers then she grimaced. "Isn't that weird, buying your sister sex clothes?"

"Eww, I just meant a nice, sexy underwear set or something. It can be her 'something new' on the day. Get your mind out of the gutter," Kieran told her laughing.

"Hello! It's her wedding night. What do you think she and Jack will be doing, holding hands?" Chantelle asked as she moved around the shop.

Kieran blushed as they passed the over-eighteen section that was partially shrouded with a heavy black velvet curtain.

"I'd rather not think about it."

Chantelle rolled her eyes.

"It's a shame Christina isn't coming to the wedding. She's always wanted to go to Jamaica as well," Kieran said as she thought about her friend, who couldn't make the trip as she was in a middle of her teaching degree. She picked up a black lace bra and thong set with blue ribbons around the edges. It was simple, yet sophisticated, not too girly and definitely Corey's style.

"I know, but this time next year she'll be a teacher," Chantelle said with excitement.

"Yeah," Kieran agreed as she picked up a 36C cup size for Corey. "We'll make up for it when we go to Greece."

Chantelle nodded and picked up a blue and white bra and thong set.

Kieran eyed her suspiciously. "Is there something you want to tell me?" she asked as they made their way over to the till and joined the queue.

"Nope," Chantelle answered, though a secretive smile played on her lips.

"Who are you sleeping with?" Kieran asked not beating around the bush.

"Ask me no questions and I'll tell you no lies," Chantelle said pretending to study the item in her hand.

Kieran studied her face for a few seconds and decided to let it go. If Chantelle was seeing someone, it would come out eventually. They blitzed through the sales and got some great bargains.

Kieran stocked up for both holiday trips then complained when they returned to her home laden with bags, "See that's why I don't like going shopping with you. You encourage me to spend."

"Don't blame me because you have no self-control." Chantelle teased. Kieran poked her tongue out at her friend but didn't argue – in truth Chantelle was right.

The Girls' light-hearted mood was cut short when they heard Darren and his friends' voices before they'd even opened the front door.

The boys were engaged in a football game on the PlayStation and making the most noise. Kieran wished for once she could come home and not have it full of noisy boys. To add, Melanie was also there. She was sat reading a magazine, which Kieran thought was strange. Usually she was in the thick of things.

"What brings you here Mel?" She asked as she perched on the arm of the sofa next to Darren. He paused the game, stood up, kissed her on the nose and headed into the kitchen. Chantelle barely acknowledged the boys and outright ignored Melanie.

"I was in the area, so I thought I'd pop in," she explained. Kieran nodded. She spent the next couple of hours chilling and sneakily taking the piss out of the boys with Chantelle until she realised the time, and reminded everyone she had to prepare for work the following day. She'd also noticed Darren's mood had turned sour as he threw her dirty looks. Kieran knew he was going to accuse her of something or another, which was another reason why she'd emptied her house of people in a hurry.

Melanie hovered and was the last to leave to her annoyance. Considering she popped round to see Kieran, she'd hardly spoken to her though Kieran was relieved, she did not have the energy or patience to deal with her.

With work on her mind, her thoughts turned to the press release she had to write the following day. It was the first time she would be writing without supervision and she felt the pressure. As she tidied up the kitchen, she thought about her role as Junior Publicist. Her job was basically to help create and control the public's perception of a product, person, or event, by creating as much positive exposure around them as possible. It was hectic at times, but Kieran loved how unpredictable and challenging it was. No two days were ever the same. She especially enjoyed meeting new people and assisting with organising events. She wasn't thrilled with the market research aspect. Nonetheless, it was part of the job. Kieran had learned a vast amount over the two years she was employed. However, she was ready for more responsibility and wanted to branch out on her own, organise more events, and be more involved with PR and advertising. She had out-grown the junior in her job title. New York would've been perfect for her.

With a sigh she finished in the kitchen and went to organise her work clothes before taking a shower. She was rummaging through the wardrobe when Darren entered the room. He sat on the bed watching her with a scowl. Kieran ignored him. Not getting any reaction, he walked over and stood next to her.

"What is it?" she asked with a sigh.

"You know what."

"No, I don't."

"Yea you do."

"Whatever. You know this will go a lot quicker if you just tell me what's bothering you, I know you're pissed off about something."

"Who are you talking to?" he asked gruffly.

There's only one jackass in the room.

Kieran counted to five.

"What were you and Jordan grinning about earlier?" he asked, as he glared at her. Kieran frowned and tried to remember what he was referring to. She didn't remember communicating with Jordan.

"I don't know what you are talking about. I spent most of my time talking to Chantelle, as you well know," she said pulling a sundress out of the wardrobe. The weatherman promised sunshine and a warm twenty five degrees the next day.

He shut the wardrobe door when Kieran stepped away from it; she marched over to the window where the ironing board stood and lay her dress down on it.

"You haven't answered my question." He said from behind her.

"I did. I said I don't know what you are talking about."

"I saw you," he snapped banging his fist against the wardrobe. Kieran raised her eyebrows. She was reminded of a child throwing a temper tantrum.

"What did you see?"

"You and Jordan obviously sharing a private joke,"

"What? Like last week when you got annoyed that Anthony was looking at me?"

"He was. I can't trust any of them," he spat.

"You are mad," Kieran said shaking her head in disbelief. She bent down and plugged in the iron. When she straightened, Darren was next to her glaring. Kieran took a step backwards.

"Are you trying to piss me off?" he growled.

Remembering how quickly he lost his temper, she realised she needed to calm him down. "Darren you're being silly. I was not grinning with Jordan about anything. I promise," Kieran told him. She reached out and touched his arm.

"I saw you!" he snapped pulling his arm away.

"What is wrong with you?" she asked with a sigh. He didn't answer, so she turned her attention to ironing her dress. She couldn't win with him.

"You're not wearing that to work tomorrow are you?" he asked suddenly changing the subject.

"Yes, I am." Kieran replied not looking at him. She ran the iron over a section of material then placed the iron down as she moved the fabric over the board. Before she could pick it up again Darren stopped her.

"Don't you think it's a bit revealing?" he grabbed the dress off the ironing board and stepped away from Kieran. She reached out to grab it from him; he moved so he was out of her reach. She felt the tears in her eyes, as her blood began to boil. It was going to be one of those nights. Of course, he was going to complain about the dress. She usually waited for him to leave in the mornings before she picked out her clothes. She should've known better.

"Give me my dress," she said and stepped towards him. She managed to grab a bit of the material and held it tightly in her fist. He tried to pull it away from her. Kieran felt the jolt in her arm from the force, but she refused to let go.

"Who's in the office tomorrow?" he demanded.

"The usual," she snapped pulling the dress again. She heard a ripping sound and winced.

"So then why do you need to wear this? Are you really going to work?" he glowered.

Kieran couldn't hold back her frustration, "Because I want to! Why do you have to be suspicious about everything I do? For the hundredth time, I am not your ex-girlfriend, so stop accusing me of things!" she screeched at him.

They glared at each other for a few seconds, both still clutching the dress.

"I told you not to mention her. Why the fuck would you do that?" he shouted.

"Because you don't listen. When I'm at work you don't trust me, when I'm right here under your nose you don't trust me, so what do you want me to do? Never see anyone again and stay at home with you all the time?"

He yanked the dress again. Kieran's arm felt as if it came out of the socket. She let go of the dress. A look of triumph passed over Darren's face.

"I do trust you. It's men I don't trust. Do you think anyone cares that you have a boyfriend? They'll still try it with you, and wearing stuff like this is only going to draw attention to yourself."

"It should make you happy that other guys find me attractive. I've chosen you. I live with you, why isn't that enough?" she rubbed her arm and rotated her shoulder in circular motions to relieve the pain.

"So, you like men looking at you?"

"Oh my God!" Kieran cried in exasperation.

Darren didn't reply. He marched over to the ironing board and threw the dress on it before picking up the iron. Kieran gasped as she realised what he was about to do. She screamed as he put the iron down onto the fabric and held it there.

She rushed over to pry his hand from the iron. He pushed her away roughly; he was a lot stronger than her. Feeling helpless she turned and sat on the bed where she burst into tears. She could smell the fabric burning.

He lifted the iron off the dress and held it up to admire his work. Kieran couldn't look. He chuckled once, clearly pleased with himself, turned and walked towards the door throwing the dress on the bed next to her.

Kieran brushed the angry tears away and forced herself to look down at her dress; a big, brown iron mark stained the sunshine yellow fabric. Not being able to control her emotions she allowed herself to cry quietly for a few minutes before taking a few deep breaths to calm down. She would not give him the satisfaction of seeing how much he had upset her. She couldn't believe he was so spiteful.

This isn't love.

3 CHAPTER THREE

Kieran danced to the beat of loud music, as she selected her holiday wear. She was in good spirits after returning from babysitting her eleven-year old twin sisters, Cameron and Charlie, while her parents went out for dinner. Darren was also sitting, though of a different sort. His parents were visiting the Lake District for the weekend. So he had been put in charge of looking after their house. Kieran refused to join him.

After the dress incident two weeks before, he had returned home with flowers because flowers made everything right in his mind. Their situation became further strained after his pathetic attempt at an apology didn't work. They had hardly spoken and that suited Kieran just fine.

Her mobile vibrated in her back pocket. She fished it out and turned the volume on the stereo down. Kieran didn't recognise the number, but said, "Hello," in a cheery voice.

"Kieran?" The voice sounded familiar however the caller eluded her.

"Who's this?" she asked still moving to the music.

"It's Joshua."

Kieran froze. "Why are you phoning me?" she asked in an abrupt tone after his name sunk in.

"I'm back in London, been back a few months now and I've been thinking about you."

"Really." She did her best to sound bored, it wasn't really a question and he didn't have an answer she was interested in.

Suddenly her face grew hot from the anger.

"Yes really. How you been?"

He's still an arrogant bastard. Why would I care that he's back from Leicester? Idiot.

"Is this a bad time or something?" Joshua enquired when she didn't answer him.

It wasn't, but she said, "Yes, it is actually."

"Okay, I'll call you back another time."

"Don't bother, I have nothing to say to you," she said and ended the call. She leant against the wall and slid down onto the floor. Her mind raced a hundred miles an hour. Taking a deep breath, she dialled Christina's number. "You will never guess who just called me," she told her.

The evening was warm and sticky with barely a breeze in the air. Kieran put her sunglasses over her eyes and looked up at the sky. The sun was getting ready to set, though wisps of pink clouds signalled that the next day would also be a warm one. She loved England in the summer time. She put her foot down on the pedal enjoying the drive. Before she knew it, she was parked outside the house of the address she was given. It was a typical Victorian house that appeared to be split into three flats.

The biggest butterfly floated around her stomach as she walked up to the door and rang the bell. Within seconds the door opened. Kieran inhaled. She couldn't believe how incredibly gorgeous Joshua looked. She had always thought so even though her friends didn't agree. He was a pretty boy and used to have a constant string of female admirers. She bet nothing had changed.

"Hey," he greeted her with a smile.

Kieran felt her knees tremble. Darren never made her knees tremble.

"Hey," she said in a calm tone that belied her nervousness. In fact, Kieran felt as if she was about to wet herself. "I don't mean to be rude, but could I use your bathroom?"

"Sure," Joshua said, stepping aside to allow her to enter. "Straight ahead, first door on the right," he told her as he looked at her up and down.

Once Kieran was in the bathroom she fixed her hair and re-applied her lip gloss in an attempt to compose herself. Her mind flew back to a conversation she had with Christina and Chantelle when she told them Joshua was back in London.

"… It's been five years since you broke up. I thought you were over him," Christina had said in a shocked tone.

"I should be over him, but since he called…"

"I don't know what to say. If one phone call from Joshua has got you acting stupid, you can't be over him," Chantelle chimed in.

"If things were different between you and Darren, would you be thinking about Joshua, much less thinking about meeting up with him?" Christina challenged.

"First, things are different between Darren and me, and second, I honestly don't know."

"We all know you've been questioning your relationship with Darren for a while," Christina reminded her, "but that's not the point."

"Yea, I know. It's not over until it's over. Why is he back now?

"There's only one way to find out," Chantelle said.

She had needed to find out, so she'd called him back and here she was.

By her second glass of wine, they had caught up on events that had taken place during their separation. Joshua was now working as a Civil Engineer which is what he studied at university. To Kieran, it felt as if they had never been apart; being with Joshua felt natural and comfortable. Their tête-à-tête took a different turn when Joshua suddenly said, "I've missed you." and reached for her hand.

"I've missed you too," Kieran mumbled. She was sure she was tipsy, and with that thought her head began to spin. Wine went to her head quicker than spirits. Kieran knew she had reached her limit, except she needed the wine to calm her nerves. She sat still unable to move, she was vaguely aware that her heart rate had picked up a little.

"I've been questioning since you got here why I ever let you go?" Joshua said as he entwined his fingers with hers.

"You know why, you got bored with me,' she said looking at their hands.

"And I've never regretted anything as much as that," he said in a serious tone.

"Why did you call me?" Kieran looked at him. His caramel complexion was still the same but the boyish looks she remembered had been replaced with a fuller, mature face. The goatee he now sported suited him. He wore his hair slightly longer, which highlighted the curls he once hated. What a difference five years made.

"Being in Leicester was easy living. I didn't have to think about anything that much. I was busy at university and work," he avoided Kieran's eyes. "When I moved back to London and met up with my old friends, I wanted to see you, too," he continued.

"Yea, but you know what you've done, don't you?" she said looking away from him.

"What?"

"You've made feelings reappear that I thought were dead." The room spun again and Kieran realised she was more than tipsy. She switched to water. She had to drive back home.

"Is that so wrong?" he asked.

Kieran felt her heart hammer inside her chest. "Yes, it is. I have a boyfriend."

"Kiki, you know what we had and still could have, no-one is ever going to replace that."

Kieran's stomach lurched at the sound of his pet name for her. No one else called her that, and hearing it again made her remember the good times they shared. The memories made her realise she'd missed him.

Kieran was afraid that he may be right and perhaps that's why her relationship with Darren was erratic – he could not compare to Joshua. She was silent and could feel his light brown eyes on her.

"Why are you staring at me?"

"I've missed seeing your face."

Kieran wondered how he could be so confident. He spoke as if nothing had changed between them. "Well, stop staring."

"You know I do it because I know you don't like it," he teased.

Kieran gave a nervous laugh, took a few mouthfuls of water, stood up and proceeded to put on her new summer jacket. She had gotten it in the River Island sale to cheer herself up after the dress burning incident, plus four new dresses, two pairs of shoes and a new bag.

"Leaving so soon?" he asked with disappointment.

"Yea," she said ignoring the look on his face. She was, in a sick way, happy that he was upset about her departure.

"You sure that's what you want to do," he said standing up.

"Don't tempt me J," she whispered.

"I'd be lying if I said I didn't want you to leave."

"And I'd be lying if I said I want to go. Either way, I'm going," Kieran fastened her jacket and picked up her bag.

Joshua walked her to the door. "When am I going to see you again?"

"I'm off to Jamaica in two days. Corey's getting married. You remember my sister Corey right? I'll call you when I get back."

He stood close to her, too close for Kieran's comfort. "Of course, I remember Corey, tell her I said congratulations. How long will you be away?"

"Two weeks." She would not be passing on any messages to her sister.

"Is your man going with you?" he asked looking into her eyes.

"Why?" she asked. It was none of his business; she was enjoying the fact that he was not in the know, though.

"Just wondering," he said with a shrug.

"If I didn't know you any better, I'd think you were jealous," she teased folding her arms across her chest. When they had been together she was the jealous one. Now the tables were turned, she couldn't help but feel smug about it.

"I am," he admitted.

Kieran wasn't expecting that reply. She took a deep breath when she saw his expression that she recognised only too well. "You're going to kiss me aren't you?" she said.

Joshua didn't answer. He pulled her close and bent his head towards hers. Kieran closed her eyes as she felt his warm, soft lips press against hers. She pulled away almost immediately.

"We shouldn't do that," she told him.

"Call me when you get home," Joshua said squeezing her hand and ignoring her statement.

"Okay." She agreed, although she knew she wouldn't.

"I want details!" Chantelle shouted down the phone the following morning.

Kieran groaned and she rolled over almost falling out of the bed. "There's nothing to tell," she grumbled.

"Liar."

"It's too early," she groaned rolling over again.

"Unless you want me to come knocking on your door, talk now," Chantelle threatened.

Kieran knew she wasn't joking. "We ate, drank wine, said how much we missed each other, then he kissed me. End of story," Kieran hung up the phone before Chantelle could say anything. She could almost hear her cursing. Chantelle would make her pay for it.

She did exactly that an hour later, as she woke Kieran a second time by knocking down her door. She strolled through the door and slapped Kieran playfully on her head. "That's for hanging up on me."

Kieran glared at her, walked into the kitchen, flicked the kettle on and joined her in the living room. "Why are you up so early? It's Sunday."

"Hello, we are going to Jamaica tomorrow. I'm going to get some last minute shopping,"

"More shopping? Why couldn't you disturb me on your way back?"

"Don't get fresh and don't ask me questions, you know why I am here. The quicker you tell me what happened, the quicker I will leave. Where's your other half by the way?"

Kieran rolled her eyes. "He's playing football," she told her and headed back to the kitchen to make them tea.

By the time Chantelle left, Kieran was wide awake. She spent most of the day packing. She had managed to fill two suitcases. She found it impossible to travel light. By the time she was through, it was early evening. She showered, fixed something to eat and after, curled up in bed to watch a movie. The next thing she knew, Darren was kissing her neck and whispering,

"I'm really going to miss you."

Kieran opened her eyes, but lay still. She wouldn't miss him. She was looking forward to the break.

"I'm going to miss you too," she lied, thankful the room was dark.

"Really?"

"What do you mean really?" she asked pretending to sound hurt, "Don't you think I will?" He was more observant than she gave him credit for and she was a better actress than she gave herself credit for.

"It's just that lately I feel you don't want me around."

"Oh don't be silly," she said, he sounded sad and suddenly she felt guilty. "Maybe some space would do us good, we can start over when I get back?" she said turning to face him.

"Are you tired?" he asked ignoring her comment and kissing her.

Clearly he didn't want to talk about it.

4 CHAPTER FOUR

The sun had risen only a few hours before and the heat was intense. Kieran looked around with a sense of contentment. She had never visited anywhere so beautiful. The island was everything a holiday brochure claimed. The sea, the greenery, the sky, the flowers, the beach, palm trees; it was picturesque.

The wedding ceremony had been a few days before. Corey was nervous before her big day and true to form was a complete cow, a trait she couldn't seem to help whenever she was nervous or anxious. Kieran and her mother received the brunt of her tantrums, and her rants increased right up to the morning of the wedding. She complained that the flowers for the wedding were not the right shade of blue, and she threw a fit when the wrong champagne was delivered. Kieran's dress had more diamante's than it was meant to, and the twins got a tongue-lashing too when their over-zealous excitement seemed too much for her.

Kieran understood the term bridezilla and came close to letting Corey know what she thought about her behaviour. She refrained when her mum asked her to be nice. She concentrated on her maid of honour duties for the small ceremony that consisted of thirty six guests; close family and friends from both the bride and groom's side. Kieran wore a beautiful, turquoise, halter neck dress with low back to compliment Corey's white dress. Though the style was the same Corey's had spaghetti straps with white diamantes that also covered the bodice. They sparkled in the tropical sunlight. Matching diamante pins held her hair in place that she piled on top of her head in an elaborate bun. She finished off with a diamante tiara, and when Kieran placed small diamond studs into her ears and whispered that they were from Jack, Corey shed tears at the gesture.

She looked serene and beautiful. Kieran quickly got over her annoyance, and was proud of her sister. The ceremony went ahead without a hitch. Kieran was happy for Corey and Jack, who had been together for five years. She couldn't hide her emotion and her dad promised her that she could have the same experience when she decided to get married.

Kieran wondered what her honeymoon would be like. Furthermore, who would she marry?

"I can't believe two weeks are over so quickly," Chantelle complained interrupting her reflections.

"I know. Back to boring, dry London," she said.

"Back to Darren and Joshua," Chantelle reminded her as she placed a hat on her head.

"You would bring that up wouldn't you? I've hardly thought about them all week," Kieran told her as she squirted factor thirty suntan lotion into her hands, and rubbed it over her arms and legs. Its cooling effect lasted for a split second. She looked at the sea of turquoise water. It was calling her.

"Liar." Chantelle teased as she too covered herself in lotion. They were extra careful after they got burned on their arrival. Full of excitement and eager to show off their new bikinis, they planted themselves on the beach without sun cream and if it wasn't for Kieran's mum calling them for lunch, they would have ended up having to spend the remainder of their holiday indoors.

"Shut up! I don't want to think about them." In truth, Joshua had been on her mind ever since she'd seen him.

"You can't run away from the situation. I know how you feel about Joshua and you know what we think about him. He's manipulative and will take advantage of you, because he knows he can. However, let's hope he's grown up some, because if he still pulls the crap he used to, there's no point in even going there."

"That's not true," Kieran protested. Though in retrospect, there was an element of truth in what Chantelle said. He was no worse than Darren though. Kieran gave serious thought about ending their relationship after he continuously called her, full of accusations. The last had been a rant about her not really being with her family when she missed two of his calls. Of course, he thought she was up to something, or was with someone, like she had made up her sister getting married.

Darren amazed her in every way possible, and it was not in a good way. She was glad she would be going to Greece after Corey's party, which was planned in London on the couple's return from their honeymoon in Mexico. It was another reason to spend time away from him. She wasn't sure how she had let it go so far and why she still tolerated him.

"Joshua was an asshole at times, but he was not insecure like Darren. We were good together before he got bored with me," she finally answered Chantelle who made a face.

"You're right, let's not talk about it," she said standing up and pulling Kieran to her feet, "let's enjoy our last day on the beach.".

5 CHAPTER FIVE

Kieran checked her watch. She was scheduled to meet Christina and Chantelle in Westfields to shop for an outfit for Christina's sister's eighteenth birthday party that night. She saved the file she was working on, clicked the mouse over the email icon and drew in a sharp breath. She was already signed in. Darren had been snooping in her emails again.

When Kieran first realised this had been happening, she thought about changing her password, but decided against it because it would lead to another argument. She had already deleted her Facebook account because every day he found something to jump to conclusions about, it was just easier if she didn't have an account anymore. Since he realised she wanted to relocate to New York, he no longer trusted her. As far as he was concerned, someone else - a man - was involved, because after all, why would she be so bothered about her career?

Anger bubbled inside her and she felt the urge to throw something; she took deep breaths to calm her nerves. She shouldn't have been surprised, he checked her phone too, so it was only a matter of time before he upgraded.

Kieran felt like a prisoner in her own home. She couldn't do anything without him questioning, or checking up on her. She found herself monitoring what she said and did. A part of her hoped, somewhat naively, that he would change; another part of her felt as if she was deluding herself. She logged off; too pissed to read her emails. She grabbed her jacket and handbag and headed out.

As they walked into Accessorize Christina announced, "I saw Joshua while you were on holiday."

Kieran felt the now familiar hammering in her chest at the mention of Joshua's name. She had spoken with him on several occasions since her return and their conversations were turning serious, emotional even. Kieran felt as if she was cheating on Darren emotionally and wondered if cheating stress could cause someone to have a heart attack.

"Is it," she managed to sound uninterested and was quietly impressed with herself.

"He asked about you," Christina added as she looked at some beach bags.

"Why would he? He didn't care what I was doing when I was with him and now he's interested in my business," Kieran scowled as she looked through a rack of sarongs.

"Babe, that's men for you," Chantelle said trying on a large straw hat.

"Some men," Christina corrected and gave Chantelle the thumbs up indicating she liked the hat.

Kieran nodded in agreement. "Yea, I guess there are a few good ones out there," she added.

"I'd like to meet one," Christina said in a tone that caught Kieran's attention.

"What's wrong?" she asked her friend.

"I'm alone. I haven't had a man for six months and I miss being in a relationship. I can't believe I'm admitting it." Christina explained rolling her eyes as they joined the queue to pay for their garments.

"It'll happen," Kieran said to reassure her. She wasn't sure how much of that she believed. Her thoughts were flickering between Darren and Joshua. She had promised to try and make things work with Darren, getting involved with Joshua would cancel out that promise, and she couldn't do that to him or herself. She had sacrificed too much.

They both continued to dominate her thoughts right up until she arrived at the party. She needed something to steady her nerves; she headed straight to the bar, ordered a Disaronno and coke, then joined Christina and Amelia who were sat at a table. A group of girls hurried past them on their way to the dance floor clearly excited about the song that was playing. Kieran smiled as she remembered when she was young and carefree. The smile disappeared when she saw Joshua walking through the bar, followed by his younger brother Jarrell.

"Remember your boyfriend," Christina nudged her.

Kieran took a sip of her drink. It warmed her chest. "Whatever," she told her. "I need some air."

Joshua smiled at her as she walked past. She nodded hello and headed outside. There were a group of girls smoking; she smiled at them as she made her way over to the wall away from them so she could have a few minutes to think. The cool air hit her and she felt better, focused. She rummaged in her bag and pulled out her secret box of cigarettes. She had given up the habit a while back but when she was out drinking sometimes she still liked to have a smoke, although she knew it was a bad habit. She had just taken a drag when Joshua appeared next to her.

"Hi," Kieran said turning to face him.

"I thought you quit?" he asked smirking.

"I have, this is a figment of your imagination," she told him grinning. Joshua laughed. "I didn't expect to see you here tonight." Kieran admitted.

"I don't usually go to eighteen year old parties, but Jarrell bugged me and I didn't have anything else planned. You look beautiful," he told her as he took the cigarette from her; he took a drag before throwing it away.

He had never agreed with her smoking.

She felt awkward as his eyes took in her bare legs and for the first time that evening, she was conscious of her short skirt. She put it aside and launched into the spiel that she had been practicing most of the day..

"Joshua, I've given a lot thought about us." She emphasised the word, us, "And I'm not going to let you ruin my relationship with Darren, because you now realise I'm worth something." she said looking at him.

"I told you I was stupid about that," he said moving closer to her.

"Well, you never know what you've got 'til it's gone," she replied taking a step backwards.

Neither of them said anything for a few moments.

"So, where's Darren tonight?" he asked.

"What's it to do with you?" she scowled. She didn't mean to; it annoyed her that he ignored her statement.

"I just wondered,"

She was sure she could see the hint of a smile on his lips. "Well don't. It has nothing to do with you. Just leave me alone. We were a long time ago. Deal with it." She shifted her weight from one foot to the other; her heels were starting to hurt.

Joshua took her hand and squeezed it. "Whatever you want," he said before walking back inside.

Kieran stared after him.

Did I do the right thing? Why was he so calm? How dare he act like he's not bothered, who does he think he is?

"Why are you out here?" Chantelle's voice broke into Kieran's thoughts and she spun around. Chantelle was with her brother Reece, who gave Kieran the once over appreciatively and grinned at her before heading over to the group of girls who were still smoking.

"He thinks he's so slick." Chantelle mumbled about her brother.

"You finally made it then," Kieran said re-arranging the expression on her face.

"Where's Darren?" Chantelle asked.

"At home."

"What? He allowed you to leave the house showing off your pins without him?" Chantelle raised her eyebrows.

"Please do not go there; ages ago it wouldn't have bothered me to wear something like this; now I feel self-conscious and I know it's because of him, Kieran said as she tugged at the hem of her skirt pulling it down.

"It isn't even that short. He's making you paranoid and it's affecting your confidence. He's no good for you, break up with him"

"I wish it was that easy," Kieran mumbled, more to herself than to Chantelle.

"What are you scared of?"

"I don't know. Guess who's here?" Kieran asked sort of changing the subject.

Chantelle looked at her shrugging her shoulders and then almost immediately after a knowing look passed over her face gasped "No way."

Kieran nodded.

"Did you know he was coming?" Chantelle whispered.

"No, why are you whispering?"

"I don't know," Chantelle said laughing.

"Bloody wonderful isn't it? I don't see or hear from him in years and now all of a sudden he's everywhere I go."

"Maybe it's a sign you should break up with Darren?"

"Do you think Joshua deserves me after everything he did, and after everything I went through because of him?" Kieran asked seriously.

"I don't know, that doesn't mean you should settle with Darren though."

Is that why I'm with Darren? Am I settling?

"Let's go inside," Chantelle said changing the subject.

Kieran nodded and pulled at her skirt again. "I'm sure a certain person in there doesn't mind how you look," Chantelle teased.

Kieran ignored her friend and walked inside.

Kieran's mood lifted when she heard the sounds of 'The Jackson Five' and fell in with her friends dancing. The DJ followed with more Michael Jackson songs and other classic tunes that had the house literally rocking. Kieran recaptured her teenage years, as she and her friends sung loudly and danced to the music. For the next hour, Kieran let her hair down without having to be aware of who she spoke to or how she looked at someone. She certainly didn't miss Darren's presence.

She glanced around looking for Joshua and saw him talking to a modelesque dark-skinned girl. She couldn't help but feel jealous. At intervals, she noticed that he kept looking in her direction.

"Joshua's eyes are following your every move," Chantelle said to her.

"Are they?" Kieran replied smirking.

"Don't even try it. I know you. You like the fact that he can't have you," she teased.

Kieran sipped her drink to hide her smile. It was true.

She noticed Joshua heading outside hand-in-hand with the pretty girl. She knew he was trying to make her jealous and even worse was that it was working.

An upbeat song came on and Kieran began dancing with her friends. She was soon doubled over with laughter as they were trying to recreate a dance routine they had made up in their younger years. She had just composed herself when she felt hands around her waist.

"What the hell?" she spun around and came face-to-face with Darren.

"Hey," he said before kissing her.

Kieran tried to look happy and hugged him. "You changed your mind!"

"I got bored. Now I'm here it's as I thought, not my scene, too many youngsters."

Translation: He's come to check up on me.

As long as she was in his line of sight he could relax.

"Oh, so you're not staying?" she said finding it hard to believe.

"What's all that stuff on your face?" he evaded her question and asked.

Here we go.

Kieran frowned. Darren didn't like her wearing make-up. She usually put it on in her car before heading to work and took it off when she knew he would get home before her. It made for a quiet life.

"What?" she asked playing dumb.

"The make-up," he said raising his eyebrows.

She felt like one of those teenagers being reprimanded by their father. She didn't answer him. "Well?" he pressed.

"Well what?" Kieran snapped.

"Don't get pissed. I'm just saying. You know you don't need it." he said in a more quiet tone and pulled her into him.

Kieran said nothing. His hands moved south down her back, to her waist, her hips, over her skirt and its layers of frills and netting, her bum then stopped at her thighs.

He stepped back and looked down at her outfit. "What are you wearing?"

"Clothes," she replied in a tetchy tone. He missed nothing

when it suited him. It was bullshit and she was not in the mood for the third degree; she hoped he knew better than to cause a scene.

"Don't you think your skirt is a bit short?" he asked taking her hand. Maybe, but she wasn't about to admit that to him. Plus it was a nice skirt, black and frilly, almost like a tutu. She got lucky finding it in the sales.

"No," she replied, "let's get some fresh air."

Darren held her hand and led her towards the entrance outside. From the corner of her eye, Kieran saw Joshua at the bar sipping a beer as he watched them. She avoided looking in his direction.

Once outside, Darren continued. "You know I don't like when you go out half naked."

"I am not half naked," she protested folding her arms across her chest.

"And since when did you start wearing make-up again? You know I don't like it. When did you get that skirt?" he asked looking down at her bare legs.

Kieran sidestepped the make-up issue. She would lose her temper otherwise and she refused to cause a scene.

"Ages ago."

"I haven't seen it before."

"I didn't realise I had to show you every item of clothing I buy," she snapped, her patience beginning to slip. What was he, the fashion police? "Darren. Can you hear yourself?"

"Was that Joshua in there?" he asked ignoring her question.

"Yes." She'd hoped he hadn't noticed him. Now that he had, it was another reason for him to complain, another reason not to trust her.

"Did you know he was coming? Is that what this is in aid of?" Darren pointed to her face and clothes.

She caught sight of Chantelle and Christina in the doorway listening to them and making faces at her.

Kieran turned away from them before she laughed in his face "No, I didn't know he was coming and you are being ridiculous."

"Look, all I'm saying is cover up a bit more. You know what I think about women who dress like that."

"Yes boss," Kieran said scowling at him. He was amazing sometimes and she didn't know what else to say without starting an argument.

"I'm not being a prick. I just don't like guys looking at you. Dressing like that is only going to encourage them."

"Don't worry about it Darren."

"You look nice though," he said softly.

Kieran gave him a false smile and mumbled, "Thanks." Why couldn't he just say that in the first place and leave it at that? Why did he have to make her feel bad for looking nice? His compliments meant nothing. He was never going to change.

"So, are you coming home with me? I'm ready to roll."

"No, I'm here with my friends and I don't know what time I'll be home,"

"Okay, I'll walk you back inside."

Before he could turn around Kieran noticed her friends dash back inside. She bit her lip to stop herself from laughing. As she and Darren walked back inside, he held her close to him. Kieran knew it was for Joshua's benefit; he was marking his territory.

"Not too late, call me when you are on your way, okay," he told her once they had re-joined her friends at the table.

Kieran nodded and pulled him close for a kiss – also for Joshua's benefit. She didn't want him to know there were issues in their relationship. Kieran felt his eyes on her as she sat down.

"What did Darren say?" Amelia asked. The four of them huddled together, so it would be easier to talk over the music.

"Basically, I'm dressed like a whore and I have on too much make-up," she told them.

"What?" Chantelle asked raising her eyebrows, "Darren is brave. I'll give him that much."

"Yep, Apparently I need to cover up a bit more."

"End it now," Christina told her as she sipped her drink.

"Look, can we not talk about it," Kieran told them, as one of their old college friends, Steven, came over and asked her for a dance. At the same time, Joshua walked past, their eyes connected and Kieran gave him a flirtatious smile and accepted Steven's request.

"Very mature Kieran," Chantelle said shaking her head when she re-joined them breathless.

"What?" Kieran asked with a look of innocence.

"You know you did that to make Joshua jealous."

"Yea, so, he's out there doing the same thing," Kieran pointed out while fanning her face with her hand.

"Yes, but how old are you two? I'm literally having déjà vu. You did this when you were fourteen and couldn't admit you liked each other." Chantelle reminded her.

"Did we?" Kieran asked downing her drink.

"You were kids then; it was less pathetic, completely different to now."

Kieran didn't know whether to laugh or cry. Her eyes followed Joshua as he walked over to his brother who stood by the DJ.

"Oh, would you sleep with him and get it over with."

"Chantelle Williams!" Kieran gasped.

"What? It's the perfect solution. Sleep with him and if you don't feel anything, move on."

Kieran stared at her in disbelief. "You need to stop drinking," she told her.

"I'm not drunk. It makes sense. Do it once, if there's nothing there then you know," Chantelle repeated.

"I cannot believe what you are saying. What is wrong with you?"

"I'd do it," she said with a shrug.

"I don't want to cheat on Darren."

"Oh my God, you are so Charlotte!" Chantelle exclaimed, a smile on her face.

Kieran was confused. "Sex And The City?" she questioned after a minute.

"Yes. You are such a goody, goody sometimes. Live a little. You've kissed him, so why not do the rest. I won't tell anyone," she said with a mischievous grin and a twinkle in her eyes.

"I am nothing like Charlotte."

"Whatever," Chantelle said rolling her eyes. "Are you worried about Darren finding out?" she asked seriously.

Kieran shook her head. She was worried that she might feel too much for Joshua, and she swore he would never get a second chance.

The DJ slowed things down and within seconds Joshua appeared by her side.

"Would you like to dance?"

"Sure." She replied before handing Chantelle her glass.

Joshua took her hand and she followed him into a corner. He held her close. Too close. He smelt good; familiar and comforting. Suddenly she didn't trust herself. Kieran pulled back a little and Joshua loosened his grip. By the time the song finished, however, she was right back where she started; with his arms wrapped tightly around her. Joshua released her. Kieran looked at him and shook her head indicating that she still wanted to dance. Joshua smiled and pulled her back towards him. This time Kieran didn't pull away. She closed her eyes and inhaled his smell of cocoa butter and Cool Water cologne.

A thousand memories of them as a couple raced through her mind, causing her stomach to twist. Her knees trembled and Kieran took a deep breath to help her stay steady.

Joshua pulled her closer, as if he knew she needed the extra support. She looked over at Chantelle who gave her a grin. Five songs later, they were still dancing. By this time Kieran needed some air.

"Do you want company?" Joshua asked after she told him about her lack of oxygen.

"I don't mind."

The front area was empty, as everyone was still dancing to the slow jams. The night air had turned chilly; it was soothing. She looked up at the sky. It was a clear night and the stars were out. Joshua stood next to her and took her hand, "Don't say anything," he said.

Kieran stayed silent. Soon she felt uncomfortable. There were too many unsaid things between them.

"It's kind of cold now." She wasn't sure she was sober enough to tell what the real temperature was. Joshua placed his arm around her shoulder and Kieran looked up at him, feeling that familiar sensation in her chest.

"We could go back inside? I want you to myself for a while though," he whispered into her ear. His breath tickled her.

"Why?" she asked.

"I don't know."

"Liar," she teased as she entwined her fingers with his.

"Can I kiss you?"

Kieran's heart danced harder and faster; she couldn't speak, so she nodded.

Joshua bent his head and Kieran closed her eyes as soon as she felt his lips on hers. She responded with an urgency she had not experienced in a long while and the dancing in her chest escalated. When they separated Kieran smiled.

"Why are you smiling?"

"I don't know." Kieran said, she honestly didn't know what had come over her.

"Liar," he teased.

Kieran grinned. "I like kissing you. I remember at times it was all I wanted to do."

"And now?"

Kieran didn't verbalise her answer, instead, she put her arms around his neck and kissed him again. She wasn't worried about being caught, which was silly of her but at that moment she just didn't care.

"Did that answer your question?"

"Are you drunk?" Joshua asked raising an eyebrow in surprise.

"Perhaps I am. Would that make a difference?"

"I don't want you to wake up tomorrow and tell me this only happened because you were drunk," he said searching her eyes for some honesty.

"I don't think I will regret it."

"Why?"

"Because ever since you came through that door tonight I've wanted to kiss you," It was as much honesty as she could give him. "I want to spend tonight with you. Can we go back to yours?" she asked before she could stop herself.

Joshua gave her a curious look.

"I don't want to have sex with you. I just want to stay up and talk like we used to," Kieran explained, she realised just how much she had missed him.

"I'd like that," Joshua told her nodding.

They returned to the party to say their goodbyes. Kieran was ready for the barrage of questions she knew would come from her friends.

"I'll meet you outside," Joshua said before disappearing into the crowd to find his brother.

"What do you think you're doing?" Amelia asked her face was

coloured with disapproval.

"They were only dancing," Chantelle rolled her eyes at Amelia's reaction.

"It didn't look like that from here, anyone would think that they were a couple, does she not remember what he put her through?" Amelia protested.

"Oh, I don't know. Do you think you'd forget if your first love did that to you?" Chantelle asked sarcastically.

"I wouldn't be dancing cosily with him at a party if he did!" Amelia snapped.

"She's not about to jump into bed with him for God sake," Chantelle replied.

Kieran thought to herself that her statement might not necessarily be true. She could see that Amelia's holier than thou attitude was winding Chantelle up. It was different for her. She married her first love, and now they had a family. Amelia had no idea what it was like trying to find 'the one'. Kieran didn't hold it against her. She was glad she was happy, but wished she remembered her friends were still looking for what she had.

"It didn't look like that from here." Amelia repeated and sipped her drink.

"You're so supportive," Chantelle said before walking off.

"I actually think Amelia has a point, you would be crazy to give him another chance," Christina said.

"Have you completely forgotten what you went through? We were there. He wasn't. Does he even know?" Amelia asked staring at her.

"I don't want to think about it let alone tell him about it." Kieran grimaced.

"Well, you will have to if you get back together," Amelia added.

"Would you really take him back after everything Kieran?" Christina asked.

After listening to their lecture, Kieran didn't feel Christina's question warranted an answer. She hugged her, then Amelia. "You guys seem to have all the answers. I'll call you," she said and went to find Chantelle.

"I will call you tomorrow," she told her.

"Why? Are you leaving?" As soon as the words left her

mouth, she gave Kieran a knowing smile. "Make sure you do and be good."

"I will," Kieran replied.

Kieran awoke and realised she was not in her own bed, bleary eyed she looked at the masculine decorated room of pale blue walls and black iron furniture.

Where was she? She remembered Christina and Amelia bitching at her... leaving the party with Joshua.... they were going back to his flat.....she didn't remember the journey. Turning her head slowly, she saw Joshua asleep next to her.

Shit, shit, shit!

"Josh, wake up," she nudged him. He groaned, but didn't move. "Why are we in the same bed?" she could hear the panic in her voice.

"You crashed out in the car, so I carried you. I have a one bedroom flat remember?" he replied not opening his eyes.

"You undressed me too?" she asked looking down at the oversized t-shirt she was wearing.

"Did you want to sleep in your clothes? It's not like I haven't seen you naked before," he said smiling, his eyes still closed.

"Joshua Simmons that is so not the point," Kieran said.

"You, my dear, don't have a point, so shhh and go back to sleep."

Kieran poked him in his side.

Joshua opened his eyes and screamed.

Kieran laughed out loud, "You still scream like a little girl."

Suddenly he had pinned her down under him. Kieran looked up at him and the smile disappeared from her face. She was in dangerous territory. What was she doing?

"I have to go," she said as she tried to move.

"Why?

"I don't trust myself with you," she mumbled avoiding his gaze.

"We haven't done anything."

"And if I stay any longer, I don't know how long that's going to stay true. We kissed, that's too much," she said sitting up and looking around for her clothes.

"I don't want you to go."

Kieran looked at him and sighed. "Josh, don't do this, okay. It's hard enough for me without you creating more pressure."

"You don't think it's hard for me?"

Kieran smirked at him. Joshua shook his head and chuckled. "You have a dirty mind."

"I didn't say anything." She protested, her eyes wide and innocent

"You didn't have to. I know you, remember?" he leaned over to kiss her. Kieran let him for a second. It felt nice – too nice.

She pulled away. "Don't J," she mumbled.

"You're the one that's making this hard." This time he smirked.

Kieran laughed. "Now who's being dirty?" she teased

"Seriously, I'm not trying to make this worse for you."

"I have to go."

"If that's what you want." he said shrugging.

"I don't know what I want." Kieran admitted.

Joshua leaned over and kissed her on the cheek. He got out of the bed and left the room.

Darren paused the game he was playing on his PlayStation when Kieran entered the flat.

"Where did you stay last night?" he turned to her and asked.

"At Chantelle's obviously," she replied as she walked over to him and kissed his cheek. The more she could do not to cause an argument the better.

"Why didn't you phone me?" he asked reverting back to the game.

Kieran was relieved. He seemed to accept her blatant lie.

"I was drunk and tired," she said going over to the PC. Her email log in box was on the screen. Clearly he didn't even care if she knew he was snooping through her emails. Her mobile started ringing.

"Hey it's me," Joshua said when she answered.

"I know," she said turning the volume down.

"Are you home yet?"

"Yea," she said walking into the kitchen. She flicked the kettle on and leaned against the counter.

"Is Darren there?" Joshua asked.

"Yea, it's okay though," she said quietly.

"He didn't say anything about where you were?"

"I'm going in the bath now, I'll call you later." She wasn't in the mood for questions.

"Okay, I miss you. Talk to you soon then?"

"You too, Bye."

"Who was that?" Darren asked studying her face as she entered the front room.

"Chantelle," she said avoiding his gaze and picking up her bag. Kieran knew he was suspicious, he may have been overly possessive but he wasn't stupid..

6 CHAPTER SIX

It was eight in the evening and their flight was leaving at one in the morning. Kieran, Chantelle and Christina had a long night ahead of them. She was partied out after Corey and Jack's belated wedding reception the night before and would be lucky if she got any sleep, she was so full of excitement to finally be off on holiday with her friends.

She had no idea where Darren was. He had been out all day and she couldn't believe he was not going to show up to say goodbye. When he realised that she was actually going to Greece, he stopped talking to her and avoided her by either leaving for work before she got up, or he came in after she went to sleep. Kieran hadn't seen him in days. She wished he'd stop being pathetic and grow up.

She checked she had all her luggage and was about to join her friends, who were waiting in the living room when Darren walked into the bedroom. He closed the door behind him. Kieran felt his stare, but refused to acknowledge him.

"So, you're really going?" he asked as she tried to side-step around him.

"Yes."

"Don't you care how I feel?" Darren asked sitting on the bed.

"Right now, not really Darren," she said.

Before he could continue, Chantelle tapped on the door, "The cab is here." she called through it.

"I'm coming," Kieran said. She finally looked at Darren. "I

have to go," she told him and walked towards the door
pulling her suitcase with her.

He stood up and grabbed her arm, "If you go Kieran then whatever happens is your fault," he said towering over her.

The lengths he would go to intimidate her were textbook. "Are you seriously trying to emotionally blackmail me?" she pulled her arm free.

"No, I'm not blackmailing you. I'm saying if this relationship means anything to you, you would consider my feelings and stay."

Kieran reached for the doorknob, "You've used that one before," she reminded him. She opened the door and walked out of the room with her suitcase.

Darren followed her. "Is that it then? You're going?" his voice was slightly panicked, as if he'd only just realised it.

"Damn straight," Kieran replied picking up her rucksack and putting it on her back.

"On your head be it." he said then glared at her friends. They glared back at him "Don't look at me like that!" he barked at them.

"Who are you shouting at?" Chantelle asked one hand on her hip.

"I don't know who you think you are." Christina hissed at him.

"Let's go," Kieran said quickly not wanting an argument to start. She grabbed the handle of her suitcase and wheeled it out the front door. Her friends thankfully followed. She cast a glance at Darren. He pretended to ignore her by picking up the joy pad and turning on the TV.

Kieran slammed the door closed without saying goodbye; as far as she was concerned, for the next week at least, she didn't have a boyfriend.

As much as she tried to erase Darren from her mind, he dominated her thoughts on the way to the airport and right up until they landed in Corfu. Only then did she push him to the back of her mind, determined that he would not stop her from having fun.

After an hour clearing immigration and a half hour drive to their resort, Kieran was excited even though she was overcome with tiredness. She glanced at Chantelle and Christina, who couldn't keep their eyes open, and dozed in the back of the taxi.

Kieran turned to admire the sun as it rose creating a yellow orange glow in the sky. She sat up when her eyes caught sight of the sea beyond the tall palm trees that lined the sides of the road. She made an involuntary squeal from excitement. This was her first girly holiday ever and excitement crept in.

"Why are you squealing?" Chantelle asked without opening her eyes.

"The sea, the sun, the beach, and the trees it's all beautiful," Kieran replied.

"Gay and boring," Christina mumbled also not opening her eyes.

Kieran laughed as the taxi pulled up outside the hotel. "We're here."

The girls walked through big tinted glass doors into a pale yellow marble reception area, and checked in. As they followed the concierge to their apartment, Kieran caught her breath when she realized that they were at the top of a cliff. Below was a breath taking view of the blue sea. She smiled when Chantelle and Christina caught sight of the view.

"Wow!" they simultaneously chorused

"It is beautiful, ah," the concierge said in a heavy Greek accent, when they approached a large gate. Kieran heard pride for his island in his voice. He pressed a button and a whirring noise started along with the creaking of metal, as the contraption in front of them came to life. Kieran exchanged an ominous glance with her friends as a cable car ambled up the side of the cliff towards them.

"Erm, are we getting in that?" Chantelle asked the concierge.

"Yes, it will take you down to your apartment." he replied with a smile.

"Our apartment is on the side of the cliff?" Chantelle asked. Her eyes showed disbelief.

"I think so," Kieran said as she climbed into the small cable car pulling her case behind her. Chantelle had an aversion to heights. It didn't help that the cable car was over water. Christina followed Kieran and they steadied themselves when the cable car rocked before they took their seats. Kieran watched Chantelle's eyes widen in horror as she stared at the sea below.

"It's perfectly safe," the concierge said resting his hand on her back to coax her into the cable car.

"Do you see how it's attached to a metal rope? It could snap at any time."

Christina laughed at her friend.

"Chan, come on, it's safe," Kieran said as she pulled her friend's case into the car. It rocked again.

Chantelle's eyes opened even wider. "Aren't there stairs?" she asked turning to face the concierge.

"Yes, but this way is quicker," he said in a slightly impatient tone.

"I don't care. I'll take them," she said heading in the direction of the stairs which were hidden behind a thick green bush.

"Fine, we'll see you there then," Kieran told her.

"I will take her. Press four and it will take you to your floor," the concierge said. Kieran followed his instructions. As the cable car moved off, she saw him shaking his head as he started down the stairs, Chantelle following.

Kieran cast a roving eye through the apartment window while they waited for Chantelle. The entire floor was tiled red. To the left, was the bathroom with a closet on the opposite side and straight ahead were large double doors that Kieran assumed led to the bedroom.

"The stairs were not fun," Chantelle announced once she joined them she was a little breathless.

"You should've have just gotten in with us," Kieran said unlocking the door.

"Are you mad? Did you see the drop?" Chantelle asked they walked past the bathroom.

Kieran took a quick look. It was spotless – which was a relief to her. She hated dirty bathrooms. She followed Christina into a large room and gasped. It housed two beds on the left and a sofa bed on the right. The walls were a lemon colour with two framed pictures that hung on either side. A kettle and four cups sat on a small dresser. The room itself was not the reason why she gasped. She was mesmerised by the view that stared at her through the glass sliding door ahead.

Kieran dropped her bag and ran to open it. She stood on the balcony that accommodated a small table and four chairs. A warm breeze greeted her and the salty smell of the sea hit her nostrils. The sun had risen, showing off flecks of yellow and orange in the sky which reflected in the sea making it sparkle like diamonds. It was beautiful. The smell of food coming from the hotel's restaurant above overtook the salty sea air and made her belly grumble.

"Wow! Girls, this is going to be a fabulous holiday!" Kieran announced with excitement. She was going to make sure of it.

"My God, can't we make a living doing this?" Chantelle asked a few hours later as she leant back in a sun lounger by the huge pool situated at the top of the cliff next to the restaurant. The sun was directly above them.

"One day Chan, one day." Kieran sighed putting down the book she had been reading since she left London. The Shopaholic series was her favourite holiday reading. Even though she had read them many times over, they still entertained her.

She looked across to her right. The hotel entertainment crew were playing darts with a group of people on the other side of the pool. She lay her head back on the sun lounger and closed her eyes, enjoying the feel of the sun on her skin. She heard kids splashing in the pool screaming with laughter, and conversations in different languages from the other tourists. Kieran opened her eyes and looked into the sky that was clear blue, not one cloud was visible. She exhaled.

This is what Darren had wanted her to give up, to sacrifice – for him. She had no regrets about leaving him behind; she knew it was going to take him a while to forgive her. At that moment, Kieran didn't care if he did.

Though she wanted to lie in, Kieran awoke the next day earlier than was necessary, probably because she realised that she would have to break up with Darren. Their situation was heavy on her mind and she couldn't justify being in a relationship with him any longer. She said as much to no one in particular when the three of them sat by the poolside later.

"We would make you even if you weren't planning to," Christina turned to face her.

"He really went too far this time," Chantelle said sipping a bright red cocktail.

Kieran took a sip of Pina Colada, savouring the coconut

creaminess and the hit of rum. "Why do you think he's changed so much?"

"This is what men do; they hide who they really are for the first year then the truth comes out," Chantelle offered in a loud voice.

Christina suppressed a giggle. Chantelle was already tipsy.

"It's true, look at Joshua," Kieran laughed and concurred.

"He was young, so it's not really the same as Darren," Chantelle challenged.

Kieran kissed her teeth. She still couldn't get over the cheek of Darren giving her an ultimatum. Did he really think it would work and that she'd choose him a second time?

Chantelle sat up and pushed her hat off her face, "You know why Darren's the way he is? Because he's realised he's not good enough for you and he's trying to keep you close so he doesn't lose you. He's an asshole," she said with a grin.

Kieran laughed and felt a tiny bit of guilt; she shrugged it off. He did not deserve her sympathy.

"It started when you got that job offer. Some men can't deal with their girlfriends or wives doing better than them, it's their male pride, or some crap like that," Christina added rolling her eyes.

"But why can't he be happy for me?" Kieran asked exasperated.

"Because he's selfish, arrogant, insecure and childish," Chantelle said.

"Oh, like all men then!" Christina said laughing.

"Men are hard work," Kieran added.

"I'm thinking about getting my boobs done," Chantelle suddenly changed the subject.

Kieran choked on her cocktail. Christina said nothing but was sat with her mouth wide open.

"What?" Chantelle asked looking at them as if she had said something obscure.

"Why do you want to get your boobs done?" Kieran asked trying to keep a serious face. She clutched her cocktail glass harder than necessary.

"Duh, because they are small."

"Chan, you have perfectly fine boobs!" Christina said in a

loud voice that caught the attention of a few people who looked over at them. She slurped the remains of her baileys cocktail oblivious to them.

"Thanks for that," Chantelle said lowering her hat over her almond shaped face.

Kieran felt light-headed all of a sudden. The cocktails had gone to her head; yet she was planning on having a third. "Can you even afford it?" she asked frowning.

"I can't at the moment, but I have about a grand saved."

"What?" Kieran spluttered.

"You heard me. I'm seriously thinking about it."

"Why didn't you mention this before?" Christina asked.

"Because I knew this would be your reaction, you two have well-proportioned boobs, so you don't understand."

"Chan you're hardly small," Kieran told her.

"I am a B you are both D's!"

"Actually, I'm an E," Christina corrected.

Kieran glared at her.

Chantelle scowled. "See what I mean? I feel like they are too small for my body."

"Don't go there," Christina told her rolling her eyes.

"It's true." Chantelle said standing up, she wobbled. The effects of drinking in the sun were taking its toll on her too.

"Chan, you have a great figure and your boobs are just fine," Kieran reassured her.

"Yes I agree, I do have a great figure; but my boobs are not fine."

Kieran looked up at her; she had an athletic figure and was well toned from being a dancer. Chantelle had been training for four years professionally, and was currently studying to be a dance teacher. She always appeared confident and Kieran hadn't known she was insecure about her breasts. Kieran and Christina were naturally slim and had curves in the right places, though not as toned as Chantelle, who worked out every day. Kieran wasn't happy with her arms; she thought they were fat and her stomach wasn't washboard flat.

She knew that Christina wasn't overly happy with her calves; she felt they were fat and her thighs small. The two of them hardly worked out. Kieran did like to go for a swim every now and then, she used to go regularly; it had been another thing that she had stopped doing when she started living with Darren. Like many women, she had insecurities; but she didn't let them get in the way.

"Chan, sometimes its good not having big boobs, you don't get backache for one, and you'll never have a problem with clothes." Christina advised.

"For real," Kieran agreed.

"Am I being shallow?"

"No, you're feeling insecure. We all feel that way from time to time. I just don't think you need to get a boob job though," Kieran explained. "You don't like pain as it is, so how will you cope?"

"I don't know. I haven't thought that far ahead yet," she said as she sat back down.

"Thank God you don't have four grand saved yet," Christina said shaking her head.

"Anyway," Chantelle changed the subject again, "What are we doing tonight?"

"I think we should take a taxi into town, have dinner and then find a club," Kieran said sitting up. Her sunglasses slid down her face and she squinted as the brightness of the sun hit her eyes. She pushed them on top of her head as she rummaged around in her bag and pulled out a box of cigarettes, she ignored Christina's glare. Her friend didn't approve of her smoking, but it calmed her down. Being in a relationship with Darren had changed her in many ways. She lit a cigarette and took a long drag.

"Smoking kills you know." Christina told her

"Yep that's what it says on the box." Kieran replied as she blew out a puff of smoke.

"It's a disgusting habit." Chantelle chimed in.

Kieran rolled her eyes behind her sunglasses; they weren't telling her anything she didn't know. "We were talking about tonight." she reminded them.

"Sounds good to me," Christina said standing up.

"Where are you going?" Chantelle asked her voice hopeful.

"To get another drink," she said sliding her toes into her flip flops.

Kieran giggled as Chantelle drained her glass and held it out to her. "Thanks."

"I believe the word you're looking for is please," Christina said seriously.

"Thanks." Chantelle repeated grinning and pulled her hat over her eyes.

"Raas." Christina cursed in patois.

Kieran followed suit and said sweetly, "Please?"

"You two are taking the piss."

"Chop, chop," Chantelle said clapping her hands before closing her eyes and lying back on the sun lounger.

Christina walked over to the pool, bent down, scooped up some water in an empty glass and walked over to Chantelle.

Kieran seeing what her friend was up to, stifled a giggle, put her cigarette out and picked up her camera waiting for Christina to strike. As Christina held the cup above her friend and poured it onto her stomach, Kieran took shots trying to steady her hands from the laughter.

Chantelle let out a high pitched scream that echoed around the pool, and jumped up from the sun lounger when the cold water touched her skin. Kieran collapsed in fits of giggles. Christina was in a heap on the floor, also doubled up with laughter. Chantelle stood open mouthed. She was less impressed when she noticed people laughing at her expense.

"You bitches, everyone is looking at me!" she hissed trying not to laugh, but couldn't help herself and joined them. "I will get you both back." She vowed.

Tears streamed down Kieran's face, while Christina clutched her stomach.

"You bloody lightweights, drunk after two cocktails; you should be ashamed of yourselves. I'll get the drinks then shall I?" Chantelle offered.

"Chop, chop!" Christina said doing a perfect imitation of Chantelle, as she collapsed back onto the lounger. Kieran burst into a fresh fit of giggles.

Fully recharged the following day after an early-ish night, Kieran suggested they bum around and do some light sight-seeing then hit the town in the evening. They had a cocktail at the hotel and shared two bottles of wine over dinner at an Indian restaurant that was disappointing. One of Kieran's favourite pastimes was to eat good food.

"At least we have an excuse to eat again later," she joked, she stepped between Chantelle and Christina and linked arms with them as they strolled down the street.

"Are you forgetting it's us? We never need an excuse to eat," Chantelle said laughing.

Kieran felt her phone vibrate in her bag. She ignored it. She knew it was Darren. He'd called her at stupid o clock and when he heard she was less than happy being awaken so early, he accused her of being in bed with someone. Kieran was so infuriated she squawked an obscenity at him and hung up. He'd been calling every hour since, much to her annoyance.

She looked around the area that was crowded with people enjoying the warm evening's light breeze. Bars, clubs and restaurants were everywhere. The smell of hot dogs, burgers and fried onions wafted around them from the food carts. She heard a mixture of music coming from the clubs as they strolled by. After walking down the road and back up, they found themselves in a bar with shocking pink neon lights playing loud music.

Kieran and her friends stood at the bar and bopped along to the music, casually checking out their surroundings. After ordering cocktails, they walked through the swarms of people trying to find an empty space near the DJ stand.

"Kieran!" a voice shouted. Kieran turned around recognising the voice.

"Oh my God!" she squealed as she threw her arms around a former college friend's neck. "Christina! Chan!" she called out to them as they walked ahead. "Look who's here!" Soon they were all having a group hug.

Courtney had been in the year above them at college. They hadn't seen him in a few years.

"Of all the bars in all of Greece, you had to walk in this one," he said laughing and taking Christina's hand.

"Gay," she said rolling her eyes and pulling her hand back laughing nervously. "I can't believe you're here," she told him shaking her head.

Kieran and Chantelle exchanged glances.

Christina and Courtney had been dating for about a year until Courtney decided to move away to study at university and broke off their relationship. Christina had been heartbroken and Kieran knew she still missed him.

"So who are you here with?" Kieran asked to lessen the tension.

"The boys from my football team, there's about twenty of us."

"Wow!" Chantelle grinned raising her eyebrows.

Kieran observed her smiling at some of his friends who were eyeing them with curiosity.

"Causing havoc as usual then?" Christina teased.

"Yes, I'm sure you three are as well," he told them. "How long will you be here?" he asked looking directly at Christina.

"We leave in four days," she replied then took a large gulp of her drink.

Kieran cleared her throat, "So maybe we should arrange to meet up tomorrow or something. You can introduce us to your single friends," she said with a grin.

"How much have you drunk tonight Kieran?" he asked nodding at her almost empty glass.

"Not that much," she lied.

"Well, I, on the other hand, haven't drunk enough, so let's swap numbers and we'll talk tomorrow," Christina told him.

Courtney took out his phone and she put her number in, said bye and rushed off. Kieran stared after her confused. They said bye to Courtney and she and Chantelle hurried out. They found Christina outside smoking a cigarette.

"What are you doing?" Kieran asked pulling it out of her mouth and throwing it away.

"I didn't know what else to do! Why is he here? Why would God do this to me now?" Christina asked sounding on the verge of hysteria.

"I guess it would be silly of me to ask how you feel about seeing him," Chantelle joked.

"It's not funny!" Christina wailed. "I wasn't ready to see him again. If I don't see him then I can pretend he doesn't exist like I have been doing for the past four years!" she held her head in her hands. "And now he probably thinks I'm mad. I just didn't know whether I was going to vomit, or cry, and I didn't want him to see me doing either. Oh why is he here?!" she wailed.

Kieran and Chantelle tried to calm her down, but her emotional state, mixed with the alcohol was not helping them.

Kieran noticed people staring as they walked in and out of the bar.

"I'm not going back in there. We have to find somewhere else to go," Christina told them as she walked off.

Kieran and Chantelle followed without saying a word and stopped walking when she did. Kieran watched as Christina took a deep breath and said, "I didn't think it would be this hard when I saw him again."

"I know, kind of takes your breath away doesn't it," Kieran said hugging her. She had felt the same way when she had seen Joshua that first time after so many years.

"I'm over it now. Let's go have a good time and forget about men. They're all useless selfish pricks."

Kieran and Chantelle laughed and nodded in agreement. They linked arms and found another bar.

Kieran had never seen Christina drink as much as she did that night. Seeing Courtney had clearly traumatised her. She told them it made her realise that she was not over him, and she didn't know if she ever would be.

Christina got so drunk that Kieran and Chantelle had to carry her most of the way back to the hotel; not before she threw up all over herself and on the floor in the back of the taxi. Neither the driver, Kieran or Chantelle were impressed, especially when he made them clean up. Christina had been too drunk to help.

The next morning, Kieran and Chantelle donned sunglasses to hide their hangovers. Leaving Christina in bed, they went up to the hotel restaurant for breakfast. Kieran managed to persuade Chantelle to get in the cable car. Maybe she was too hung over to realise what she agreed to; after, she refused to do it ever again. It hadn't helped that it had stopped suddenly mid journey and to make matters worse they had been stuck between floors even Kieran had felt slightly anxious.

An hour later, Kieran and Chantelle returned to the room to find Christina gone. Confused, Kieran left Chantelle and went back up to the restaurant to see if they had crossed paths and missed each other; she wasn't there either. She went back to the room taking the stairs as the cable car was being serviced.

Kieran picked up her phone to call her and saw ten missed calls from Darren. She kissed her teeth and called Christina. She got her voicemail, left a message and plugged the phone into the charger.

"Do you think she went to meet Courtney?" Chantelle asked.

"I thought she never wanted to see him again?" Kieran said as she walked out onto the balcony and sat at the table. She heard Chantelle put on some music before joining her.

"When did she say that?"

"In the taxi."

"You actually understood what she was going on about?" Chantelle asked surprised.

Kieran laughed as she started painting her nails. "After a while, yea."

"She's so funny when she's drunk." Chantelle flicked through a book.

"She always ends up crying somehow."

"And vomiting," Chantelle added with a scowl.

Kieran grimaced. Her phone started ringing. "That better be Christina and not Darren," she grumbled as she got up.

"Still not talking to him then?"

She stood at the doorway as she checked her phone; she sighed and put the phone back down. "I guess its Darren," Chantelle said.

"He is driving me mad, seriously," Kieran said rubbing her temples and sitting down.

"Relationships aren't meant to be this hard," Chantelle mused.

"I know, and he's making this one harder. It's always about him and what he wants. I always feel like I have to think about making him happy before myself." Kieran sighed and studied her nails on the hand she had just painted.

"A woman need never feel obligated to please a man," Chantelle read from her book.

"Men really understand that as well don't they?" Kieran rolled her eyes. "What is that anyway?" She asked looking at the cover of the book, "Three hundred and sixty five ways to keep your love alive by John Gray. Interesting?"

"It's okay, some of the quotes are good and some just make you roll your eyes."

"Like?" she started painting her other hand, while Chantelle thumbed through the book for a few seconds looking for a quote.

"When we mistakenly think men and women are the same our relationships are filled with unrealistic expectations." Chantelle read.

Kieran snorted then asked, "So it's unrealistic for me to think my boyfriend should be happy of my success, but I should be happy for him if it was the other way round?"

"Yes, if he got a promotion and a big opportunity, you are meant to support him and treat him like a king; you got the promotion and it dented his male pride, so how can he possibly make you feel good about yourself when it's your success that's making him feel bad?"

"It's not an unrealistic expectation, he's just an asshole," Kieran stated.

"Check this one out, 'A man will often ignore his feelings of attraction unless a woman looks a certain way.'"

"What?!" Kieran shouted in amazement jolting the table and almost knocking over the bottle of nail polish in the process.

"That is so rude. Basically if you're ugly then you have no hope."

"That is a great book Chan," Kieran said with sarcasm, "very uplifting for women."

"I told you some of them will make you roll your eyes," Chantelle reminded her.

"Yea, but that's shocking."

She and Chantelle spent the next hour discussing the book and men and then Christina appeared in the doorway.

"Oh, alive are you?" Kieran said clearly unimpressed.

"Come on, you knew I was fine," Christina told them as she sat down.

Kieran observed that she had been crying.

"Where were you?" Chantelle asked closing her book.

"With Courtney."

"Told you so!" Chantelle trilled before bouncing up and down in her chair.

"What happened?" Kieran asked ignoring Chantelle's excitement.

"He called me this morning and said he wanted to have breakfast together to catch up. We talked about what we've been up to and that was about it. We could meet up with him and some of his friends later if you lot want," she took her glasses off her head and covered her eyes.

"That's it?" Chantelle asked clearly disappointed.

"What did you think he was going to do? Tell me the four years apart have been torture and seeing me has made him realise how much he's missed me and he doesn't want to lose me again, and can't live without me?" Christina said in one breath. Evidently she had hoped the same thing.

"Stranger things have happened," Kieran offered.

"Sometimes you are way too naïve," Christina gave her a dirty look.

"You know he's still crazy about you, he always has been," Kieran reasoned.

"Do you realise who you are?" Christina asked with a smirk on her face.

"Who? Kieran replied.

"Charlotte, Sex and the City," Christina said with impatience.

Chantelle laughed in agreement. "I did tell you."

Kieran thought about the theory. Was she like Charlotte? The eternal optimist as she was referred to in the programme. Kieran wouldn't describe herself as such; sometimes she hoped things worked out how she liked. Everyone deserved a happy ending, plus Charlotte could be quite judgemental, a little bit of a prude and she had a lot of rules she adhered to. Kieran wasn't quite that strict with herself, although maybe if she was, she wouldn't be in the situation she was in.

"I'm not Charlotte," she corrected her.

Christina gave her a dismissive nod.

"I'm not!" Kieran protested trying not to laugh.

"You're Miranda," Chantelle told Christina.

"So does that make you Samantha then?" Christina asked her.

"I wish I could be like Samantha. She is a legend. I'm not that brave, plus I let my emotions get involved too much. I guess I'm more of a Carrie."

Kieran clapped her hands together with excitement.

Chantelle and Christina looked at her.

"What's wrong with you?" Christina asked her eyes narrowed.

"Courtney is Steve," Kieran giggled.

Chantelle smirked.

"Kieran, shut up," Christina said seriously. "It's not funny."

"I'm not joking; Miranda didn't believe in Steve's feelings for her, and look how that turned out."

"It's a TV show. Stuff like that doesn't happen in real life," Christina snapped throwing Kieran a dark look.

Kieran exchanged glances with Chantelle acknowledging Christina's overreaction.

"Where do you think they get the stories from? Sometimes people experience things they write about," she replied before sipping her drink.

"Sometimes you live in a dream world," Christina scowled.

"Sometimes you are too cynical for your own good," Kieran hit back.

Chantelle picked up her book and cleared her throat interrupting them before it turned into an argument.

"No more quotes Chan," Kieran laughed.

"Why not? She could do with three hundred and sixty five ways to keep her love alive," Chantelle said with a grin.

Christina glared at her. "It is alive enough thank you, too alive," she said, reached over and picked up Kieran's glass, took a mouthful and screwed up her face in shock when she realised it was alcohol.

"You lot are alcoholics I swear." she said handing the glass back to Kieran.

"Quite often a man feels his love when he is directly faced with the possibility of losing a woman," Chantelle read ignoring her.

"Well how is that relevant? He lost me already and he didn't care much then," Christina said in a bitter tone, she leant forward resting her chin in her hand.

"Yes, four years later he's seen you and maybe now can't face the possibility of losing you again. Maybe breakfast was his way of getting things moving?" Chantelle suggested.

"Why are you even reading that?" Christina looked at her like she had gone mad.

"It's interesting."

"Hardly, you missed out the quote that if you're ugly a man will pretend he feels nothing for you," Kieran scoffed. Her stomach rumbled reminding her lunchtime had approached.

Christina took the glass out of Kieran's hand, "Well that's pretty obvious, men can be fickle," she said sipping Kieran's drink again. Kieran was about to remind her about her alcoholic comment when Chantelle laughed.

"This one is going to crack you two up. 'Men respond much better when they are not seen as the problem but as the solution,'" she screeched.

"You can tell a man wrote this book," Kieran said shaking her head in disbelief.

"Half the time they are the problem. Why should we make them feel otherwise?" Chantelle asked.

"I think you should get a refund on your book Chan," Christina told her.

"What crap!" Chantelle exclaimed.

"It's true, if you piss me off then I'm not going to sit here and tell you it's not you," Kieran agreed.

"So it's okay to lie to spare their feelings?" Christina asked.

Kieran laughed. "Pretty much,"

"They respond better when they are not seen as the problem," Chantelle repeated laughing. "It's the same thing all the time, we have to mother them and boost their egos, but God forbid we do anything for ourselves just in case we make them feel bad."

"Women respond better when men aren't assholes. Maybe that quote should be in the book?" Kieran laughed.

"We should write our own book," Chantelle suggested.

"It's true, 'Three hundred and sixty five ways to keep yourself alive, a must have for all men,'" Christina added.

Kieran spat out her drink unable to contain her laughter. This made Chantelle and Christina laugh too and pretty soon they were all collapsed in giggles.

7 CHAPTER SEVEN

The three girls set off after breakfast, joined the queue outside the front of the hotel and waited for the shuttle bus that would take them to the beach. They agreed to spend the last day there having only visited once before. Kieran was in heaven, the early morning sun was already blazing in the sky, it felt great on her skin.

"So, did Courtney say anything about last night?" Chantelle asked Christina, "I know you had a wake-up call from him."

Kieran's mind flashed back to the previous night when they met up with Courtney. She and Chantelle had shamelessly flirted with a few of his friends that had joined them; it was harmless fun, and she'd had a great time. Christina spent all her time with Courtney and at one point, Kieran had seen them kissing.

"No." Christina replied sullenly. The bus came along the gravel path causing the dust to rise; Kieran covered her face and hurried onto the hot bus.

"From my observation, looks like he's still crazy about you. He hardly paid anyone else any attention," Chantelle told her as they took their seats.

"I think it was the alcohol. He probably thought I'd sleep with him," Christina replied through the gap in the seats. Kieran and Chantelle were sat behind her.

"He's not like any of Darren's friends," Kieran reminded her.

"If you remember, Courtney hated them at college."

"It's true, hmm, birds of a feather…" Chantelle said.

"Yea, I know they flock together. Maybe he is just like them." Kieran mused.

"Still breaking up with him?" Christina asked turning around and kneeling on the chair so she faced Kieran and Chantelle.

"Yep!" Kieran said looking out of the window at the swaying palm trees. Her phone bleeped and she smiled as she read the text message.

"Oh yea, who's that from?" Christina asked grinning.

"What?" Kieran asked innocently.

"It's not Darren, you would've kissed your teeth already," Chantelle pointed out.

"Whatever," Kieran retorted rolling her eyes

"It's Joshua isn't it?" Chantelle asked.

"Yes, it is, he's just saying hi, hoping I'm having a good time and he can't wait to see me again."

"What do you think Darren would say if he knew you were talking to your ex- boyfriend?" Christina asked.

"He'd accuse me of sleeping with him. What do you think?"

"Hmm, maybe he's not so stupid after all," Chantelle teased.

Kieran hit her friend playfully and laughed. "I'm not sleeping with him!" she protested in a loud voice that caught the attention of the other passengers, who craned their necks to stare at them disapprovingly. Kieran hid her head in shame; not before noticing Christina hiding in her seat as she stifled her laughter.

"Maybe you should test the waters?" Christina suggested once she had composed herself.

Chantelle spluttered in shock next to Kieran.

"I am not sleeping with him," Kieran hissed through the chairs to Christina.

"Yet," Christina said over her shoulder with a smile.

"No. I am not sleeping with him in the near future either; a lot happened in the past, stuff he doesn't even know about and that needs to be dealt with, before I even consider going back down that road." Kieran explained.

"Oh, so you haven't given it much thought then?" Chantelle asked sarcastically.

"No, not much," Kieran replied in an equally sarcastic tone. She had thought about it every day, but she wasn't about to admit that.

The bus pulled up at the beach severing the conversation much to Kieran's relief.

After splashing around in the sea, Kieran stretched out on the sun lounger relaxing to the music on her iPod. In her opinion, the holiday had gone well and she'd had a great time. A holiday she would always remember. She smiled with satisfaction.

"What shall we do on our last night?" Christina asked.

"Dinner and hang out at a bar I guess. We don't want to overdo it. Flying with a hangover is not the greatest feeling," Kieran replied turning over onto her stomach. Her skin felt like it was cooking, she was sure she could feel her organs roasting. She loved feeling the sun on her body, however.

"Why can't we live in a hot country?" Chantelle complained.

"We should've stayed for two weeks," Kieran said, thinking she needed to take another dip in the sea.

"I couldn't afford to, not working part time," Christina replied closing her eyes.

"Are you nervous about getting your results?" Kieran asked her. Christina had taken her final exam and her results were expected in a few weeks.

"Kind of; I'm trying not to think about it," she said sitting up.

"Where are you off to?" she asked when Kieran stood up and put on her flip flops.

"To get a drink, I suppose you two want one as well?"

"Please," Christina and Chantelle said at the same time. "Chop, chop!" They chorused and collapsed with laughter.

Kieran rolled her eyes at her friends. She made her way over to the beach bar and joined the busy queue. She had only been standing there a few minutes when she noticed a big hairy man walking through the bar wearing red speedos and carrying a bright pink lilo. She bit her lip as she tried not to laugh. Who had told him that was a good idea? She spotted a young blonde woman behind him. As she walked past Kieran she gave her a dirty look. Kieran's face flushed in embarrassment, clearly the woman was his girlfriend and she had seen Kieran staring at him. Kieran quickly averted her eyes and looked in the other direction.

She stood on her tip toes to try and see over the queue of people in front of her. Fortunately, it looked worse than it was. She became aware of someone standing next to her when she felt an arm brush against hers. She turned and her eyes connected with a well-tanned chest. She was so shocked, she took a step back and looked up to see whom it belonged to. She had a second shock when she looked into the greenest most beautiful eyes she'd ever seen.

Oh sweet Jesus.

He was tall, with an athletic build, olive skin and dark brown hair that was cut close to his head. He wore a five o'clock shadow that gave his pretty boy looks a rugged edge. The word gorgeous sprung to Kieran's mind and her body tingled.

He looked down at her while a smile played on his lips and said, "Hey," in a pleasant deep voice.

Is his accent English? No way!

She'd never seen anyone so gorgeous from London; he looked like he should be dressed in a tuxedo working a red carpet in LA or New York. "Hi," she managed.

Obviously he was not hitting on her. She must be hallucinating; she had been out in the sun for too long. He was completely out of her league. Only in her dreams could she find someone so good looking with perfect sun kissed skin that complimented his toned body.

He held out his hand, "I'm Rome."

Kieran felt her face flush. He was from London. She ignored the butterflies in her tummy "Rome? That's unusual," she said as she took his hand then winced.

Was that rude?

"You have no idea," he said tightening his chiselled jaw. He was stunning.

Say something then.

"Is it... spelt like… the capital city of Italy?" she asked. She noticed his long thick eye lashes and the way his eyes sparkled in the sunshine.

"Yep, R-O-M-E."

"Cool."

"What's your name?" he asked smiling.

Kieran didn't know at that moment... he was still holding her hand.

Why is he staring at me like that? Oh right my name...

"Kieran," she replied shaking his hand. It was soft and she

wondered what field of work he was in. Thank God he didn't appear to bite his nails, she really hated that. She extracted her hand.

Definitely too much sun, why am I checking out his hands?

"Where are you from Kieran?" he asked leaning on the bar.

"London, North London," she replied sitting down on a bar stool, she needed the extra support her legs were shaking so much – which was ridiculous. After ordering her drinks she looked up at him.

"What about you?"

"I live in Woodford," he said also sitting down on a vacant stool. "Would you mind if I asked you to have a drink with me?" Kieran looked at his full, inviting lips.

It would be amazing to kiss him. Her eyes widened from the thought.

"What's wrong?" he asked.

"Nothing, of course, I'd love to," she said with a smile; she couldn't refuse even if she had wanted to. She could feel Chantelle and Christina's eyes burning into her back.

When the bar man placed the drinks before them, Rome said, "I've got this."

"Thank you," Kieran told him, "Let me give these to my friends and I'll be right back."

Chantelle gave her the thumbs up as she approached them.

"Oh my effing God! Did you see what just happened?" she screeched at them.

Christina rolled her eyes.

"Hurry up and get back over there!" Chantelle hissed as she took the drinks out of Kieran's shaking hand.

"I don't know what to say!" she wailed looking over her shoulder towards the bar, her stomach knotted. He was looking in her direction.

"Kieran, don't be stupid, he's just a man," Christina snapped.

"He's a beautiful man," Kieran corrected taking a deep breath. She smoothed her hair down and put on some lip gloss that Chantelle handed to her at lightning speed.

"One of us needs to get some on this holiday," Chantelle said winking.

Christina made a disgusted sound, which they both ignored.

"Wish me luck," Kieran called over her shoulder as she left.

"Don't come back here without his phone number," Chantelle teased.

Kieran waved at them as she walked back to the bar.

Within ten minutes of Kieran joining Rome, she learned that he was twenty five years old and a fireman. They talked about their lives back home, and what they'd been up to while they had been in Greece. Kieran omitted to tell him that she had a boyfriend albeit soon to be ex-boyfriend. He was with friends and had been there three days longer than the girls; he was also flying home the next day -and whether coincidence or fate - on the same flight. She felt as if someone was testing her and all she knew was given the chance, she would happily fail. She smiled as she sipped her drink.

"Why are you smiling?" he asked curiously.

"No reason," she said trying to look as serious as possible.

"So, do you have a boyfriend?"

Kieran put her glass down. "Well that only took you over an hour to ask, I'm impressed," she teased.

He smiled. Kieran was sure she saw a dimple. She hadn't noticed before, because she was mesmerised by the way his eyes spoke to her. She had a weakness for men with dimples – she was definitely being tested.

"I wanted to know if it was relevant first. Now that I've spoken to you properly, it's very relevant," he said looking into her eyes.

Kieran shifted in her seat. "Do you have a girlfriend?"

"Nope, I am single; I've been single for about a year now, see how easy that was?" he teased.

Kieran poked her tongue out at him.

He laughed. "Well?"

"Yes, I have a boyfriend." she said in a tone that surprised her.

"Wow," he chuckled and took a sip of his drink.

Kieran watched the muscles ripple in his arm and shifted in her seat again. She was lusting after a stranger. It was so unlike her. "It's complicated… long story," she added.

"I'm not in a rush," he replied, as he called the barman over and asked for two refills.

Kieran gulped. "I don't want to talk about him. So who came

up with your name? I've never met anyone with the name of a city before; although the Beckham's named one of their sons Brooklyn where he was apparently conceived, well that's what I read in a magazine." Kieran knew she was babbling, she couldn't help it, he made her nervous on so many levels, and that was not good. She was, however, genuinely interested in his background.

An uncomfortable look clouded his face and he shifted in his seat. "Do we have to talk about it?"

"Not if you don't want to. I have an unusual name, too. I know constantly repeating yourself is annoying," she said with a shrug though she wondered why the history of his name would make him feel uncomfortable.

"Kieran is not unusual," he pointed out. The smile returned.

"It is for a girl, my sister's name is Corey. I think my mum had a thing about boy's names for girls," she said rolling her eyes.

"It's unique," he said and swallowed a mouthful of beer.

"So is Rome." Kieran noticed the uncomfortable look returned.

"It's not that unique. It's actually an abbreviation of my full name." His face flushed and Kieran wondered whether he was embarrassed.

"What is it?" she asked intrigued.

"I don't want to say." He said with a shy smile.

Kieran made a criss cross pattern over her heart and said, "I won't laugh, promise." She couldn't imagine it was that bad. He looked at her, swallowed another mouthful of beer and mumbled something Kieran didn't understand. "What did you say?"

"Romeo," he mumbled again.

"Your name is Romeo." She said slowly. She was not sure how she felt about that. There were too many connotations. Not all of them good. She didn't even know what to say.

"Stupid isn't it?" he said as if he knew exactly where her mind went. The expression on his face reminded Kieran of a sulky child. He was pouting.

She couldn't help it, suddenly she was laughing. "I'm sorry," she said in between breaths.

He was laughing too. "You said you wouldn't laugh!"

"It was the look on your face," she explained.

Rome chuckled "Yea I hate it so much it shows,"

"You shouldn't," she said smiling "It's cute,"

Rome stared at her.

Kieran had no idea what was going through his mind, she didn't know what his expression meant. Her nerves made her keep talking. "Why Romeo though? Who chose the name, your mum, or dad?"

"My mum, she had a thing for Shakespeare," he said rolling his eyes.

"And you don't like it?"

"Nope. I actually tried to change it legally when I was fourteen; they wouldn't let me, so I go by Rome instead."

"It could be worse, she could have named you Mercutio," she teased.

Rome frowned "She tried; it's actually my middle name…"

Kieran stared back at him in shock. She could not remove the expression she knew was on her face.

"I'm joking." Rome announced with a grin.

Kieran literally breathed a sigh of relief.

Then they were both laughing.

Thank God!

Once Rome caught his breath he continued. "My dad didn't like Romeo, he would've let me change it if it was down to him. He's the only one in the family who calls me Rome."

"I like it though," Kieran said after regaining her equilibrium. She took a sip of her drink. She liked him.

He gazed at her and Kieran's stomach flipped. "I like you," he said reaching across the table and stroking her hand.

Kieran blushed. From the corner of her eye, she noticed someone approaching them; she turned to see this tall, dark and muscular guy grinning at them. She looked back at Rome; who was smiling too, though his face looked a little red.

He removed his hand from Kieran's "I'll be two seconds," he said standing up to talk to his friend. Kieran smiled at him and nodded. While they were distracted she looked over in the direction of her friends, this new guy was exactly Chantelle's type.

Chantelle was one-step ahead of her and already on her way over. "We're going back to the hotel in a bit," she said when she reached Kieran.

"Why?" she was in no rush to leave.

"We are going into town remember?"

Rome turned back to her, and she said, "This is my friend Chantelle. Chantelle, Rome." Kieran looked at his friend.

"Luke," he said smiling at Chantelle.

"What are you doing on your last night?" Rome asked while looking into her eyes.

"Dinner and a bar probably," she replied finishing the remains of her drink.

"Which bar? Maybe we could meet up with you?" Luke said still smiling at Chantelle.

"That's a great idea!" Kieran cheered. She hadn't meant to sound so excited but she knew that's how it had come out. Chantelle looked at her and shook her head.

"I like your enthusiasm," Rome said laughing. "I thought my name would've scared you off."

She giggled girlishly and touched his arm. "Don't be silly."

It's gonna take much more than that.

She was grinning at him, she realised that, but she couldn't seem to stop. It didn't help that he was grinning back at her.

Chantelle suddenly cleared her throat.

"What?" Kieran asked still smiling.

Chantelle rolled her eyes.

"Okay, well swap numbers and get on with it," Luke said with a hint of impatience.

Kieran and Chantelle looked at him, both surprised by his tone.

"Dude, Chill," Rome said frowning at his friend

"This is long, come on we can meet up with Simone and her friends," Luke said. Kieran was sure she saw him wink.

Rome was glaring at his friend. "What are you doing?" he asked him.

"Being rude," Chantelle said before Luke could reply.

"Who's Simone?" Kieran asked looking at Rome. He looked like he was about to reply but Chantelle cut in.

"Does it matter?" She asked.

"Yes." Kieran said raising her eyebrows.

"He just said it to piss us off, he's probably trying to make us jealous, or something equally as stupid." Chantelle said giving Luke a dirty look

"Pardon?" he asked clearly in shock.

"You heard me," Chantelle said looking straight at him.

Rome was biting his lip; Kieran was looking from Chantelle to Luke in shock. What had she missed?

Luke glared at Chantelle and without a word turned and walked off.

"Not sure who he thinks he is," Chantelle exclaimed loudly.

"I think he just got a taste of his own medicine." Rome chuckled.

Kieran turned to the barman to order another drink.

Chantelle waved him away "I think you've had enough."

"It's our last day!" Kieran protested.

"And if you want to make it to tonight, I think you should stop for a bit."

"I think you should listen to your friend," Rome added with a smile. "If you're like this after two…."

She poked her tongue at him; and he laughed, flashing his dimples. He seemed to be enjoying their childish banter. He took his phone out of his pocket and handed it to her, she added her number to his phone book and handed it back to him. As she hopped off the bar stool, she slipped, Rome reached out to steady her and somehow she ended up with her body pressed up against his, his arms around her. Shocked, she looked up at him; his eyes were talking to her, inviting her in.

"Had enough now?" he asked seriously.

Kieran felt a warm pleasurable tingle down her spine as he held her there, close to him. She could smell his cologne, and the warmth of his body on hers, his strong arms around her. It did things to her, and before she could stop herself she said the first thing that came to her head.

"Definitely not." From her tone of voice they both knew she wasn't talking about alcohol. Rome made a sound of appreciation and bent his head slowly towards her. Kieran's heart began to pound, she hadn't prepared for this to happen, but she was open to it, lost in the moment, lost in him, oblivious to everything around her, she closed her eyes, his lips had just touched hers, when Chantelle cleared her throat and forced herself in between them.

"Sorry to interrupt!" she said loudly.

Kieran glared at her friend.

Chantelle laughed. "Don't look at me like that, I'm not the only one who doesn't want to see you two kissing in the middle of the beach bar, there's plenty of time for that." she told them. Rome laughed and looked slightly embarrassed. "Let's go Kieran," she stepped out from in between them so that they could say their goodbyes.

Kieran looked up at Rome, he smiled back at her. "See you tonight?" she said.

"Definitely," he vowed.

She could still feel the tension of their almost kiss fizzing between them, she wanted that moment back. Chantelle was right though, they had to be alone for that.

I'm actually a little bit drunk.....

Kieran began to walk away with her friend. Smiling over her shoulder at him as they headed back to Christina.

"Welcome back, remembered me have you?" Christina asked in a sarcastic tone when they approached.

Kieran flopped down next to her in a daze. A huge smile plastered across her face, she couldn't even hide it. "Wow." She breathed.

"Are you for real?" Christina asked rolling her eyes.

"Is he looking over here?" Kieran asked ignoring her. She looked at Chantelle, who did a quick check and nodded. "He is freaking sexy!" Kieran announced.

"Boyfriend at home," Christina reminded her.

"Asshole at home you mean," Chantelle said grinning "He's pretty much accused her of sleeping with every man she encounters, so she may as well make the headache worth her while."

"Oh my God!" Christina exclaimed looking back and forth at them.

"What?" Kieran and Chantelle asked at the same time.

"You can't." she told Kieran.

"Did I say I was going to?" Kieran asked as she fanned herself. She wasn't sure if it was the sun, the alcohol, or Rome that had her hot and bothered.

"You are thinking about it," Christina pointed out.

"Of course I am. Did you not see him? He is beautiful... and when in Rome...although technically....." she said and collapsed in a heap of laughter.

Chantelle laughed too "You are such a pervert." she told her friend.

"What's his name?" Christina asked.

Their laughter rose as Kieran and Chantelle hugged each other unable to stop themselves.

"Rome." Kieran gasped between giggles.

"You're not in Rome," Christina chided her, clearly not getting Kieran's joke.

This made Kieran and Chantelle laugh harder.

Christina huffed impatiently waiting for them to calm down. Kieran pulled herself together first. "Seriously, his name is Rome, well Romeo actually."

"Ha! How original is that?" Christina asked laughing.

"Are you serious? Chantelle asked.

"His mum had a thing for Shakespeare. He doesn't like Romeo, so he goes by Rome."

"It's a stupid name, what was his mum thinking?" Chantelle asked.

"It's not that bad." Kieran told them. It wasn't the worst name she had heard, and the Beckham's also had a son called Romeo.

"Could you really take a guy called Romeo seriously?" Christina asked.

Kieran ignored her friends and looked over to where her crush was. He was engrossed in a game of football with his friends. He must have felt her eyes on him, because he looked over at her.

Kieran looked away quickly. "He is going to get me into trouble," she mumbled.

"He is pretty fly for a white guy," Chantelle acknowledged.

"Greek God. My Adonis," Kieran corrected; a gleam in her eyes.

"Kieran!" Christina exclaimed.

"I don't care," Kieran said grinning.

"Yea, you're not drinking anymore either," Christina told her.

"Shame, I told you," Chantelle said smugly, picking up her iPod.

Kieran tutted and stood up. "Anyone for a dip?" she needed to cool down and the water had never looked more inviting. "Well?" she repeated as she ran towards the water, smiling because she knew Rome was watching her.

Not long after, Kieran and her friends headed back to the hotel and packed most of their belongings so as not to be in a rush the following day. Kieran lit a cigarette as she sat on the balcony waiting for Chantelle and Christina to finish dressing. She felt nervous about meeting Rome again. She wasn't even sure if he would call, and anxiety replaced her nervousness.

She took a drag of the cigarette and watched the sun set behind the mountains. The peachy glow and wisps of pink and orange clouds signalled that the next day would also be beautiful. Kieran sighed. She was sad to leave; and now thanks to Rome, her holiday suddenly had the potential of being extra special.

She was excited about possibly spending the last night in his company. She felt like a sixteen-year-old around him. It had been ages since she had felt nervous and excited all at the same time over a man. Kieran realised even more, that there was a spark missing from her and Darren's relationship. She didn't know how it had gotten so bad between them; if she was honest with herself their relationship had never meant to be 'forever and ever' serious.

Kieran hadn't gotten over Joshua when she invited Darren to live with her. He was a distraction from the reality that she and Joshua were over, and the thoughts that haunted her. She loved him in her own way, but she knew deep down she was always looking for a way out and moving to New York would've given her that chance, if she hadn't been such a coward.

Her phone made a noise alerting her to a message. Her stomach lurched. It was Rome. She read the text a few times, looking for any hidden meaning that might tell her that he was as intrigued about her as she was about him.

"Rome is going down to Venus Bar. Said we can meet him there after we've eaten," Kieran told her friends.

"Venus is the Greek Goddess of love isn't she?" Chantelle called from inside.

Christina cackled.

Kieran ignored their taunts. "I didn't think he'd text," she mused.

"Hmm, he's keen," Chantelle said appearing at the door.

Kieran grinned, "So am I," she said raising her eyebrows

mischievously. "Let's get out of here already." They made their way to a Greek restaurant that they had sampled a few days earlier and quite liked.

"Oh My God, you really like him don't you?" Chantelle said as she sat down in the restaurant. "You haven't stopped talking about him since we left the hotel."

"I think so, he makes me giddy, and I don't think I've ever felt like that before," Kieran said as she browsed through the menu. She wasn't sure what she felt like. She was hungry the sea air always made her hungrier than usual.

"Really?"

"Well, Darren and I were friends first, so that instant spark wasn't even there, and with Joshua I was fourteen, so it's hardly the same as meeting someone in my twenties. I'm an adult now. To feel this way is almost like being fourteen again; though way more intense and I like that feeling. It has a certain kind of mystery; you know the je ne sais quoi."

"What about Joshua?" Christina asked looking up from her menu.

"What about him?"

"I thought you had feelings for him."

"I do," she admitted.

"So then what are you doing?" Chantelle questioned.

"Making it uncomplicated. I don't know if I have the energy to go back down the Joshua road and drag up the past. I'd rather not deal with it yet, so if that means forgetting what we could have then fine. Anyway, I'm sure Rome is out of my league long term, so I don't think it's even an issue. He's probably only after one thing," Kieran said with a shrug. "I just want to have some fun. I'm on holiday after all and right now I'm famished. What are we ordering?"

She was perplexed as to why Rome walked into her life then. Kieran had no expectations. She just had the impulse to go with the flow. The best part was Rome knew nothing about her past. He was fresh and new, and maybe he was what she needed to move on from the lovers in her past and present.

"You can't run from it forever though, you know you're going to have to deal with it before you can move on, and he is not out of your league," Chantelle told her ignoring her question.

"Can we get back to that later? I'm hungry." Kieran insisted.

"Me too," said Christina.

"You're quiet tonight," Kieran said to her while getting the waiter's attention.

"I have my own drama to deal with; I can't cope with all this excitement." Christina replied closing the menu.

"You know you're happy about seeing Courtney later, so don't try it," Chantelle told her smirking.

Christina pressed her lips together to hide a smile. "A little maybe," she admitted, "Still, I don't see what the point is if it's not going anywhere,"

"Maybe you should try and be a little bit more like Charlotte just for once," Kieran suggested.

"I prefer Miranda thank you," she hit back. The waiter came to their table before Kieran could reply.

They ordered a Meze platter, which consisted of different types of meats, fish, rice, pitta bread and a variety of dips. After tucking in and eating way too much, they left the restaurant. Kieran slotted between Christina and Chantelle and linked arms. They made the ten minute walk to the Venus Bar. Courtney had called Christina during dinner and she told him to meet her there, turned out he was heading there to meet to meet his friends. It had all worked out well.

As they got closer, the music grew louder and Kieran saw people queuing to get into the bar. Out-of-the-blue, Christina squealed, pulled away and started to dance in the middle of the street to the music that filtered out of the bar. "I love this song!" she cheered.

"What are you doing?" Kieran hissed grabbing her hand as if she was a naughty child.

"Yea, people are staring," Chantelle told her in disapproval.

Christina pulled herself away, ignored them and continued to bounce to the music. Embarrassed, Kieran and Chantelle joined the queue. When they reached the door, Christina joined them. The bouncer gave her a funny look.

"She likes dance music, it's her happy drug," Kieran explained to him.

"We like that kind of drug," the bouncer said with a chuckle, as he stamped their hands.

"Right you two, keep an eye out for Rome; I'm going to act like I'm not looking if he spots me first," Kieran told them as she checked her reflection in the mirror that lined the walls. She didn't need to look far. Rome and his friends were standing at the bar. Kieran felt a rush of heat when she saw him. Her neck and face flushed when he gave her a warm smile. She waved as she made her way over to join him, ignoring the shaking in her legs. After the introductions and drink orders, Courtney arrived, and after greeting the girls he approached Rome with familiarity. Kieran looked at Chantelle and Christina in confusion.

"You two know each other?" Kieran asked trying to sound indifferent.

"Yea, I told you there was about twenty of us here." Courtney told her.

"And how do you know each other?" Rome asked looking from Kieran to Courtney.

"We were at college together." She explained. She was sure he looked relieved.

"Rome is on our football team," Courtney explained.

"Oh! So you're the Christina he keeps talking about," Rome said turning to Christina who broke into an uncomfortable smile.

"Dude," Courtney said and shook his head.

Rome grinned, but said nothing else.

They indulged in light conversation but it wasn't long before one of them started talking football and sport in general. With an entourage of twenty men, not that Kieran and her friends were complaining, it was no surprise to Kieran. However, though she loved football, there was a time and a place. In the bar on the last night of her holiday was neither the time, nor place. She made eye contact with Chantelle and Christina and nodded towards the dance floor. To Kieran's delight, the DJ switched to eighties soul music. The girls were in their element and took over the dance floor.

After a few songs, Kieran looked over at Rome, who was still standing at the bar. She could see different women at the bar, trying to get his attention, smiling at him, trying to get him to make eye contact. He was studiously ignoring them as he tried to get the barman's attention. She hoped it was because of her.

It was as if he could feel her eyes on him, because suddenly he looked over at her, Kieran couldn't turn away quick enough, so she held his gaze and smiled at him, he smiled back, flashing his dimples.

"I'll be back." She told her friends over the music.

Feeling brave she made her way over to him, she didn't want him paying attention to anyone but her.

No sooner was she at his side, she felt awkward.

I should flirt with him a little.....How do I do that again?

It had been way too long and he made her way too nervous for her to flirt confidently with him.

He bent his head and asked, "Would you like a drink?"

Kieran felt his breath on her neck and nodded woodenly. "What would you like?"

She tried not to stare into his eyes because she knew she would probably kiss him then and there, and she wasn't ready for that. He moved closer to her and Kieran got a whiff of a familiar spicy, yet sweet scent. The same scent that she had noticed on him earlier that day.

"What cologne are you wearing?"

He smiled, "Armani Code. You like it?"

She nodded; it was one of her favourite perfumes. She was wearing the women's version herself. *Ha! We match!*

He was still smiling at her. She tried not to stare at his lips; the fullness and the curve of them made her want to kiss him. In the brief contact they had shared earlier she knew his lips were soft. After replaying the scene in her head more than few times and remembering the way he had made her feel she knew he would be a good kisser.

The barman approached them.

"Drink?" Rome asked again.

She looked back at the cocktail menu and against her better judgement said, "A seductive kiss, please."

"Coming right up," he said grinning at her. He ordered a beer for himself.

"Thank you," she said when he handed her the drink. She took a sip, it was tasty although she had no idea what the ingredients were. She was just being a hussy. She cringed in shame as her conscience tutted; a now familiar sound.

"So do you like seductive kisses?" Rome asked her. Kieran's face flushed before she could answer him. "I was talking about the drink." he said and chuckled at the look on her face "Do you want to go outside for some air?"

"Sure," Kieran straightened her shoulders to mask how nervous she was feeling. It was as if every fibre of her body was aware she was stepping out of her comfort zone. He took her hand and led the way. Kieran felt the chemistry flowing between them. She was not in the right place in her life to be falling for someone. She had too much baggage. Chantelle was right, she could run from it; it'd only come around to bite her in the rear at some point. But this…this… whatever she was feeling for the complete stranger she'd met on the beach, the intensity of it was making her stupid.

They found a table and Rome pulled a chair out for her. After Kieran took a seat, she shivered.

Rome sat next to her, "You cold?" he asked putting his arm around her.

Kieran shook her head and looked at him. She was far from cold. He was staring at her and his head began inching closer to hers. The seductive wood and musk smell of his Armani code drew her in and Kieran felt her head moving towards his, she couldn't even stop herself, she was hypnotised by everything about him.

Their noses touched. He inclined his head, and his mouth met hers in a soft and gentle kiss. Kieran felt his arms around her pulling her closer to him. She allowed her body to move into him. His eyelashes tickled her face and she found it hard to concentrate; their lips were still locked and moving eagerly in synchronisation. Her phone started ringing startling them from their intimate moment.

Kieran pulled away with a crash back to reality. She had just cheated on Darren – again, and when she checked her phone, it was him calling. She turned the phone off and looked up to see Rome staring at her, as if searching her face for an emotion he could recognise. A part of her wanted to continue kissing him, to hide away from the reality of her situation; the sane part told her to stop right then and not confuse her life any more.

"Wrong number?" Rome asked breaking the silence and the tension with a mocking smile. He brushed a loose strand of hair off her face.

Kieran shivered as his fingers lingered at the base of her jaw.

"I told you it was complicated," she mumbled as she looked into his green eyes. *Screw it!* She leaned into him for another kiss. Kieran could hear the tutting in her head; though it soon disappeared when Rome kissed her urgently.

As they were about to return to the bar, Chantelle and Christina were on their way out, followed by Courtney. Chantelle looked at Kieran smirking. She couldn't help but smile in response.

"What are you two grinning about?" Courtney asked loudly.

Kieran glared at him. Sometimes he was so obvious and she knew him well enough to know he had asked on purpose.

"Are we leaving already?" she asked her friends ignoring Courtney who was touching fists with Rome, she imagined they did the same thing during their football games. Kieran felt like telling him he hadn't scored, but left it alone – it was clearly written all over her face anyway.

"We thought we'd bar hop on the way to the hotel," a friend from their group called Tom said. He had his arm draped around a blonde. Kieran observed that it was the first thing he had said all night. He seemed to be the quiet one out of the group, drinking brought him out of his shell.

"Oh, okay," she said.

The boys walked ahead as the girls trailed behind.

"So, dish the dirt. Is he a good kisser?" Chantelle asked.

"Hell yes! Amazing." Kieran grinned "Good doesn't do him justice."

"I can't believe you kissed him!" Christina exclaimed loudly.

Without turning, Kieran whacked her hard. "Shut up!"

"Ow!" Christina screamed dramatically.

"Serves you right," Kieran hissed.

Before she could say anything else, Rome fell in step with her, threw his arm around her shoulder and said to Christina, "So why can't you believe she kissed me?"

Kieran was mortified and her face grew hot. She shot Christina a warning look and told him, "Ignore her."

Rome stopped walking and pulled Kieran into him. She looked up at him curiously. His mouth was upturned into a smile, the dimples in his cheeks visible. Kieran wanted to kiss him again. As if he read her mind, he bent his head and kissed her.

As the night wore on, they became more and more intoxicated, Tom had already been sick, yet he continued to drink. They were in their fifth bar. Kieran had lost count of the amount of drinks she had consumed. She knew she would be sick at some stage and she also knew she would vow never to drink again. It was the same whenever she had a hangover; she always seemed to forget once she was out with her friends though.

At intervals, Rome whisked her off for private kisses. Kieran observed Chantelle and Luke dancing by themselves; they looked like they were having fun. Kieran scanned the room for Courtney and Christina. She couldn't see them anywhere, this meant they were together which made Kieran happy.

Rome had his arms around her as they waited at the bar, and Kieran rested her head on his chest.

"Tired?" he asked.

"Thirsty, but I'm having water this time."

Am I slurring?

He laughed, "You are an amateur; you're meant to follow every drink with water," he kissed her neck.

Kieran smiled – his kisses were amazing. "Whatever." She managed to respond. He was very good at distracting her.

"It's true, that's what I've been doing; I think you've been too tipsy to notice."

Kieran had wondered how he was the most sober out of them all. "I need to go outside." She announced, suddenly she didn't feel so good.

"Do you still want that water?" Rome asked her.

"No, no thanks."

Rome led her up the stairs and outside. He pulled a chair out and she sat down. Kieran noticed the sky was getting lighter and checked the time. It was almost five in the morning.

"Feel a bit better?" he asked kneeling down in front of her and looking concerned. Kieran looked into his eyes and nodded.

This isn't helping the nausea... he's too close to me.

She groaned and held her head in her hands. She felt her stomach churning and a burning sensation saturated in her chest.

"I should tell you now I don't do very well with vomit, so please don't be sick," he teased.

Kieran tried not to laugh, her stomach churned again. She put a hand over her mouth, she knew it was coming, but she didn't want the gorgeous man to see her being sick. She would die of shame first. She scanned the area for somewhere to escape. She should have gone to the toilet; it would have been a lot easier. But there was no time for her to go back into the bar. She spotted an alleyway to the side of the building and jumped up as her stomach turned again. *Run!*

"Excuse me," she muttered and ran as fast as she could in her heels. She crouched down with one hand on the wall in front of her for support, as she tried to vomit quietly which wasn't helping the situation. She could feel tears and snot running down her face, she had no tissue and was still heaving as her body brought up more liquid. It was not one of her finest moments.

Kieran cringed when she felt Rome rubbing her back in sympathy.

Why? Why is he here?

She couldn't believe she'd been sick. How the hell was she going to clean her face? It was bad enough him seeing her in that wretched and unladylike state, but not with snot all over her face.

Please God, if you get me out of this I will never drink again.... well, in theory.

Rome suddenly pushed a tissue into her hand.

Wow that was quick. Thank you!

Once she wiped her face, she stood up and took a deep breath. She couldn't make eye contact with him. Kieran couldn't bear to think about what he thought of her, and further, what she looked like.

"Don't be embarrassed," Rome said taking her hand and leading her back to the table, "I've had my moments, too."

Kieran sat down and held her head in her hands, mostly in shame, Rome sat next to her. She refused to look at him. She needed her compact mirror first.

"Are you ever going to look at me?"

"No." Kieran told him and she was serious.

"Don't be silly," he laughed as he put an arm around her shoulders.

"It's better that way trust me, God knows what I look and smell like right now. Could I have that water now, please?"

"Sure. You'll be okay on your own?"

"Yes," she told him as she rummaged in her bag for her cigarettes. The box was empty. He took his box out of his pocket, lit one and gave it to her.

"I'll be right back," he said.

As soon as he left, Kieran whipped her compact out. Thankfully, she didn't look as bad as she felt. She fidgeted with her hair and dabbed the shine off her face then she sat back and took a drag of the cigarette. It tasted disgusting and she put it out. Now she had sobered up a bit, she needed to brush her teeth.

"Do you want to get out of here?" he asked when he returned.

"Shouldn't we wait for the others?"

"We can text them and tell them we've gone."

"Okay, give me a sec please." Kieran headed back to the alleyway and rinsed her mouth out. "So, where do you want to go?" she asked once re-joining him.

"Your place or mine?" he grinned at her.

"Pardon?"

"Come on, I don't mean like that," he said chuckling as he draped his arm around her shoulders.

"You better not," she jokingly threatened him.

"We'll go to mine, you can freshen up and then I'll walk you home."

Kieran nodded in agreement. At least she got to spend more time with him. What harm could it do?

8 CHAPTER EIGHT

The next morning Kieran awoke feeling groggy, as she knew she would. She stretched. "Oh my God!" she shrieked when her leg brushed against something and she realised it was Rome and that they were both naked.

"What's wrong?" he asked sitting up in a panic.

"What do you mean what's wrong? Why didn't I go back to my room?" she demanded.

Rome visibly relaxed when he realised there was no emergency. "We got distracted." he grinned.

Kieran stared into his eyes that twinkled before he closed them and lay back on the pillows. Her stomach knotted as she remembered the night's events; after she had freshened up, she returned to join him in the bedroom. He had fallen asleep, she had only meant to stay a little while, just so she could be close to him, but he had kissed her and now she was naked in his bed.

Kieran grabbed the sheets and brought them to her chin. She'd known him all of five seconds and they'd already done the dirty. Her friends were going to kill her, well Christina would. Chantelle would applaud her. She bet he thought she was loose giving it up on the first night. Kieran buried her face in the sheet.

It's official. I'm a slut.

"This isn't how it was meant to happen!" she groaned.

Rome opened his eyes again and looked at her in confusion. "How what was meant to happen?" he yawned as he tried to pull her back towards him.

"This... us... you know what I'm talking about!" she snapped pushing him away.

"Come on, don't freak out. We are adults."

"So? I'm not the kind of woman that meets someone then sleeps with him on the first night despite what you might think," she said rounding on him.

She stared at him as he sat up and rubbed his temples. He knitted his brows, even in his tired and confused state he was sexy. What did he want with her?

Duh! Sex was what he wanted and you gave it to him!

Kieran wanted to slap herself. She couldn't blame the drink, because she'd thrown most of it up. She shuddered at the memory and groaned. What had she been thinking? She had never been that reckless before. Now she had potentially ruined something good with Rome all because she had slept with him on the first night.

He sat up and put his arm around her, this time she let him. "Look, I am not judging you," he said, "we, you, didn't do anything wrong."

"You should judge me, I'm judging me right now," she told him. She couldn't bring herself to look him. The shame she felt was too much to bear.

He turned her face towards his. "I'm not judging you, and you shouldn't judge you either, it happened. There's nothing that you or I can do about it now, so stop beating yourself up." he leaned in and kissed her on the lips.

"I have a boyfriend and I hardly know you," she protested.

"Those are two things that can easily be rectified," he said and kissed her again.

"Stop doing that!" She jumped out of bed taking the sheet with her, leaving Rome lying naked. In frustration she turned to face him. "Why aren't you taking me seriously?"

Standing in full view of him, Kieran's eyes almost bulged out her head. Defined muscles and dips in all the right places made her mouth fall open. She caught sight of parts she had missed in her drunken haze and salivated. Kieran caught herself and clamped her mouth shut. Embarrassment flooded through her when he grinned at her knowingly. Kieran closed her eyes and resisted the temptation to look again. She could hear Rome and her conscience laughing at her for two different reasons.

She opened her eyes and scanned around the room to locate her clothes "I need to go," she told him.

"Kieran, seriously, stop freaking out," he got out of bed and walked towards her.

Kieran wanted to turn and run. Before she finished the thought, his arms were around her. He looked down at her and kissed her on the forehead and took her face in his hands.

"Please don't regret last night," he said softly.

She felt herself dissolving. "I... don't."

"Good, because it was amazing, I don't know what's going to happen with us, but I definitely want to find out."

"I have a boyfriend." The more times she said it, the feebler an excuse it sounded, since in her head, she had broken up with Darren a million different times.

"I would hazard a guess that you are not happy with him, if you were, you wouldn't be here. Am I right?"

"No…. yes…. I'm confused." She admitted.

"So, then you know what you have to do, unless you don't want to?"

"This wasn't meant to happen!" She wailed again as she pulled away and sat on the bed. Rome followed and sat next to her. Kieran wished he would cover up, it was literally staring her in the face and she couldn't focus.

"It has happened, so we need to deal with the consequences, or forget about it and move on," he said lying back down.

"I don't want to forget about you." Kieran said turning to face him.

"Good," he said motioning for her to lie next to him.

Kieran studied him trying to figure out if he was genuine. Could it really be possible he was not judging her? She'd never met a guy like him. Darren had names for females' who behaved the way she had. Then again, this was a first for her. There were women who did that all the time. She tried to calm herself down by rationalising that he wasn't a complete stranger. But what did she know about him apart from the fact he was beautiful and a good kisser?

She lay down next to him and he rolled onto his side to face her. "Calm now?" he asked smirking.

No. Kieran nodded.

"So, do you want to sleep for a bit longer?" he yawned again. "We don't travel for another twelve hours."

She eyed him with suspicion. "I mean sleep," he said laughing at her expression.

"You'd better," she said as she threw the sheet over him. He pulled her closer. Kieran's stomach did a back flip; as his scent and touch triggered memories from the night before and flooded her mind. His naked skin was soft and warm against hers. Her skin tingled in response, like a small electric current running through her body.

"We will take this as slow, or as fast as you want," he said softly.

"Well technically I don't think we could go any faster," she joked.

"Yea, but we don't have to do it again until you've sorted out your stuff back home," he said yawning again.

Kieran yawned, too and nodded. She liked the way he said we, like they were in it together. Could she believe him? It was too early for this drama. She would rather not think about anything until she had to, she just wanted to lie in the comfort of Rome's arms. And she did until her ringing phone woke her.

"Where the hell are you?" Christina asked abruptly.

Kieran squinted as she looked at the screen of her phone to see the time. She had been asleep for nearly two hours. "I'm alive and I will be back soon," she told her.

"That didn't answer my question."

"Go girl!" she heard Chantelle shout in the background.

Kieran held in her laughter; it would only piss Christina off. "I'll be back soon," she repeated and hung up quickly. It was then she realised Rome was not in bed.

She sat up and looked around, his clothes were gone. Her initial fears that he had only been after one thing were realised. He'd left her there to avoid a scene. Kieran could hear a voice in her head on repeat. I told you so. Tears stung her eyes; she held them in. It served her right really and crying was not going to bring him back. She got out of bed, picked up her clothes shaking her head in disgust as she went into the bathroom. She scowled at her reflection in the mirror. Her hair was all over the place and her eye make-up was smudged.

No wonder he changed his mind.

She grabbed some toilet roll, wet it under the tap and removed as much smudged make-up as possible before she washed her face. Her one silver lining was that she had managed to fit a small brush and hair band into her bag, after brushing the frizzy mess into a pony tail, she felt a bit more human. She used the same toothbrush Rome had given her the night before, put on her clothes and refused to look in the mirror again. She didn't want to face the disappointment she would see in her eyes.

She opened the door to see Rome sitting on the bed reading a newspaper. Kieran froze; he looked up when he heard the door open. "Morning beautiful, I got you breakfast."

For a moment she forgot how to form a sentence.

I'm going to cry, God I'm so pathetic.

"Are you okay?" he walked over to her and planted a kiss on her forehead.

She nodded. It was better she stayed silent.

"You thought I left didn't you?" he walked across the room and picked up a cup of coffee.

She nodded again. The shock of him actually coming back had thrown her and she was genuinely lost for words.

"I was going to leave a note, but thought I'd be back before you woke up," he explained. She didn't respond. "I told you I wasn't judging you. If I judge you then I have to judge myself. It takes two to tango and all that, right?" he said holding out the cup of coffee to her. "Kieran?" he studied her face.

She exhaled, and realised that she had been holding her breath all the while. No wonder she couldn't speak. She took the cup from him, her hands shaking

"I just find it hard to believe you're being normal, who knew men like you existed?"

"Oh, so you haven't suddenly turned into a mute?" he teased.

Kieran laughed. He didn't miss anything. He took her free hand and led her out onto the balcony and they sat at the table for two. He opened a container of fruit and gestured for her to tuck in. What planet had he come from?

"Why are you so quiet?"

"I don't know what to say; I didn't think you would be back, you just caught me off guard and then to top it off you got me breakfast. That's so thoughtful." It may have seemed like a normal gesture to him; to Kieran, it was more.

"Have you been let down a lot by men or something?"

He didn't know the half of it and she was not about to go telling him her deepest secrets, although she felt she could trust him. She bit into a piece of banana and stayed silent.

"I'll take that as a yes."

"I'm not saying that I have been. I guess I'm just used to being treated a certain way, and this isn't one of them," she said with a shrug. Kieran looked away as Rome gazed at her. At the same time her phone rang. She bet it was Darren.

Maybe he knows.....

She thought about her reality back home, no holiday romance was going to change the fact she had to end their relationship. Rome or no Rome it was time for her to move on.

"Your loser boyfriend? Aren't you going to answer the phone?"

Kieran felt the sudden urge to defend Darren. Rome knew nothing about him to make that judgement. She said, "No," instead.

"He doesn't deserve you if he doesn't know how to treat you—"

"I know."

"So, why are you still with him?" he leaned over and rubbed her back.

"It's not that simple, we live together for one..." her voice trailed off. Kieran couldn't actually think of another reason. She felt his eyes on her waiting to learn more. She wasn't ready for that, not when things were so complicated.

"Is that the only reason?"

"I know it sounds easy to end it; it's not. I'm not sure how he's going to take it." It was a slight lie - she knew exactly how he was going to take it, which was why she was stalling. She should've ended it ages ago, but familiarity and routine with someone was a hard thing to let go of sometimes. Kieran knew it had a lot to do with her not wanting to be alone. She'd made a lot of bad decisions because of that; eventually she would have to grow up and face her fear.

"I don't know anything about you two; I'm not here to

criticise you either, I just want to get to know you. I really like you Kieran and I can see us really going somewhere. It's been a while since I met someone I've had real chemistry with. It's pretty intense, but in a good way," he explained.

Kieran finally met his gaze. She felt a flutter in her stomach as his words sunk in. It was too soon for them to be feeling that way, too out-of-the-blue.

"I want that, too, and I feel the same," she admitted, but she kept her doubts to herself.

"I'm glad," he took her hands in his and kissed them one at a time. She felt the softness of his lips on her palms and wanted to kiss him again. She couldn't find the courage to make the first move. Why did he make her so nervous?

"Don't you think this is weird?" she suddenly asked.

Rome looked at her quizzically. "What?"

Kieran found his confusion endearing, it calmed her down a little. "This... thing between us, it's making me feel uneasy," she admitted as she looked out over the balcony. The view was nowhere near as breath taking as the hotel where she was staying; the sea was visible in the distance, however.

"Me too," he laughed like he was relieved. "Like I said, it's been a long time since I met someone who blew me away."

Kieran felt herself getting hot. She was uncomfortable with his compliments. He must have seen it in her body language, for he laughed and squeezed her hand reassuringly.

"Doesn't your boyfriend say stuff like this to you? Why do you get nervous when I compliment you?"

"I don't know." It was another lie. It was because he seemed too good to be true. Kieran didn't want to believe anything he said until she knew he was not taking the piss.

"We will have to work on that," he teased.

Kieran smiled and tried to relax. She found it a lot easier to talk to him after she'd had a drink or two. Now she felt self-conscious, insecure, even.

"Do you want to go for a walk or something?"

She nodded. Kieran wasn't sure why or how real whatever chemistry they were sharing, was. She did know, however, that if her relationship was good, while she found Rome attractive, there was no way she would've cheated. That wasn't Kieran's style. She hated cheaters. Now she carried that title.

Rome took her hands and pulled her into him; he wrapped his arms around her and kissed her again. Kieran responded and their kiss grew urgent, passionate, it wasn't long before they had forgotten about their walk and were back in bed. Kieran couldn't stop herself even though she knew she should. Her conscience was screaming at her, but Kieran was too wrapped up in the arms of Romeo to pay attention.

When she got back to her hotel room she was greeted with a death stare from Christina. Chantelle ignored Christina and dragged Kieran onto their balcony. She had cocktails waiting almost like a celebration. Kieran laughed.

"Details!" Chantelle demanded and clapped her hands like an excited child. Kieran sat down. She felt like she'd been dreaming. She didn't know where to start. Christina sat down in silence. Kieran knew she was dying to hear the details as well, though she pretended to be disgusted by her behaviour. Before she could think, her phone bleeped. It was Rome telling her he missed her already. Kieran smiled, she missed him too. It was an emotion she knew she shouldn't have been feeling so soon.

"This is bad," she announced to her friends, dropping her head into her hands.

"He was bad?" Chantelle asked, her face showing clear disappointment.

"No," Kieran said aghast. She shivered as a memory of that morning flashed through her mind. It had been the best and most intense sexual experience of her life if she was honest. "Far from it actually, I mean the situation is bad. I really like him and I think he really likes me; it just feels too good to be true."

"Why?" Christina asked.

Kieran and Chantelle looked at her. She hadn't taken long to break her silence, which was unusual. She could be stubborn when she was ready.

"When does this happen ever? When does someone go on holiday and meet the perfect guy? And he is perfect; he says and does all the right things. I am convinced he's out of my league though, seriously, what does he want with me?"

"Oh my God, freaking out already," Chantelle teased.

"It's not funny. I feel like I'm going to have a breakdown," Kieran sighed and then filled her friends in on some of the details. By the time she was finished, Chantelle had the hugest grin on her face. Christina was grinning, too, even though she tried to hide it. They agreed that maybe Rome had happened for a reason and Kieran deserved someone better than Darren.

"Come on, it will be fine," Chantelle told her with reassurance as she sipped her cocktail.

Kieran was surprised that she could absorb any more alcohol after what they had put away the night before then she realised when she sipped hers, that it was virgin. She was thrilled when Christina told her that she and Courtney were talking about getting back together, and she was even more shocked when Chantelle told her that Luke had kissed her.

"I see we were all pretty busy last night then."

"Not as busy as you," Christina said with a smile.

"Shh. I can't believe I did that. I was mortified this morning," Kieran said rolling her eyes.

"What if this is how it's meant to be?" Chantelle said.

"What?" Christina asked, confusion clouding her face.

"None of us have great track records with guys to even compare; maybe this is how a guy is meant to be when he wants to be with you. No games, no bullshit, just honest and up front."

Kieran looked at her. *Ha, and I thought I had it bad.*

Chantelle was alarmingly positive all of a sudden, and she knew it was because of her kissing antics with Luke.

"Yes, Chan, this is how it's meant to be, when has that ever meant anything?" Christina answered.

"I think it's white guys who are like that. Black guys would not be filling your head so fast, they always keep their options open," Chantelle said.

"Guys will be guys, Black, White, Asian, they're all the same. I give Rome a week once we get back to London to do a one-eighty on me."

"You never know. Men are unpredictable, just when you think you've figured them out they surprise you."

"That isn't another quote from your book, is it Chan?" Christina teased.

Kieran laughed and turned her attention to responding to

Rome's message. Thereafter, she showered, finished packing and then after dinner they headed to the airport to be greeted by a long queue leading to the check in desk.

"I bet the plane is delayed," Kieran said rolling her eyes.

"Wouldn't surprise me," Chantelle added as they walked around to the side of the coach to collect their suitcases.

It was almost midnight. The air was humid and Kieran fanned herself with her passport, although it didn't help much. After collecting her luggage, she and the girls made their way into the airport. Her eyes caught sight of a pile of empty suitcases by the door.

"Do you know what's going on?" someone asked from behind them.

She shook her head, no. Kieran observed people emptying their suitcases into black bags. Some were setting up camp on the floor and on chairs, taking items of clothing out of their cases to use as pillows and blankets. Clusters of people stood around looking confused and angry. There were couples, families with babies and small children, groups of boys and girls, many of them still wearing their holiday t-shirts emblazoned with their nicknames, the name of the island and the year. Many of the girls looked like they might cry; some were actually in tears and being consoled by their friends.

"This doesn't look good," Kieran mumbled as they approached the check in desk. She spotted Luke near the front of the queue and nudged Chantelle.

"I'll go ask him if he knows what's going on," she said and hurried off. Her face was grim when she returned. "Bad news or bad news?" she asked.

Kieran sighed, "Go on, what's wrong?"

"There's a baggage strike. If you want to go home today you have to empty your suitcase into a black bag, throw away whatever doesn't fit, leave the suitcase here and carry the bags on yourself. If you don't want to do that, you wait two days until the strike is over," she relayed.

"I am not throwing my stuff away and there's no way it will all fit into a black bag," Kieran said with defiance. She completely understood why there were girls crying. She would cry too if she was forced to throw away her possessions especially her dresses.

"Me neither," Christina agreed. "Do you think our insurance will cover us if we stay?"

"What are Luke and the others doing?" Kieran asked turning to Chantelle. This delay could mean more time with Rome if he decided to stay and that was not something she wasn't going to complain about.

"They're staying; they're trying to see if the airline will put them up in a hotel," Chantelle told her.

Kieran couldn't hide her smile.

"I guess that pleases you," Christina teased.

"Well, two extra days in a hotel preferably with a pool is not going to kill us, is it?"

Her phone rang. She looked at the screen and grinned. "Hey Rome, what's up?" She answered.

"Hey beautiful."

Kieran blushed and hid her face from her friends who stood watching her. "Do you guys want to come down to the front of the queue? We've told them we are all together, so they're paying half of the hotel cost because there's so many of us, plus Courtncy threatened them with Watchdog, he recorded everything they said." he said laughing.

"There had to be a catch for them to agree to that. Okay cool, we're coming." Kieran relayed the terms to her friends and Chantelle complained in a loud voice as they headed over to the boys.

"Damn straight, they could have informed us before we left a perfectly good hotel overlooking a beach."

Kieran heard people tutting as they passed, obviously wondering why they were special enough to be going to the front of the queue. Rome greeted Kieran with a kiss on the forehead. His action did not go unnoticed. Kieran saw Chantelle raise her eyebrows and grin. Christina looked bemused at his open display of affection.

"How are you?" he asked pulling her towards him and wrapping his arms around her, it felt like he had missed her. Kieran inhaled his scent and felt an odd sense of relief at being close to him again. She had missed him too.

"I'm good. Kind of glad we don't have to go home yet."

"Me, too, so does that mean you want to share a room with me then?" he asked smiling.

Kieran blushed and gave him a shy nod, yes. She wasn't expecting his suggestion and glanced at Chantelle who was still grinning. Kieran knew her friends had heard.

"If you abandon me to share with Luke I will never speak to you again," Christina warned Chantelle.

"You could always share with Courtney?" Rome suggested.

Kieran and Chantelle giggled.

"That is not funny," Christina said glaring at the three of them.

Before Rome could reply Courtney approached them. "Okay, they've found us a hotel about half an hour away. We need to be back here in two days. Our airline is the same and so is the flight time."

"How are we getting to the hotel?" Chantelle asked.

"There's a coach going that way. They've given us tickets so we are sorted," Courtney told them.

"Who are you sharing a room with?" Chantelle asked him casually.

Christina elbowed her hard in the ribs before he could reply. Courtney eyed the two girls suspiciously. Kieran and Rome cracked up laughing.

"I was just asking!" Chantelle said rubbing her side. Christina was mumbling under her breath about not being able to trust her friends.

They eventually retraced their steps to the outside of the airport and filed onto the coach.

Kieran could not stop smiling as they entered the hotel reception and checked in. The hotel was part of a chain, so there was nothing special about it. The colour scheme was beige and white that did nothing for its character. The hotel was however rated four stars and that made Kieran happy. She could think of nothing worse than staying in a grotty hotel. They booked out eleven rooms between twenty three of them.

It was almost two in the morning when everyone agreed to call it a night and meet for breakfast in the morning. Kieran said goodnight to her friends.

"Have fun," Chantelle teased.

"We will," Rome replied with a grin.

The room was nothing like the previous hotel which was

similar to a villa. Kieran walked toward the double doors and out onto the balcony. She had told Rome she was terrified of bugs, so he was checking out the room.

"All clear," he said joining her and wrapping his arms around her. Alone with him once again, Kieran wondered what the hell possessed her to agree to such an arrangement. She felt the butterflies in her stomach fluttering and pulled away. She found she could concentrate better when he wasn't touching her. Kieran had never been so aware of someone before.

"Are you okay?"

"I'm fine." *Translation: I'm nervous and I can't stand it.*

"You're quiet; I haven't done anything, have I? You know you didn't have to say yes to us sharing a room if you're uncomfortable? I just want to spend as much time as I can with you."

"Seriously, I'm fine," she reassured him. "I'm glad you suggested it actually, I never would have." That part was true.

"Why?"

"I'm shy."

"Of course," he said rolling his eyes playfully.

"I am!" she protested.

"Let's make a deal," he suggested leading her inside. Kieran took the opportunity to divert her attention and switched on the kettle.

"What?"

"We should say what's on our minds, no shyness, no over thinking or analysing. Let's just go with whatever happens. I want you to tell me how you feel."

"Okay." Kieran agreed.

"I know you're humouring me. I don't think you will ever tell me what you're really feeling," he said walking over to his case. He opened it, took out his toiletry bag and headed into the bathroom kissing her as he passed.

Kieran was silent. He was right; but what did he expect from her? No matter what she thought she felt, she would not admit it to him. She knew guys who took advantage of how a girl felt about them so they could get away with certain behaviour; she was determined not to give away her power. The kettle finished boiling and Kieran busied herself making a cup of tea. The bathroom door opened and Rome appeared in his boxers.

Oh dear Lord!

"Tea?" she offered shakily, as he climbed into the bed. She watched him through the mirror.

"No, thanks babe," he said yawning, his torso rippling as he did.

Is it hot in here all of a sudden?

"I'm going to take a quick shower," she announced.

"What about your tea?"

"I won't be long. It'll be just right by the time I get back." She grabbed some personal stuff, headed into the bathroom locked the door and turned the shower on. She sat on the floor with her phone and called Chantelle.

She answered after one ring. "What's wrong?"

"I'm freaking out!"

"Why? And why are you whispering?"

"I don't exactly know," Kieran replied holding her head in her hand ignoring the last part of the question.

"You don't know why you're whispering? What is wrong with you?" Chantelle asked laughing.

"I'm losing my mind, clearly!" Kieran hissed. "I can't believe you're laughing at me."

"What's happened?"

"He wants me to tell him how I feel."

"No, don't do that," Chantelle said in a serious tone.

"You don't have to tell me twice, I'm cringing at the thought of it."

"He's either trying to get you to give away your power so he can decide how to play it, or he wants to know if you are feeling the same way he is."

"How do you think he's feeling?"

"I think he really likes you. He's oblivious to everyone else when you're around."

"No, he isn't," Kieran said rolling her eyes.

"Yes, he is, look at how he was at the airport. I'm still waiting for a hello," Chantelle teased.

Kieran smiled. "You may have a point. I just don't know how to be around him. His gorgeousness makes me nervous."

"What is wrong with you? Seriously, yes he's cute, but you've already slept with him, why are you being weird now?”

"Because I'm not drunk now!" Kieran said loudly, "Shit," she cursed looking towards the door.

"What?"

"He's going to think I'm talking to myself," she said dropping her voice back to a whisper.

"Where are you?"

"On the bathroom floor."

"Ah, so that's the shower running?"

"Yes," Kieran admitted. She knew she sounded crazy and rested her head on her knees.

"Bye Kieran," Chantelle laughed.

"No, don't go!"

"You will be fine. Come on, you wanted to spend more time with him so don't waste it."

"You are no help to me," Kieran grumbled as she stood up.

"Because I don't know what your problem is, you're with a gorgeous guy who seems to be crazy about you. From your behaviour I can assume you are crazy about him, so why the hell are you hiding in the bathroom?"

"I'm scared," she admitted chewing her thumb nail.

"Of?" Chantelle pressed.

"Falling for him."

"I think you're counting your chickens before they've hatched."

"I wish I was, this just feels different, and it's not like with Joshua or Darren. It feels so real, intense. I don't know how else to explain it."

"Well, just see what happens after these two days together. Maybe you should use the time wisely instead of just being in bed."

"Excuse me, when did you hear me say that's all we would be doing?"

"Kieran, I wasn't born yesterday, why else did he suggest sharing a room?"

"He wanted to spend time with me actually," she said pacing the bathroom floor.

"You do have it bad don't you? Listen to you defending him already."

"Bye Chan," Kieran said sighing in frustration. She didn't wait for a reply. She hung up the phone, undressed and stepped into the shower.

Already she knew the more time she spent with him the more she would fall in love with him. Now their paths had crossed, her life would change, she knew that, she just wasn't sure whether it would be a good change.

Kieran did not believe in love at first sight. It was too much of a naïve concept for her. It only happened in films and fairy tales, and she'd had a bit more life experience to know that in reality perfect men, if there was such a thing, didn't just turn up on the beach. But Rome had a certain affect. He had the power to contradict every thought she had ever had about the myths of love at first sight; she wasn't sure how she felt about that.

A full half an hour passed before Kieran turned the shower off. She hoped Rome had fallen asleep. She knew she was being childish in avoiding him. Anyone else would've been happy. Why was she so uncomfortable being alone with him? She opened the door and tiptoed out of the bathroom glancing over at him. He seemed to be asleep. Kieran made another cup of tea and took it out to the balcony. She decided it was as good a time as any to break the news to Darren about her late return home. He would throw a fit, so she turned her phone off after she sent the message. She was not in the mood to hear his noise.

It was just after four by the time she got into bed; Rome moved closer to her and pulled her against him.

"You smell good," he mumbled as he kissed the back of her neck. She ran her fingers up and down his muscled arm.

"Thanks."

His breathing slowed as he drifted back off to sleep. Kieran listened to him breathing for a while; snuggled in the warmth of his arms it didn't take her very long to fall asleep.

9 CHAPTER NINE

Kieran opened her eyes to see Rome lying propped up on one arm looking at her. She made a face "What are you doing?"

Please God don't let me have slept with my mouth open.

"Morning beautiful," he said before kissing her on the lips. "I was watching you sleep."

"Why?" she asked sitting up. She smoothed down her hair with her hands and rubbed her eyes.

Also Can I ask that I don't have morning breath? Thanks.

"You look beautiful when you sleep."

"I doubt that very much," she said laughing.

He pulled her against him and kissed her again, stroking her face. As he did, Kieran held her breath.

"It's true," he said looking into her eyes.

Kieran felt as if she would melt. It wasn't fair that he was able to do that to her. "What time is it?" she asked covering her mouth to stifle a yawn.

"Seven," he replied after looking at his watch.

"It's too early to get up."

"You are right lazy bones," he teased.

"I like my sleep, that's why I don't have children yet, plus I didn't get into bed until about three." Kieran noticed Rome grimace slightly.

I definitely have morning breath, how embarrassing!

"Well that's what you get for spending ages in the bathroom on the phone," he jibed.

So he'd heard her. "I was talking to Chantelle."

"I thought it may have been your boyfriend," he admitted.

She noticed the hint of bitterness in his voice making him sound less English, it was the first time she'd noticed it, obviously because she'd been distracted by other things. A strange look passed over his face. It was gone before Kieran could identify it.

"What was that?"

"What?"

"That face you just made."

"I don't know what you mean. I didn't make a face." He sat up and stretched "I'm going to the bathroom. Back in a min."

Kieran grinned. He was jealous she was sure. She got up, yawned again and went over to the window. The sun was dazzling and warm. She was about to close the blinds, but the sun created a warm amber glow in the room so she left them open, she liked the atmosphere. It promised another good day and matched her mood.

She turned her mobile on and was surprised to see no missed calls from Darren. She flicked the kettle on and walked over to the air conditioner to turn the temperature to a lower setting. Rome opened the bathroom door, humming as he walked out. Kieran disappeared inside.

When she returned from brushing her teeth, Rome had made her a cup of tea. She smiled at the gesture and climbed back into bed.

"What do you want to do today?" he asked as he placed the cup on the night table next to her, she promptly picked it up.

"Sleep," she informed him, taking a sip of the hot liquid.

"No, you can sleep tonight."

"It's too early to go out."

"You are an old woman," he teased.

"What?" she said in mock anger.

"You heard, sleeping till all hours, drinking tea and snoring, you're an old woman," he said with a grin.

"I do not snore."

"Babe, you do. It's cute though."

"Whatever," she mumbled. Kieran was beyond mortified. If she was snoring that meant her mouth had been open.

Bet that was attractive.

He laughed at her expression and got into bed next to her as her phone rang. She should've known it was too good to be true.

"You're awake early," Darren said without greeting her.

"Well phones don't ring silently do they?" she replied in a sarcastic tone.

"Why are you being rude?"

"For the same reason you're calling at a stupid hour; because I can," she told him taking another sip of tea.

"Don't be a bitch Kieran; I am just checking in to see if you are okay. I got your text, when you coming home?"

"If you don't like it then don't phone me. I told you I'm leaving tomorrow night," she felt Rome shift next to her. She mouthed, "Excuse me," grabbed her cigarettes and went out to the balcony.

"I went online and couldn't find anything about a baggage strike," Darren said to her.

"So what, I'm lying?" she retorted and lit a cigarette. "Darren, it's not even eight a.m. and you're already stressing me out."

"I don't believe you," he told her, "You're stressing yourself out. Maybe if you didn't lie so much you wouldn't be so stressed."

Kieran laughed. He was unbelievable.

"It's not fucking funny!" he shouted.

Kieran inhaled, determined not to lose her temper. "It is funny; I don't know what you expect me to do when you behave like a child," she said in a calm tone.

"I told you what would happen if you went on holiday, so who is he then?"

"Who is who?" she asked not feeling guilty.

"You know what I'm asking."

"I have no idea. There is a baggage strike. I don't care if you can't find news about it. If you don't believe me phone the airline." She glanced over her shoulder into the room and saw Rome getting dressed. She took another pull of her cigarette and exhaled blowing out a cloud of smoke, she watched it disperse. Darren was silent. "Have you finished?" she asked him with impatience.

"No."

"Tough, I'm going back to bed don't phone me again." she told him before hanging up and switching off the phone. She put the cigarette out and went inside.

Rome entered the bathroom and slammed the door shut.

Kieran grimaced, he was pissed. She sighed. Was there one man in her life not trying her patience? She knocked on the door. Rome opened it and walked past her avoiding her eyes.

"What's wrong?" she asked him.

"Nothing," he grumbled.

"What happened to telling each other how we felt?" she asked moving closer and standing in front of him.

He looked at her. "I can't do this," he said with a shrug and walked around her.

"You can't do what?" fear tugged at her stomach and she felt sick. If he ended it now she was sure she would cry, which in all honesty was ridiculous.

"I can't pretend that this is normal. You have a boyfriend and from the sounds of it, I don't think you have any intention of ending things with him, otherwise you would tell him," he said sitting on the bed.

"It's not that simple. If I tell him now he'll do something stupid and I can't have that on my conscience," she turned around to face him.

"Why do you care? What about how you feel? What about me?" he asked looking at her.

"You knew I had a boyfriend and you didn't care," she reminded him.

"Well, I care now. I heard how he spoke to you. What am I supposed to do, sit here and say nothing?"

"Yes actually, I don't need you to defend my honour and he's not exactly wrong is he?" she countered standing with her arms folded across her chest.

"He's an asshole for calling you a bitch."

"I know this."

"So then why do you waste your time explaining yourself to him?"

"I don't know, it's easier that way," she dropped her arms and sat next to him on the bed.

"Bullshit Kieran, you don't want to end it with him, otherwise you would have by now, even before I came along."

"I do not need you telling me how I should conduct my relationship, thank you," she snapped.

"No, because you're doing such a great job of it aren't you?"

he got up and stormed out on to the balcony.

"Where is this coming from Rome?" she asked following him. She stood in the doorway and he sat at the table.

"What do you mean where is this coming from?" he asked with a scowl, "Is it news to you that you have an asshole for a boyfriend?" his tone was full of sarcasm.

"No, but it seems to be news to you," Kieran replied snidely. She was not going to tolerate him being rude to her regardless of how much dimple he flashed at her.

"What's news to me is the reaction he got from you. If you don't care like you say, I don't see why you bother."

"Me neither. All men are strange," she mumbled before turning round and going back inside. Kieran lay on the bed and looked up at the ceiling. Cracks ran vertically along in faint lines. They reminded her of her relationship with Darren; from a distance it looked fine; up close it was a mess.

Rome came inside "Why do you pull away from me?" he asked quietly. He sat down in the chair next to the bed and rubbed his temples in agitation.

"What?" she asked sitting up.

"He talks to you like shit and yet you drop everything to shut him up. I'm here trying to show you that I'm genuine; that I care, and all you do is pull away," his eyes narrowed.

He was sexy when angry. Kieran shook her head. *Focus.*

"I actually don't have a clue as to what you are on about," she told him.

"You have no intention of this going any further because you're not trying to spend time with me. Last night, for example, you hid in the bathroom for forty-five minutes and then you go outside for another half an hour just to avoid being alone with me. I'm not stupid," he stood up again and marched over to the balcony door, picked up his cigarettes from the table and lit one. He exhaled blowing out a thick cloud of smoke.

"You think that's what I was doing?" he had it so wrong.

"I know that's what you were doing, even when I kissed you this morning, you were pulling faces. As soon as he calls he has your attention, so what do I have to do to get your attention the way he does? Do I need to be an asshole as well? Maybe you are one of those girls who like having drama in her relationship," he said taking another pull on the cigarette, then flicking it over the balcony.

Kieran realised it then, he had an American twang to his accent and it was noticeable when he was annoyed. She bit her lip. She should have been offended by what he said, but she found his vulnerability endearing. It made her feel better that she wasn't the only one anxious about their "relationship."

"As a matter-of-fact, you don't know what you're talking about," she told him.

"Really?" he challenged.

Kieran sighed. She would have to tell him the truth. She understood the expression she'd seen on his face earlier. It was an amalgamation of jealousy, anger, confusion and hurt.

"First of all, I don't need you be an asshole to get my attention. You've had my attention since we met. Second, I wasn't hiding in the bathroom last night for the reasons you think and the same for my behaviour this morning,"

He stared at her.

Kieran got up and stood in front of him, she looked him in the eyes. She noticed they took on flecks of brown in his anger, the green almost disappearing. "I told you I was on the phone to Chantelle. I was freaking out," she admitted, her face grew hot.

His face softened. "Why?" he asked reaching towards her and playing with a strand of her hair before gently tucking it behind her ear.

"Because,"

"Because?"

"Because you make me uncomfortable," she stammered. Her knees suddenly felt weak. She sat down on the bed and he joined her.

"Is that meant to be reassuring?" he asked leaning forward and resting his elbows on his knees, his face in his hands.

Kieran had the urge to run her fingers along the contours of the rippling muscles on his back; she wasn't sure how receptive he would be, given his mental anguish.

She shook her head. "No you idiot, not uncomfortable in a bad way. I just kind of forget who I am when I'm with you," she explained looking away from him.

"What?" he sat up.

"You make me nervous, I feel like I'm going to say, or do something stupid. I told you, I'm generally a shy person and I'm worse when I'm with you. I don't know why…well, I do…. never mind. I'm just not used to having to think before I do things, and I find when I'm with you I am more self-aware."

"I make you self-conscious?" he asked with a bewildered look.

"Yes, that, and I'm more of a cynic than I thought I was. I keep waiting for you to do something to prove me right. You are too good to be true and that's part of the reason I keep pulling away. Chantelle laughed at me when I told her. She couldn't believe I was hiding in the bathroom," she smiled in spite of herself. She leant back on her hands and he mirrored her movement. "I don't like feeling insecure and I don't think a guy has made me feel this way before. It's not your fault; this is just way past my comfort zone."

"How so?"

"Remember when you said we should tell each other how we feel?"

"Vaguely."

Kieran sensed he was loosening up, though his face was still serious. "Well, if I told you some of the thoughts I've been having you would probably run a mile."

"Try me."

"No, I'm not even ready to admit them to myself let alone tell you," she said sitting up.

Rome took one of her hands in his. "Please," he whispered, stroking her face and looking into her eyes. Like a chameleon, the green returned in his eyes.

"For a start, things like that," she complained pulling her hand away.

"What?" he frowned.

"I forget how to form a sentence when you look at me like that. That's what I mean about you making me nervous."

"Okay, so what about pulling faces when I kissed you this morning. Explain that."

"If you must know, that was because I hadn't brushed my teeth – morning breath," she mumbled.

"Are you serious?" he asked guffawing.

"I'm glad you find it funny," she snapped pulling her hand away and lying down. He fell back next to her.

"I do find it funny only because I got it so wrong. Well, you're not the only one who's freaked out."

"I didn't know that until your little tantrum," she teased

"It was not a tantrum. I'm sorry I shouted at you," he looked apologetically into her eyes.

Kieran's heart skipped a beat and her stomach fluttered. "It's alright, so are we okay now?"

"I guess." he said smiling flashing his dimples. Kieran would never get bored of his smile.

"Well, what are we going to do with this gorgeous day?"

"Thought you wanted to sleep?" he reminded her stroking her face.

"I did, but you're right, I can sleep tonight. Let's do something interesting."

Rome raised an eyebrow.

"Not that," she said giggling.

"Okay," he said sitting up, "You get ready I'll sort some stuff out."

"What are you going to sort out?"

"Our first date," he said with a beaming smile.

"First date? I think we're already past that," Kieran said sitting up and crossing her legs. She watched as he crossed the room and picked up his t-shirt.

"We have, but this wasn't meant to happen remember? Going out in a group doesn't count. People are there to cushion the blow if it doesn't work out. The first date is about getting to know someone and bonding; we haven't exactly done that yet, well, in some ways we have," he grinned.

"You are such a girl," Kieran teased.

"Oh come on, tell me that hasn't crossed your mind?" he said pulling the T-shirt over his head. Kieran tried not to look disappointed seeing his beautiful physique disappear.

"No, it hasn't crossed my mind." She hadn't been on a first date in ages and couldn't even remember if she and Darren had been on one.

"What? Why not?"

"I just figured we were going to hang out with everyone while we were here," she shrugged. Kieran left out the part of not expecting to hear from him once they returned home as the other reason why she hadn't contemplated a first date with him.

"Would you prefer that?"

"No, I guess we could go on a date," she was starting to like the idea; maybe it would be easier once she got used to being around him. The only thing bad about being around a person and getting close to them was missing them when they were gone. She didn't know how long he was going to be around, and she wasn't comfortable with the attachment she was starting to feel towards him. Regardless, the damage was done, it was too late for her to turn back and if she was honest, she didn't want to.

"Sure?" he asked.

"Yes, I'm sure," she nodded for emphasis.

"Nervous?" he asked and squeezed her hand.

"Yes, but it will be good for me."

"You are a crazy," he lifted her hand and kissed the back of it.

"Shut up," she said with a smile. She knew what she was talking about.

"I'm sorry, but I still don't get it."

Kieran glanced at him from under her eyelashes. "It's too soon to have this conversation." She sighed and uncrossed her legs.

Rome turned her face towards his. "Tell me, just be as honest as you can be, I promise I won't hold it against you."

Kieran bit her lip. He had no idea what he was asking of her, and she had no idea what she was doing. What good could come of her admitting how she felt? "Please?" he flashed a dimple. It was if he knew she couldn't resist him when he smiled at her like that.

"Okay, I'm only going to explain this once and only once, don't interrupt me and please don't make fun of me, even if you think I'm crazy, I'm just trying to be honest." she said quietly. She could feel herself flushing as she tried to organise her thoughts. It was truly a cringe worthy moment.

"I'm listening."

Kieran closed her eyes. She would never get the words out otherwise. Perspiration made her hands clammy and she clenched them into balls on her lap. She opened her mouth to speak and then closed it. Rome kissed her on the lips.

So not helping.

"Still listening." he reminded her.

"I don't know if I'm thinking about us too much, or not enough. I feel that if I'm completely honest with my words and actions around you I will scare you away." Rome took her hand as if to prove he wasn't going anywhere.

What was my point again? Kieran removed her hand determined not to let him distract her. She heard his quiet chuckle, but continued. "It was silly to hide from you last night, but you make me unbelievably nervous. I met you a couple of days ago and we are sharing a hotel room. I hardly know you, so I don't know how I'm meant to act around you. Sometimes I want to kiss you, but I don't in case I come across too strong, or in case you don't want me to and then sometimes I want to tell you exactly how I feel, but it'll sound girly and stupid. That's what I mean about being self-conscious."

"Babe," Rome started but Kieran shook her head and carried on.

"I don't understand why it doesn't faze you. I feel like I'm having a meltdown and you're just, so, casual about everything. You say all the right words and have been perfect about everything. The thing that makes it even worse is that I know it's only a matter of time before you get bored. You could have anyone you want, because you are gorgeous and completely out of my league, and I don't want to end up getting hurt." She couldn't seem to stop the words coming out of her mouth, even though she knew she should have. She had already said too much, yet she took another breath and continued.

"The bottom line is I'm scared of falling for you and the longer I spend with you the more likely it seems that's going to happen, if I were to lose you now I don't know how I'd go back to normal, all I really know is that I want you in my life and I hope you feel the same. I need you to feel the same; I don't want this to just be a casual holiday fling to you because already for me, it's more and I knew that in your hotel room two nights ago, so how am I meant to act normal around you when this is how I feel?"

He was still silent and Kieran was suddenly scared to open her eyes. Her mind was racing. Why was he quiet? What if she had scared him? How long could she sit there without looking crazy?

Note to self, next time say nothing!

"How long are you going to sit there with your eyes closed?" he asked as if reading her mind.

Kieran heard the smile in his voice. She opened her eyes and refused to look at him, she was so damn embarrassed. Snippets of her little speech were going round in her head.

"That was a lot of information to process. I had to take a minute," he teased reaching over to rub her back.

"Well, now you know," Kieran mumbled. She felt sick and stupid for being honest, too honest. She lay back down.

Rome propped himself up on his arm and looked down at her. He kissed her on the forehead and continued to stare.

Kieran felt him willing her to make eye contact; *dammit!* She surrendered.

"First of all, you are crazy," he told her. "It's not just you having these thoughts. I'm just better at hiding it than you. I find it difficult to be myself around you, too. I won't pretend I don't feel the same way and I always go with my instincts. If I feel like kissing you," he kissed her on the nose, "I'm going to kiss you, and I happen to like kissing you." He kissed her on the lips.

"I think I can tell," Kieran said smiling.

Rome kissed her again. "I say things to you because that's how I feel. Why would I hide that? I'm not like this with everyone; it just comes naturally with you. I care about you, if you were just a holiday fling we wouldn't be here now. You'd better get used to me. I'm not going anywhere just yet," he put his arm around her.

Kieran lay in silence for a few minutes allowing his words to sink in. She rolled onto her side and propped herself up on her arm. She traced his mouth with her index finger.

God his lips are amazing....

She wanted to kiss them all the time. Lowering her head, she kissed him then rested her chin on his chest.

He stroked the side of her face. "You make me happy and it's been a while since I've felt like that," he told her with sincerity.

Kieran was speechless.

Rome pulled her closer so they were face-to-face, up close and personal. "I am not perfect and I am definitely not out of your league. Kieran you are beautiful." She rolled her eyes. "It's true." He told her.

She traced the lines on his forehead, the length of his nose, around his mouth, his chin, and back to his lips while he stared at her. Her arm settled around his waist and she pulled him closer to her. Was he real or was she having a really good dream? She didn't want to wake up if she was dreaming. She knew she would probably do something stupid like cry.

"What are you thinking?" he asked looking into her eyes. She shrugged. She wasn't falling for that one again. "Tell me," he urged.

Kieran sighed. "There are many stunning women out there and look at you. I just don't get why you would want me..." her eyes dropped and her voice trailed off. He was staring at her as if she was a mental patient.

"You are smart, funny, sexy, and extremely beautiful; trust me I wouldn't be here otherwise."

"Nice," she said frowning as she remembered one of the quotes from the book Chantelle was reading. Men really were fickle.

"I'm serious. Beautiful women are my weakness and you have become my number one weakness. You don't know what you've done to me," he explained.

Kieran glared at him and removed her arm from around him. "Beautiful women are your weakness? Maybe Romeo suits you more than you think," she snapped and rolled away from him; not before seeing him wince at the sound of his name.

"I knew that's what you'd think. I don't even know why I'm surprised. Women always think the same thing when they hear my name," he said. Sighing in frustration he leaned over and rubbed her arm trying to get her to turn around.

"So how many women do you have then?"

"Kieran come on," he tried to pull her towards him; she moved out of his reach and climbed off the bed, she faced him her arms crossed over her chest.

"What? Beautiful women are your weakness. You said it," she reminded him, "so how many women do you have?"

"I didn't mean it like that."

"How many?" she asked again.

"I'm not a saint Kieran. I do have a past like everyone else."

"I know that. I'm asking if you make a habit of chasing women. Sorry, beautiful women. I should know what I'm letting myself in for," she said marching over to the balcony. She needed fresh air. Kieran looked out into the distance at the sea. She wished she was closer to the beach. She needed to feel the sun on her skin. She wondered whether they would ever leave the hotel room at the rate they were going. She looked over at him. "I'm waiting for your answer."

"I don't normally have to chase women."

Kieran grimaced. *What am I doing here?*

"Well, this isn't any different for you then? Because I'm an idiot you didn't even have to work that hard; I gave it up on the first night. So out of interest, do they just throw themselves at you? Do you have one night stands a lot? Beautiful women being your weakness and all."

God I'm so jealous.

"You're insane," he said following her.

Kieran's head whipped around and she saw him trying not to smile. "You're a womanizer," she hit back sitting down at the table.

The sun was warm on her bare arms at that moment. She wanted more sun. Everything was better in the sun.

"Do you really think that?" he asked, the smile had disappeared from his face.

"I don't need to hear about your past conquests," she said pretending to study her nails.

Rome laughed and sat next to her. Kieran ignored him. He turned her face towards him. It was fast becoming a habit.

"I'm not as smooth as you think I am. I've had four girlfriends my whole life and the longest one was five years. It was my last real relationship," he put his arm around her when he sensed her relax.

"When did you break up?" she asked stiffly. *Oh. My. God, I'm his rebound girl!* It made more sense than him being interested in her.

"About a year ago."

"Really." The relief in her voice was obvious. "So how many people have you slept with since?" she figured it was as good a time as any to discuss his past.

"Two," he answered.

"And in total?" Kieran asked raising an eyebrow

"Let's just say double figures," he said chuckling.

Kieran raised both eyebrows. "Oh," she replied. She didn't know what to make of that and bit her lip. Why was he being cagey about it?

"What about you?" he asked.

Kieran blushed and considered whether to lie or not. Her number was at the other end of the scale to his. "I'm still in single digits," she said smirking.

"Really?" he asked with a sly smile.

Kieran narrowed her eyes and moved away from him. "What did you think I was going to say? Contrary to my behaviour since meeting you, I'm not into casual sex," she informed him crossing her arms.

"Is that all this is to you? Casual sex?" he brushed the back of his hand against her arm.

"You tell me," she replied not looking at him. They were going round in circles.

"It's not for me. I already told you, I'm too old for that shit." he said.

Kieran couldn't help but look at him, just to see if she could tell how genuine he was. At that moment she believed him. She sighed and stood up taking Rome's hand. He followed her back into the room. She lay down on the bed. She was exhausted from all the emotions she was feeling. Rome lay next to her. Kieran let him pull her onto her side so they were spooning while his chin rested on her head.

"By the way, I could never be out of your league. Any guy would be lucky to have you, including your asshole boyfriend."

"Okay new deal," she said.

"What?"

"No more talk of the asshole boyfriend, he's not important."

Rome shifted and turned her face, "I'm so glad you said that." he said before kissing her.

"So why did you and your girlfriend break up?" Kieran had been dying to ask the question. She bit her lip waiting for the answer.

"Just wasn't working out."

"Five years is a long time."

"I know. I guess we just outgrew each other."

Kieran thought he sounded as if he was uncomfortable with her line of questioning, she could feel the doubt creeping in as her intuition flickered. "If I had a girlfriend what would you think?"

Her stomach turned. "I don't know," she shrugged, "Why? Do you have one?" she asked rolling over to face him.

"No, Kieran, we've been through this already. I am single."

"So then why did you ask?"

"Just wanted to know what you would do if the tables were turned."

Kieran thought for a minute. She was pretty sure she would have stayed away from him if he had a girlfriend. "What would you want me to do?" It was the safest reply she could think of.

"Exactly the same thing I've done. If I had a girlfriend, I don't think I'd be able to stop myself. Do you know how crazy I am about you?" he brushed the hair out of her face.

Kieran ignored the feeling that was brewing within her because of their physical closeness. "This is all going so fast."

"Which is exactly why we should slow it down and have that first date; we'll be one of those couples that does it backwards," he said grinning at her.

"So does that mean we'll do the marriage and baby thing backwards as well?" she joked.

His face went pale and was a picture of horror and amusement. Kieran wished she could take the comment back, though he hadn't let go of her, or run away screaming. She knew men his age freaked out at the thought of marriage and kids, even more so after three days. Clearly she'd learnt nothing.

"Kieran, I think—"

"I was joking," she interrupted him.

"I know."

Kieran saw the colour return to his face, "You looked scared there for a minute,"

"I was thinking."

"About?"

"The future... marriage and babies.... in that order though."

"Erm, what?"

"Maybe one day?"

What?

His eyes searched hers and Kieran hoped not for an

answer. "We hardly know each other," she reminded him she was feeling a little breathless.

Rome kissed her forehead. "I know myself and sometimes you just know who you want to spend your future with, I meant it when I said I've not felt like this about anyone before."

She had no words.

"I've scared you haven't I?" he said laughing at her worried expression.

"Just a bit," she whispered meeting his eyes.

"Sorry, I just think all of this means something. I know when we go home tomorrow I will miss you. I haven't known you long enough, so I shouldn't feel that way, and you said you feel the same, that has to mean something in the grand scheme of things." he explained.

"I get it, really, I know exactly what you're talking about," Kieran told him, their eyes communicated understanding.

"We should get ready," he said kissing her on the lips.

Kieran was tempted to tell him to screw the first date and screw her instead, but it wasn't very ladylike so she decided against it. She watched him as he climbed off the bed and bent down to put on his trainers admiring him as he moved around. The temptation in her rose again.

"And exactly where are we going?" she tried to sound interested.

"Never you mind. Get ready," he said heading through the door.

Kieran stared after him. They had just shared a lot and she should have felt reassured by his declarations; she wasn't. It was too simple, too easy, and nothing was simple or easy in her love life.

10 CHAPTER TEN

Two hours later, they were sitting on the promenade by the sea front having a late breakfast in the old town of Corfu. It was another beautiful day; a light breeze made the hot weather bearable. Kieran was impressed with the impromptu outing considering it hadn't taken Rome long to organise it. She had no clue what else he had planned, as he refused to tell her.

Rome led her over to a horse drawn carriage. Kieran in her excitement had kissed him rather passionately, oblivious that they were not alone. She had been embarrassed afterwards when she realised people had been staring, but Rome took it all in his stride, he had looked amused and slightly proud of himself for getting that reaction out of her. It was the single most romantic thing anyone had ever done for her. She admired the pure white horse and thought it quite pretty as horses went. The driver gestured for them to get into the carriage. Rome climbed in and helped Kieran up. She squealed as the horse pulled away. Rome chuckled and put his arm around her and pulling her closer to him.

Kieran couldn't believe how beautiful Corfu was. She and her friends had been situated in the busy built up part of town, mainly for the younger crowd. This old part of city was authentic and had an ancient style that she fell in love with. They rode through the cobblestone roads that were too narrow for cars, and at times Kieran was sure too narrow for the carriage. Her fears were unnecessary as the carriage driver expertly led them through without a hitch.

The streets were cleaner away from the bars and clubs. Old houses and office buildings made from sand coloured stone and bricks lined the pavements blocking out the sunlight in the streets. The brilliant blue sky, however, couldn't be missed. She looked up at Rome, who kissed her on the lips.

"You ready to tell me where we are going yet?"

"No, we will be there soon."

Kieran couldn't wait to get to their destination. The smell of the horse in the heat was off putting. Thankfully, it wasn't long before the horse came to a stop. Kieran looked around, and her eyes caught sight of a walkway ahead that seemed to go over water. It led to a small island with high walls built around the perimeter and surrounding an old building. Rome paid the driver and jumped down from the carriage; he took Kieran's hands and helped her down.

"Where are we?"

"Palaio Frourio," the driver answered, "it means old citadel."

Kieran looked towards the island. She was not sure if she would feel comfortable going over the walkway – she had an aversion to bridges and tunnels, especially if they were surrounded by water.

"The site was initially a neck of land; when the Venetians were in power, they dug a moat to convert it into an island for greater security. This was one of the reasons why Corfu, unlike the rest of Greece, was never conquered by the Turks, although they tried a number of times." The driver told them. "The houses we just passed were also Venetian inspired; some people say it reminds them of Italy."

Kieran found this brief history interesting and she was excited to learn more, so much so, that two-hours later, she and Rome were still exploring the building. They walked through high stone arches and along the maze-like hallways throughout the fortress taking in the breath taking views and old architecture. She was amazed by the artefacts and the history from centuries before in the little museum. Kieran was way up over the town when she saw the clear, sparkling, turquoise sea. Boats and yachts appeared like tiny twinkling dots in the distance.

The gift shop in the museum sold authentic Greek jewellery and replica paintings, statues, as well as traditional souvenirs.

Kieran's weakness for pretty things surfaced and she purchased a few jewellery pieces she fell in love with, as well as other souvenirs for friends and family. Rome wanted to buy something for her. Kieran refused - much to his annoyance.

"Will you at least let me buy you lunch?" he asked her as they walked hand-in-hand to an outside café and sat at one of the clustered tables.

"You bought me breakfast," she reminded him putting her sunglasses on.

"Your point being?"

"You can't buy me everything."

"Breakfast and lunch is not everything,"

"I will buy you lunch,"

He stood up and sighed. "Fine, you wait here and I will go and arrange for a carriage to take us back in a bit."

Kieran nodded and picked up a menu. She raised her eyebrows at the prices. She was not going to eat much. In fact, she wasn't even hungry and decided on a fruit salad. It was too hot to eat anything heavy. She ordered an orange juice and Rome returned claiming that he could not find a carriage to take them back. Kieran was relieved. Though riding in the horse-drawn carriage was romantic, she couldn't handle the smell of the animal again.

Rome ordered a beer and a burger. Kieran wondered how he could eat and drink all the wrong things, yet it didn't show on his perfect body.

"Where are we going next?" she asked sipping her juice.

"We are going to the old palace gardens," he informed her.

"Did I tell you I love plants and flowers?" she asked her eyes lighting up. Kieran loved green spaces.

"No, but it's a good thing we have things in common isn't it?"

"You like plants and flowers?" she asked surprised.

"I like plants and some flowers. My Grandmother taught me all about them when I was younger. I used to help her do the gardening. When I buy a house I want to have a massive garden, trees, flowers, the lot," he told her as he sipped his beer.

"Seriously?"

"Seriously," he repeated.

Kieran smiled. "My house is overrun with plants, Chantelle and Christina have actually banned me from buying anymore," she said laughing.

"Maybe one day I'll get to see it."

"Maybe," she said grinning at him. He leaned across the table and Kieran leaned forward to meet his lips. He pulled away and Kieran said, "Mmm, one more."

He kissed her again. When they separated, they were smiling.

The sun was starting to set by the time they left the gardens. Kieran had never seen so many exotic flowers and plants in one place; she had identified about five types of lilies that she knew including her favourite calla lilies. She had also spotted tulips, lilacs, orchids, lotus', about five different coloured roses, gardenias, hibiscuses and many others that she'd never heard of. She was impressed that Rome could name some of them off the top of his head.

Kieran would never forget how beautiful it had been, all the different colours of the rainbow in one place, she learned so much in one day and she loved it. There seemed to be no end to the amount of history that surrounded the island. Afterwards they had found somewhere quiet and sat and enjoyed the weather, the scenery and each other's company. It had been the most romantic afternoon of Kieran's life. She knew she would never forget it or him. Romeo by name, Romeo by nature.

As a first date, it was different and the best one she had ever had. She and Darren had never had a first date. The only places they went to were parties. He wasn't into history, or plants, or architecture, or learning about new things and maybe that was their problem. They had nothing in common anymore. Kieran had grown out of constant partying. Yes, she liked to socialise, but as she got older, it was becoming more and more of an issue to her.

"Do you want to head back to the hotel now?" Rome asked interrupting her reflections.

"Not yet," she said. She was content being snuggled up to him in the taxi.

"Cool, I want to take you to one more place before we head back to meet the guys for dinner," he said with a mischievous smile.

"Have you been here before? How did you know all this stuff existed?" Kieran asked studying his face; he broke into an easy smile making Kieran's heart flutter.

God he's beautiful.

"I did a little research while you were getting ready. This is my first visit to Corfu. I went to Zante last year."

"Boy's holiday?" Kieran asked raising her eyebrows.

"Yea, tough breakup," Rome said followed by nervous laughter.

"So you slept with someone then?" Kieran asked, before he could reply she covered her ears and said, "Actually I don't want to know."

Rome chuckled. "Don't get jealous," he teased.

"Me? Never," she gasped and smiled.

Rome pulled her towards him and kissed her cheek. "She had nothing on you," he whispered.

Kieran smiled. "Flattery will get you everywhere."

"Good thing I'm so good at it then," he grinned.

Kieran didn't argue. It was true. She was enjoying being spoilt. She couldn't remember the last time a guy had lavished so much attention and time on her and been genuine about it.

The taxi stopped at Spianada square a large cobblestone square in the centre of town. Rome told her it was the largest square in South Eastern Europe and was separated by a street into two squares. Ano Plateia and Kato Plateia which translated into upper and lower square respectively. Rome led Kieran towards the upper square.

Around the outside of the square were the usual cafés, souvenir shops and restaurants for tourists to sit and enjoy the sites. In the centre, surrounded by an iron fence was an octagon shaped gazebo, with high arches and a domed ceiling. Steps led up from the ground to the main marbled platform. A band was in the midst of setting up their instruments.

"That's the music pavilion, the band are going to play soon, do you want to walk around for a bit? I think we still have time before they start." Rome said smiling and kissing her hand.

Kieran nodded. When he smiled at her like that, she would do anything he wanted.

They walked around the square, until Kieran decided it was time to take a break. She hadn't done that much walking in ages, especially since she had been driving. They found a little café and sat at a table next to each other facing the band who were now sat under the music pavilion's shelter in silence. The sun had disappeared and the sea air made her shiver.

"Are you cold babe?" Rome asked rubbing her arms.

"A little," she admitted.

"I'm sorry; I didn't think we'd be out this long," he moved closer and put one arm around her shoulders.

"Don't be silly." Kieran swallowed a mouthful of the hot tea no sooner had the waiter placed it on the table. In an instant, she felt warm. She yawned and snuggled closer to Rome as he sipped a beer. She wasn't sure if she would have the energy for dinner.

She took in the surroundings. Twinkling lights hung from lamp post to lamp post, lining the edge of the square; it looked like a scene out of a movie. Kieran looked out towards the sea and could see the fortress. There must have been a thousand lights all pointing at it. Every inch of it was luminous and shining against the backdrop of the dark sky. It was almost as if it was floating on air, since the vast hill it sat on was almost invisible in the darkness. The boats looked like little lamps bobbing up and down on the water, while the old fortress reflected on the water's surface, breaking every now and then when a boat passed.

Kieran shook her head in disbelief; Corfu was even more stunning at night. People sat at tables that lined the outside of the square, some in groups on the floor, drinking, talking and laughing. There was a magical ambience in the air. Kieran wasn't sure if it was because of the history that surrounded them, or if people were excited about the band, or if it was the closeness she felt for Rome.

Their conversation that morning coupled with the time she had spent with him that day had drawn her closer to him. Kieran had almost accepted the possibility of him sticking around and the thought made her happy. She hadn't felt like that for a long time.

"I've had a really good day," she told Rome, "thank you."

"No, thank you."

"Why are you thanking me?"

"For experiencing all of this with me, it's been an amazing day and it wouldn't have been the same if you weren't here."

Before Kieran could respond, the harp player started playing a moving solo, the string section joining in a few minutes later adding emphasis to the emotion of the song. Kieran was not a fan of classical music, but she felt an appreciation for it. Maybe it was the setting, or maybe it was Rome; she got emotional and couldn't hide the tears in her eyes. She sniffled quietly.

"Babe, what's wrong?" Rome asked concerned.

"Nothing," she said swallowing the stubborn lump in her throat.

"So why do you look like you're about to burst into tears?"

"I think it's everything. This is all just so beautiful." The traitor tears rolled down her face.

Rome looked relieved and smiled, "I know. It's overwhelming."

Kieran knew he wasn't talking about the setting. He wiped the tears from her eyes, kissed her nose and then her lips.

"This has been one of the best days of my life." Kieran confessed looking into his eyes and stroking his face.

"For me too, you have no idea."

"Seriously, thank you," she repeated.

"Stop thanking me, I haven't done anything special."

"You have."

Everyone clapped in appreciation at the end of the first song. A gypsy man with white hair and dark leathery skin and a long nose approached their table with a bucket of yellow roses. He reminded Kieran of Dobby the house elf from Harry Potter.

"No thanks," Kieran told him and then wondered if he would put a curse on her when she observed him giving her a dirty look.

Rome looked at her and back at the man. "How much?" he asked.

"Five euros for one," The man told him with a smile.

"You don't have to," Kieran told him. He would buy her the world if she asked him and it made her uncomfortable.

"Listen to your boyfriend miss," the rose seller told her. Clearly, he wanted to make a sale. She looked at Rome who was grinning at the assumption. He handed the man five euros and was handed a single yellow rose, which he gave to Kieran. She sniffed it and inhaled its aroma.

"Thanks, again."

"You are more than welcome," he said.

The band started another song and people got up and danced in the middle of the square. Kieran noticed it was mostly locals. It was similar to a scene from another time, an old tradition which continued even with the intrusion of tourists. It was a beautiful place and as it was theirs, they continued to enjoy it. People didn't take the time to do that kind of thing home in London, and that was one thing Kieran disliked about living in a fast growing, ever changing city, sometimes it lacked that kind of culture and tradition.

"Would you like to dance?" Rome asked her.

Kieran looked at him as if he'd lost his mind. She sniffed the rose, "Dance?"

"When in Rome and all that," he said with a grin and took her hand.

Kieran didn't even have a chance to answer him before he was leading her into the centre of the square, where couples, young and old, friends and even children were spinning in circles. No one paid them any mind, but Kieran felt self-conscious. She didn't know how to dance to classical music. Rome pulled her towards him placing his arm round her waist and began to move his feet to the music.

"What are you doing?" she asked anxiously.

"The waltz."

"You know how to waltz?"

He moved her in slow circles in perfect timing to the music in answer to her question. Kieran rolled her eyes; he did, he was good at it too. "My Grandmother taught me," he explained blushing slightly.

"That is the cutest thing ever," she said concentrating on following his lead.

"Whatever," he said trying to keep his face serious.

"You talk about your grandmother a lot."

"I love her; I used to spend summers with her in New York when I was growing up."

"Ah, that explains your accent."

"I didn't think it was that noticeable."

"Only when you're angry."

"I was born in New York, moved to England when I was five, moved back to New York when I was fourteen and returned to England five years ago.

"That is pretty cool."

Kieran tried to imagine him as a kid. She bet he was breaking hearts even then.

"I've been meaning to visit my family, it's hard getting time off work."

"You should go. You made this holiday," she told him, "If I hadn't listened to Darren I would be living there now." He stopped dancing. Kieran looked up at him. "What?" she asked.

"He said you couldn't go?"

"Yes," Kieran said slightly ashamed. "My aunt wanted me to go over there for a year as Publicist for the New York office. I'm a Junior Publicist at the moment, so it would've been a promotion. I've always wanted to work and live in another country and I really want to go to New York. I shouldn't have listened to him. I regret it now," Kieran told him with a hint of sadness in her voice.

"I can't believe you let him talk you out of it. That would have been a good opportunity for you. New York is amazing," he shook his head and continued dancing. "Next time you get an opportunity like that, take it, no matter what." he advised.

This time Kieran stopped dancing. "No matter what?" she repeated looking at him.

"Yes, if he cared about you then he would've known how important it was to you and dealt with it. I understand why he didn't want you to go, but there are ways to work things out."

"Like what?" she asked as he spun her around.

"Depends, a year is long; but not that long. People can adjust, people can visit and if it gets really bad, people can move. If you want it to work it will." he stopped twirling her to kiss her.

"Good answer," Kieran said smiling up at him.

"Just so you know when you get another chance which you will, I wouldn't let you choose. We would adjust."

She was silent as she put both arms around his neck as they continued to move to the music. Her heart was pounding, reacting to what he had said. She could tell he was serious and not telling her what he felt she wanted to hear.

"Then again, if I had gone I wouldn't be here. I wouldn't have met you," she pointed out.

He looked down at her. "If this is meant to be we would've met somewhere, maybe even in New York."

Kieran smiled. "So you believe in all that fate stuff?"

"Don't you?"

She was thoughtful for a minute. Did she? She wasn't sure. Maybe it was because she'd never met anyone to prove her otherwise. Darren wasn't the one, she knew that. Was Rome? Maybe. She wasn't ready to admit that to him, yet. She shrugged and said, "Maybe. What do you believe? You didn't answer me,"

"I believe that sometimes you can want something and it can appear in your life, not necessarily there and then; but when you least expect it. I've been looking for someone like you for ages, and look what happened? The universe brought you to me."

Kieran tried her hardest not to roll her eyes. Was he for real? He sounded like someone out of a romance novel.

"I don't know if that means its fate; it just feels right, I'm not really surprised to have met you, I've been expecting you," he added.

Kieran rested her head against his chest and said nothing. What was she meant to say to that? Was he saying they were meant to be?

"You're not doing too badly," he teased changing the subject.

"I'm following you, plus it's in my genes, my parents are from Guyana and they love to waltz there, well so my Grandparents tell me," she said laughing and glad for the change of topic it was too much to think about.

"Oh, so then you'll pick it up easily. Maybe I will have to give you proper lessons sometime?"

"I think I would like that, that way if we ever came back here we could show them how it's done."

"Do you know this is the first time you've made reference to us having a future after this holiday? I do believe we are finally on the same page." he grinned. Kieran smiled at him. "I have one more surprise for you," he confessed.

"Are you kidding me?" she stopped dancing to glare at him. He pulled her towards him. Kieran refused to budge.

"Don't worry about it now. I'm just warning you."

"You are spoiling me rotten you know. No good can come of it."

"Whatever," he said and whirled her around.

"You don't have to shower me with gifts to prove anything."

"Is that what you think I am doing?"

"Why else won't you let me spend my money?"

"I am quite old fashioned when it comes to how to treat a lady. My grandfather always tells me a man pays on dates, and a man should spoil his girlfriend, that's just how it is with me."

"I'm not your girlfriend," she reminded him.

He looked into her eyes. "Yet," he said before kissing her.

"Whatever," Kieran teased rolling her eyes dramatically.

"Yea, whatever," Rome mimicked her.

Kieran laughed and then sighed. "You buying me stuff makes me feel guilty. I'm not a good person for what I'm doing to Darren," she explained resting her head on his chest.

He was silent for a few seconds then said, "You have nothing to feel guilty about,"

She didn't answer – they both knew it was a lie.

They danced in silence enjoying the closeness between them. Kieran looked up at him and saw a weird, distant look on his face. When he realised Kieran was staring at him he readjusted his expression, smiled and bent his head to kiss her. Kieran wondered what he was thinking about that made him zone out. She noticed it a few times throughout the day. Though she'd known him only a short while, she knew enough to tell that something was on his mind. There was something he wasn't saying.

The song finished and everyone clapped.

"Are you ready to go now?"

Kieran nodded and took his hand as he led her to the taxi rank on the other side of the square. As soon as she was snuggled up next to him in the back seat she fell asleep and had to struggle to pull herself awake to join their friends for dinner.

Afterwards, while Rome and his friends shot pool, Kieran filled Chantelle and Christina in on the day as they sat drinking cocktails.

As Kieran recounted, she realised she still felt somewhat insecure in spite of all Rome did for her. She was convinced that there was something not right. How could someone like him be single? Her fears were tested when a group of stunning girls lingered by the pool table vying for Rome's attention. Kieran tried not to feel jealous, but found she couldn't help it.

"Let's go over there," Chantelle suggested.

"Let's not, he can talk to who he likes," Kieran said sipping her drink and trying her hardest not to look over.

"Of course, but still—"

"No," Kieran said stubbornly. She refused to be that kind of girl. If it was ever going to work between them she would have to get over the fact that girls would find him attractive. For now, he had chosen her and that would have to be enough to make her feel better - in theory.

"Rome's calling you," Christina observed.

Kieran looked up, and sure enough he was waving at her to join him. She noticed one of the girls looking at her in a not so friendly way.

Chantelle laughed. "Did you see her face?"

"Yep, she's probably thinking the same thing I am," Kieran said miserably. She stood up and so, too, did Chantelle and Christina. They walked over to where Rome and his friends were. Chantelle and Christina gave the girls dirty looks. Kieran would've laughed if she wasn't so jealous.

"What's up?" she asked when she reached Rome.

"Nothing. Just missed you," he whispered into her ear as he pulled her towards him and held her close.

"You're not short of company," she told him trying not to sound bitter.

"True, but I'm not interested in their company."

"Well, from the look I got when you called me over I think they're interested in yours," Kieran said inclining her head in the girls' direction.

Rome laughed. "I didn't notice. You are the only person I am interested in, okay?"

"At least I'm not the only crazy one. From the look on their faces, they are wondering why you're interested in me too."

"Please, all girls like that are the same. They came over because they are confident in their looks, and think that's enough. It's not the only attractive quality."

"I would be confident if I had their looks."

"Looks only last for so long, if you have nothing to back them up with then you're screwed," he said planting a kiss on her lips.

Kieran could tell he was trying to distract her from asking further questions. It almost worked.

"So, if I didn't have a personality you wouldn't be interested?"

"Kieran, you are gorgeous. Of course, I'd be interested; but only for one reason," he pulled her even closer to him.

"So then why aren't you interested in them?"

"Honestly, I probably would be if I hadn't met you; like I said, it would only be for one thing."

Kieran nodded. He hadn't made her feel any better. Anyway, who were these girls? Courtney called Rome to the table as it was his turn to play. He let Kieran go and she joined her friends who were whispering and cackling with each other.

"What's funny?" she asked them as she sat down.

"Ah, just wondering why you would come to a bar in hardly any clothes," Chantelle said loudly over her shoulder in the direction of the girls.

"Apparently, because that's all they have to offer." Kieran replied playing with a straw.

"That's stating the obvious. That one couldn't be more naked," Christina said looking disgustedly over at the girl who was wearing the shortest denim shorts imaginable and a sparkly bikini top.

"There are plenty of guys around, why are they over here?" Chantelle asked.

"More to choose from, less chance of rejection?" Kieran suggested and noticed two of the girls whispering and looking in their direction.

"What's their problem?" Christina asked narrowing her eyes. Before anyone could reply, the two girls walked towards them.

Kieran noticed Rome's eyes following them across the room. She pretended not to see when his eyes flashed to her face to catch her reaction.

"Hi," the girls said smiling falsely at them.

"Hi," Kieran and her friends replied imitating them perfectly.

"We were just wondering something," the blonde said as she tossed her hair over her shoulder. She had bright blue eyes and was dressed in a short frilly skirt with a low cut vest top.

"Now what could that be, honey?" Chantelle asked.

"Are you with Rome?" the blonde girl asked Kieran, ignoring Chantelle's sarcastic tone.

Kieran opened and closed her mouth not knowing how to answer.

"Yes, she is," Christina answered for her.

Kieran was glad. She could not believe the brazenness of the girl. She had seen her and Rome exchange a kiss, so why was she pretending otherwise?

"Oh, Luke said he didn't have a girlfriend," the almost-naked girl told them. She had dark shoulder length hair and dark brown eyes. There was arrogance about her when she smiled.

"Why don't you go ask him?" Kieran suggested, she wanted to slap the smug smile off her face but resisted, she had more class than that.

"Okay," Blondie replied and walked confidently over to Rome with her friend flipping her hair as she followed. Kieran put her acting skills to use and tried not to look interested in his reaction.

"Bitch," Chantelle fumed and Christina kissed her teeth.

From what she could see from under her eyelashes, Rome looked irritated as the girl spoke to him while running her hand through her hair. Kieran rolled her eyes. It was so clichéd. Why did she have to find him attractive? Kieran rolled her eyes again, this time at her own naiveté.

Duh! He's gorgeous. Why wouldn't she?

Rome gave his pool cue to Courtney and stalked over to Kieran leaving the two girls standing there. They were still whispering and glancing over at Kieran.

"What was that about?" Rome asked Kieran sitting next to her.

"Apparently Luke told her you were single and she obviously got confused. I told her to ask you," Kieran explained stirring her drink with a straw and pretending she wasn't bothered by the girl.

"Luke is an idiot, You should have just told her."

"Told her what? That we've known each other for three days or that, you're not my boyfriend?" she asked still not looking at him.

"Why did you tell her to ask me?"

Kieran noted that he didn't answer her question. "Because it's your decision whether you're interested in her or not, how am I meant to know what you want me to tell her? It's not like she'd believe me. Anyway, Christina told her," she snapped, her pretence disappearing.

"Kieran, stop being stupid," he was annoyed, his American twang was back.

"Pardon?" she asked shocked by his tone.

"I already told you I wasn't interested in her. I'm only interested in you; I thought you got that after today? If you still doubt how I feel about you then what is the point in trying?" he pushed his chair back scraping it along the floor.

Kieran winced. He stood up and stalked off towards the toilets. The three girls stared after him.

"Okay, what was that?" Chantelle asked with a frown.

"I have no idea; it was only a matter of time before he started acting weird," Kieran said shrugging.

"I think I know what's wrong with him," Christina said before sipping her cocktail.

"What?" Chantelle and Kieran asked in unison.

"You make it so obvious that you're waiting for him to mess up, it probably is annoying, especially after the effort he went to today."

"She has a point. You've turned into Darren just on a less psychopathic scale," Chantelle mused.

Kieran looked at her friends horrified. When they put it like that she understood why he'd stormed off. Before she could get up to go to find him, he was on his way back over.

He sat down and took her hand. "I'm sorry."

"No, I'm sorry; you have every right to be mad."

"No, I don't," he said kissing her hand.

"Yes you do," she said in a firm tone, "I know you're trying. I need to get over my insecurities and stop making it hard for you."

"Do you want to get out of here?" he asked her.

She nodded. She was tired and the annoyingly stunning girls didn't seem to be leaving any time soon. "Are you two coming?" she asked her friends.

They stood up and said bye to the rest of the boys. Courtney left with them. Kieran heard Rome mumbling under his breath to Courtney. She couldn't figure out why he was annoyed and what it was about the girls that irritated him. He was in a much better mood once they got back to the hotel.

"I'm going in the shower," she told him as he collapsed on the bed.

"Will you be in there for forty five minutes again?" he teased.

She stuck her tongue out at him. "Surprisingly, I'm not freaking out tonight," she told him smiling.

He sat up and grinned at her. "Good," he said kicking off his trainers.

Kieran finished in the bathroom in record time, even with shaving her legs. When she entered the room the lighting had changed. Kieran looked to find the source and saw that Rome had been busy while she'd been in the shower. He'd lit candles and a small gift wrapped present was on the bed next to him. He smiled at her.

Kieran walked towards the bed eyeing the present. "So what is this?" she asked picking it up.

He pulled her onto the bed next to him. "Duh, a present, go on, open it."

"Romeo, what did I tell you?" she asked him using his full name. He deserved it.

"Ha, funny," he said attempting to keep his face serious.

"I don't want you buying stuff for me," she said as she turned the small package over in her hands.

"I don't want to hear it, just open it."

Kieran sighed and did as she was told. She knew it was one of the pieces of jewellery she'd fallen in love with. She should have known he was going to find a way to get it. How had he hidden it from her all day? She opened the tissue paper and tears sprung to her eyes. Her hands trembled as she took the silver bracelet out of the tissue paper. Six silver and turquoise charms dangled from it, spelling her name with the letters of the Greek alphabet.

"It's nothing major. I knew you liked it so I went back and got it for you," he told her.

Kieran looked at him and back at the present, "Thank you. It's beautiful," she said wiping her eyes.

"You cry too easily," he teased as he fastened it around her wrist.

She didn't answer him. Kieran couldn't find the right words to express how she was feeling. They stared into each other's eyes in silence. Kieran could feel the now familiar longing in her body surfacing and threatening to take over, before she could stop herself or give him warning, she was on top of him kissing him as if her life depended on it. No words were needed. Finally they understood each other perfectly.

11 CHAPTER ELEVEN

Rome wasn't awake when Kieran opened her eyes. She thanked God he hadn't been watching her sleep. She went to the bathroom, used the toilet, brushed her teeth and climbed back into the bed. She kissed his shoulder and put one arm around his waist. He rolled onto his side to face her.

"Morning, beautiful,"

"You're not so bad yourself," she said kissing him on the lips.

He still had his eyes closed "What time is it?" he asked.

"Eight."

"I'm not leaving this bed until twelve," he told her.

"Oh, now you want to sleep?" she teased.

"We have a long day ahead of us and since we were up until about four hours ago, I need to catch up on some sleep," he said through a yawn.

"Me and you both," she agreed also yawning.

"If you hadn't attacked me last night then we would've gone to bed at a decent time," he opened one eye to catch her reaction.

"Excuse me, I admit I attacked you once, the second, third and fourth time was all your doing."

"You started it," he said with a grin.

"And you were not complaining."

"Hell no."

Kieran stared at him. He must have felt her gaze on him, because he opened his eyes "What's wrong?" he asked.

"Nothing."

"Sure?"

"Positive. You have made me a very happy woman," she told him with a smile.

"Well someone had to do it."

"I'm glad it's you," she said kissing him for longer than necessary. Kieran couldn't help herself once she got started.

"Are you trying to keep me awake again?" he asked her through the kisses.

She didn't answer him. Rome chuckled and pulled away. "Hold that thought, I'll be right back," he told her and headed to the bathroom.

When he returned, Kieran snuggled up to him. He wrapped his arms around her, rolling her onto her back then rolled on top of her and brushed the hair away from her face and stroked her face with his thumbs. He kissed her forehead, her nose, her cheeks, her chin, her jaw line, down her neck, her collar bone and then he brushed his nose against hers, their lips centimetres away. Kieran wanted him; he was teasing her because he'd carefully avoided her lips.

He looked into her eyes. "What are you doing to do to me?"

"I think you need to ask yourself that question," she giggled wrapping her arms around him.

"I'm not doing anything, just kissing you."

"It's how you're kissing me," she told him.

"No idea what you mean," he rubbed noses with her again.

"Liar," she laughed trying to kiss his lips.

"See it's all you," he teased moving his lips away from hers and kissing her cheek instead.

Kieran turned her head to catch his mouth; but he moved. "Not quick enough," he taunted.

She put her arms around his neck and tried a different approach, "Please?" she asked sweetly.

"You'll have to try better than that."

"You're not being fair."

"Neither are you. You knew I wouldn't be able to resist even though I told you I wanted to sleep."

"It's not my fault you have no willpower," she said with a grin.

"It's not about willpower, you're naked and in bed with me."

"If you kiss me, I promise I will let you sleep."

"If I kiss you, neither of us will sleep," he told her.

"We can sleep when we are dead," she joked trying to pull his head closer to hers.

"That may be sooner than you think if I don't get some sleep today."

"You know you want to," she said in a seductive tone. Kieran liked this new found confidence.

"You have no idea," he whispered and before she knew it, he was kissing her and she was in heaven. She didn't know how she was going to get back down to earth.

At midday, Kieran and Rome left the room. Their friends had called them several times, neither of them answered the calls. They met them in the lobby; the others had gone last minute shopping.

"About time," Courtney complained looking at his watch when they approached.

"Oh shh, we are on holiday," Kieran said. She was in a great mood.

"The hotel clerk said we can leave our luggage here until the coach comes for us, so take your bags over to check in," Chantelle told her.

"Sure," Kieran replied, unable to remove the smile on her face.

"You look like the cat that got the cream," Christina observed looking up from her magazine.

"I'm happy," Kieran said looking at Rome. He kissed her forehead before going to the check-out desk with both their cases.

"Look at you all loved up with your Romeo, not freaking out anymore either." Chantelle teased.

"Don't let him hear you and I am not loved up," she informed them.

Christina and Chantelle laughed at her.

"Whatever," Courtney said rolling his eyes.

"It's been three days," she told them.

"Stranger things have happened," Chantelle sung as she stood up and stretched.

Kieran stuck her tongue out at her friends.

"We're sorted. What are we going to do for the next few hours?" Rome asked as he re-joined them.

"Let's go to a bar or something," Christina suggested closing her magazine and putting it into her bag.

"A bar with food," Kieran suggested.

"For real," Rome agreed rubbing his stomach.

"Oh, I wonder why you two are hungry?" Chantelle asked crossing her eyes.

"Shut up Chan," Kieran said and laughed out loud at how silly her friend looked.

"Okay Juliet," Chantelle said in a dreamy sing song voice. Kieran and Rome glared at her, "Okay, I was joking," she told them giggling.

"It's true though," Rome whispered in Kieran's ear. She smiled.

"Ugh, are you two going to be like this is all day?" Christina asked rolling her eyes.

"Maybe," Rome told her squeezing Kieran's hand.

"Definitely," she corrected.

He chuckled and put his arm around her as they strolled out of the hotel.

They got to the airport late that night and Kieran was glad to see that normal service had resumed, though she felt a pang of sadness that her fairy tale holiday was nearing its end. She was still enjoying herself. After checking in, Kieran and Rome walked around window shopping. They were entering a souvenir shop when Kieran saw the stunning girls from the bar. Rome ignored them and quickly pulled her into the shop. The girls smiled smugly at Kieran.

"What is your problem with them?" she asked as they walked around the shop.

"Not important," he said kissing her hand.

"It is. You get too irritated when they're around. Why?" she demanded.

"Okay, I met them before last night," he admitted not looking at her.

"Oh really," Kieran said her heart pounding.

"I kissed her," he confessed.

Kieran didn't have to ask which one. She knew it was the girl with the long, shiny, blonde hair, that's why she'd had such an attitude. "What else happened?" she asked trying not to panic; she was looking at postcards and pretending his answer wasn't that important.

"Nothing, she wanted to go further, I didn't and she got pissed," he explained, shrugging to emphasise that he didn't care.

"Why didn't you want it to go further? You did with me," She said still not looking at him.

He came up behind her and put his arms around her. "You are two completely different people. She was just after one thing and I wasn't." He said trying to reassure her.

Kieran rolled her eyes. *He must be the only man who isn't.*

"So you two kissed?" she said the words slow.

"It was nothing. I was drunk."

"I knew something was up. You were too annoyed yesterday."

"She wanted to know who you were."

"What did you say?"

"I told her, not that it was any of her business, that you are my girlfriend, so she thinks I cheated on you."

"She wouldn't be impressed if she found out the truth; you have been a busy boy this holiday haven't you Romeo?" Kieran said trying to make light of the situation; although she was not overcome with joy at the thought of them kissing.

"Don't call me that please, it was like our second night here I haven't done anything else like that until I met you," he protested.

"I can't say anything; you are free to do what you like."

"Kieran, don't be pissed," he begged.

"I'm not," she said shrugging her shoulders.

"You are," he said attempting to kiss her.

Kieran moved away and walked out of the shop. In two quick strides he was in front of her trying to stop her from walking any further.

"What are you doing?" she asked him. She couldn't contain her anger.

"Trying to calm you down," he pulled her towards him wrapping his arms around her.

Kieran let him, but snapped, "I am fine!"

"Then why are you so angry?" she could see he was trying not to smile.

"I am not," she lied, but changed her tone.

"Kieran come on, you can admit it," he said with a serious look.

"Why? Does it make you happy that I'm pissed?"

"It does actually; at least I know you care."

"Of course, you know I care," she told him looking into his eyes.

"Do I? This whole thing might just be you pretending to like me to get back at your loser boyfriend."

Kieran was stunned with disbelief. "I'm not that good an actress. Please don't try and make me feel better. Honestly I'm not at all surprised there was something between you two. She's stunning and so are you. It makes more sense than me and you."

"She is generic and false. There are hundreds of girls and more out there like her. What's to like?"

"I'm not blind. I can see what she looks like," Kieran grumbled.

"I told you, looks only last so long. There's a reason I know she's only into her physical appearance."

"Please, I do not need to hear the details!" Kieran snapped before covering her ears with her hands.

Rome chuckled and pried her hands away. Kieran let him win.

"She cannot hold a conversation. She doesn't think she needs to because of her looks. I like humble women. Women who are smart, funny, have a sense of ambition and adventure, and women who have no idea how gorgeous they are; she is not one of those women," he explained squeezing her hands. "Come on Kieran, you know I'm falling for you, she is nothing compared to you." his eyes searched hers for understanding.

Kieran couldn't look away. She knew he was being honest, otherwise he would be with that girl and the two of them never would've met. She winced at the thought; she didn't want to imagine it. She sighed and moved closer to him and he wrapped his arms around her.

"Okay, I believe you," she whispered.

He bent his head and kissed her. "You have nothing to worry about, trust me," he told her.

Kieran nodded, "Sorry," she mumbled.

"Don't be silly."

"It's pathetic. I'm jealous," she admitted.

"It's cute and everyone gets jealous."

"I bet you don't," she told him as they started walking hand in hand.

He laughed. "I get very jealous, don't you remember my tantrum yesterday?" he asked raising an eyebrow.

Yesterday? Has it only been a day?

It felt as if so much had changed in such a short space of time. Kieran felt as if she had known him longer than three days. It was her turn to laugh, "That was different."

"Jealousy is jealousy. I don't want anyone else with you."

"I don't think I want anyone else with me," she admitted.

"That makes me happy," he said smiling.

Kieran put her arm around his waist. "You make me happy, very much so," she told him blushing.

He stopped walking, took her face in his hands and kissed her slowly and tenderly, meaning every second of it. Kieran couldn't breathe; the kiss was intense and meaningful. He soothed her fear for the moment; no one could be that good an actor.

More than a few hours later, the plane touched down in London. Kieran sighed with relief. She was glad to be getting off the plane. The flight was bearable only because Rome had been there to reassure her while they flew through a storm. Kieran hated turbulence with a passion. It was nine a.m. Kieran had been awake for almost twenty four hours. Not that she was tired. She still felt as if she was on cloud nine. It had been a great holiday and she didn't want it to end for more than one reason. She was dreading saying goodbye to Rome, not knowing when she would see him again. She had decided she wasn't calling him first. In fact, she vowed not to....in theory at least.

Rome pushed the trolley with their cases. As they entered customs there was a queue. He put an arm around her, pulling her into his side. She sniffed him, taking in his scent, not knowing when she would get to be that close to him again. He kissed the top of her head. "I miss you already," he told her.

"Me too, it's going to be weird you not being there."

"You going home to someone else is weird."

"I am ending it today. I promise," she said looking into his eyes. She wanted him to know how serious she was.

"In your own time, I'm ready when you are and you have my number."

She moved closer to him and he let go of the trolley and wrapped his arms around her. Kieran responded to his kiss oblivious to everyone around them. Someone cleared their throat and they broke apart. She looked around to see Chantelle and Christina grinning behind them.

"You're holding up the queue," Christina teased.

Kieran and Rome laughed. He pushed the trolley and they exited customs, out into the airport where a sea of faces waiting for family and friends greeted them. Kieran's eyes connected with Darren standing at the barriers almost immediately.

What the hell?

He meandered around the crowd making his way over to her. Kieran swore under her breath while dropping her arm from the trolley. She moved away from Rome and glanced over her shoulder at Chantelle and Christina who had also seen Darren. They looked just as shocked as she did.

Shit, shit, shit! Why is he here?

How could she explain to Rome without Darren seeing? They were standing too close, too comfortable; he was bound to know something had happened.....but what did it matter? She might as well get it over with and tell him. Before she could think of where to start, a little voice shouting in excitement caught her attention.

"Daddy! Daddy!"

Kieran felt Rome freeze next to her. She looked up at him and saw the colour drain from his face. She followed his gaze in the direction of the little voice. She felt sick as she realised the voice was calling him, and then a little dark haired girl, about five-years-old, launched herself at him.

Rome readjusted his expression and hurried forward. He picked her up laughing and hugging her. Chantelle and Christina were immediately at her side. They linked arms with her and kept walking. She hadn't even realised she had stopped moving, stopped breathing. Her head was a blur and at that moment she forgot Darren, who had to have seen her face fall at the sight of the little girl. How could he do this to her after everything?

Kieran turned casually to see a slim, beautiful woman with long, wavy dark hair hug and kiss Rome on his lips. Kieran's face fell even more.

Asshole! He has a child and a girlfriend? I'm so stupid!

She laughed bitterly and yanked her suitcase off the trolley.

"Let me help you," Rome said suddenly at her side.

"Don't touch me." She couldn't look at him. She would not let him see the hurt in her eyes.

"Kieran, it's not what you think," he had his hand on her suitcase. "Please let me explain."

"My boyfriend is on his way over. Since things have changed, I guess I should work on my relationship," she told him trying to stay calm, what she really wanted to do was slap him.

She watched as Darren approached scowling at Rome. Kieran rolled her eyes. No doubt he could see the tension between them.

Rome took the case off the trolley, "It's not what you think," he said again.

"Goodbye, Romeo," Kieran said in a voice that sounded dead in her ears. Rome looked hurt by her words. He turned and walked away without another word.

Kieran barely had time to comprehend what had happened before Darren was in her face.

"Who was that?" he asked staring after Rome.

"Hello and welcome home to you too," Kieran said with as much sarcasm as she could manage. She wasn't going to pretend she was in a good mood when she was far from it. Her thoughts were whirling out of control. She berated herself for believing him even a little bit when she had known all along he was too good to be true. He must have been laughing at her and she couldn't blame him. She was an idiot.

A smile appeared on Darren's face, as if he saw her for the first time. "I thought I'd surprise you. I missed you babe," he said hugging her.

Kieran couldn't hug him back with the same enthusiasm; it was lost. She felt the tears filling up in her eyes and had to get away – for a few minutes at least to compose herself. "I need to go to the toilet," she told Darren as he took her suitcase from her. Kieran knew if he hadn't seen Rome help her he wouldn't have taken it.

"Can you hurry up, the parking fee here takes the piss," he grumbled.

Kieran took a deep breath and walked off towards the toilet. Chantelle and Christina were behind her. Rome's friends were still coming through. Kieran put on a brave face as they said quick goodbyes. She had to hold it together until she got to the toilets. She couldn't let Darren or anyone see her break down. Kieran didn't even look at him and would deal with his barrage of questions when they were in the car, if he could wait that long.

She caught Rome staring at her with a mixture of emotions on his face. She knew he was trying to tell her something; she didn't know what and she didn't know if she wanted to know. His daughter and his girlfriend were beside him - a happy family reunited.

Kieran felt the tears again and hurried off to the bathroom. As soon as she was behind the doors she burst into tears. Other women eyed her curiously as Christina and Chantelle tried to console her.

"I told you he was too good to be true," she sobbed. Christina reeled off some paper towel, her face a picture of concern.

"Why didn't Courtney say anything? How could he let this happen? I'll be having words with him later." she said handing the paper towel to her friend. "Don't worry Kieran," she soothed.

Chantelle was unusually quiet. Kieran had to look up and check she was still there. She was scowling and livid. "What a complete bastard," she fumed.

Fresh tears welled up and spilled down Kieran's face. She allowed herself to cry for a few minutes then took a deep breath and washed her face. She vowed that was the last tear she would shed for him. He did not deserve her and he did not deserve her tears. Her phone bleeped and her stomach flipped she knew it was him. She took her phone out of her bag and took a deep breath, read the message and threw her phone back into her bag, not speaking, as she let the words sink in. After a minute or so she told the girls what he had said.

"He promises everything he said about how he feels about me is true. He knows he owes me an explanation. He doesn't want me to think I was right all along. He wants us to meet up tomorrow."

"Is he crazy? We all saw them kiss!" Chantelle shouted causing the women in the bathroom to stare.

Kieran just wanted to go home and forget he ever existed. "I don't care what he has to say. It's pretty obvious what he wanted. I'm so angry for falling for it. Of course, he has a girlfriend. Look at him," she laughed even though it wasn't funny. "Romeo by name, Romeo by nature."

"She's not even that pretty," Christina added.

Kieran smiled at her friend's attempt to make her feel better. She took a deep breath and looked in the mirror. Her face was covered in red blotches and her eyes were puffy. She wondered if Darren would notice – probably not. He was too busy memorising all the guys' faces he'd seen.

"Let's go," she told her friends.

"You sure?" Chantelle asked with a worried look. "Can you hold it together in front of Darren?"

"I have to," Kieran told them. She knew if she cried again she wouldn't be able to stop. She was more hurt than she would ever show. Darren was waiting by the car park exit. So, too, were Rome and the other boys. Kieran allowed herself to look at him one last time. He stared at her with hope in his eyes. She turned away and carried on walking, her head held high. As far as she was concerned, he did not exist.

Later that day, Kieran lay in bed with a massive headache; she was too upset and annoyed to sleep. Darren and his friends were in the front room playing music and the PlayStation. She sighed; she was in no mood for them to be there all day and all night. Kieran imagined that's all they'd been doing while she'd been away.

Her phone rang again. She'd been ignoring it all morning. This time she answered. "What is it Romeo?" she asked rudely.

"I thought you weren't going to answer," he said sounding relieved.

Kieran was silent.

God I miss him.

She was so livid at the thought she pushed it to the back of her mind. "I almost didn't; since you won't stop harassing me I may as well humour you," she told him.

"Are you okay?" he asked concerned.

"Peachy," she replied with indifference.

"Kieran it's not what you think," he started.

"You're full of shit," she hissed at him.

"I know you think that; I swear to you she's not my girlfriend."

"Oh really? Just like you swore you weren't taking the piss out of me and that you felt exactly how I was feeling?" she asked sitting up and brushing away the angry tears that rolled down her face.

"She's the one I broke up with last year."

"I don't want to hear it. You lied to me and made a fool out of me. No wonder those girls were looking at me like that. They must think I'm 'Idiot of the Year.' You probably slept with that girl, too, for all I know."

"Kieran come on, you know me. I didn't lie to you. I have a kid with her and that's it," he said.

She could hear in his voice that he was upset; she didn't care. "I know you? You are incredible! I have no idea who the hell you are because everything I thought I knew was bullshit!" she shouted at him.

"No, it wasn't Kieran; I meant what I said about wanting to be with you."

"How does your girlfriend feel about that?" she asked bitterly. Her throat tightened at the image of her kissing him at the airport, their daughter looking up at them happily. She struggled to fight back the nausea in the pit of her stomach.

"Kieran stop it," he pleaded.

"Stop what? Am I making you uncomfortable? I knew there was something wrong. I knew it! And you told me that I was being silly, all that shit about wanting us to get married and have kids when you already have a child! You could've told me then. It was the perfect opportunity!" she said her voice getting louder. She didn't care if Darren heard her, she had nothing more to lose.

"I didn't know how to tell you. I didn't want to say anything in case we didn't go anywhere; then the more I fell for you the harder it got to tell you. I meant every word I said about how I feel about you Kieran. I need you to believe that."

"Why? To ease your conscience? Don't worry about me. I'm fine." She wasn't fine. Far from it.

"Are you? I'm not. I miss you already and I'm scared that this is over and I don't want it to be. I really did fall for you, you know," he told her.

Kieran made a noise that was meant to be laughter; it came out like a strained cough instead. "You don't miss me and you don't care about me! You are just some full-of-shit-guy, and I'm the fool who fell for your lines! Well done. Brilliant performance by the way."

"Kieran just calm down and listen to me," he begged.

"Fuck you! I listened to you for three goddamn days and you lied to me the whole time!" she shouted. Suddenly she was worried Darren might hear her, so she lowered her voice. It would be easier if she didn't have to explain any of it to him. "I don't care what you have to say about it now and I won't care in the future. As far as I'm concerned you do not exist. Me and you never happened! I wish I never went to the beach that day. Have a nice life Romeo." she spat before hanging up the phone.

Before she could stop herself she broke down in tears. She wanted to call him back and tell him she'd meet up with him and talk, but she couldn't. It scared her how much she cared and how much she missed him. She would not give him another chance to make her feel that way again.

After much crying, Kieran managed to pull herself together to go into the kitchen and get herself a drink. If anyone asked why her face was red and blotchy she'd tell them she wasn't feeling well.

"Hey, Kieran, welcome home," Anthony said as soon as she entered the front room. She smiled a genuine smile, but didn't answer him. Kieran could feel Darren's eyes on her and did her best to avoid eye contact with him.

"What's wrong?" he asked her.

She glanced at him and shook her head. If she spoke she would cry. Kieran looked around the front room and saw all the mess the boys had made and then she spotted Melanie. Seeing Kieran staring at her she waved.

"What are you doing here?" She didn't care if she sounded rude she had no patience left.

"I was passing by," Melanie replied.

"Do you mind calling next time?" Kieran snapped at her.

"Chill Kieran," Darren told her.

She looked at him like he'd lost his mind. "What?"

"I said chill, she's your friend."

Kieran looked at him with apprehension. If it had been

Chantelle or Christina she had spoken to like that, he wouldn't have defended either of them. Why was he defending Melanie?

"My friends always call before they come here," she said looking at him and then Melanie, who wasn't looking at Kieran. She was staring at Darren. Kieran's intuition flickered.

"So, where were you coming from?" she asked Melanie as she sat down on the arm of a sofa. Melanie hesitated one second too long and Kieran knew she was lying. She stood up. "Everyone get out," she said calmly.

Darren was the only one who looked at her. His friends were too engrossed in the computer game to hear her.

"I said get out!" she screamed. She got their attention then and they looked at her, all of them wore the same shocked expression on their faces.

"Shit Kieran, what is wrong with you?" Darren shouted at her.

"I want everyone out of here. My house is not a fucking adventure playground, get out now!" she yelled again.

The boys started getting their things together.

"You lot cotch man. I live here too. She can't chuck you out," Darren told them.

Kieran glared at him, marched over to the PlayStation and ripped the plug out of the socket. All eyes looked at her like they couldn't believe what they were seeing. She couldn't believe it herself, but was too incensed to care.

"I said get the fuck out!" Kieran knew she'd lost it.

The boys stood up, said bye to Darren and left the flat in a hurry, apart from Melanie. "What didn't you understand about get out?" Kieran asked turning to face her.

Melanie looked at Darren. He shrugged. "What the fuck are you looking at him for? This is my house get out!"

Melanie scowled at her, picked up her bag and walked out the house slamming the door behind her. Kieran was about to go and shout some more abuse at her for slamming the door when Darren grabbed her by the arm roughly before she could leave the room.

"What the fuck is wrong with you?" he growled.

She yanked her arm away from him. "You're what's wrong," she spat.

You're not Rome and you will always be wrong to me.

No. She couldn't tell him that. "Look at the state of my

house!" she yelled at him pointing to the empty packets of crisps and biscuits and cans of beer that littered the floor.

"It's not even that bad," he argued, and he was right. The boys always cleaned up after themselves because they knew what she was like.

"It is that bad and it's my house, so I'll say and do what I like," she told him.

"So it's just your house is it?" he asked her.

"I'm quite sure I pay the rent," she said folding her arms across her chest daring him to challenge her.

"I pay the bills."

Kieran laughed, "You pay the water and gas bills. The rest of your money goes on alcohol, computer games and raving with your stupid friends."

"Excuse me for not earning the same as you."

"Maybe if you weren't so ignorant and immature you could earn as much as me, or would you be happier if I earned less than you, so you could feel better about yourself?"

"My wages weren't a problem before," he said ignoring the question.

Kieran knew that meant he would be happy if he earned more money; he would be in control. "Yea, well, it's a fucking problem now!" she snapped at him.

"Why, what's changed?" he asked her.

"Me," she said before storming into the kitchen.

He followed her, "You're not lying. What is wrong with you?"

"I'm tired. I don't feel well and for one day couldn't you have thought that maybe I wanted the flat to myself. I've just got back from holiday, I don't need a bunch of boys making noise in my house," she shouted as she slammed the fridge door shut. She heard the glass jars rattle from the force.

"I think I'm going to stay at my mum's tonight," he told her.

"Good," Kieran told him. She didn't want him anywhere near her or touching her. The way she felt, if he tried to even kiss her, she would assault him. The rage she felt frightened her, and she could tell it frightened Darren too. He'd never seen her conduct herself that way and he'd never given in to her so easily.

Kieran felt guilty for a split second and then it was gone. She felt something was going on between him and Melanie. There was no point asking him about it; he would deny any knowledge and so would Melanie. What could she say about it anyway? She'd cheated on him. It was karma. She wondered how long it had been going on, not that she cared. As long as it wasn't in her house, he could do what he liked.

"Is there anything you want to tell me?" he actually looked concerned.

Kieran glared at him. "Yes, if you let that whore in my house again you can move out!" she snapped before stalking off back to the bedroom. She heard the front door slam a few minutes later.

Kieran curled up on her bed and cried herself to sleep.

12 CHAPTER TWELVE

Carnival weekend approached at the end of August. It was an occasion that Kieran and her friends attended ever since they were eighteen. Amelia, too, was joining them. It was one tradition that Kieran hadn't left behind with her single life. For her, it was a time when she could party the entire weekend and not worry about anything. She and Corey had taken the twins to the children's carnival the day before. She was glad to be out of the house. It made the pain easier to deal with when she was occupied.

The occasion coincided with Christina celebrating passing her exams with flying colours and securing a teaching post at a primary school. Her relationship with Courtney was developing, and that was another excuse for a celebration. Of course, she had given him hell about Rome; from what Christina said, Kieran deduced that Courtney had only known Rome about six months, and he didn't talk much about his personal life.

Chantelle, in a show of solidarity had not spoken to, or seen Luke even though he tried numerous times to contact her. Unfortunately for him, once he confirmed that he had known about Rome's situation, Chantelle wanted nothing more to do with him. "Birds of a feather," she reminded Kieran. Once they relayed their findings, neither of them mentioned Rome again. Rome continued to text her asking to meet on several occasions. Kieran stubbornly refused.

It had been three days since she had last heard from him. She would not allow him the chance to make a fool out of her again.

She put on a brave face and threw herself into work pretending that the episode was a meaningless holiday romance.

What she still couldn't understand was why he had lied when she had been honest with him. At least she knew she wasn't crazy. The weird facial expressions that she couldn't identify, his mind wandering, refusing to accept Kieran calling him perfect, it all made sense to her after the fact.

Kieran hadn't broken up with Darren as planned. She was not ready to deal with any more stress. She, however, was distracting herself with Joshua. As long as she didn't have to think about Rome, she was content. She would survive.

She and her friends arrived at Westbourne Park station. As expected, swarms of people in amazing colourful, eye-catching outfits added to the carnival atmosphere. Kieran saw a blur of the familiar carnival colours, red, green and yellow. She smiled in recognition, as those were the colours that represented Guyana.

Kieran disliked crowds and carnival wasn't an exception. It was estimated that almost one million people attended every year, although the numbers decreased over the years due to violence. This made Kieran quite sad because the carnival could have been bigger and better every year but due to those odd few who ruined it for everyone else it seemed to be going the opposite direction. She walked along Portobello Road, a popular street market. The distinct market sections included antiques, fruit and vegetables and fashionable shops. It was an attraction for both Londoners and tourists alike. The road stretched for two miles and was busy at the best of times, let alone during the carnival weekend.

After an hour's stroll taking in the feel, sights and sounds, Kieran grew hungry. The intoxicating aromas of West Indian food tickled her taste buds. She found a food stall and sticking with her Guyanese tradition, Kieran ordered lamb curry and roti. The food was nowhere near her grandmother's recipe, but it was tasty. Chantelle, Christina and Amelia ordered ackee and salt fish with fried dumplings, jerk chicken with rice and peas and stew chicken with rice and peas respectively. They washed their meals down with a large glass of Guinness punch each.

Fuelled with food, Kieran and her friends followed the crowd and found themselves on All Saints Road, where many sound systems played music of every variety including soca, calypso, reggae, hip-hop and R&B. The street was packed with revellers and before Kieran knew it, she was caught up in it. She couldn't move. Popular, catchy songs had people dancing as if their lives depended on it.

Kieran and her friends fell in as they got into the carnival groove and danced to their favourite sounds. Not long after, four cute guys joined them, Kieran and her friends grinned at each other. She was not in the mood to flirt, but allowed one of them who made a beeline in her direction to dance with her. Though the weather was not hot, she dripped with sweat from non-stop dancing and fanned herself with her hand. It was then she caught a whiff of Armani code. The impact was instantaneous. Her mind flew to Rome and her stomach churned. She was half tempted to look around to see if it was him but decided against it, she wasn't sure how she would cope seeing him.

Motioning to her friends that it was time to move on, she said goodbye to her dance partner, and wormed her way through the crowd, pushing any thoughts of Rome to the back of her mind.

As they strolled along, Chantelle sniffed the air.

Kieran looked at her and grinned. "Yes, I can smell it too,"

"What?" Christina and Amelia asked one after the other.

"Weed," Chantelle giggled.

"Ooh, let's get some," Kieran suggested.

Chantelle followed her nose to find where the smell was coming from. Christina looked aghast and frowned. "Do we have to?"

"I'm a mother, I can't be doing that stuff anymore; you guys go ahead," Amelia said with a smile.

During their college days it would have been Amelia taking the lead. How things had changed; it was just what Kieran needed.

"Don't encourage them," Christina told Amelia.

"You don't have to smoke it. Chan and I will. Come on, it's not like we do it every day," Kieran said rolling her eyes.

"Sometimes you are such a goody two shoes," Chantelle told Christina.

"I don't see the fun in it."

"If you weren't such a stick in the mud you would," Chantelle argued.

Kieran and Amelia exchanged glances.

"Children, please," Kieran teased.

They looked at her and laughed. It often got like this between the two of them, although their bickering never lasted long.

They followed the sea of people that were moving at a snail's pace behind the many different floats. Kieran loved when people from all over the world came to visit London's biggest carnival. It showed how diverse the city was. Seeing them and the revellers dressed in costumes in all the colours of the rainbow caught her attention and she forgot about the weed as the scene reminded her of dancing in the square in Greece among the locals and tourists. Though it was a different atmosphere, Kieran felt proud that London still managed to uphold its own traditions despite the feelings that surrounded events like carnival in more recent times.

After much dancing and more eating Kieran and her friends agreed it was time to leave. As she walked from the station toward the side street where she parked her car, her phone rang.

"Hey," she said to Joshua.

"You sound cheerful,"

"I've had a good day. I'm heading home from the carnival."

"So what are you doing now?"

"Heading home as I just said. Why?"

"Just wondering. I'm all alone and bored."

"I'm going home. I'm tired. I've been on my feet all day."

"How about tomorrow?"

"Maybe, I'll call you later."

"Promise?"

Kieran agreed before hanging up. She got into her car, tuned into a radio station and drove home. As she pulled up outside her house she felt her body tense, preparing for the fight she knew she would have with Darren They'd hardly spoken over the last few weeks. It was Kieran's defensive way of dealing with her hurt feelings - creating arguments. Sometimes she worked herself up to the point she forgot all about Rome. Kieran was well aware that she was not doing herself any favours; she had, however, reached the stage where she was past caring.

She was punishing Darren for pushing her towards Rome in the first place. He deserved it. He had no idea she cheated on him. Of course, he'd accused her of the act. Kieran hadn't expected anything less. She still suspected he was cheating on her with

Melanie; without proof though, there was no point bringing it up

They had argued before she left that morning, like they did almost every morning. He did not want her to go to the carnival, and further, he'd caught her putting on mascara which set him off. He had a cheek as far as Kieran was concerned.

"Hello," she said not looking at him as she entered the front room. She placed her bag on the sofa.

"Hi," he said not looking up from the TV.

"Are you hungry?" she asked. Not that she cared.

"Nope. I'm going out."

Kieran wondered when she would be brave enough to tell him it was over. It had to be better than the charade they played. Neither of them was happy. "Where?" she asked.

"Just out!" he snapped and turned up the volume on the TV.

"Don't talk to me like that. I asked a simple question," she said over the din of the game.

"And I gave you a simple answer," he said looking at her.

"Fuck it. I can't be bothered with you today," she said picking up her bag and headed towards her bedroom.

"You are never bothered so why change?"

"Just go Darren. I'm tired and not in the mood for your shit," she called over her shoulder.

"Oh, but I'm meant to take your shit?" he asked her.

She turned around to glare at him. "Fuck you," she said and entered her room slamming the door behind her.

Kieran wondered if she needed counselling. She'd developed serious anger issues over the last six weeks. She'd never sworn so much in her life. She'd have to give that more consideration she thought as she entered the bathroom and turned the tap on. She gave the bath a quick clean before adding bubbles to the water. She unzipped her dress and walked back into the bedroom to see Darren sitting on the bed with her phone in his hand.

"What do you think you are doing?" she demanded holding her hand out for her phone.

"Nothing," he replied tossing the phone onto the bed.

"Prick," Kieran mumbled under her breath pushing past him.

"Pardon?"

"You fucking heard me! Why are you going through my phone? Have you never heard of the word, privacy?" she shouted as she picked up the phone. She scrolled through her messages to see what he had seen. Glad she was always one step ahead of him. She had deleted anything conspicuous.

"Privacy doesn't exist in a relationship," he told her.

Kieran turned around to stare at him in amazement.

Where did he come up with this crap?

"I am entitled to my privacy; I don't have to share every little detail of my life with you, especially when I can't talk to you without you flying off the handle."

"As your boyfriend I am entitled to know what you are up to," he sneered at her.

"Maybe you shouldn't be my boyfriend then, since we see things differently."

"Is that what you want Kieran?"

Yes! She thought, but said, "I don't know Darren," she threw the phone back on the bed. Kieran didn't understand what it was that stopped her from ending their relationship.

"Fucking bitch," Darren hissed before storming out of the room.

Kieran stared after him. She wasn't sure who he thought he was talking to. She marched after him. "What did you say?"

"You heard me, if you don't know what you want, why are we together? Do you know how much I've sacrificed to be with you? Yet you don't know if you want to be with me."

"How much you've sacrificed? Are you taking the piss?" Kieran spluttered.

"I could be out living the single life; instead I'm stuck here with you," he said narrowing his eyes.

Kieran chuckled. "Trust me I am not stopping you from going out and living the single life if that's what you want."

Before she could say anything else, Darren pushed her onto the sofa and was on top of her shouting and swearing.

Kieran was stunned. She didn't understand what he was saying apart from the swear words. With a quick reflex, she slapped him in the face and pushed him away from her.

"Are you crazy?" she screamed at him.

"It's you, you make me this way. If you just did as I said we wouldn't argue and we would get along fine," Darren shouted at her holding his face.

"If I did what you said? Do you hear yourself?" she asked as she stood in front of him. He marched into the kitchen. Kieran followed him calling him every name she could think of, Darren turned suddenly and pushed her against the fridge. Rage coursed through her veins and Kieran pushed him back, her strength surprising both of them. They stood breathing heavily staring at each other.

Kieran cut her eyes at him and made her way toward the bedroom; she'd taken no more than a few steps when she heard the smashing of glass. She spun around to see Darren standing with his fist in the full length mirror on the wall. It took her a second to notice his hand was dripping with blood.

"What the hell did you do?" she shouted hurrying over to him. His face was pale and he looked dazed. He pulled his hand away from Kieran when she reached out and pushed past her hurrying into bathroom. Kieran stared at the droplets of blood that oozed down the mirror onto the floor. She took a deep breath and walked into the bathroom. Darren stood at the sink holding his hand under the tap.

"You might need stitches," she told him as she turned off the tap in the bath.

"This is your fault," he grumbled not looking at her.

"I didn't tell you to punch the mirror."

"You drove me to it."

Kieran didn't answer him. He might have had a point. Though blaming her was his way of not dealing with his issues.

She reached over to take a look at his hand; he yanked it away from her, wincing in the process. "I'm going to the hospital," he announced.

"I'll drive you." she said feeling a pang of guilt.

"I think you've done enough, thanks," he said giving her a stone cold look as he wrapped his hand in a towel and left the bathroom. Kieran heard the door slam. Alone with her thoughts and the blood, she began to shake. The gravity of what had occurred made her aware that their confrontations were getting worse. She wondered what it would take for them to accept enough was enough. The next punch could be aimed at her. With Kieran's temper and the animosity she felt towards him, she would kill him if he dared.

Kieran didn't want to be in the house when he got back. After a bath, she got dressed and was soon standing outside Joshua's front door. He looked happy though surprised to see her. It was the reaction she was hoping for.

Once inside, Joshua asked her what had changed her mind. She didn't know. Kieran wasn't sure if she knew her mind anymore.

"Like you, I got bored. You don't mind me turning up do you?" she asked even though she knew he didn't.

"Of course not, I enjoy your company."

"Good, I enjoy yours, too," she said as she sat down on the sofa.

He dithered and Kieran felt smug, glad to see he was nervous.

"So what do you want to do? Are you hungry?" he asked, still dithering.

"Yes, starving."

"Okay, I'll order Indian."

Kieran smiled. Joshua knew Indian food was one of her favourite cuisines. It felt like old times, familiar, comforting; she liked that. The best part was she didn't have to think about what she was saying or doing. Joshua had known her too long. After dinner, they sipped wine as light music played in the background and talked about the old days.

Kieran took in Joshua's large one bedroom studio flat, which she didn't take any notice of on her previous visit. The walls of the front room were painted sky blue, and Joshua's Bachelor's Degree certificate that was encased in a framed glass, was displayed on the wall, as well as his graduation picture. The opposite wall displayed a picture of New York's Brooklyn Bridge. The brilliant white skirting board enhanced the dark navy blue carpet, while the three-seater, black, leather settee that they sat on, and a small wooden black coffee table that housed a bottle of wine, sat on a navy blue centre rug completed the room's decor. She vaguely remembered the kitchen and bedroom from her previous visits. She felt a sense of satisfaction that he'd done alright for himself.

"This is cosy, like old times" she told him and picked up her glass.

"I know. Sometimes I really miss us," he said sitting back in the sofa with a smile.

"Only sometimes?" Kieran teased.

"I miss talking to you," he said moving closer to her and rubbing her back. Kieran suddenly remembered Rome had been the last person to give her a massage. She grimaced.

Shit why did I go there?

"And what about the rest?" she asked him She would not think about Rome.

"I miss that all the time. I miss you all the time."

Kieran put her glass on the table. She took his hand and squeezed it. "I miss you too."

"Really?"

"We were together for four years and I knew you inside out. You know what we had. Nothing or no one will ever compare to it, and of course, I miss you. You were the most important person in my life at that time."

"And what about now?" he looked into her eyes.

"What about now?" Kieran wasn't sure if she could feel that way about him again. A lot had happened; there were things he didn't know. She looked up at the framed picture of New York. The irony of it being there taunted her. He could've chosen any other picture; but no - it had to be New York. If she had gone she would not be in such a mess. She never would've met Rome.

He never would've broken my.... don't say it. Do not even think it.

"Am I still important to you?" Joshua asked interrupting her inner babble and moving closer to her.

"We will never be how we were for a lot of different reasons. Mainly because I've learnt how not to love you, and I'm not going back to get hurt again." Kieran could not handle another emotional let-down.

"Kieran, I've changed. I was so much younger then. We both were. Now I know what I want."

"Let's just see how things go. There are other people to consider," she said letting go of his hand. The conversation was getting too serious for her and she wasn't in the best frame of mind.

"I'm sorry, I shouldn't have said that," Joshua apologised.

Kieran didn't answer him. He shifted and increased the distance between them. "So, you feel the same then?" he asked leaning forward and picking up his glass.

"J, at this moment I don't know what I feel, or what I'm feeling means. I don't know if it means I love you any more or Darren any less. I'm confused," she half lied. She didn't love Darren anymore; that didn't mean she was ready to be with Joshua.

"You take all the time you need. I'm not going to rush, or pressurise you, I'm sorry," he said looking into his glass.

"Stop apologising."

"I want you to know I'm telling the truth. I miss you and I want us to try again. I'm still in love with you Kieran."

What was she meant to say? A part of her would always love him; was it enough to be with him? She wasn't at all sure if she could rely on him. It hadn't been a bad thing that they had broken up once she'd gotten over the heartache. Though they were older now with different life experiences.

"I'm scared about getting into this with you again," she finally answered.

"I don't want you to be scared of me," he put his glass down and took her hand. Kieran looked into his eyes. Maybe it could work between them. What did she have to lose? He was a much better option than Darren and they used to be happy.

She moved closer to him and closed her eyes, as she pressed her lips against his. Rome infiltrated her thoughts once again.

"What about Darren?" Joshua asked pulling away.

"Darren isn't here," she replied. *Neither is Rome.*

His eyes made her want to kiss him more. It was like reliving her teenage years before everything got messed up and complicated. Maybe this time they would have a better chance of a relationship. She'd already cheated on Darren. The end for them was inevitable, regardless of what he may have been doing with Melanie. She closed her eyes and kissed him with more passion and unable to say no, Joshua responded.

Kieran pulled away. Joshua opened his eyes, "What's wrong?" he croaked.

"Nothing."

"Are you sure?" he ran his finger across her lips.

"No."

"What is it? What are you thinking?" he dropped his hand; his eyes searched hers.

"Kiss me again," she said.

Joshua put his arms around her, held her close and kissed her. Once again Kieran pulled away. It felt different. It wasn't like his kiss. It wasn't Rome's kiss which made her feel as if she was melting every time he kissed her. She could not, under any circumstances tell Joshua that. Kieran wanted to pretend he never happened. He would not ruin her life. Kieran wasn't sure if she'd ever get over him; although she was determined to try.

"Let's go to your room," she whispered. Joshua held her face and looked into her eyes.

"Are you sure?"

"Yes, I'm sure."

Joshua took her hand and pulled her up out of the chair. Kieran let him lead the way. She wouldn't think about him. She could do that. Kieran knew that nobody could make her feel like Joshua did. It was a different kind of love, and at that moment it was what Kieran needed and wanted. They made love in the darkness and Kieran cried.

A little bit of her tears were for Darren, a little for Rome; mostly it was for herself. As far as she was concerned neither of them were a part of her future, and even though her actions did not make sense, she knew sleeping with Joshua was her way of letting both of them go.

"Morning," Joshua said.

Kieran opened her eyes to see him staring down at her. "Hey," she whispered as she stretched.

"How'd you sleep?" he asked as his fingers traced circles on her shoulder.

"Good and you?" she asked rolling onto her side to face him.

He put one arm over her and pulled her closer. "Like a baby."

"Would that be for any particular reason?" she asked with a smile.

"I'm not sure," he teased her.

"And how can I make you sure?" she flirted as she pulled away from him, her morning breath fear kicking in.

"Kiss me," he said. Kieran smiled and kissed him on the lips. "Okay, there was a reason," he admitted with a nod.

"What?"

"You being next me. I haven't slept that well in ages."

"Yea right," Kieran said rolling her eyes.

"I'm serious."

Kieran was about to reply when her mobile rang. She motioned for Joshua to be quiet. "Hello," she said in a casual voice.

"Where are you?" Darren asked.

"Why?"

"Because you're not here," he snapped.

"What time did you get in last night?" Kieran fished.

"About four, why?"

"Because I wasn't home at four and it's now eleven and you're only just checking to see where I am."

"I was tired," he said in a dismissive lie.

"So for all you knew, I could've been lying dead somewhere and because you were tired you didn't notice I wasn't there?" Kieran knew she was picking a fight with him on purpose because she was trying to find a way out. She ran her fingers through her hair. Why didn't he just break up with her? She would feel less guilty.

"Kieran don't start."

"You do not want me to start," she retorted. It was strange how their arguments felt natural. The same things were always said. They never argued about anything new.

"Where are you?" he asked again.

"You weren't bothered last night, so why the hell do you give a shit now?" she snapped.

"Who are you talking to like that?"

"You," she said into the phone before disconnecting him.

The phone rang again. She and Joshua looked at each other and at the phone. Kieran switched it off.

"Are you okay?" Joshua asked taking her hand.

"Yea, fine. He just pisses me off," she said pulling her hand back. She was irritated.

"Calm down. You don't have to worry about him now. Just relax."

Kieran took a deep breath and nodded. "Okay."

"Good," he said leaning over and kissing her on the cheek. "I'm hungry. Would you make me some breakfast and wake me when it's done," she ordered before turning over with a smile.

"You're the only person I'd let order me about like that," he said before getting up.

Kieran chuckled. All the guilt vanished and she was glad to be with Joshua.

13 CHAPTER THIRTEEN

When she got home, Darren was sprawled on the sofa watching TV. Kieran's eyes caught sight of a can of beer on the floor next to the remote and an empty packet of biscuits. She wondered how long he had been lying there and if he had been to bed at all.

"Hello," she called out.

"If you aren't going to say it like you mean it don't bother," he grumbled, before Kieran could reply he sat up. "Who's Rome?" he asked.

Kieran froze. A million thoughts whizzed through her head while she tried to think of a response. How the hell did he know his name? "Where did you hear about him?" she asked stalling for time.

Do not admit anything. Find out what he knows first.

She marched over to her computer and switched it on before sitting down in front of the screen.

"Does it matter?" Darren asked his eyes not leaving her face.

Kieran maintained eye contact with him as she answered, "Yes, it does matter. Did you go through my phone?" she asked glaring at him.

"Yea, I did," he finally answered.

"Why?" she asked clicking her mouse to start up her email.

"Because you were acting strange when you got back from Greece, you're still acting strange," he said as he picked up the control and flicked through the channels. "Maybe I've been acting strange because you're a paranoid control freak."

"Who is he Kieran?" Darren asked turning to look at her again.

"Someone Chan met on holiday," she lied.

"So why is he texting your phone?" Darren asked throwing the control down in frustration.

Kieran knew he knew she was lying, but he couldn't prove it. "Because Chan didn't want him to have her number," she said shrugging. She clicked a few more times on her screen. She wasn't looking at anything in particular. She was occupying herself to make it appear less obvious that she was lying through her teeth.

"You're a lying bitch."

"Pardon?" she asked raising her eyebrows.

"You heard me. Do you expect me to believe that?"

"Yes. What exactly did you see in my phone to prove otherwise?"

"He told you to meet him at a bar."

Kieran tried her hardest not to smile. He had nothing. She had deleted all the messages Rome sent her barring one to remind her of how things had started between them. "The message was for Chantelle. I was the go-between," she said rolling her eyes for extra effect.

She stood up. She could feel Darren glaring at her trying to decipher whether she was telling the truth.

"If I find out you're lying, I swear to God—"

"You swear to God what? Don't threaten me Darren. It is not my problem that you went searching through my phone and jumped to conclusions, just like it is not my problem that you go through my emails. You have serious problems and maybe it's because you're judging me by your actions why you're so paranoid," she said as she folded her arms across her chest and looked at him accusingly.

"Now who's being paranoid?" he switched places and took a seat in front of the computer. He was hiding something.

"Stop going through my shit Darren," she told him before picking up her bag and jacket.

"When you give me reason not to, I will," he retorted.

"You don't need a reason, you just can't help yourself," she replied heading into the bedroom and slamming the door.

She called Christina. Darren had not been the only one trying to track her down.

"Where the hell have you been?"

Kieran laughed at her friend's tone of voice. "I'm fine,"

"You think it's a joke? I called you so many times last night and you weren't picking up either of your phones. I thought all kinds of things."

Kieran rolled her eyes. Her friends were worried about her mental state. She wasn't that depressed. "I can't talk now. Let's meet for lunch," she whispered.

"Okay, where?"

"Cottons?" Kieran suggested as her stomach grumbled. It had been a while since she had eaten. She smiled as she remembered why she and Joshua had skipped breakfast.

"Hello?" Christina called interrupting her brief memory.

"I'm here," Kieran said opening her wardrobe.

"I said an hour."

"Okay," Kieran replied as she rifled through her cluttered wardrobe.

"Don't be late. I'm hungry," Christina warned.

"You're the one who's always late Chris," Kieran reminded her.

"Just hurry up," Christina said laughing.

"Bye," Kieran said before hanging up. She closed her wardrobe. She would decide what to wear after her shower when she could concentrate better. She floated off into the bathroom smiling.

"Oh My God!" Christina screamed after Kieran told her about her night with Joshua. Her excitement surprised Kieran as she had been expecting a telling off. Kieran laughed and told her to be quiet. People would complain. On past occasions, restaurant staff would regularly ask them to be quiet when they got excitable, or they would see the looks of disapproval from other customers, sometimes though, this made them louder.

"It was nice, kind of like old times," Kieran said with a smile. She had enjoyed herself. Prior to then, Kieran hadn't imagined being content again. It had seemed impossible.

"So what happens now?" Christina asked playing with a napkin.

"I think we'll go with the flow and see what happens. Last night was a good start. I haven't felt like this, since… in a while," Kieran said as she picked up the drinks menu. "Is it too early to have a cocktail? It's barely one."

"What about Darren?" Christina asked ignoring her question.

And here comes the lecture.

"What about him?" Kieran asked raising her eyebrows at her friend, "You know my theory about him and Melanie. I know you guys' think my guilt is making me paranoid, but come on Chris, our female instincts are usually right. He's my boyfriend, we live together, how could I not know when it's on my doorstep?"

"Okay you might have a point,"

"By the way, he found a text from Romeo. I told him Chan met him while we were away if he should ever ask, though I doubt he'd approach either of you since you would both tell him where to go," Kieran added. It was easier when she used his full name, it made it feel like she was talking about someone else. Plus she knew it would irritate him.

Christina rolled her eyes, "He is such a loser, speaking of Rome, what about him?"

"Why would you ask me that?" Kieran asked in a nonchalant tone and avoided Christina's prying eyes by studying the drinks menu again. Alcohol was definitely needed.

"Kieran, who do you think you're fooling?" Christina asked with a serious look.

"What?" Kieran placed the menu down and folded her arms across her chest.

"You've practically been a zombie since we've been back. You haven't been yourself. I'm sure Darren has noticed too."

"It was a silly holiday fling it meant nothing," she said studying her nails. Sometimes Kieran hated that her friends knew her so well. "And yes, Darren has noticed my change."

"You don't even talk about Rome anymore, and I know you think about him,"

"I don't actually, well I try not to, it was a holiday fling for the one hundredth time!"

"Keep telling yourself that it was only a holiday fling. One day you'll believe it," Christina warned as a waiter walked towards them. Kieran saw Christina's face light up then fall as he served the food to a couple at the table next to them. "Still deluding yourself?" she turned her attention back to Kieran.

"Christina please, can we drop it?" Kieran was getting annoyed.

"No, we cannot. Maybe you should call him?" Christina suggested before sipping some water.

"What for?" Kieran almost shouted. The couple who were lucky to be served glanced over with raised eyebrows.

"I don't want you running back to Joshua just to get over Rome, that's not going to do you any favours," Christina told her.

"Please stop saying his name. There's nothing to get over," Kieran replied.

She would never admit how much she was hurting over Rome. He had lied to her and pretended to be someone he wasn't. He made her look like an idiot in front of his friends, as well as hers, and she wasn't going to forgive him for that. She was glad she hadn't been more vocal about where she thought their relationship would go. She sighed. She had literally lost her head in the space of three days and allowed herself to believe in the fairy tale of holiday romances turning into serious relationships.

"Okay, so you are going to break up with Darren and get back together with Joshua, is that what you are saying?"

"I don't know about that yet, the getting back together with Joshua part, that is," her lack of a concrete plan was not helping her plead her case.

"But you slept with him."

"You told me to!" Kieran reminded her in frustration.

"That was before you met Rome and honestly, if you know that what you feel for him is real, why are you running back to someone who broke your heart?" Christina asked looking confused.

Kieran drew in a deep breath then exhaled. She didn't want to argue and had no clear answers. "Well, maybe Rome broke my heart, too," she said quietly as her eyes welled with tears.

God I'm pathetic.

"What?" Christina asked her eyes wide.

Before Kieran could reply, a waiter approached their table and set their plates of food in front of them. Kieran had lost her appetite. Christina thanked the waiter, sliced a piece of jerk chicken, savoured it and said, "Well?"

"I don't want to talk about it anymore. I was stupid enough to believe it was a possibility. Joshua and I were heading this way before we went away; why should it change?" Kieran answered. She ate a forkful of rice and peas. It was better than nothing.

"Okay fine. All I'm saying is be careful. I was there the last time he fucked up. I saw what it did to you and I don't want the same thing to happen again."

"It won't." Kieran wasn't sure how much her friend believed her argument. It was true, Joshua broke her heart, and after that experience, Kieran knew better than to believe him. She also knew nothing could make her feel any worse than she already did.

14 CHAPTER FOURTEEN

Two months later, Kieran was still seeing Joshua. The feud between her and Darren continued, though they had good days intermittently. On those good days, they ended up sleeping together. For Kieran, it was an act to pacify him and their situation, or rather her guilt, and she didn't want to prove he was right about her. Further, Kieran genuinely didn't want to hurt him. They had been good friends once upon a time.

Kieran was off work, she hadn't been feeling well. Darren had been banished from the house. She had told him she didn't want him to catch whatever it was she had, but really he was irritating the hell out of her and she needed space.

"You look like shit," Chantelle greeted her when she visited. She had already had the bug, Kieran had caught it from her.

"Thanks. Makes me feel a whole lot better hearing that," Kieran grumbled as she collapsed back on the sofa.

"Glad I could help," Chantelle sat across from her.

"I do feel like shit and I've got the worst stomach ache, I think my period is due." she complained wrapping herself in a blanket.

They watched TV in silence for a few moments, while Kieran felt sorry for herself. She hated being sick.

"Erm aren't you late this month?" Chantelle suddenly asked.

Kieran shook her head dismissively "Nope, you know I'm like clockwork every month."

Chantelle was silent and focused her attention back to the TV.

Kieran took a deep breath and looked at hers. *Fuck!* "No!" she wailed as she saw the indicator with two blue lines indicating she was pregnant.

Christina looked at them shocked as they stared at each other and back at the tests. The dripping tap sounded loud all of a sudden "So you're both up the duff then?" she said.

"I'm pregnant," Chantelle whispered. Disbelief clouded her face.

Kieran sat down on the edge of the bath tub next to her. "What a mess," she mumbled and stared once again at the clear blue digital response test, as if hoping it would miraculously change.

"So what happens now?" Christina questioned looking at them; Kieran noticed she was just as pale as Chantelle.

"I don't even know who the father is," Kieran whispered.

"Look, you know whatever happens, we are here," Chantelle told her.

"Are you still thinking about abortion?" Kieran asked Chantelle.

"What?" Christina asked standing up.

Kieran pulled a face; she had forgotten Chantelle had left that bit out.

"What?" Chantelle asked Christina. Kieran knew Chantelle was stalling for time.

Christina glared at her. "You heard me. Are you really getting rid of it?"

"Do you want me to have that idiot's child?" Chantelle asked scowling at her.

"Well you should've thought about that before you slept with him! We aren't sixteen anymore, don't you remember what Kieran went through? How we swore we would never go through that after seeing all the pain she was in? Abortion can't automatically be the answer because you were stupid enough to get pregnant!" Christina ranted throwing her hands up in the air in despair.

Kieran had never seen her so angry. She looked at Chantelle, judging from the frown on her face and the way her mouth hung wide open, she knew what was coming. She took a deep breath, preparing herself.

"Excuse me? Things change. What did we know at sixteen? Life gets complicated and sometimes you have to do things that you don't want to do, and for your information, I'm on the pill and fully aware of how old I am!" Chantelle shouted at her as she stood face to face with Christina.

Kieran looked at them, "Please, you two, not now," she interjected holding her head; she couldn't handle them arguing.

"When then? I cannot believe you two are pregnant. One of you doesn't know who the father is and one is getting rid of it because she slept with an asshole - again!" Christina shouted.

Kieran was glad Chantelle's family were not at home.

"I do not need a lecture from you!" Chantelle hollered back, one hand on her hip.

"Oh, dear God," Kieran mumbled under her breath and closed her eyes.

"Maybe if I had lectured you months ago you wouldn't be here right now, but no, you didn't tell us because you knew what we'd say," Christina pointed at Chantelle.

"My God, sometimes you are so judgemental," Chantelle told her. "Accidents happen."

"Well, I'm not the one who's pregnant; maybe you two should be a bit more judgemental. Maybe these "accidents" wouldn't happen to you," Christina said crossing her arms over her chest in a defiant manner.

"Can you two not do this please?" Kieran asked as her head continued to explode. What the hell was she going to do? She didn't need to fall out with her friends as well. Things were bad enough.

"Why? Scared I'm going to start on you?" Christina turned to face Kieran.

"No, I don't actually care what anyone thinks. I didn't plan it," Kieran said staring boldly at her.

"Yea, but you still slept with both of them and didn't use protection."

"For your information I used protection with both of them, maybe not all the time with Joshua but most of the time."

Her knuckles were white where she was gripping the edge of the bath. She was trying not to lose her temper. "Shit happens; condoms aren't a hundred per cent safe."

"It's probably not Darren's," Chantelle told her.

"What if it is?" Christina asked.

Kieran stood up and sighed. "Regardless, I can't have another abortion," she said lowering her voice.

Chantelle turned to Christina, "If all you're going to do is look down your nose at us, then why are you here? Is this what you call being a friend?"

"I'm telling you the truth, that's what I call being a friend."

"I've had enough of this. See you later," Kieran said walking over to the bathroom door and opening it. She hurried down the stairs, grabbed her jacket and put it on. As she walked out the front door, she could still hear Chantelle and Christina arguing.

Kieran walked to her car, forcing herself not to cry; as soon as she sat in the car and started the engine, she broke down in tears. She drove to Joshua's flat. If she had to choose who to tell between him and Darren about her situation, it was Joshua. He would handle it better. Well, she hoped he would anyway.

She took a deep breath to calm herself down; but as soon as he opened the door she burst in to tears again.

"Take a deep breath and tell me what's wrong," he said when they were sat on the sofa.

"I'm pregnant," she sobbed into her hands unable to look at him. It felt surreal to her that they were even having that conversation.

"Really?" he asked in a shocked, but happy voice, much to Kieran's annoyance. She knew he would make it easy for her; that was why she wanted to tell him in the first place.
He pulled her hands away from her face.

"No, I just said it to get a reaction," she replied in a sarcastic tone, wiping her face with the sleeve of her jacket.

"Sorry, stupid question. Have you decided what you're going to do?"

"Whatever happens, I'm keeping it, I think," she said biting her lip. She hadn't exactly told Joshua she was still sleeping with Darren. She wasn't sure how he would handle it if the baby might not be his. Kieran didn't want to risk him walking away when she needed him.

"Ki-Ki, I'm sorry," Joshua said bowing his head, "I should have been more careful. I can't believe this is happening."

"What have you got to be sorry about?" she asked taking his hand. They were both to blame, her, more so when it came down to it.

"For putting you in this situation."

"Are we really going to do this? Are you ready to be a father?" Joshua was silent, thoughtful, Kieran's palms began to sweat and she wiped her hands on her jeans anxiously. How was this happening? She wished she was dreaming and could wake up.

"If that's what you want. This baby is here and we can be a family and make this work and I'm ready for that. It's you Kieran, of course, I'm ready," he said smiling at her.

Kieran nodded. "Well, I guess now is a good time to tell Darren it's over."

"Do you want me to come with you?" Joshua asked putting his arm around her.

"Nope, if you're there Darren will feel like we're ganging up on him," she said resting her head on his shoulder. Plus he would start a fight and she didn't want that happening because of her. Kieran couldn't run the risk of Joshua telling him she was pregnant either. The less Darren knew the better.

"I don't care about Darren. I just don't want him to do anything stupid to hurt you." Joshua said with a worried look. He kissed her forehead.

"I'll be fine. I'll be back later," she said smiling up at him.

He bent his head and kissed her on the lips. "Promise?"

"I promise," she said and responded to his kiss.

Twenty minutes later, she was getting back into her car. She waved to Joshua and drove off. The guilt of the secret she was keeping from him started to creep in but she ignored it.

Kieran walked into her front room and saw no sign of Darren. He was not at his usual spot on the sofa. A noise in the bedroom caught her attention. She placed her bag on the sofa, walked across the room and opened the door. Her mouth fell open. Karma was indeed a bitch.

"What the hell do you think you're doing?" she asked calmly.

"Oh shit! What are you doing back?" Darren pushed Melanie off of him and jumped out of bed.

"What is that whore doing in my bed?" she asked raising her voice. She was suddenly annoyed she had wasted her time trying to protect his feelings; he was just as bad as she was.

"Who are you calling a whore? You bitch!" Melanie screeched.

Kieran looked blankly at Melanie. Was she seriously making noise in her house – in her bed? She had known that Melanie hung around her and her friends for a reason; she was not stupid enough to believe that the girls liked her; they tolerated her because they didn't want to be mean.

Well that's going right out the window....ha! I cannot wait to tell the girls I was right!

"Listen I have to talk to Darren, Alone. Please leave." Kieran said surprising herself at how calm she was. She wasn't angry. She felt a lot better about their situation. She picked up Melanie's clothes off the floor.

"Are you going to let her throw me out like that?" Melanie asked Darren raising her eyebrows.

He was muted. Kieran looked from him to Melanie who sat in her bed with the duvet around her. She threw the bundle of clothes at her with as much aggression as she could muster.

"Technically, this is my house; it's not up to him, so get the fuck out!" She didn't shout but her patience was wearing thin. Melanie kissed her teeth as she untangled her clothes and began to put them on while glaring at Kieran.

Darren stood hovering by the door looking as if he was deciding whether to make a run for it or not. Kieran found the scenario amusing. When Melanie was dressed, she kissed Darren and left without a glance at Kieran. Once the front door slammed shut, Darren opened his mouth to explain.

Kieran held up her hand to stop him, "I don't want to hear it," she told him.

"But—"

"No buts Darren. Listen I'm not bothered about her; you can do what you want. Things haven't been right with us for ages, and it's because of this we've both been cheating," she admitted as she sat down on the bed.

"You've been doing what?!" he shouted as he picked up his t-shirt off the floor and pulled it over his head.

"I think you should calm down. I'm not pissed at you so you have no right to be pissed at me," she said as she picked up the pillows and began taking the cases off. Kieran thought about burning them and had a vision of dancing around a bonfire with her friends in celebration.

"Why not? How can you call Mel a whore? Look at you!" he snapped.

"Oh, Mel now is it?" she threw the pillowcases on the floor and started undoing the duvet cover.

I'm burning everything she touched. The tramp!

"She was actually paying me attention," he protested as he opened his drawers and began pulling items of clothing out and stuffing them into a bag, Kieran resisted the urge not to jump for joy. Finally, he was leaving.

"Darren you are such a child!" she snapped and marched over to her wardrobe. Throwing open the doors she didn't know what she was looking for. She was trying not to throw something at Darren.

"Yea, blame me."

"I'm not blaming you!" Kieran snapped. He was silent for once. "It's the principle of it - How dare you have sex with her in my bed." She lowered her voice. It would do no good to shout.

"Don't go there," Darren replied looking at her.

"Don't go where? At least I didn't do it here where we do it, you actually make me sick."

"Who is he then?" Darren asked and stopped packing.

"None of your business."

"I think it is, since you've been sleeping with me and him."

"Joshua," she said sighing. Now the fireworks were really going to start.

"Your ex?" Darren asked wide eyed.

Kieran looked at him. He was livid she could tell. The vein in his forehead pulsated and anger radiated from him. Kieran could practically see the wheels in his head turning, putting everything together.

"Yes. Is that a problem? At least he wasn't your friend."

Darren started to laugh, he sounded hysterical. Kieran turned from the wardrobe and stared at him. "What are you laughing at?"

"She has never been your friend, and he's either really desperate, or just sad."

"How would you know? At least he treats me like I'm important to him," Kieran's hand rested on a shoe box. She had a picture in her mind of the box connecting with Darren's head. She smiled in spite of herself.

"You were, and still are important to me; I just don't think things are working out and I kind of have feelings for Melanie."

"I'm glad you feel that way and that this is going to be a clean break up. I was so scared of hurting you," she said sitting down on the bed relaxing finally.

"Me too," he said sitting next to her.

"So what now?" Kieran asked fiddling with the buttons on the duvet cover. She screwed up her face, she could smell Melanie's cheap perfume.

"I guess I'll move out."

"You don't have to rush. I'm not going to be here for a few days anyway."

"Where are you going?" he asked looking at her.

"Staying at Joshua's."

"I hope he's going to make you happy."

"He does. He loves me," she said not looking at Darren. She didn't want to rub it in his face.

"I love you too," he told her.

Kieran shook her head, "You do not love me Darren."

"How can you say that?" he asked taking her hand.

Kieran looked down at their hands. She'd forgotten how it felt to hold his hand. He was like a complete stranger to her. "If you really loved me you would've understood what going to New York meant to me. You would have put how you felt about it aside. You didn't even want to compromise, and I think that's a big part of loving someone. You can't always have your own way and you always feel you should," she said pulling her hand away.

"So do you."

"No Darren, I don't. Do you not get that we are here because of you? Everything I do you have a problem with. You can only be happy if I'm right under your nose where you know what I'm doing. You'd be happy if I gave up everyone in my life just to make you happy, that is not love."

"You can't tell me I don't love you, you don't know how I feel."

"I know how I feel. You ruined anything that I ever felt for you with your paranoia, possessiveness, and jealousy, you have drained me and tried to change the person I am and that's why I started distancing myself from you a long time ago. It just got way too much for me."

"But you know why I was like that. I thought I was going to lose you when you started going on about moving to New York. If you had gone, I would've lost you; it wouldn't have been long before you met someone else."

"That was your insecurity and you made it my problem. Over the past few months, all you've been doing is grinding me down so that I don't go anywhere and I've had it."

"I haven't been trying to grind you down. Don't flatter yourself that I care that much," he said glaring at her.

Kieran thought he could fake nonchalance all he liked; it was just another tactic to make her question what she was saying. He really thought she was dumb. "You have and you know it, criticizing my clothes, my friends, going on holiday, none of that was actually to do with me, it was all about how me having a life outside of you made you feel. If you loved me, you would understand that it's good for me to be my own person and have my own life and interests. And most importantly, you would've encouraged me to take up a work opportunity either in New York or anywhere else," she explained remembering Rome's words.

She smiled sadly at the thought of him. How come he understood and the person she'd been living with for years was too ignorant to get it?

"Wait, so I was meant to let you run off halfway across the world?"

"This is your whole problem. It's not down to you to let me do anything. I don't need your permission. I'm an adult, and I do what I want when I want!" she snapped.

"You're so selfish," Darren said shaking his head.

"Me? Are you kidding me? These past few months have been like living in a prison. You go through my emails, my phone. Do you think that's normal behaviour? I shouldn't have to think about the way I dress in case you don't like it, or watch who I talk to in case you get the wrong idea. This whole fucking relationship has been about you, and I told you, the reason you were so paranoid about me was because you were judging me by your standards and I wasn't wrong!"

Kieran jumped off the bed. She'd had enough of talking to him. She was wasting her time. He would never admit she was right. She threw the duvet cover on top of the pile of pillowcases and went back over to the wardrobe. She took out some clothes and put them in an overnight bag.

"It's not like you helped, is it? You know what I'm like and instead of just doing what I asked, you always had to argue and do what you wanted. Anyway, I knew you would cheat on me eventually," Darren said angrily.

Kieran sighed. He would never admit his faults. He would blame her for everything. She was the reason why he behaved that way. He continued to rant; *blah, blah, blah.* "Get over yourself Darren," she said without looking at him. She zipped up the bag and left it by the wardrobe.

Darren stood up and marched over to her. Kieran backed away unsure of what he was about to do. She backed right into the wardrobe. "Why don't you get over yourself? You think you're so much better than me don't you?" he growled grabbing her arm.

Kieran considered telling him that yes, she did think she was better than him, but thought better of it when she saw the crazed look in his eyes.

"I'm not claiming to be. I just think you have a cheek to tell me shit like that. In the beginning I thought you were so much better for me than Joshua and look how wrong I was? What you've put me through is nothing short of mental abuse, and I can see now what a huge mistake we were. Love really is blind," Kieran was being spiteful; she did not care. She pulled her arm away roughly and it hurt but she didn't let it show.

"Joshua must be fucking stupid to want you back."

Kieran glowered at him. She thought about telling him about Rome just to wipe the smug smile off his face; though it would only make matters worse.

She exhaled "Why do I even bother having conversations with you? I want you out of my house today, get all your stuff and get out."

"You don't have to tell me twice. I'm going," he said kissing his teeth and moving away from her.

Kieran was done being nice. "I don't know what I ever saw in you," she mumbled rubbing her arm.

"You're a hoe. You know exactly what it was. It's the only thing you were ever really good at," he said before spitting toward Kieran's feet.

She looked down at the thick glob of saliva sitting on her wooden floor. He was insulting her, taunting her, it was the worst thing he could've done and he knew it.

Rage like she had never felt before bubbled inside her and before she could stop herself Kieran charged at him and slapped him hard in the face. Darren looked at her; first in shock and then rage.

Kieran suddenly felt intimidated and took a step back. "Go now please," she whispered her hands shaking.

He grabbed both of her wrists, pushed her onto the bed and straddled her. Kieran screamed as Darren shouted abuse at her and all she knew was that she could feel the spit from his mouth spraying in her face. Her temper sky rocketed again, she didn't know where she found the strength; she pulled one of her hands free and scratched him hard in the face. She felt when her nails broke his skin, almost like she was piercing fruit.

He cried out in pain and clutched his face releasing her hand. Kieran pushed him, rolled off the bed and hurried over to the door, throwing it open. She ran into the kitchen and yanked open the kitchen drawer to look for a weapon. She was blinded by rage and fear. Before she could find something to protect herself, Darren appeared at the doorway. The scratch that started from his eye down to the corner of his mouth oozed blood.

He took a step towards Kieran. Her hands grabbed a glass that was on the sink and she hurled it in his direction. He ducked and it hit the wall and shattered.

"Have you lost your mind?" he shouted.

Kieran's reply was calm and so honest it scared her a little. "Probably, so if you come anywhere near me I will kill you," she warned him.

Darren looked at her, smiled and walked into the front room. Kieran fought to control her breathing, she could feel a panic attack starting.

Why did I think this would end normally?

The sound of glass shattering made her breathing stop. "What the hell?" She took a step towards the kitchen door. Another crash of glass sounded. Kieran stepped over the broken glass on the kitchen floor, there was another crash, she hurried into the front room. Darren stood by her bookshelf and was smashing the photos there one-by-one. Three frames were at his feet, two pictures of him and Kieran and one of her sisters.

"What are you doing?" she yelled at him.

"What? Do you think you're the only person who can smash things?" he asked grinning manically.

He's lost the plot.

She watched as he picked up another photo, one of Kieran and her friends, and he launched it against the far wall. Kieran shrieked and covered her ears as it flew past her. He laughed and picked up another - this time of her parents - and smashed that as well. Glass scattered over the floor.

Kieran marched over to the TV. She picked up his beloved PlayStation three and hurled it against the wall. It made a loud crack from the impact. She hoped it was the console and not the wall.

"What the fuck are you doing?" he roared hurrying over and shoving her away. Kieran cried out again as she lost her footing. She put her hands out to break her fall and felt a sharp pain in one hand as she landed on all fours in a pile of glass. She lifted her hand up and saw an angry, deep cut in the middle of her palm. Blood surfaced. She tried to pull herself up; before she could, Darren was next to her.

"You are going to regret that," he spat as he towered over her.

Kieran looked up at him. She was terrified he was going to batter her; she refused to let him see how scared she was, she would not give him the satisfaction. Not even thinking about it, her remaining good hand searched around on the floor. Her fingers closed around a large shard of glass, she grabbed it and held it out towards him. Her other hand went to her stomach protectively.

"If you touch me, I will kill you. I mean it," she said in a calm and firm tone.

He seemed to believe her, because he backed away and entered the bedroom. Kieran heard things smashing as they hit the ground. She stood up, careful to avoid placing her hands in the broken glass. She felt crunching under her feet as bits of glass stuck between the grooves of her shoes. She looked around the room and for the first time the tears stung her eyes. She wiped them away.

Darren was back in the room. Kieran watched as his eyes surveyed the damage. He looked pleased with himself which angered Kieran more. She was still gripping the shard of glass and could feel it digging into her palm. She wondered if she had pierced the skin, but refused to look. She didn't trust Darren not to attack her while her attention was diverted.

"I'm going now," he said as if they had spent a casual, social evening together. He put his jacket on and picked up his bag of clothes.

Kieran didn't answer him.

His eyes looked down to her hand and the sharp bit of glass she held. He smiled. "See ya, Kieran," he said before turning and walking out of the room.

Kieran heard the door slam shut minutes later, she dropped the glass and burst into tears. When she felt calmer, she walked into the bedroom to assess the damage. He had emptied all her drawers, smashed two more photos, the dressing table mirror and Kieran's Aloe Vera plant. Clothes, soil and glass covered the floor.

Kieran decided she would not tell another soul what Darren had done. Things would get a lot worse for him if she did. Joshua would kill him and so would her family and friends. She dried her eyes with the back of her hands and walked into the bathroom. She cleaned and bandaged her wounded hand, got the dustpan and broom and set to work.

An hour later, her home was in its original state. She was happy that Darren was no longer her boyfriend. He had proven what an unstable person he was and she was better off without him. Kieran rubbed her stomach. She hoped she was not carrying his baby; after his behaviour, and seeing what he was capable of, she wanted nothing more to do with him.

By the time Kieran got to Joshua's flat, she was too tired to go out, it had been a long day. She could not stop yawning and was stretched out on the sofa.

"Are you hungry?" he asked sitting next to her.

"No but I'm eating for two now,"

"Hey, what's wrong, I thought you wanted this baby?" he said noticing the pained expression on her face. He took her hand.

"I do, I'm scared and worried I guess; this is a huge thing to get my head round."

"I'm scared too, but we will be fine."

"Why do you always have to be so rational?"

"I'm not just a pretty face you know," he said with a grin.

"I know, you have a pretty big head too," she said rolling her eyes.

"That's what all the girls say," he said with a proud look.

"I may be pregnant, but I can still hurt you," she threatened playfully.

"I was joking," Joshua smiled and kissed her on the forehead.

Kieran winced. It reminded her of Rome when he did that. Was he going to haunt her forever?

"Ki, what did you do to your hand?" Joshua asked breaking her thoughts.

Kieran's stomach turned "I broke a glass," she lied.

Joshua kissed the palm of her hand. "Does it hurt?"

She shook her head, no. "I guess I should make an appointment at the doctor's," she said distracting him from asking her any more questions about her hand.

"Let me know when, and I'll take time off work to go with you," he wrapped his arms around her.

Kieran inhaled his familiar sweet smell, "What did I do to deserve you?" she questioned.

"Nothing, all you've ever done is been you."

Kieran was silent. If only he knew.

"Don't start crying," he teased, kissing her on the forehead again.

Kieran tried her hardest not to wince. "I won't, let's go to bed."

Joshua nodded, turned off the TV, stood up, pulled Kieran up and led her into the bedroom for their first night as an official couple.

15 CHAPTER FIFTEEN

Chantelle sat in the passenger seat of Kieran's car sulking and pouting as she drove to Christina's house. Kieran forced herself to hold in her laughter. She felt as if she was a mother bridging her two daughter's dispute to kiss and make up. Christina opened the door with a look of surprise.

"Hi, "Kieran smiled.

Chantelle tutted.

Christina smiled at Kieran, ignored Chantelle and said, "Hi, I'm glad you came."

"Me too," Kieran said following her inside.

Chantelle trailed behind them. Christina led the way to her room and Kieran got to the reason of their visit.

"It's silly us fighting, we've been through worse than this before," she said taking a seat.

Chantelle stood silent by the window.

"So, did you break the news?" Christina avoided Kieran's statement.

Kieran looked at Chantelle who huffed.

"Darren has moved out," Kieran told her feeling smug that her intuition was right. "I caught him in my bed with Melanie."

"What?"

"Yep, in my bed," she reiterated.

"What a skank," Christina said and shook her head in disbelief and disgust.

"Now I know the reason she was always passing by. Darren's

so pathetic; he relished the attention when I stopped caring."

"What about Joshua?" Christina asked.

Kieran looked over at Chantelle again. She glowered at her. "He doesn't know I was still sleeping with Darren so he has no idea the baby might not be his. I don't know how to tell him."

"You know you could do a paternity test?"

"If I wait until the baby is born it will kill him if it turns out not to be his."

"No, you can do an amniocentesis," Christina informed her.

"Isn't that a test for downs syndrome?" Kieran asked confused.

"Usually, yes; you can get paternity results from it as well. You should check it out."

"That's good to know. I will. Joshua has been great about it. He's excited and wants us to have this baby." Kieran told her.

"Really? Wow, he has grown up hasn't he?"

"Yes, he has, I don't want to ruin it this time, and I will if the baby isn't his; I guess there's always a way to make it work if we want to," she grimaced at Rome's words.

"Chan, have you decided what you're doing?" Christina asked in a hesitant tone.

Chantelle looked at her for the first time. "You know what I'm doing," she said frostily.

"Have you booked it?"

"Yes, the appointment is in two weeks," she replied and looked out of the window again. Chantelle was being difficult. Kieran knew she couldn't help it and was still hurt by the way Christina had spoken to her.

"Do you need us to come?" Christina asked.

Chantelle's face softened and then she burst into tears. Kieran and Christina exchanged looks; it took a lot to make Chantelle cry. It must have been far worse for her than she was making out. She sat down and when Christina reached out to her, Kieran restrained her. It was best to let her cry for as long as she needed.

After a while, Christina spoke. "I'm sorry I was so rude to you guys. You are like my sisters; I'm just worried about you." She too had tears in her eyes as did Kieran. She didn't have to say anything else. No matter what happened, they would be there for each other and their friendship would remain strong.

Kieran could tell it was the middle of Autumn, it was barely six in the evening and the sky was already starting to darken. She was on her way to Courtney's house. The football team he played with had asked Kieran's company to sponsor them, Janet loved helping out the community so had jumped at the chance. Since Kieran and Courtney lived in close vicinity, she agreed to drop off some paperwork.

She looked at the clock on her car's dashboard. She could spend no more than fifteen minutes before she had to leave to prepare for Chantelle's twenty-fourth birthday party. Chantelle had the abortion a few days before. Although she didn't regret her decision, Kieran knew she still felt bad about the procedure. She was impressed with how well she was coping. Perhaps it was because she hardly had time to get used to the idea of being pregnant; that had no doubt helped.

The previous week had been calmer for Kieran since she didn't have to deal with Darren. She visited the doctor, who confirmed she was six weeks pregnant, because they calculated from the day of the woman's last period. It didn't really make sense to her how they worked it out. She was still going through a guilt trip about Joshua not knowing the truth. The longer she left it, the harder it would be. However, the thought of losing him when she needed him most kept her from telling him. History could not repeat itself.

She hurried up the stairs to Courtney's flat. He greeted her with a bear hug. They hadn't seen each other in a while; he and Christina had been busy with work and romance. She followed him into the living room and froze when she saw Rome sitting on the sofa looking as beautiful as ever. Kieran's stomach lurched and she inhaled sharply.

Damn, I've missed him.

Regaining her composure, she said, "Thanks for the heads up Courtney." She was sure she saw a sly smile playing on his lips.

"Hey Kieran," Rome said smiling slightly.

Kieran turned to Courtney as if she hadn't heard him. "I'm not staying. Here's the promotional literature, I'll see you at the party later." She handed him the envelope, turned and walked out the door.

Her feet barely touched the first step when Rome called after her, "Kieran wait!"

"Go away." she said hurrying forward.

"You never returned any of my calls. I never got to explain properly," he blurted out.

"I don't care what your explanation is Romeo," Kieran said over her shoulder, she reached her car, unlocked it, and jumped in. Before she could lock the doors Rome got into the passenger seat. "What do you think you are doing? Get out now," Kieran trembled.

"I just want to explain," he said in a soft voice.

"Why? What difference does it make? I've moved on," she said. She was scared to look at him. Scared of what it would do to her.

"I know you have. I know I hurt you and I know I should've told you the truth; I didn't know what you'd say and I just wanted you to get to know me first."

"Well you know how that turned out." She refused to make it easy for him; she didn't want him to know how angry she was either. She needed to be nonchalant for as long as possible. She couldn't believe he was there.

"I can't handle you thinking that I lied about how I feel about you," he said.

"Felt you mean," she corrected playing with her keys.

"No, Kieran, I still feel the same way. I practically had to bribe Courtney to allow me to see you."

"He will be punished."

"Go easy on him, he's protective of you, but I gave him no other option. I told him I'd camp outside all day," he smiled as if he was proud of himself.

"Well explain then," Kieran said; her resolve breaking, though she still wouldn't look at him, it would only break her heart again.

He turned her face towards his: a familiar habit. Their eyes met for a second and her stomach lurched. He was so beautiful. Her heart started to pound. Kieran couldn't handle the close proximity between them. She pushed his hand away and glared at him.

"First of all, I'm sorry I hurt you and made you doubt what we have."

"Had, and for lying to me about your child," she reminded him.

"I didn't lie to you Kieran, I just didn't tell you. I have never lied to you."

"So why did she kiss you like that?" Kieran asked. The image was embedded in her head.

"I know what it must've looked like. We have a kid together, but we are not together. It's just that sometimes things happen between us for old time's sake I guess. I told you we were together for five years." His eyes never left her face. Kieran wanted to believe him. She wanted to believe that she hadn't misjudged him; she couldn't. It would mean admitting the horrible mistakes she had made based on those judgements.

"Sometimes things happen between you two?" she repeated.

"Yes, but I swear to you nothing happened for a few months before I met you."

"I don't care when the last time was. I don't like being lied to and taken the piss out of," she said. Her voice sounded strong, like she meant it.

"I know, but what was I meant to say?"

"You could've tried the truth. I told you everything."

"So who's Joshua?" he retorted. Kieran flinched as Courtney popped in her head – two things she'd have to tell him off about. She stayed silent. She didn't have a leg to stand on.

"So you didn't tell me everything," he told her.

"I wasn't sleeping with him. He wasn't my boyfriend, there wasn't anything to tell. Don't you dare try to twist this, if you're finished get out. I have to go," she started the engine.

Rome sighed. "I don't want to argue with you Kieran. I would've told you eventually. I just didn't know how to. The more time I spent with you the harder it was to say it. I didn't want you to judge me because I have a child and I'm not with her mother. I know how women look at guys like me."

"How?" Kieran mumbled.

"Like we are absentee dads with kids all over the place, irresponsible, can't hold down a relationship, you know what I mean."

"Everyone is different, shit happens, that's life, and how could

I judge you when I cheated on my boyfriend?"

"It's not the same thing as having a five-year-old."

"She's five. Wow." Kieran said nodding.

"Her name is Alana, she's almost five," he said with a proud look.

"Why did you break up with her mother?" she changed the subject. She wasn't ready to talk about his child.

"It wasn't working; you can't be with someone just for the sake of kids. It doesn't always work that way. We tried; in the end we were both unhappy," he explained and leaned back.

Kieran looked at him in her peripheral vision. This wasn't fair. Why would he come back into her life now she'd moved on?

Why isn't he over it? He's meant to be over it.... Regardless, we are so done.

She'd made sure of that. Yet there he was, wanting her to know everything, as if her life couldn't get any more complicated.

"Why are you still sleeping with each other, doesn't that confuse you?" she wasn't really sure she wanted to know the answer. The thought of him sleeping with anyone made her burn with jealousy.

"When you're familiar with someone sometimes it's hard letting go, not because you're still in love, or because you want to be with that person. Sometimes it's easier than starting again, well, it was until I met you," he said looking at her, he reached out stroked her face.

Kieran understood. That had been why she hadn't broken up with Darren, and if she was honest, that was what drove her back to Joshua; although she loved him in her own way, and they were having a baby.

She took Rome's hand. "I get it."

"Do you?" he said, his eyes searching hers.

"More than you know,"

"I fucked everything up and I'm sorry. I didn't think it would be an issue then. I wasn't even sure if I'd see you again and then she turned up at the airport."

"You didn't think you'd see me again?"

"I didn't think you were going to end it with your asshole boyfriend," he admitted.

"After everything?"

"It would've been too easy for everything to just work out," he said with a shrug.

"So what were you going to do if I did end it?"

"I was planning on telling her everything, anyway I did tell her in the end."

"Really?"

"Yes, I was in a shit mood for weeks. She got it out of me eventually. I wanted to tell you about Alana so bad. I tried a few times, but couldn't get the words out. I was scared. I know it's too late for us. I just had to explain. You were so angry with me, and I knew I wouldn't feel better until we sorted it out, or tried to at least."

Kieran felt the tears forming and a lump in her throat rising. She wanted to tell him it wasn't too late; it was.

"The worst part is I've missed you. I've never connected with someone so fast. I wished I told you from the beginning, who knows where we'd be now," he said.

"I've missed you too, more than you know," Kieran admitted. She looked away from him as her voice broke and she knew she was going to cry.

So much for nonchalance.

"I'm so sorry Kieran."

"Me too," she whispered.

They sat in the heaviness of silence for a while. Just holding hands, neither of them moved. Neither of them talked. There was so much Kieran wanted to say; although it was irrelevant at that moment.

"So, I hope this new guy is treating you better than the last one. He really was a loser. I saw the way he was looking at me at the airport," Rome said smiling.

"He was actually cheating on me; I caught him in bed with some chick, at least now I know why he was so paranoid."

"I told you he didn't deserve you."

"I knew that. I knew it for ages; like you said, it's hard to let go of familiarity."

"I wish things weren't complicated. I'd like to say we could be friends; I think it would be hard for me. Is that selfish?" he asked. Kieran shook her head. If she spoke, she would not be able to control the tears. "I don't think I could handle it feeling the way I feel about you," he continued.

Kieran heard the sadness in his voice and it hurt her heart. "Stop it, please," she choked.

He gave her a worried look and asked, "What's wrong?"

"Nothing and everything, and the more you say the more I hate myself for not answering your calls, or replying to your messages. I've made a mess of everything and I wish I could take it all back if it meant we could start over; I can't, it's out of my hands now," she was crying. She swore as the tears rolled down her face. She wiped them away; more replaced them.

Rome leaned over and hugged her. The warmth of the hug and the familiar scent of his cologne made Kieran's heart ache and she sobbed even more. She pulled away after a few minutes.

"It will be okay," he soothed taking her hand.

Kieran nodded. *No it won't. Not like this.*

"Do you want me to go now?"

She looked at him torn between her answer. She wanted to scream in frustration. "I don't know what I want," she admitted, "I've never been so confused or felt so lonely in my life."

"This isn't just about me is it?"

"No. It's been a tough couple of months. I made stupid pathetic decisions to prove to myself I didn't care that you lied, that you didn't tell me about your situation. I hid how hurt I was and forced things to happen so I would forget; now I can't seem to find my way back from it. I should've listened to Christina when she told me I was being an idiot. I didn't because of my pride. I feel trapped and I don't know what to do…" her voice trailed off as she started to cry again.

Rome wiped her face with his hands and pulled her closer to him.

"Don't," she mumbled, but she didn't move away from him.

"Why?" he whispered into her hair.

"Because," she sniffled.

Rome laughed quietly, as if he knew exactly what that because meant. He sighed and moved away from her, but continued to hold her hand. She looked at him, unable to hide her emotion.

I wish you could stay with me….

"I think you should go now," she whispered. It hurt her to say it, more than he would ever know.

"Yea, I think so, too."

"I won't be able to stop crying if you stay."

"And I won't go if you don't stop crying," he said.

Kieran smiled sadly and squeezed his hand. "I'm sorry," she told him.

"Me too," he let go of her hand and stroked her face with the back of his hand. "I'll still miss you."

Kieran kissed his hand. "Me too," she said fighting back another wave of tears.

"Take care of yourself, okay. Everything will work out the way it's meant to."

"I wish I had your optimism," she said wiping away a tear.

"Come here," he said as he leaned over and hugged her for a long time. Kieran closed her eyes and held onto him, not wanting to let go. She wanted to always remember how it felt to be close to him, it would never be like that between them again.

She sniffled. *He has to let go first, I can't do this.*

He sighed and let go of her as if he'd heard her. They looked into each other's eyes and Kieran knew what was coming. She closed her eyes as their faces moved closer. She felt his lips press hers, and she pulled his face closer and kissed him with passion and tenderness. She wanted to let him know everything in that kiss. He was holding her face when they separated. He rubbed his nose against hers and smiled sadly. Kieran fought back the tears this time.

"Will you be okay to drive home?" he asked her.

She nodded as he kissed her forehead, her cheeks, her nose, her jaw line, taking in every inch of her face and the way her skin felt on his lips. To Kieran, it was as if he wanted to enjoy her for as long as possible. He kissed her on the lips again then let go of her.

"You know I said we couldn't be friends, but I'm here anytime you need me okay?"

She nodded again. He touched her face again; she smiled and took his hand from her face squeezing it reassuringly to let him know she would be fine.

"Bye, Kieran," he whispered.

"Bye, Romeo" she managed a smile to try and lighten the situation. Rome didn't return her smile, instead he opened the car door and climbed out. As soon as he shut the door Kieran put the car in gear and drove off. No sooner had she turned the corner, she parked the car and let the tears consume her.

16 CHAPTER SIXTEEN

Kieran blamed her hormones for her tears when she got to Joshua's flat and he asked what was wrong. There was no way she could tell him that it was because she had said goodbye to someone who could have been more important to her than anyone else, including him.

"I'm sorry," she apologised again.

"Don't be silly, do you still want to go to the party?"

"Of course, Chan's my best friend, I can't miss it," she sniffled and stood up. "I'm going to have a quick shower."

"See you in three days then," he teased.

An hour later, they were ready to leave, "You can drive," Kieran told him as she threw him the car keys.

Music was blaring and Chantelle stood at the door looking vexed when they arrived.

"Smile girl, it's your birthday," Kieran told her as she approached her.

Chantelle gave her a sarcastic smile.

Kieran laughed.

"What's wrong?" Joshua asked her, "Why are you standing at the door?"

Chantelle motioned for them to follow her. "I asked that rat of a brother of mine to do one thing and one thing only; what does he do? Mess it up, he is such a fool," Chantelle fumed.

Kieran tried not to laugh; she knew it was going to be a funny story. It always was with her brother, Reece. "What did you ask him to do?" she asked leaning against the kitchen counter.

"Move the damn furniture," Chantelle grumbled as she poured herself a shot of Sailor Jerry's Rum and swallowed it in one gulp.

Kieran raised an eyebrow as she poured another.

"What happened?" Joshua pressed.

"What didn't happen? He got all his stupid friends to come and help him. They ended up wrestling in the living room, broke my mum's vase, smashed my dad's eyeglasses and one idiot who decided to smoke and wrestle at the same time burnt a hole in the carpet."

Kieran bit her lip hard to hold in her laughter. "Don't you dare laugh," Chantelle scolded trying not to smile.

"I'm not!" Kieran protested innocently.

"What do you want to drink? Disaronno?" Chantelle asked.

"No, I can't drink that stuff anymore. I'm with child, remember?"

"Oh, yea, juice?"

Kieran nodded. They joined a few people they knew. Kieran however, wasn't in the mood for small talk. She left Joshua to chat and followed Chantelle outside where Christina and Courtney were. As soon as Courtney spotted her, he made a quick exit. Kieran laughed as Christina stared after him in confusion.

"What's with Courtney?" Chantelle asked sitting next to her.

"He's avoiding me," Kieran informed her.

"Avoiding you, why?" Christina asked surprised.

"Didn't he tell you he betrayed me this afternoon? Rome was waiting for me at his flat when I hand delivered some promotional stuff," Kieran explained sipping her drink.

"What?" Christina and Chantelle said in unison.

"Shh," Kieran placed a finger to her lips and looked around.

"What the hell happened?" Chantelle asked wide eyed.

"Basically, I've been an idiot and now it's too late," she surmised. They didn't seem as surprised as she expected them to be.

"What did he say?" Chantelle asked.

Kieran explained while trying not to break down. "You can say you told me so," she said to Christina when she had finished.

"That's not going to help."

"The thing that annoys me the most is that I was too stubborn to listen to him. I was convinced I was right.”

“Yea, when you expect bad things to happen they usually do.” Christina mused.

“Even though I got it wrong, I should’ve listened to him at the time; I was so annoyed that I couldn’t bring myself to give him the time of day. When he told me everything, it hit me how stupid I’ve been. We could be together know if I had just listened. Now it’s too late.”

“Oh Kieran,” Christina said putting an arm around her.

“Don’t,” Chantelle said seeing her eyes fill up with tears.

“Sorry,” she said dabbing her eyes.

“So, you and Rome are finished, not even friends?” Christina asked.

“He said we couldn’t be friends because he would find it hard knowing I’ve moved on.” She straightened. “I told him that things had changed and I couldn’t go back on them now. He seemed to get it. He didn’t argue or anything, so either he knows and isn’t saying anything, or he’s moved on too.”

“He hasn’t,” Christina told her. Kieran stared at her. “He told Courtney it’s going to take him a while to get over you; until then he’s taking time out from women. He wants you to be happy and if that means you being with someone else then fine, but it’s not going to be easy for him to just pretend you didn’t exist,” Christina told her.

A lump rose in Kieran’s throat. She hoped he knew it wasn’t easy for her, and that she was in her situation out of desperation to end the pain he caused. As much as she pretended he didn’t exist, not one day went by without her thinking of him; she hadn’t even been able to watch him walk away. He’d never know how much she would miss him, more than she’d ever missed anybody. She wanted him in her life more than anything but now she would have to get over him all over again; this time would be harder, because it was final. She had just been biding her time in punishing him, making him sweat, deep down she had been planning on giving him a second chance, once the anger had subsided. Now her plan had backfired, the baby had put a stop to any future with Rome she may have had.

“When did you come by this information?” she asked.

“A few days ago, now I know why Courtney was fishing,

Rome had obviously been bugging him for a while; he was asking me if you still had feelings for Rome."

"And what did you say?" Kieran asked as her eyebrows rose.

"I told him not to ask stupid questions, you're having a baby with Joshua." Christina replied.

Kieran didn't answer her.

"Have you decided about ..." Chantelle inclined her head towards Joshua who was talking to group of people.

Kieran shook her head.

"You have to decide soon. If it's not his, he needs to know sooner rather than later," Christina told her.

Kieran nodded. She was still stunned by what Christina told her. She rubbed her stomach.

Please let this be Joshua's baby, it's the only good thing that will come out of this situation.

They returned to the party and Kieran amused herself listening to Chantelle barking at Reece and his silly friends. She was talking with Joshua when she heard someone sneer, "Oh look who it is."

Kieran turned to see Darren staring at her. "What do you want?"

"That's no way to talk to an old friend," he grinned at her.

"Darren, do not push your luck," she threatened. Though she hadn't told anyone about what he had done, it didn't mean she wouldn't if he pushed her. She glanced up at Joshua who remained silent although his jaw was clenched.

"There's no need to get rude. I just wanted to say, hello," Darren added.

"Say it then say goodbye and leave," Kieran said coldly.

"I just got here."

"And?"

"I was invited," Darren looked at Joshua and smiled.

"By who? I know Chantelle didn't invite you, she doesn't like you, and in fact I'm sure no one here does," Kieran told him looking around.

"Why are you being such a bitch?" Darren asked.

"What did you say?" Joshua asked before Kieran had a chance to reply.

"You heard," Darren replied.

Kieran was well aware that he was trying to start a fight.

"That's funny; my hearing must be playing up. You could never have said what I thought you said. You are not that brave and not that stupid," Joshua said his voice was suddenly aggressive.

"I'm just telling it as it is. Your girlfriend is a bitch," Darren taunted him.

Kieran was not going to let him get away with it, "How's your face?" she could see the faint scar on one side of his face.

His face darkened and she couldn't help but grin, her smile soon disappeared when he retorted "How's your hand?"

"What is he going on about?" Joshua asked turning to face Kieran.

She saw that he was getting angry. "Ignore him," she told him and squeezed his hand.

"Yea, do as the bitch says," Darren said laughing and looking around at his friends. They didn't look as amused as he was.

Joshua punched him in the face. Kieran would never forget the sound of bone connecting with bone; she was pushed out the way before she could register what was going on. Darren's friends stepped in to separate them as they tumbled about.

"Stop it!" Kieran screamed as she forced herself between them.

Joshua glared at her "What are you doing. Have you lost your mind?" he shouted and pulled her out of the way.

Kieran noticed a semi-circle form around them as the other guests gathered to watch the commotion. "Have you lost yours? What are you fighting him for? He isn't worth it!" she screamed, she was livid.

"He shouldn't have called you a bitch," Joshua growled.

"It doesn't bother me. I don't care what he has to say, he chats shit all the time. I don't need you to fight my battles. That's what he wants you to do. Ignore him. It's not hard!"

Chantelle and Christina walked over to Kieran when they realised there was a scene. "What's going on?" Christina asked looking around at their angry faces.

"Mind your business," Darren told her.

Kieran spun around seething, "Listen, you are really pissing me off. Please shut your mouth for five seconds. Christina wasn't talking to you, so don't use that tone with her."

"Who do you think you're talking to?"

"Darren, do not push me," Kieran warned him. She was tempted to tell everyone about his behaviour the last time she had seen him and made sure he saw it in her eyes.

"Who do you think you're talking to?" Joshua asked stepping forward. Jarrell and Courtney held him back as Kieran stepped in front of him and tried to calm him down.

"Will someone please tell me what is going on?" Chantelle asked annoyed.

"Ask him," Kieran said looking at Darren with disgust.

"You know what Darren, I don't have a problem with you being here; if you want to stay, do you mind acting like an adult for a few hours?" Chantelle asked.

"It's cool. He hit me first. I'm going to retaliate innit? Yea, it's done. I'll behave," he said with a shrug and rubbed his jaw.

"Joshua?" Chantelle asked raising her eyebrows.

"Hey, I was just defending Kieran. He stepped out of line and I wasn't having it." With all that said Kieran took Joshua's hand and glared at Darren as they walked past him into the house.

17 CHAPTER SEVENTEEN

Christmas day arrived too quickly for Kieran's liking. She felt much better about Rome since they cleared the air. It helped her to move on with Joshua and that was all she could ask. She was over two months pregnant and only her close friends knew. Kieran wanted to tell Corey she wasn't sure what her reaction would be. She would be mortified if she found out her sister had been sleeping with two guys at the same time. Kieran also knew she would be disappointed and hurt if she didn't tell her, since they told each other everything. She just wasn't sure she could handle her questions.

Kieran was also considering doing the paternity test. Her research told her that she had up until she was twenty weeks to do it; it was risky, as there was chance of infection and damage to the baby. She felt the chances of it being Darren's were slim, as they always used protection. However, she couldn't wait until the baby was born. Joshua would be heartbroken if the baby wasn't his. She had to find out. Worst case scenario, she would do it alone. She had no other option. Kieran consoled herself that many women did it, and she had her family and friends around. She would be fine.

She rolled over and watched Joshua as he slept. He had turned her life around. For a while, Kieran had been worried she would be miserable after seeing Rome; however she was actually happy and felt loved. Joshua would do anything for her and most importantly, their relationship was void of any abuse. She kissed him on the lips. He opened his eyes and smiled.

"Hey."

"Hey," he said.

"Happy Christmas."

"Happy Christmas," he repeated and kissed her.

"Are you hungry?" she asked. She was starving.

"Yes, I'll make breakfast," he told her as he stretched. Kieran smiled. He looked extra cute when he did that. It was amazing how fast they had re-bonded. In some ways, it was like they had never been apart.

"I want to make breakfast for you."

"Okay, we'll do it together," he suggested and moved closer to her.

"Why are you looking at me like that?" Kieran asked rubbing his back.

"You look beautiful this morning," he said moving the hair off her face.

"Thank you."

Joshua pulled her towards him. Kieran grinned at him, "Breakfast can wait an hour or so can't it?" she said suggestively.

"Definitely," he whispered as he threw the quilt over their heads. Kieran giggled. Joshua wasn't laughing. He looked into her eyes and stroked her face, "I love you."

Kieran felt tears in her eyes. She not only heard the sincerity of his words; she felt it. It was the first time he said it since they had been back together.

"I love you too," she whispered. And Kieran did love him. She had done since she was fifteen.

"My mum is going to kill me. We are so late," Joshua complained a few hours later as they rushed around getting dressed.

"They won't eat without us will they?" Kieran asked as she put on her make-up. They were having dinner at his parents' then dessert, and hopefully more dinner at Kieran's parents. She'd been eating like a trooper for the past few weeks. The symptoms of her pregnancy had kicked in and she was thankful that the morning sickness was short-lived. She was not showing yet, but Kieran could feel her body changing. She was excited, though it didn't feel real to her yet.

Joshua looked at her and laughed. "Why didn't we get up earlier again?" he asked as he put on his trainers.

"You were the one who wanted to go back to bed," Kieran teased.

"You were not complaining."

Kieran smiled. It was a good Christmas day so far. She looked at the white gold bracelet that was on her wrist. She loved it. Joshua had been good to her. He came up behind her and kissed her neck, "You look beautiful, now can we go?" he asked.

"Yep," she told him before turning around and kissing him on the lips. She hoped he couldn't see the guilt in her eyes. She hated keeping secrets from him.

"Doing that is going to make me want to get straight back into bed and we can't do that," he said smiling.

Kieran let go of him. "Okay, I'll be good but you better watch your back when we get home," she called after him. She turned back to the mirror to inspect her hair.

"Kieran come on," Joshua called.

"I'm ready," she said brushing her hair.

Joshua was in the bathroom again staring at her through the mirror. Kieran hurriedly tied her hair up. He wiggled his fingers threatening to tickle her if she didn't get going. She glared at him daring him to do it. He stepped closer and she half giggled half screamed. He laughed slyly.

"Let's go," he said wiggling his fingers again.

Kieran hated being tickled more than anything else and he was the only person who knew it. "You are mean," she said pretending to be angry and stomped after him.

He picked up her jacket and helped her into it, grabbed her bag and said, "Yea, but you love me."

"Sometimes," she told him trying not to smile, as he double locked the door.

"Ha, you're so funny."

"Yea, but you love me," she said mimicking his earlier jibe.

They walked down the stairs and out to the car. The weather was cold with a light frost on the ground and the air was crisp. Kieran shivered.

"Sometimes," he said nodding.

Kieran hit him playfully.

Jarrell answered the door when they arrived at Joshua's parents' house. They touched fists in greeting, and Kieran kissed him on the cheek.

"Don't get too happy," Joshua teased him. Jarrell laughed and shut the door. He followed them inside.

"Joshua, what time do you call this?" His mum asked as he kissed her.

"Just gone three, Mum," he replied cheekily.

Kieran shook her head and kissed her. "Sorry we are late Donna. Your son couldn't get out of bed."

Her closeness with the family did not alleviate her guilt. She pushed the thoughts to the back of her head. She would deal with it when she had to. She grinned at Joshua. He opened his mouth to protest; Kieran put her hands over his mouth to quiet him.

"Too lazy, like his father," his mum joked.

"I've been up since nine this morning," Joshua's dad, Patrick protested from the table where he and Jarrell were peeling potatoes.

"Makes a change," Jarrell mumbled.

His dad glared at him. Jarrell said nothing and continued peeling the potatoes. Donna made her way back into the kitchen and seeing his opportunity to escape, Patrick swiftly left the table and hurried into the living room. Joshua laughed and helped himself to some Christmas cake.

Joshua and his mother shared the same almond shaped eyes and their facial expression relayed a softness when they smiled. They also shared the same jet black curly hair. Joshua wore his short, so the curls were visible only when he grew his hair, which he hadn't done since he left school. He inherited his dad's hazel coloured eyes.

Jarrell's features, however, were those of his dad; round face and cheeky grin. The brothers were mixed-race; their mum Trinidadian and their dad Irish. Joshua's nine year-old sister, Jasmine, ran and flung her arms around Kieran who bent down to hug her. The little girl adored her and Kieran felt the same way about her. "Happy Christmas Jaz!." she said cheerfully.

"Come and see my presents!" Jasmine said bouncing up and down excitedly, before Kieran could reply she was being pulled towards the door.

"Is it true you couldn't get up, or were you in bed for obvious reasons?" Jarrell asked his brother as he picked up what felt like his one hundredth potato.

"You need to mind your business," Joshua replied trying not to smile.

"I'll take that as a yes, then," Jarrell said grinning. He flicked a potato skin at his brother that hit him square on the forehead.

"Jarrell!" Joshua warned.

"Yes J? I'm not stupid; I see how you look at her. I'm happy for you. It's about time you settled down. Try not to mess it up this time, she's good for you," Jarrell knew how much Kieran impacted Joshua's life, before and now.

"It won't happen again, she's perfect," Joshua said as he threw the potato peel back at Jarrell. It missed him and landed on the floor. Neither of them made a move to pick it up.

"So when you getting married?" Jarrell teased rolling his eyes as he picked up another potato to peel.

"Listen, don't tell Mum and Dad, she's pregnant," Joshua whispered.

"Really?" Jarrell exclaimed loudly.

Joshua elbowed him and nodded.

"That's wicked. Congrats."

"Thanks bro," Joshua said with a proud grin.

"What are you two making noise about?" Their mum asked entering the room with a bowl of salad; she placed it on the table and looked at her sons.

"Nothing, I'm going to save Kieran from Jaz," Joshua said before quickly leaving the room.

"What's he hiding?" Donna asked. Her eye caught the potato skin on the floor; she kissed her teeth.

"Nothing," Jarrell lied.

"Why is there potato skin on the floor?" she asked one hand on her hip.

"I think it was Dad," he said and rolled his eyes.

As soon as Kieran saw Corey, she knew she was drunk. "Hey Corey, Happy Christmas!" she said kissing and hugging her sister.

"Happy Christmas little sis!" Corey squealed throwing her

arms around Kieran. "Hey Joshua, looking good as usual," she told him winking. The twins, Charlie and Cameron ran towards them squealing. If Kieran didn't know any better, she would have thought they'd been drinking too. She hugged and kissed them before letting them drag her in the direction of the living room.

The TV was on and there was music playing. A board game sat on the centre table. Her family appeared tipsy and Kieran's grandparents, still in their Christmas hats, were asleep on the sofa through the din.

Some things never changed. Her dad sat by the stereo playing vinyl records. Her mother and her sister, Janet, sat holding a glass of wine each, while singing along to the music and cackling.

"Hey everyone, Happy Christmas" Kieran shouted over the noise and introduced Joshua to her relatives who hadn't met him before. Once the introductions were over, Kieran's attacked her presents in a matter of minutes. After her squeals of delight for the perfumes, CDs, and jewellery she had received she looked at Joshua. "What are you waiting for? Open yours or I will," she threatened playfully.

He shook his head at her and tore off the Christmas wrapper revealing a DVD. He thanked Corey and Jack and unwrapped another present, revealing a bottle of Armani Code. Kieran froze, not sure how to react.

"That's from me and Alex, Kieran has the female version so we thought it would be nice if you matched, you can take it back if you don't like it, there's a gift receipt," Kieran's mother Denise told him.

"I was going buy this the other day, thanks so much," he said, leaning over and kissing her on her cheek. He shook Kieran's Dad's hand.

Kieran watched as he opened the bottle and sprayed the scent on him. The fragrance wafted over to her and she closed her eyes and inhaled. Her stomach lurched and she felt like crying as a rush of memories whizzed through her mind.

I should be here with Rome.

She grimaced at the selfish thought.

"Kieran are you okay?" Joshua asked quietly as put the lid on the bottle.

She gave him a fake smile. "I'm fine," she lied, "it's a bit strong," she wiped her eyes.

"I won't use it when you're around," he said looking concerned, which made Kieran feel guilty.

"I'll be fine," she said before getting up and hurrying to the bathroom. She splashed her face with cold water and composed herself before she re-joined Joshua. They made their way into the kitchen. "Would you like some desert?" she asked.

"Depends what it is," he grinned raising his eyebrows.

"Not here, wait till we get home." she leaned forward and kissed him.

"Okay, if I must. What's for desert anyway? I don't like Christmas pudding," he told her screwing up his face then picked up a newspaper that lay on the table and turned it to the sports page. Kieran saw his eyes rove over an article about Arsenal – his favourite team.

She smiled. They were alike in many ways. "Neither do I. Mum makes me strawberry cheesecake. I don't usually share. Since it's you, I guess I can manage that," she said making a face.

"You're greedy," he told her and returned the newspaper to the table.

Kieran poked out her tongue and walked over to the fridge. Joshua came up behind her and put his arms around her. He placed both hands on her belly. "Next Christmas we'll be a family," he whispered.

Kieran smiled. She decided to put the idea of the amniocentesis out in the open. "Have you heard of an amino?" she asked him, as she took the cheesecake out of its container. She hoped maybe he'd never heard of it and wouldn't know about the risks.

"That's the test they do for Down 's syndrome."

Oh crap.

She sat down at the table. Joshua did the same. "I was thinking of having one," she said looking at him.

His face darkened and he shook his head. "No Kieran," he said firmly.

"Why not?"

"It's risky."

"How do you know?" she asked unable to hide her annoyance at his knowledge.

"My mum had one when she got pregnant with Jaz, because of her age the doctor recommended it to make sure the baby was okay."

"Things turned out fine there," she reminded him as she cut the cheesecake.

"It was still a risk. My dad wanted to leave it to chance. If there was something wrong with the baby, they would deal with it."

"But wouldn't you rather be prepared, just in case?" she argued.

"Not at the expense of our baby Ki," he said leaning forward.

Kieran fed him a piece of cheesecake. "Okay, I won't have one," she lied.

"Good," he said and rubbed her stomach.

Kieran's heart skipped a beat. She was a bad person. How could she lie to him so easily? Karma was sure to catch up with her - again.

A week later, Kieran and Joshua made their way over to Courtney's house for a New Year's Eve party. Kieran was looking forward to seeing in the New Year with her friends and Joshua. The thought crossed her mind that Rome may be there and she was terrified of seeing him. She grimaced when the car pulled up outside Courtney's, as she remembered their last encounter.

Christina opened the door before they even knocked, she glanced at Kieran and nodded slightly, she knew that was her friend's way of telling her Rome was there. She took a deep breath to prepare herself. It was going to be a long night.

She walked into the living room and tried not to look for him. Kieran spoke to a few people she knew then followed Christina out into the garden where there was a gazebo with outdoor heaters. She spotted him standing under a heater wearing a leather jacket and gloves; his cheeks were red. Her eyes went to him like a moth to a flame. Kieran had never seen him look more gorgeous. He turned, as if sensing her presence and a smile spread across his face; his dimples prominent.

Shit, shit, shit!

Kieran's stomach lurched. He still had the same effect on her. She felt herself squeezing Joshua's hand. He looked at her questioningly. Kieran smiled at him. She looked back at Rome and their eyes never left each other as she walked over to where he and a group, including Chantelle, stood.

"Hey everyone," she said trying to sound cheerful.

God I want to hug him.

Instead, she hugged Chantelle who whispered to her "Just be cool,"

"Hey," Rome said smiling. She returned his smile and ignored the way her heart danced.

"You guys are late," Courtney told them. His eyes flickered from Kieran to Joshua to Rome and then back to Kieran.

"She takes ages to get ready," Joshua informed him.

Kieran rolled her eyes. She glanced at Rome, met his eyes, and looked away. A lump was forming in her throat and her stomach was going crazy. She felt as if she wanted to be sick or start crying. "I'm going to get a drink. Want anything?" she asked turning to face Joshua. It was safer if she looked at him.

"I'll come with you," he suggested.

"No, it's fine," Kieran said quickly. She needed to compose herself and she couldn't do it with him around.

"Okay, I'll have a beer please," he said and kissed her.

Kieran hoped Rome didn't think she was rubbing his face in it. That was the last thing she wanted him to think. She flashed a smile at Joshua before turning and going back inside.

Kieran went straight into the bathroom. She closed her eyes and leant against the door trying to calm her pounding, aching heart. She should have stayed at home, which was her original plan, because she was scared Rome would turn up. Christina reassured her he wouldn't do that to himself, and yet, there he was, torturing the both of them. When she felt better, she opened the bathroom door.

Rome stood outside; he too looked as if he was fighting with himself whether to be there or not. She saw which decision won as soon as their eyes met. "Hey," he said taking her hand and pulling her close.

Kieran was shocked by his action, but soon she was hugging him back. "I've missed you," she whispered into his chest, inhaling his scent.

"Me, too," he said kissing her forehead.

"How are you?" She looked up at him and saw sadness in his eyes. They were not sparkling like they used to.

"Surviving," he said with a shrug. His eyes went to her stomach. At fourteen weeks, she was barely showing, but there was no mistaking the look on his face. He knew. She was going to kill Courtney. "You look good, How you doing?"

Same old Rome, always saying the right things, she did not feel she looked good. In her opinion, she looked fat.

She rubbed her belly and met his eyes. "Surviving," she finally answered.

"Happy?" his jaw was taut, his eyes careful, like he was trying to hide the sadness there.

Kieran hesitated, and then nodded. She was as happy as she could be, though that happiness was nowhere near what she shared with him; He moved a step closer and stroked her face. His fingertips were cold. Kieran shivered.

"That's all I can ask for then." he said quietly.

Kieran was lost for words, and scared that if she spoke she would cry. Why did he keep doing this to her? How was she ever going to get over him when he kept showing up in her life? "How many months are you?" he asked interrupting her thoughts.

"Almost four," she mumbled. She didn't want to have this conversation with him. It was wrong.

"Is Joshua happy?"

"Yea."

"I hope he knows how lucky he is," he said looking into her eyes.

Kieran didn't know how to respond to his statement. Whatever she said would be rubbing salt into their wounds.

"Pregnancy suits you," he added with a smile. It didn't quite reach his eyes.

Kieran felt the lump in her throat rise again and swallowed. *Don't you dare cry.*

She wouldn't stop with the way her hormones were playing up, and how would she explain that to Joshua? "Do you still think we can't be friends?" she asked. She had to get back to Joshua soon.

He kissed her forehead. "I can't babe. I can't pretend to be happy that you're with someone else and having his baby. That doesn't make me a friend. We were never friends and we never could be; not because I don't want to be, but because I have feelings for you. I don't know how to have you in my life and be your friend," he explained.

Kieran admired his honesty. He was right. It would be madness for them to try. The temptation would always be there, she couldn't imagine a time where she wouldn't want him.

"It's good seeing you," she said stepping away from him. It was now or never.

"You too, I'm glad you're happy Kieran," he said with sincerity.

She didn't look at him – she couldn't. She would break Joshua's heart right then and there, so she stayed silent just enjoying the proximity between them.

He leaned forward and kissed her cheek, close enough to her lips to make her want to turn her head to kiss him. He moved his head away from hers so that their eyes met. Their faces were centimetres apart. Her eyes flickered to his lips; still perfect, still kissable.

"I think we should go back downstairs," she buried her head into his chest smelling him one last time.

"Yes, your boyfriend will be wondering where you are."

Kieran nodded as tears balanced on the edges of her eye lids, threatening to spill over at any moment. Her lip trembled and she saw a pained look flash across Rome's face. "Don't, Kieran please," he whispered taking her face in his hands.

"I'm sorry. I just miss you. It feels like it's been months since I saw you last, not a day goes by when I don't think about you and I want you to know that I haven't forgotten you. I will never forget you," she said stroking his face.

He kissed her hand. "I don't know if that makes me feel better or worse. I came tonight to see you. I almost changed my mind at the last minute, but I had to come, just to see that you were okay. I was hoping maybe you'd changed your mind," he said with a bitter laugh.

"I'm so sorry."

"Don't be. Maybe in time we can be friends. It's not your fault."

"It is. Don't try and make me feel better, we both know it's my fault."

"Don't be silly," he said, still cupping her face. He moved his head towards hers.

Kieran held her breath. She should stop him shouldn't she? But it was their last kiss for sure this time. She wanted him to kiss her. She didn't care if they got caught, if that was all they had left it would be worth it. His lips brushed against hers, gentle and tentative.

Kieran knew he was holding back, not wanting to kiss her the way he wanted out of respect for her and Joshua's relationship and the child she was carrying. She also felt every ounce of his emotion. Tears rolled down her cheeks as she closed her eyes. She was disappointed, but grateful that she got to be that close to him one last time. Their lips touched again before he sighed and dropped his hands.

Kieran stepped away from him. No more words were said between them that night. He turned towards the stairs, waved then disappeared. She returned to the bathroom and burst into tears. After composing herself for a second time, she fixed her make-up before heading downstairs.

She looked around searching for Rome. He was gone. It was better that way; she knew that; though his leaving didn't stop the hurt. He hadn't even said goodbye. Then it hit her. That's what the kiss had been, his personal goodbye.

Kieran joined Joshua and her friends and forced herself to get caught up in the party atmosphere. No-one knew her heart was breaking all over again.

Before she knew it, they were into a new year.
"Happy New Year!" Everyone joyously shouted at midnight through the noise of party poppers and sprays of champagne.

Kieran was whisked into a corner by Joshua. He was completely oblivious to the emotional rendezvous she'd had upstairs a while earlier. "Happy New Year Ki," he said.

"Happy New Year to you, too," she said kissing him.

"We will have a great year. We become a family this year," he said proudly as he hugged her.

Kieran smiled and nodded. She hoped for his sake that was true.

18 CHAPTER EIGHTEEN

Kieran stood outside Oxford Street Station waiting for Corey. Their intention was to browse through the January sales. She shivered and looked at her watch. A woman almost bumped into her.

"Sorry," she apologised.

Kieran nodded, and caught sight of a snow white Jack Russell terrier with a brown patch of fur over one eye. His tongue hung out of his mouth to one side and Kieran could swear he was smiling at her.

"Oh, he's so cute;" she said smiling at his owner.

"Isn't he? Thanks." The woman hurried out of the cold and into the station.

Kieran wondered why she said that. She wasn't a dog lover. The notion of walking them every day put her off. She dismissed the thought and looked at her watch again. Her sister arrived half an hour later. Kieran saw her jogging up the stairs.

"Sorry I'm late, Jack wouldn't let me go," Corey explained grinning as she hugged her.

"That's too much information. If I've missed out on any bargains it'll be your fault, and you're buying lunch." Kieran told her.

"I'm not buying you anything, so don't even go there," Corey said giving her a playful push.

An hour and several shopping bags later, they were still shopping. Kieran needed maternity outfits. Her waist line seemed to expand with each day. However, she still hadn't told her family she was in a family way.

"Corey?" Kieran said as she looked through a rack of dresses that she had no intention of buying.

"Yea," she replied, as she held up a dress against herself and looked in a mirror.

"Let's head over to Next when we leave here."

"Since when do you shop there?" Corey asked as she checked the price tag and made a face indicating she wasn't prepared for the price.

"I know, but that's the only shop that sells decent maternity wear," Kieran said not looking at her.

"If you want," Corey replied examining another dress. Clearly she wasn't paying attention. Kieran waited; Corey frowned as she processed what she heard and turned to look at Kieran.

"Why do you need maternity wear?"

"I'm…three months pregnant."

Corey let out a loud squeal that caused people to stare. Kieran hid her face in embarrassment. Corey then threw her arms around her and jumped up and down. Kieran wasn't expecting this reaction. She took her by the hand and led her out of the shop.

"Why didn't you tell me before?" Corey asked with excitement.

"I thought I'd wait in case anything went wrong," Kieran was relieved her sister was happy for her.

"Do Mum and Dad know?"

"No, come on, if Mum knew, you would've known," Kieran said rolling her eyes.

"True," Corey said with a fond smile, "When will you tell them?"

"I don't know. Soon, I guess."

"You don't seem very excited."

Kieran shrugged. "I am. It just happened so fast. I'm still trying to get my head around it"

"Yea, I can imagine, but you should tell them."

"Do you think they'll freak out?" Kieran asked as they passed a toy store. She tugged Corey and they entered the shop.

"They'll be cool. It's not like you're sixteen. Is Joshua happy?" Corey asked picking up a Dalmatian soft toy.

"Yea, the waiting is killing him."

"I'm going to be an aunty!" Corey squealed again.

Kieran smiled and touched her stomach. She anticipated everyone's excitement, but was ashamed to reveal that she wasn't sure who the father was – especially to Corey who always had her life together.

She'd never be in a situation like her little sister. Kieran didn't want to disappoint her and omitted that detail. She had to deal with the amino sooner rather than later. The more she thought about the test, the more scared she became. Kieran couldn't bear the thought of hearing what she didn't want to hear, so she buried her head in the sand, for the moment at least.

Kieran opened her eyes when she felt Joshua kiss her forehead. He had officially moved in with her and things were going well. "Morning," he said.

"Why are you up so early on a Saturday?" Kieran asked before yawning and stretching. Her hand went instinctively to her stomach. She was four months pregnant and was having a relatively easy pregnancy. She felt flutters as the baby began to move. She couldn't wait for it to start kicking.

"I'm going shopping."

Kieran sat up, "What kind of shopping?"

"What kind of shopping do you want it to be?"

"Clothes."

Joshua shook his head and smiled. "I'm going to Camden," he told her.

Kieran got out of bed, "I'll be ready in twenty minutes." Shopping she loved. Shopping in Camden was even better, and there was an Aldo shoe store which made Kieran even happier.

"If you do it in fifteen, I'll treat you to something pretty," he told her.

Kieran grinned and entered the bathroom. She had the quickest shower and was dressed, make-up and all in fifteen minutes flat. "Don't ever tell me you need hours to get ready again," Joshua told her as they got into her car.

"I do when it's special. This is casual," she explained with a yawn. As of recent, she grew tired easily. She rubbed her stomach.

"And don't ever tell me you don't like getting up early,

because I've seen you do it now."

"That's because it's shopping, so don't get excited. You know my main purpose in life is to shop."

Joshua laughed.

By the time Kieran returned home, she was in a bad mood after bumping into an ex-girlfriend of his who Kieran knew of well. He hadn't even noticed she was pissed off as she stood and watched while they talked and laughed like old friends.

Kieran excused herself, telling him she would meet him in half an hour and left them to reminisce. She deliberately didn't show up and when he called after an hour, Kieran was ready to blow a fuse. Her only consolation was the clothes and shoes she purchased for herself and clothes for the baby. Her face softened as she looked at the cute baby wear. Kieran would prefer a girl first, though the health of the baby was more important. She caressed the cute little pink dress with pink and white flowers. She was having her first scan in a few days, and debated whether to find out the sex. Still, if it wasn't a girl, she would keep the dress until she did have one.

"Do you want to go out for dinner tonight?" Joshua asked breaking her maternal thoughts.

"What for?" she asked, her jealous mood returning.

"What's your problem?" he questioned.

"Like you care," she snapped.

"What did I do?" he asked with a confused look.

"What didn't you do?"

"It's Vanessa, isn't it?"

"Yea, pretty much. You didn't even have the decency to introduce me as your girlfriend. You didn't meet me on time. What the hell were you doing for an hour?" Kieran hadn't realised she was shouting until she finished her sentence. Why was she overreacting?

"We were just talking. We haven't spoken in ages and as for me and you, it has nothing to do with her," Joshua said.

"It has everything to do with her. I want her to know that you and I are an item again, so this time she doesn't get any ideas," Kieran said. Though she didn't shout, there was anger in her voice and she felt emotional, like she had been feeling over the past week for no particular reason.

"What ideas?"

"Are you stupid? Have you forgotten that she's the reason we broke up in the first place? You cheated on me with her and then you spent an hour with her today. Do you really expect me not to be pissed off? What is wrong with you?" Kieran glared at him.

"You have to trust me. I was younger then. I know what I want now and it's not her. I want to be with you and only you. Don't you know that yet?" he asked in a soft voice and hugged her.

Kieran took a deep breath. "I'm sorry. I don't know what's wrong with me. It still freaks me out, I guess."

"There's no need to be freaked out," he reassured her. Kieran wrapped her arms around him. She wanted to trust him more than anything. "Okay." she said. Kieran put the episode behind her and spent the next few hours relaxing before preparing to go out to dinner.

"I have a surprise for you," Joshua announced over dessert.

Kieran placed the glass of virgin Pina Colada on the table. "Really? What is it?"

He handed her an envelope. Kieran gave him a curious look as she opened it. "Oh my God," her mouth fell open.

Joshua laughed. "Do you approve?"

"Are we really going on a cruise around the Caribbean?" she asked looking at the two tickets.

"Yep."

"Well, hell yea!"

"I'm glad you're excited," he said smiling.

"Can we afford this?" Kieran frowned, they were having a baby and a cruise around the Caribbean wasn't cheap.

"Yes, I want to do this for you before the baby comes," he said kissing her hand.

"You sure?"

"Ki, its fine."

"Well then of course, I approve. Joshua Simmons, I love you."

"I love you too, that's why I was gone for an hour today. You made it easy when you stormed off. Anyway, I wanted it to be a surprise, plus it'll be the last holiday we have for a while," he explained. It was the best news Kieran had heard in ages and she shrieked with excitement. "Okay, people are staring," Joshua told her looking around the restaurant.

Kieran didn't care, "I'm so excited!" She looked at the tickets again. "Hang on, today is Friday, we leave Tuesday, the scan is Monday and what about my work?"

Joshua grinned at her. "I know that. I already spoke to Janet. She agreed to let you go for the ten days, no problem." he looked so proud of himself.

Kieran wasn't worried about getting time off. Didn't he know her at all? She needed to go shopping. She rolled her eyes. "I don't have anything to wear."

"Any excuse to shop huh?" Joshua teased shaking his head. "You have two wardrobes full of clothes and then some."

"I need pregnancy holiday clothes," she told him.

"What the hell are they?"

"Pregnancy holiday clothes," Kieran rolled her eyes again.

"Do you want company?" he asked humouring her.

"Are we going to run into any more of your ex's?" she questioned

"No."

"Well then, sure," Kieran smiled then squealed again.

Joshua hid his face behind a menu.

Before Kieran knew it, she was packing to leave. Chantelle and Christina shared their excitement and jealousy with her.

"You are so lucky," Christina said for the fifth time in an hour while Kieran packed.

"We've gathered that," Chantelle replied.

Kieran laughed and closed the suitcase. She couldn't get the zipper round. "I think I may have packed a bit too much."

"You think?" Joshua said.

"Take some stuff out." Christina suggested. Kieran looked at her like she was crazy. "I take it back," Christina said laughing at Kieran's expression.

Joshua raised his eyebrows. "Who do you think is carrying that?" Kieran smiled sweetly at him. "I'm not breaking my back so you have a full wardrobe," he informed her and returned his attention to the computer.

Kieran heard his serious tone. He'd been on the computer most of the afternoon. She wondered what he was up to. He hardly ever used it. She tutted and unzipped the case. What should she take out? Did she really need a bikini for every day? Yes, yes, she did.

"I'm going to the shop. Do you guys want anything?" Joshua asked standing up and stretching. They declined, and as soon as he was gone. Kieran unzipped his suitcase.

"What are you doing?" Chantelle asked.

"Nothing."

"You sneaky bitch," Chantelle laughed.

"I'm not leaving any of my stuff behind; he can take it for me," Kieran said with a mischievous grin.

"He'll find out," Christina told her.

"And it will be too late," Kieran told them as she added some clothes and two pairs of shoes in the bottom of his suitcase. She zipped the case. "Done," she said, sat down and rubbed her swollen stomach.

"What time's your flight?" Chantelle asked.

"Nine in the morning."

"Looking forward to the flight?" Christina asked.

"When have I ever liked flying, especially in turbulence? Ask Chantelle how I was when we went Jamaica?" she grimaced.

"I thought I was going to have to knock her out to keep her from getting hysterical," Chantelle told Christina.

Kieran chuckled and went into the kitchen. She had her head in the fridge when Joshua returned.

"What are you doing?" he asked and kissed her on the nose when she turned to face him. Kieran couldn't answer. She was busy chewing the chocolate she had crammed into her mouth. "I can't wait to have you all to myself."

She swallowed. "Me too. Thank you again."

"You are very welcome. You deserve a break," he said.

Kieran leant against the counter. "J, how about we get a puppy?"

"That's out-of-the-blue. Why?"

"I just thought it would be nice." she shrugged.

"I don't like dogs' babe, neither do you."

"I like the little ones."

"Is this some kind of maternal instinct thing kicking in?" he raised his eyebrows.

"I don't know," Kieran thought maybe he had a point. "Can we get a little one please?"

Joshua thought for a second, "Sorry."

"It's okay." Kieran sighed. It was probably a good thing. It would be manic enough when the baby arrived.

Not long after, Kieran said goodbye to her friends who couldn't leave without a last minute jibe.

"Don't get up to too much mischief," Chantelle told her.

"Would I ever?" Kieran asked with a look of innocence.

"Yes!"

"Shut up, I'll call you after my scan tomorrow."

"Good luck," they chorused.

Joshua was out cold on the sofa when she entered the living room, his mouth hanging open. She smiled and woke him up.

"How long have I been sleeping?" he asked rubbing his eyes.

"Not long," she explained as she straightened up the magazines on the coffee table and picked up the used glasses.

"I'm knackered and we have to get up early," he groaned.

"I'm too excited to sleep."

"You're such a big kid," he teased.

Kieran grinned and disappeared into the kitchen, disposing of the dirty glasses in the sink. She switched the light off and walked back into the front room.

"I was thinking, when we get back I'm going have an amnio. I know you don't want me to; except I will feel better knowing everything is fine," she blurted out. That was not how she planned on telling him.

"What's with all this out-of-the-blue stuff? Haven't we already been through this?" he asked with a hint of impatience.

"I need to do it," she said walking into the bedroom.

He followed her and sat on the bed, "Well, I don't think you should risk it."

"Don't you want to know if the baby is okay?"

"Of course, I do, but I don't want you to risk losing this baby. Whatever happens we will deal with it," he told her.

Right. Sure. Even if it's not your baby?

"I'd feel better knowing," she argued as she threw a pile of the clothes she'd decided not to take on the clothes hamper. She'd deal with them in the morning.

"Let's not make any decisions now. We'll talk more when we get back, okay?"

Kieran nodded. Regardless of what he said, she had already made her decision.

The following day, she and Joshua sat in the hospital waiting room. Kieran tried not to stare at some of the heavily pregnant women who looked close to giving birth. Were they scared?

You better come out quickly little one, no pain, no problems and no pushing. Please God, no pushing!

She was dreading the pushing part and terrified of the pain. The nurse called her name. She took Joshua's hand and walked into a small room that housed a bed and a few machines beside it. The doctor had a pleasant smile. She made Kieran comfortable then explained what she would do. She squirted gel onto her stomach. Its coldness made her jump and she squealed. Kieran's heart pounded as the screen flickered and her womb appeared showing a small round shape.

"That's your baby," the doctor said pointing to an area on the screen.

"Really?"

Why does my baby look like a potato?

"Yes, it has its back to us."

Kieran nodded at the screen. The baby moved and Kieran saw an arm, a leg and a head. The baby lay on its back with a knee up and an arm bent. She gasped and tears sprang to her eyes. She looked closer to see if she could see any indication of its gender. Nothing obvious caught her attention.

"Wow." Joshua breathed after a while.

"Your baby is a healthy size from the looks of it," the doctor said.

"It should be the way I've been eating," Kieran joked.

The doctor smiled as she turned a knob on the machine. Kieran heard the muffled heartbeat as it filled the room. She gasped again and this time she started crying. Joshua kissed her forehead. His eyes glistened with tears.

"I'm so proud of you," he whispered into her hair.

"Would you like to know the sex of the baby?" The doctor asked.

Kieran looked at Joshua. He shook his head. Kieran tried not to look disappointed. "No, thank you. We'll leave it as a surprise," she told the doctor.

"Has anyone spoken to you about an amniocentesis?" she asked.

Kieran's eyes widened. "Is something wrong?" she grabbed Joshua's hand.

"No, no. Sorry, I was just asking," the doctor said reassuringly.

Kieran and Joshua exhaled hard.

"We won't be having one," Joshua said.

Kieran looked at him and looked at the doctor.

"Are you sure?" she asked Kieran.

Kieran hesitated. "Yes," though her stomach flipped confirming her lie. She couldn't worry about it then, instead she focused on the image of her baby on the screen and smiled. Finally it felt real, she was going to be a mother.

19 CHAPTER NINETEEN

Joshua kissed Kieran's hand as she sat with her eyes closed, preparing herself for take-off. It was the worst part of flying for her.

"You'll be fine," he told her.

She didn't dare open her eyes to look at him. Suddenly the plane surged forward down the runway and graduated into a lift. She squeezed her eyes shut and covered her mouth as she tried to control her breathing. When the plane levelled, she relaxed, slightly, she just hoped there was no turbulence.

Ten hours later, they landed in Miami. Kieran was the first person off the plane. She was grateful for her feet to touch concrete.

Joshua couldn't stop laughing at her. "You are so dramatic," he told her.

Kieran didn't respond. It had been alright for him, he had entertained himself with the free alcoholic drinks and had passed out for most of the flight. As she was pregnant she never had that luxury, so when they had flown through a storm somewhere over the Atlantic ocean, Kieran had suffered in silence for twenty minutes, Joshua snoring peacefully next to her completely oblivious. He woke up afterwards declaring what a smooth flight it had been. Kieran had never wanted to punch someone more.

After another two hours, they reached the white ship. Kieran was amazed by the size of vessel. It was huge and reminded her of the Titanic. She gulped, as images from the movie flashed through her head. She probably should have thought about it before she had flown ten hours to get there. Kieran hesitated as she thought that the majority of the week she would be surrounded by water. She gulped again. During her research, Kieran found that the ship had six levels, boasted two swimming pools, a gym, four different restaurants, a grand dining hall and shops. She looked at the round cabin windows on the side of the ship. They grew bigger the higher up the ship. She knew those were the expensive rooms. She wondered where they would be situated, as she followed Joshua and the porter to the cabin.

"It's not bad," she whispered looking around the average size room, much like a standard hotel room. The décor was neutral and simple, with a standard sized double bed in the centre of the room. Kieran figured they were in the middle section of the ship which made her feel better. She did not like the thought of being below sea level where the cheaper rooms were. All the poor people had died on the Titanic.

"We hope you enjoy your stay," the porter told them as he put down their luggage. Joshua tipped him and said, "Thanks."
Kieran threw her arms around him. "I love it here and it's ours for ten whole days."

"Ki-ki, calm down," he told her laughing, "I'm glad you like it," he said kissing her on the lips.

"You, Mr. Simmons, have made me very happy."

"And you, Miss Taylor, deserve it."

"We have at least an hour before dinner. Have you ever done it on a boat before?" she asked grinning as she put her hands under his t-shirt.

"Are you hinting?" Joshua wrapped his arms around her.

"What do you think?" she said lifting the t-shirt over his head.

Kieran woke up to hear Joshua showering. She stretched and rubbed her belly. They were halfway through the holiday and it was Valentine's Day. Kieran looked forward to sharing the day with Joshua, which they would spend in Barbados. They had already visited Jamaica and the and were due to visit Antigua and St. Lucia over the next five days, before they docked back in Miami. Kieran was enjoying spending time alone with Joshua.

They loved the weather, the food, the shops and the ship itself, and when on board, they spent most of their time lounging by the pool. When the ship berthed, they explored the islands and resorts. She got up and headed to the small airless bathroom that had a basic shower and a toilet.

"Morning J," she called.

"Morning. Happy Valentine's Day." he said poking his head out of the shower.

"Happy Valentine's Day," she grinned "How long have you been up?" she asked looking in the mirror. She frowned at her reflection; her skin was suffering because of her hormones. The good news was, her tan hid the blemishes.

"Around eight," Joshua said and turned off the shower.

"Have you had breakfast yet?" she asked holding out a towel.

"No, I was waiting for you."

"I'll be ready in twenty minutes once you move out of the way."

"You could always join me," he said raising his eyebrows and turning the shower back on.

"Did anyone ever tell you that you are a pervert?"

"No, actually," he said with an innocent look.

"First time for everything."

"Kieran, get in the shower," he said pulling back the shower curtain. She grinned, took off her night-shirt and joined him.

Twenty minutes later Kieran stood tying a blue sarong around her waist, she accompanied it with a matching bikini top. Joshua appeared at the doorway. He stopped and stared at her.

"What?" she asked.

"You look beautiful," he said, walked over and took her in his arms.

"Thank you," Kieran said unconvinced. She felt how she looked – fat. Joshua told her she was merely keeping the baby warm. He knew how to say the right things, that was for sure.

They spent most of the day on the beach. The Caribbean had the most beautiful beaches she had ever seen, white golden sand, turquoise sea and breath-taking sunsets. Kieran loved being by the water and would have happily stayed there all day. Sadly, they had to return to the vessel. The ships staff was preparing a special Valentine's dinner and dance for their guests.

Kieran wore a long, black, halter neck maxi dress. She took a pair of wedges out of Joshua's suitcase and was about to give herself a pat on the back for not getting caught when Joshua cleared his throat making her jump guiltily.

"You are so sneaky." he was shaking his head in disbelief from the doorway. She smiled as she walked over to him and kissed him. "Don't try to get out of it," he warned, "I know what you're trying to do," he told her through the kisses, though he didn't stop her.

"I have no idea what you're talking about," she said.

"Yes, you do."

"Do you forgive me?" she asked trying to look innocent.

"If I must," he said rolling his eyes.

"Good," Kieran said, "If you really forgive me I might make it worth your while," she winked at him.

He chuckled and kissed her once on the lips. "Oh yea, how?"

"I'll show you when we get back from dinner," she teased putting her arms around his neck.

"How about we skip dinner?" He kissed her again.

Kieran's head whirled from the thought, but her stomach rumbled reminding her that she was still eating for two. Their sexual cravings could be dealt with another time.

"How about we go and have dinner and then we can have desert back here?" she suggested.

"You are nothin' but a tease," he said letting go of her and picking up the room key.

Kieran gasped and pretended to be offended.

Joshua laughed. "Let's go, I'm hungry."

Kieran looked around the grand dining room that was transformed. The main lighting was dimmed creating a romantic ambience. A huge glitter ball rotated in the centre of the ceiling. Red balloons adorned the room from ceiling to floor; the normal white table cloths were replaced with red and white tablecloths and heart shaped confetti was sprinkled over them; red heart shaped candles sat in the centre of each table. The waiters wore red waistcoats and black trousers and the waitresses black pinafores with red roses in their hair. It was a pretty sight, and Kieran, being Kieran squealed with delight after she took it all in.

An hour later, she was trying to stifle her laughter. Joshua complained about the ship's poor taste in music, and he wasn't being quiet about it. He mimicked the songs - badly, which made Kieran laugh harder. His silliness made her feel like a teenager again. He was always able to make her laugh.

"I'm ready for desert," Kieran said looking around for a waiter. Joshua raised a mischievous eyebrow and grinned. Kieran rolled her eyes, "I meant real desert," she said smiling.

"Before we get to that, there's something I want to ask you," he said his face turning serious.

"What are you up to?"

He appeared nervous playing with the salt shaker. Kieran was sure his hands were trembling. Her stomach twisted. Something told her it wasn't going to be good.

"Can you be quiet and listen until I'm finished."

"Okay," Kieran agreed.

"Okay," he said fidgeting in his seat. "Since we've been back together things have been going great. I've realised that I really do love you and that I never should have let you go. It was the most stupid thing I've ever done. Now you're pregnant and I don't want to lose you or the baby. You are the most important people in my life now, so I'm asking you to be my wife," he said while taking a small box out of his pocket and flipped it open.

Oh. My. God.

Kieran saw his hands were trembling. She looked at him as he grinned back at her expectantly. She didn't know what was happening, What should she do? Why hadn't he discussed it with her first? What should she say?

"Oh J," she managed looking at the ring. It was a beautiful high set, princess cut diamond on a white gold band. Simple, but beautiful. "It's so beautiful, but I.....I can't," she stammered.

"What?" he asked his smile fading, "Why not?"

He snapped the box closed and shoved it into his pocket before anyone else could see.

"I am just not ready for that yet."

"We are having a baby. How can you not be ready?" he glared at her.

Kieran saw that he was furious and embarrassed. Someone must have seen his gesture. Kieran allowed her eyes a quick glance around to see if anyone had indeed seen, and sure enough, a group of people at the table next to them had stopped talking and stared in their direction. Her face flushed with embarrassment.

Great. Witnesses to me breaking his heart. Why did he have to propose in front of people?

He was staring at her waiting for an explanation. Unless she told him the truth, no explanation was going to be good enough. She was nowhere near ready to open that can of worms. She started with the part that was most true.

"It's just not right for me now. I'm not ready to get married. Please don't be mad J," she said touching his arm.

He jerked it away. "Hey it's cool. Just forget it," he said with a shrug.

His nonchalance was not lost on her. He was hurt.

"I'm sorry," Kieran said looking down at her hands.

"Look, I don't feel so good. I'm going to lie down. You have your desert and I'll see you back in the room," he said before getting up and walking off.

Kieran stared after him. She could've said yes; it wasn't fair to him though. She couldn't make a promise to him when he didn't know the truth. She lost her desire for dessert and joined him in the cabin. He ignored her and his attitude changed towards her thereafter. He didn't speak to her much for the remaining days. He hadn't even wanted to be around her, which ruined the rest of their holiday.

They were far from the happy couple when they returned home. Unable to take any more tension, Kieran showered, changed and told Joshua, "I'm going to see Chan and Chris, I'll be back soon."

"Yea, whatever," he replied.

He was lying down on the sofa staring at the TV screen. Kieran walked over and bent down to kiss him. He moved his head away, his action hurt Kieran as intended. She straightened and made her way out of the door without another word.

By the time Kieran got to Chantelle's house she was in tears.

"Honey what's wrong?" Chantelle asked.

"Joshua asked me to marry him and I said no. Now he hates me," she sobbed.

"Why did you say no?" Chantelle asked confused as she took her friends hand and led her inside the house.

"I didn't want to commit before I find out if the baby is his. It would kill him if it isn't."

"What's going on?" Christina asked wide eyed when they entered.

Kieran looked at her and burst into tears again.

20 CHAPTER TWENTY

By the time Kieran entered her fifth month of pregnancy, things hadn't improved between her and Joshua and she didn't know how to fix it. She couldn't give him what he wanted and while she understood his point, the bottom line was, she was not ready to get married and he would have to come to terms with that. It was, however, hard sharing a house with someone when you were not on speaking terms. It made everything that much harder to organise.

They were scheduled to go over to Christina's for drinks to celebrate her birthday. Kieran was looking forward to socialising with her friends; she just wished Joshua would speak to her. She hated pretending everything was fine between them in public and he was better at acting, which pissed her off.

They drove in silence. Kieran had given up trying to make conversation with him; he only ignored her. Before she could park the car outside Christina's house, Joshua got out and walked towards his brother who had arrived at the same time. Kieran stared after him open mouthed. Instead of calling him out on it, she switched off the engine, rested her head against the steering wheel and started to cry. She didn't know how much more she could take. She jumped and wiped her eyes when she heard a knock on the window. She powered the window down.

"Hey, what's wrong?" Jarrell asked concerned.

"Nothing," she sniffed.

"So, why are you crying?"

"I'm okay. I swear," she lied, "Just my hormones playing up." She pulled down the mirror from the visor.

"I don't believe you. Have you and J had an argument? He's been a bit moody recently."

Kieran started crying again.

Jarrell leaned through the window and gave her a hug. "He'll come round, he's stubborn you know, always has been, always will be," he soothed.

"I hope so. He hasn't spoken to me in weeks. I miss him."

"Do you want me to go get him?"

"No, I'll be fine, I'll be in soon," she said drying her eyes.

"Sure?"

"Yea, thanks Jarrell," she gave him a smile.

"Anytime." He said.

Kieran took out her make-up and re-applied some lip gloss and mascara before getting out the car. As she locked the door, Joshua appeared.

"Are you okay?"

Kieran tried to keep her mouth from dropping to the floor. It was the most he'd said to her in weeks. "I'm fine."

"Jarrell said you were crying," he reached out and took her hand.

"Don't worry, I didn't tell him why," she snapped pulling her hand away.

"Maybe you should've. He'd talk some sense into me."

Kieran softened a little too quickly for her liking, "I know you're upset about me saying no, can't you understand that I'm not ready?" she asked him, her voice breaking.

"Yes, but I thought you loved me enough to trust me," he reached out to take her hand again. Kieran let him.

"I do trust you, that has nothing to do with it," she explained leaning against the car.

"So what is it?

"I'm not saying I never want to marry you. I love you and I want to be with you. All I'm asking is for you to wait a few months until I'm ready."

"I don't want to wait a few months; I want people to know we are serious about each other."

Kieran looked at him, "We don't need to rush into marriage

for that. Who cares what people think? We know how we feel. Unless you don't trust me and you think that by getting engaged it will be harder for me to leave if things go wrong?" He dropped his gaze. "Oh my God, That's what you think isn't it?"

"You can't blame me can you, given how we got back together?" he said in a bitter voice and stepped away from her.

Kieran raised her eyebrows; she hadn't seen that one coming. He was scared she was going to do the same thing to him that she had done to Darren. The same thing he had done to her.

"So you don't really want to marry me, you only asked because you don't want anyone else to have me?" she shouted completely losing control of her demeanour.

"It's not like that," he protested holding up his hands to pacify her.

"Don't even try to deny it. So much for you not being able to live without me, you couldn't live with the fact that I might do what you did to me four years ago!"

"Kieran stop shouting," he told her looking around.

Kieran stepped towards him, her hands clenched at her side. "No, I will not. For three weeks you have ignored and treated me like shit you scraped off the bottom of your shoe, all because I don't want to rush into marriage! Excuse me for trying to be smart. You said you'd matured, but right now you're being the same immature little boy you were when we first got together. I have news for you, I'm not the same naive little girl I once was, and you are not putting me through the same shit. I'm not letting you do it a second time!" she pointed at him like a mother would to her naughty child.

She could see he was too stunned by the volume of her words to argue, so she continued, "If you don't want me, and I mean really want me, tell me now and we can go back a few months and pretend none of this happened."

"Kieran, don't be stupid. You know I want to be with you and our baby," he said pulling her towards him.

She winced at the mention of the baby. Reality hit her. "So why doesn't it feel that way?" she asked into his chest. She was an awful person. How could she lecture him after what she had done? After what she was still doing; Lying.

"Because I'm an immature little boy apparently," he chuckled.

"This isn't a joke J, you hurt me," she said looking at him.

"I'm hurt too. I do want to marry you even if part of the reason is wrong," he said and kissed her forehead.

"It's not a good reason to marry someone. I chose you and you have to trust me enough to know that I'm not going anywhere. I don't want you to ask me again, because until I'm sure that you want to marry me for the right reasons, I'm going to keep saying, no." She moved away from him. She wasn't going to forgive him that easily.

"Kieran, that's harsh," he said sounding wounded.

"Even harsher than finding out that your proposal wasn't one hundred per cent genuine? How do you think that makes me feel?"

"I've said I'm sorry. I don't know what else to do."

"Why didn't you talk to me first? How do you expect us to have a proper relationship if you can't be honest with me?" she asked looking into his eyes. Kieran couldn't believe the conversation they were having, it was basic relationship etiquette, and she shouldn't have to explain it to him.

Kettle, pot and black! Her conscience shouted at her.

"I'm being honest now," he told her.

"Well, now's a little too late, because you've already let me down," she said, disappointment in her tone.

"What are you saying?" he asked with a worried look.

"That you've made a mistake and even though it hurts, everyone's allowed to make mistakes. If you continue to lie to me and let me down, we will not have a future, so it's up to you to decide how much you want me." Kieran knew she was being self-righteous, since she hadn't been totally honest with him; but she honestly couldn't believe he had proposed to her for the reason he had given her.

"I want you more than you know."

"Really?"

Joshua pulled her towards him and hugged her tightly "I'm sorry Kieran," he whispered.

"Let's go and have some fun," she told him changing the subject. In all honesty she couldn't blame him for his theory. He knew her better than she thought.

"Okay," Joshua agreed following her up the stairs to the house. He pulled her back by the arm before she went inside.

"What now?" She was irritated, more with herself than with him.

"I love you."

"I love you too." But she wasn't sure if that was enough.

The following day, Kieran went to see her obstetrician. "You know there is a slight risk of getting an infection or miscarriage with this test don't you?" the doctor asked her.

Kieran bit her lip. "Yes, I know, one in two hundred women though, isn't it?"

"Yes. It's a very small risk and you will have to sign a consent form to show you are aware of the risks," the doctor told her. Kieran nodded. "I'll book you in for Friday because you're in your twentieth week. If you want to cancel, don't hesitate to phone the hospital."

Kieran nodded again. No way was she cancelling.

When she got home Joshua met her at the door with a wide grin. "What are you grinning at?"

"It's a surprise. Close your eyes."

Kieran looked at him with apprehension, but did as she was told; she hoped he wasn't proposing again, she'd have to say yes this time and didn't think she could do it. Joshua took her hand and led her into the living room and sat her down on a chair. He placed something in her lap. It wasn't heavy or bulky. "Okay, open."

Kieran looked down and back at Joshua.

What the hell? Is he serious?

"It's a picture of a dog." she stammered

"I know, don't you like it?" he asked clearly pleased with himself.

"What am I meant to do with it?" she asked trying not to show her annoyance.

"Keep it, of course," he said leaning over and kissing her cheek.

"It's a picture," Kieran reminded him. She had the urge to tell him where he could put his picture. She bit her lip.

"It's a cute dog though. I thought it would be nice for you because I said we couldn't get a real one," he explained, holding the picture up for her to see.

"Thanks," Kieran said trying to sound appreciative. She got up, walked in to the kitchen and switched on the kettle.

"Hey, are you making tea?" Joshua called.

"Yes, why?" her voice sounded shrill.

"Could you make me a cup please?"

"How about I just take a picture of it for you," she mumbled.

"Pardon?" his voice called from the living room.

"I said okay, I'll get it for you," she lied before kissing her teeth. Irritated, she didn't want to be around him when he thought that a stupid picture of a dog was a great present for her. She decided to go to Chantelle's instead. She left the kettle to boil, picked up her shopping bags and headed towards the bedroom. She opened the door and stopped in her tracks.

Lying on the bed was the cutest Jack Russell Terrier puppy with a pink bow around its neck.

"J, you got me a puppy!" she squealed before throwing her bags down on the floor. She ran over to the puppy and picked it up. Joshua appeared at the door grinning.

"So you like her then?"

"Much better than a picture. When did you get her?" The dog wagged its tail and sniffed her face; Kieran kept it at arm's length, which was hard as it would not keep still.

"This morning. Jarrell helped me choose her," Joshua explained taking the struggling dog out of Kieran's arms. She couldn't believe he had done that for her. A part of her knew he was also sucking up for the proposal farce. Lucky for him it was working.

"She's gorgeous. Thank you, baby," Kieran said kissing him on the lips.

"So are you making the tea?" he questioned as he put the dog down. She scampered off into the front room to investigate her surroundings.

"In a sec," she said following the dog.

"And I'd like a real cup please, not a picture," he added.

Kieran glanced over her shoulder at him. "You heard?"

"Loud and clear. I knew you were pissed off, you held it in well. I'm impressed," he teased rubbing her shoulders. They stood watching the puppy sniffing everything in sight, the pink ribbon trailing behind her.

"I'm not pissed any more. This is the best present ever," she turned to face him and wrapped her arms around his waist.

"It's an 'I'm sorry and I love you present,'" he said kissing her.

Kieran knew this. "You are forgiven. Let's forget the tea, let's go out for dinner. I'm feeling like Chiquito's," Kieran said naming her favourite Mexican restaurant.

"Whose house do you want to drive by first?" Joshua asked rolling his eyes.

"You know me too well," she giggled, "we'll go to Chan's, Christina is there."

"Show off," he teased as he patted his pockets looking for his car keys.

"Jarrell will have to look after her while we are eating," she said ignoring his taunts. She hurried over to the corner of the front room where the dog was sniffing one of her plants. She was sure it was getting ready to lift its leg and pee. She scooped her up.

"I'll call him and let him know," Joshua said as he switched off the TV.

"What is that?" Christina asked alarmed when Kieran, Joshua and the dog entered.

"This is my dog. I haven't named her yet. Joshua got her for me," Kieran said looking proud.

"She is the cutest little puppy," Chantelle said taking her out of Kieran's arms.

"Just keep her away from me," Christina warned. Like Joshua, she wasn't a fan of dogs.

Kieran and Chantelle cooed at the dog that was lapping up the attention.

"Anybody would think it was a baby you lot were passing round," Christina said flicking through a magazine.

"We will be in about four months," Joshua said rubbing Kieran's belly.

"Good, then we can forget about this stupid dog," Christina said in a more cheerful tone.

"Don't call my dog stupid," Kieran said laughing.

Christina made a face and carried on flicking through the magazine.

"So what are you going to call her?" Chantelle asked.

"I'm thinking Lily," Kieran said grinning.

"Gay." Christina said rolling her eyes, Kieran rolled hers in response. Christina thought anything girly was gay.

"Come on, we'd better go. Jarrell has to go out later," Joshua interrupted before she could reply to Christina. He picked Lily up.

"Where are you going?" Chantelle asked tickling behind the dog's ear.

"Chiquito's. I felt like Mexican food."

"You don't even eat Mexican when we go there. You always have a burger or something," Christina told her.

"Nobody asked for you to comment," Kieran joked as she and Joshua headed towards the door, "see you later," she waved.

"If you two aren't doing anything after you've eaten come back, we'll be drinking and watching DVD's," Chantelle told them.

"Without the dog!" Christina said loudly.

Kieran laughed "I'll text you and let you know," she said following Joshua outside.

Later, when Joshua had taken Lily for a walk, Kieran called Chantelle while she washed some dishes. "I have a hospital appointment on Friday morning."

"For the test?"

"Yes, Joshua doesn't know though," she spoke in a quiet voice. She was paranoid that he would return and she wouldn't hear while the tap was running.

"Are you sure you want to go through with this?" Chantelle asked.

Kieran heard the concern in her friend's voice. "Yea I have to do it," she replied as she switched the phone over to her other ear and cradled it in between her neck and shoulder.

"Don't do this because of Joshua."

"It'll be better for all of us. I can't settle with him properly until I know."

"What time on Friday?"

"Eleven."

"Christina is working; I will be there."

"You don't have to Chan," Kieran said touched by her friends support. She rinsed the dishes, put them in the drainer and wiped her face with her sleeve as the tears started. She couldn't believe what was happening.

"Did the doctor explain the procedure?" Chantelle asked.
Kieran turned off the tap and dried her hands. She felt her back crack, as she straightened her neck and held the phone in her hand.

"It's done between the fourteenth and the twenty-fourth week of pregnancy. They stick a needle into my belly and take a sample of the foetal cells from the amniotic fluid," she explained sitting down on the sofa.

"That's the water around the baby right?" Chantelle questioned.

"Yes. After they've taken samples, they will compare it with Joshua's DNA, they told me I'd need to get his consent." Kieran said sighing.

"Shit, so you have to tell him?" Chantelle asked.

Kieran was silent for a moment, "No I'm not telling him,"

"How are you going to get his consent?"

"I will forge his signature or something," Kieran said dismissively.

Chantelle gasped. "I'm quite sure that's illegal."

"Probably, but I can't tell him now, I'd rather just get it done and see what happens, what other choice do I have?"

"I guess, you won't need to tell him unless it's Darren's." Chantelle said.

"Exactly, let's just hope it doesn't come to that."

"Don't you think it will be worse if you wait until then?"

"I really don't know. Anyway, let's change the subject before he gets back." Kieran said. They chatted for a while and Kieran spent the rest of the evening bonding with Lily.

The following day Kieran visited Amelia. Since they had motherhood in common, Kieran welcomed any tips on the subject. Amelia answered the door and handed Kieran her eleventh month old baby. Kieran took her and followed Amelia into the house as the baby started to scream for her mother.

"These kids are driving me crazy," Amelia said rolling her eyes as she threw toys into a plastic container. Alicia, Amelia's four-year-old was asleep in the middle of the floor on a blanket with toys around her. Kieran chuckled and sat down on the sofa trying to calm down the crying baby.

"Does she want a bottle or something?"

"Probably, she doesn't stop eating," Amelia joked.

Kieran laughed, "Do you want me to sort her out?"

"Yea, you may as well get some practice," Amelia said as she picked up Alicia and took her up the stairs.

Kieran carried Frankie into the kitchen on her hip. She felt the temperature of the kettle, poured the water into a bottle and added formula. Frankie started to cry again.

Kieran tried to soothe her. She wondered what it would be like when she had her own screaming baby.

Hey little one, you better have more patience than this, or we won't get on.

She smiled to herself as she continued making the bottle. By the time Amelia returned Frankie was half asleep, her bottle still in her mouth.

"Wow, you're a natural," Amelia told Kieran as she sat on the sofa next to her.

"I think maybe she was tired and hungry," Kieran whispered.

"She's an impatient little imp," Amelia said and stroked her daughter's head fondly.

Kieran smiled. "Wonder where she gets that from?" she teased.

"You're lucky you're holding her," Amelia said pretending to be annoyed.

"You can't hit a pregnant woman," Kieran bantered.

Amelia rolled her eyes, "Wanna bet?"

They laughed and Frankie opened her eyes startled by the noise. Kieran rocked her. She sighed and closed her eyes again, pushing the bottle out of her mouth. Kieran smiled. She couldn't believe she was going to have her own baby soon.

"So, are you excited?" Amelia asked studying her face.

"Yea, a bit scared of the labour pains though."

"You should be," Amelia said wincing.

Kieran's eyes widened. That's not what she wanted to hear. "You don't regret it though do you?" she asked looking down at the sleeping baby.

Amelia smiled and took her daughter's chubby hand in hers, "Never. Motherhood changes you in ways you can't imagine. I never thought I would settle down this young. I wanted to travel and meet people; I wouldn't change my life for the world. You won't either. Once that little is one is born, he or she will be your life and everything else will be secondary."

"I'm so scared I won't be able to cope," Kieran mumbled, staring at Frankie's dimpled chin. She couldn't imagine what it was going to be like having her own little person to look after.

"You will be fine and you have Joshua. I'm telling you, I don't know what I would've done if I didn't have Kyle."

Kieran sighed. Amelia knew who her children's father was. She didn't have that luxury yet.

"What's wrong?" Amelia asked noticing her pained expression.

Kieran filled her in with the details.

Amelia's eyes were wide with shock, "You have to tell him, fast."

"I know." Kieran agreed. She looked down at Frankie again, still asleep without a care in the world. She wished she hadn't a care in the world either. Sometimes it was way too hard being an adult.

21 CHAPTER TWENTY-ONE

Kieran read the card stapled to the cellophane that hugged the sunflowers on her desk. She smiled, picked up her phone and left a message on her aunt's voice mail. She was so sweet.

By midday, she took a break from work drumming her fingers on the desk, as she thought what to have for lunch. She looked around her office. It was okay as offices went, neutral, wooden furniture, a window overlooking the dreary grey car park ten floors below. Her mind drifted to what her office in New York would have looked like. She imagined tall ceilings, marble floors and expensive furniture, maybe a view of Central Park. It seemed like a million years ago that it had been an option for her. Now she was having a baby.

Would she ever have the opportunity to go there again? How would that even work with a baby and Joshua? She wasn't sure how she felt about giving up her career goals to be a mother. Part of her would always wonder what if? What if she had ignored Darren and taken the job? How different would her life be on the other side of the Atlantic?

Kieran looked down at her stomach and rubbed it. She thought about what Amelia said. Her life was about to change. Though she was excited, she wished it happened later - when she was ready. There was so much she wanted to do and see before she settled down. Now it was on hold. Her priorities were different. Would her old priorities be relevant after the birth of her child? She sighed; she'd made her bed; now she had to lie in it.

Her breathing quickened at the thought that the baby would depend on her for everything. How was she going to cope with the pressure? It was a little too late to worry about that now; this was her life for the foreseeable future. Before she had a full scale panic attack, she called Joshua.

"Hey J," she said happy to hear his voice. It soothed her. Of course she made the right choice in having the baby and being with him.

"Hey Ki, you okay?"

"Fine, just thinking what to get for lunch," Kieran replied. Then she heard a female talking in the background and the tinkle of cutlery.

"I'll have what you're having," Joshua said to the other peson.

"Where are you?"

"Having lunch."

"With who?"

"A friend."

"Which friend? You didn't tell me you were meeting anyone." Kieran heard how silly she sounded.

"She was in the area, it was impromptu."

"By she I take it you mean Vanessa," Kieran snapped

"So?"

"So? So she asked you to jump and you said how high. You were supposed to go and sort out the pushchair," Kieran said raising her voice. She couldn't believe her ears.

"I don't want to argue now. I'll sort it out tomorrow. It's not a big deal Kieran."

"Oh, I'm sorry, lunch with your precious ex-girlfriend is more of a big deal than your baby," Kieran hissed before slamming the phone down. It was a low blow; but she didn't care. She wondered if she had made the right decision after all.

Her mobile rang. She looked at the screen. "Yes?"

"Why do you always fly off the handle whenever I talk to her?" he asked annoyed.

"You know why."

"That was four years ago."

"That doesn't make it any easier to deal with."

"I love you and you're the only person I want to be with. I'm not stupid enough to risk losing you twice," he declared.

"That's all fine and dandy; does she know this? Do you think that's going to stop her?"

"Stop her from what, exactly?" Joshua asked sounding frustrated.

"Trying to get you back!" Kieran said. Honestly, how dumb was he?

"She never had me. The whole experience was stupid and meant nothing," he tried to reassure her.

"Do you realise that makes it even worse?"

"How?"

"I was supposed to be the most important person in your life, but you risked that for a meaningless fling. That does not make me feel very important!" She had the urge to throw something. Her eyes settled on the pen on her desk; she picked it up and threw it across the room. It hit the wall and landed on the carpet without a sound. It was not the effect she'd had in mind.

"It's in the past!" Joshua shouted.

Kieran's mouth fell open. He had never shouted at her before. Did she push him too far with her tantrum? At that moment she didn't care; she was not tolerating his attitude. "Don't you dare speak to me like that."

"I'm fed up of having the same argument with you. What don't you understand about it?" he patronised her.

"Do not talk to me like I'm a child," Kieran warned him.

"You are acting like one."

"Why? I'm telling you how I feel. You are meant to care."

"I do care. Fine, explain it to me," he said in a bored tone.

"I don't understand how you could cheat on someone you love." She was aware she cheated on Darren, but clearly she hadn't loved him at the time.

"Well, maybe I didn't love you then," he told her.

Kieran paused, "Remember you said that." She slammed the phone down and burst into tears.

Suddenly someone cleared their throat and knocked on her open office door. She looked up and her heart stopped.

"Shall I come back at a better time?"

Kieran couldn't speak. Standing before her was her favourite footballer in the world, whom she referred to as her French fancy, like the little cakes, she had been obsessed with both during her teenage years.

She took a deep breath and switched into professional mode.

"Um, no it's fine, I'm sorry. How can I help you?" she questioned wiping her eyes. Why, oh why did he choose then to enter her office?

Shit, shit, shit! How long was he standing there and what the hell did he hear?

Her cheeks flushed. It was one thing for Joshua to hear her lunacy; it was another for a celebrity, a crush and client to hear. He bent down and picked up the pen. Kieran tried not to stare at certain body parts as he retrieved it and wondered what else she could throw down for him to pick up.

"Are you Kieran Taylor?" he asked in a deep French accent as he approached her desk and put the pen down.

"That's me," she squeaked and stood up. He made her name sound sexy. She held out her hand and he shook it.

"I just finished a meeting with Janet. She tells me you will be handling my PR."

Kieran couldn't believe her aunt hadn't accompanied him to her office; neither included her in the meeting, which was the norm. She had a feeling Janet deliberately sent him to her office knowing how much her niece loved Arsenal, the London team he had played for.

Kieran was about to speak when her mobile rang. It was Joshua, she silenced it and her direct line rang. It was her aunt's secretary. She had reserved lunch for the two of them at Sardo Canal, a Sardinian restaurant located on the banks of Regent's canal in London's chic and Charming Primrose Hill. A taxi was waiting outside.

Kieran wanted the floor to open up and put her out of her misery. She was not, in her opinion, appropriately dressed for such a lavish lunch with such a lavish client.

"We have a taxi waiting," she told him.

"Ah, good, I am hungry. I hope you like the restaurant. I chose it."

"I'm sure I will. I haven't had lunch yet either." She smiled, picked up her bag and walked with him out of her office; her friends were going to die when she told them.

An hour later, after they finished lunch of Battuta d'agnello alla griglia—grilled lamb fillet marinated in olive oil and herbs served with potatoes, leeks and Zuppetta di pesche con sorbetto di fragola, a puree of fresh peaches served with a strawberry sorbet for desert, they got down to business. Kieran was busy taking notes when she suddenly gasped and touched her stomach.

French fancy looked at her. "What is it?" he asked concerned.

"My baby, I think it just kicked," she touched the area where she felt the jolt.

"You are pregnant?" he asked.

Kieran nodded. Maybe she didn't look as fat as she felt, or he was humouring her. "Five months," she said with a smile.

"Congratulations," he toasted with a glass of Perrier water.

Even that sounded sexy. "Thank you," Kieran said blushing. She had to pinch herself on occasion to make sure she wasn't dreaming. He was easy going and made Kieran feel at ease. Soon, she felt as if she was having lunch with an old friend.

"I should phone my boyfriend to let him know; I don't particularly like him at the moment though," she said. She hoped she wasn't stepping out of line. Easy going and friendly he may be, he was still a client.

"Relationships," he paused, "they are okay I guess."

"If you're with the right person," Kieran added.

"Are you with the right person?"

"I guess," she rubbed her belly hoping for another movement.

"How long have you been together?"

"We've just gotten back together. We were apart for over four years."

"Why were you apart?" he probed.

"He cheated on me. That's what we were fighting about when you showed up. He is still friends with the girl."

"Do you trust him?'

"I do; it's hard though. I keep thinking that he's done it before and you know what they say about leopards." Ha. She was a leopard too.

"Leopards?"

Kieran explained the metaphor.

He smiled, "Un léopard ne change jamais ses taches."

Kieran stopped breathing and stared at him dumbfounded. *Oh my freaking gosh*!

"It sounds better in French," she managed to splutter and threw a smile at him so she didn't look weird.

He laughed and sipped some water. Kieran tried not to stare at him. "You're expecting his baby. I don't think he would want to lose you," he continued.

Kieran tried not to sneer. In a perfect world, he was right. In the real world some men were unpredictable and stupid.

"When will you marry your fiancée?" Kieran turned the table on him. She had enough of talking about her situation. Living it day-to-day was more than she could take. Like many other girls, she was heartbroken when she read about his second engagement in the tabloids.

"We are getting married next month," he said laughing.
Kieran knew he picked up on the deliberate switch. She joined his laughter. They were going to get along fine; she would enjoy working with him.

Back at the office, she, French fancy and Janet were finalizing negotiating contracts and discussing an approach for a charity event he was headlining. They looked up when they heard a knock on the door.

"Come in," Janet said.

Kieran tried not to roll her eyes when Joshua walked in. She said in a polite tone, "I'm nearly done," and looked at her watch. It was just after 5 p.m. he'd left work early. Sucking up, she thought.

"Hey, Joshua," Janet called out.

"Hey, Janet," he replied with a wave.

Kieran looked back at him and his eyes opened wide when he caught sight of her client.

Kieran introduced the two men. She tried not to laugh at Joshua's expression as they shook hands. They finalised the contract soon after and Kieran and Joshua left the office.

On the way out, Joshua said, "I didn't know you were working with him?"

"I don't feel like cooking tonight, do you want to get take-away?" she asked ignoring his question. She didn't want to talk to him.

"Sure."

They hardly spoke on the way home. Kieran went straight to her room with her dinner and was eating when Joshua entered and said, "We need to talk."

"I'm busy," she replied turning up the volume on the television.

"Ki-Ki, I'm sorry. I didn't mean what I said. It just came out."

"I believe you didn't love me then anyway so don't worry about it," she said in a dismissive tone.

"How can you say that?" he hovered by the doorway.

"Easy. You used to tell me back then how special I was, how much you loved me and how lucky you were that I was a part of your life. Then just like that, you go and have meaningless sex because it was offered to you. I accepted it and tried to pretend that it wasn't a big deal, because everyone gets cheated on sometime in their life. I gave you nearly four years of my life and you repaid me by having sex with someone else!" she snapped.

"You haven't forgiven me, have you?"

"No, I haven't. I did everything for you, whenever you needed me I was there. For ages after we broke up I believed that you cheated on me because I wasn't good enough, or pretty enough, or perfect enough to keep you happy. When we were at school, every girl there liked you and I was proud that out of all those girls you picked me. You used to tell me I had nothing to worry about because you thought no other girl could compare to me. If all that was true, why the fuck did you do it?"

It had been in her system for the last four years and she was going to tell him exactly what she thought. It needed to be said, or she'd resent him forever. "It's not like you weren't getting sex on a regular basis. If you weren't, I could understand why you were such a bastard. I thought you were different. I used to see your friends with different girls every week, and I used to think I was so lucky that you didn't feel pressured to copy them; all the time you were." She put her plate down losing her appetite.

"Kieran, please just listen." He took a few steps towards the bed.

"No, you listen. You had your chance to explain when it happened and I accepted everything you told me. I should have kicked your ass for what you did to me. So what was it? Why did you cheat on someone who was so perfect?" She didn't give him a chance to answer her. "Wasn't the sex good enough? Did it make you feel good knowing that you had your pick of two girls? Did it make you feel like one of the boys? Did you ever stop to think about how it would make me feel? If you didn't want me anymore, you should have just said!" she shouted, she was livid because she remembered all too well how she had felt at the time.

"Where is all this coming from? Why are you still so angry?"

"You don't know why I'm angry? Are you stupid or what?"

"I cheated on you because I was eighteen and dumb. I didn't know what I wanted."

"That's funny, because you were always the one to convince me when I had doubts," she reminded him.

"In the beginning it was cool. I was the only one out of my friends who had a proper girlfriend, so when they used to go out looking for girls I felt left out. It seems stupid now; we were young. What did we know?" he sat down on the bed and reached for her hand.

Kieran pulled away. "You are pathetic. You do know that don't you? You were the one who convinced me to have sex with you. I wasn't sure about it and you spent months trying to make me see that you were my knight in shining armour. As soon as I turned sixteen I took that step and suddenly it wasn't a challenge anymore right?"

"It wasn't like that, Kieran."

"Yes it was. That's all I was to you. It took you two years to get me into bed. You were satisfied for about a year and then you got bored."

"Now you're being stupid. How can you say all this? You know how much I worshipped you."

Kieran glared at him and took a deep breath. She wondered if she would traumatise the baby by shouting.

Are you okay little one? Mummy's sorry. She rubbed her stomach and lowered her voice.

"You never worshipped me. You worshipped your friends, and you didn't want them to think you were pathetic for being with one girl. You ignored what you felt to fit in. You are weak and that's why I don't know if I can trust you again. I thought I could, but you still have her in your life. If she isn't important to you why the fuck is she still around?"

"Why are you so jealous? Look at you. I'm not the one who's pathetic! You need to look in the mirror. I'm fed up of this abuse."

Joshua stood up. He was clearly pissed off.

Kieran jumped up as fast as she could. "I am jealous if you must know, because she took you away from me. She ruined everything we had. She must have something that I didn't to be able to do that. We had a perfect relationship before you met her. You used to tell me she was just a friend and how she was nothing compared to me blah, blah, blah. Months down the line, you were screwing her. You took everything you felt for me and shit on it for somebody that meant nothing to you. You got bored of me and ran to her and that's why I'm jealous. So maybe that is pathetic. I was in love with you and I never thought you were capable of hurting me like that!"

Lily whined at the loudness of Kieran's voice, she jumped off the bed and ran out the room. Joshua was silent; Kieran knew he was in shock at her outburst, even at the time she hadn't let him know how angry she was. She'd had more important things to worry about.

His voice was quiet when he eventually spoke. "I didn't know how to deal with what I felt for you. After I slept with her I got even more scared when I realised what I'd done; then it happened the second time. I stopped feeling scared because I thought that if I was in love with you I wouldn't be cheating on you. It wasn't until after you refused to acknowledge me, I knew I'd made a mistake," he explained.

Kieran looked up at him and saw the concern and confusion etched on his face. She realised she had to tell him the truth, it was the only way he would understand her emotional turmoil and why she was behaving that way, she'd already kept it from him for too long. She sat back down on the bed and took a deep breath. "The night I caught you, I came to tell you something," she said quietly.

"What were you coming to tell me?" he asked frowning.

"That I was pregnant," she whispered. The baby kicked as if showing her a sign. Kieran rubbed her stomach and looked at Joshua who was staring at her open mouthed.

Kieran's vision blurred from the tears that sprang to her eyes. She never spoke about that time in her life. It still haunted her. "I was two months pregnant and I was coming to tell you because I didn't know what to do. You'd been distant with me for months and I stupidly thought maybe the baby would bring us closer. Then all that stuff happened and I realised you didn't want me or a baby. I did the hardest thing I've ever had to do and had an abortion. I could never forgive you for making me do that and that's why I wouldn't speak to you." she croaked.

Suddenly he was beside her, his arms around her "Kieran baby, I didn't know. I'm sorry," She sobbed into his chest. "You never should have had to go through that on your own," he told her as he stroked her head "I'm so sorry,"

"Corey, Chan, Chris and Amelia were there. They're the only ones who knew." Kieran sniffled.

"So this is why you're angry?" he asked studying her face.

Kieran nodded. "Yea, I guess. I just thought that because you loved me, you might be okay with it. I knew you wouldn't let me get rid of it. Then when I found you two, I felt completely stupid and let down, and I didn't want you to be with me because you had to. I couldn't go through with it. I was only eighteen," she dried her eyes with her sleeve.

"I get it now. You think history is going to repeat itself? I can't believe you didn't tell me this before." he said shaking his head in disbelief.

"Here I am with you again, pregnant, and who shows up all of a sudden? I feel threatened by her. She ruined my life once already. I can't let her do it again," she said starting to cry again.

"It's not down to her. It's down to me," he said as he reached out to comfort her.

Kieran pulled away from him. "It was down to you last time. She knew about us. I can't let myself be made a fool out of again. I won't do it."

"I'm not here to make a fool out of you. You don't need to feel threatened by her, not this time. I promise."

It was too much for Kieran to think about; whether she could believe him or not. She needed time to think, time to calm down.

"I'm taking Lily for a walk," she announced as she dried her eyes and stood up.

Joshua nodded; he didn't try to stop her.

Kieran walked for hours and didn't return home until almost midnight. Joshua met her at the door.

"Where the hell have you been? You're soaking wet. I walked

around for an hour looking for you." he shouted at her.

Kieran gave him a blank look, took off her jacket, went into the bathroom and turned the tap on ignoring his sanctimonious crap.

Joshua followed her into the bathroom. "Kieran, I asked you a question."

She continued to ignore him and began taking her wet clothes off. Joshua stood in front her where she couldn't ignore him and waited for her to answer him.

"I needed some space and time to think." she said without looking at him.

"I was worried sick; I thought something happened to you. How could you be so selfish?"

Kieran slapped him in the face. The rage she felt frightened her; though she knew it had been a long time coming.

Joshua held his face from the sting.

"Don't you ever lecture me about being selfish, if you weren't selfish I wouldn't have had to have an abortion! If you weren't selfish and actually thought about talking to me about what you were feeling instead of sleeping with someone else, we would not be having this fight."

"I'm not going to keep apologising for something that happened when we were kids," he said dropping his hand from his face.

Kieran continued to take off her wet clothes ignoring the urge she had to hit him again…violence wouldn't solve anything.

"So, tell me, if you hate me so much, why the hell are we even bothering to make a go of this? Let's face it, you are never going to trust me and I'm never going to convince you otherwise, so why are we wasting our time? You'd be better off with someone you know won't cheat on you, and I'd be better off with someone who trusts me. We're obviously not meant to be. I'll do the best thing for both of us and leave," Joshua said.

Kieran watched him. Her eyes narrowed, knowing if he walked through the door she would not take him back. A fresh wave of rage washed over her and before she could stop herself, she picked up a glass off the bedside table and threw it at him. It sailed past him and landed with a loud thud on the rug near the door. Amazingly it didn't break. Joshua stared at her wide eyed.

"If you want to go, go!" she screeched storming past him into the bathroom. She locked the door and stood with one hand on the handle as she tried to control her breathing.

Kieran heard the front door slam and Lily barking. She slid down to the floor and burst into tears. She was not sure how long she sat there. She was numb and exhausted. Eventually, she crawled into bed. Joshua was still not back and she wasn't expecting him to return. She was falling asleep when she heard him calling her name.

"J?" she questioned as she groggily switched on the lamp. She squinted at its brightness and looked at the clock. It was three in the morning. She threw her arms around his neck. She could tell he was taken aback, but he hugged her.

"Look, I'm sorry I left, I just think we should take a break for a while until we both calm down," he said.

"You're right about me needing to forgive you. I don't want to lose you, not again," she whispered ignoring what he said. She didn't want to take a break.

"You won't lose me, but I have to know that you are over what happened and I know it's going to take time."

"Don't go. I'm sorry, I know I'm being a bitch to you. I'm just scared and my hormones aren't helping,"

"I know you're scared. I'm scared too, but you have to talk to me not scream at me," he said pulling away and drying her face with his hands.

"I'm so sorry I lost it with you."

"I'm sorry too. I never even apologised for cheating on you at the time, I was such a dick to you." he said kissing her forehead.

She closed her eyes, "Like you said, it's in the past," she said feeling calmer.

"It should never have happened. You were the best thing that happened to me, and I should have treated you with the respect you deserved. I never should have slept with Vanessa. Yes, I should have spoken to you. You never should have had to have an abortion. That's going to haunt me for the rest of my life."

"Me, too," Kieran said sadly.

Joshua hugged her tightly. "I love you so much and I'd never intentionally hurt you, not now, not ever, I promise."

"I know," she whispered. Kieran realised this time she was the one hurting him, and felt like the world's biggest hypocrite.

"So, are we going to forget about it now?" he asked.

"I'm going to try," she was trying to be reasonable; she would need him to be the same if the results came back with bad news.

"I won't be friends with her any more if it's going to make you feel better," he suggested.

"Really?" Kieran asked looking at him.

"Yes, if that's what you want."

She wanted to tell him he couldn't see her, but she had no right to do that. The truth was Vanessa wasn't the reason why she was arguing with him.

"It's fine, you can see her. I'll just have to learn to trust you again. I can't watch you twenty four seven," she admitted, she looked down at her hands and pretended to study her nails.

"I won't let you down." he promised.

"You'd better not," she said trying to sound perky.

"I love you, you know that don't you?" he asked lifting her face to look at him.

"I know J. I love you too."

Joshua smiled and kissed her. They were silent for a few moments until he yawned.

"I'm knackered. I'm cold and I need sleep. I've been sitting in the park since I left," he confessed.

"Why didn't you come back sooner you muppet," Kieran teased as she lay back onto the pillows.

"I was scared you might throw another missile at me," he joked.

"Sorry about that," she said feeling ashamed.

"I deserved it for what I said."

"So, are you getting into bed or what?" Kieran asked changing the subject.

"Yes," he pulled his hoody over his head.

"Good, but first get me some food please, I'm hungry," she gave him a sweet smile.

"What's wrong with your hands and feet?" he teased throwing his top at her. It landed on her head.

"I'm pregnant," Kieran said before throwing it back at him.

"No, you're lazy," he replied catching it. She stuck her tongue out at him. He bent down and kissed her on the forehead, "I'll be back in a minute."

Kieran held his face and kissed him on the lips before he left the room. She was glad he knew the truth about their past. Now there was just one other thing standing in their way

22 CHAPTER TWENTY-TWO

Kieran and Joshua were on their way to meet with Jarrell to celebrate his twenty-first birthday. Not long after arriving at the party, Kieran realised she left Jarrell's birthday card in the car and returned to get it, only to bump into Darren.

She cursed. Was he ever going to get out of her life?

Maybe it's an omen the baby is his... shit.

It had been two weeks since she had the amniocentesis, but had not yet been called in for the results. Darren stared at her stomach. Kieran ignored him and walked off.

"What's wrong?" Joshua asked when he saw her not too happy facial expression once she had re-joined him.

"Darren's here." she grumbled.

"I'll break his neck if he says anything stupid," Joshua threatened.

"No, you won't," Kieran told him, "You don't have to fight to defend my honour. If he wants to be an asshole, let him, okay?"

"Yes boss," he teased.

Shortly after, Chantelle and Christina arrived. "About time," Kieran said.

"I noticed Darren's here, has he said anything?" Chantelle asked.

"No, it's only a matter of time, I don't know how he manages to get invites to places where no one likes him, it's like he does it on purpose just to torture me." Kieran complained..

"I wouldn't put it past him." Chantelle said shaking her head.

"What did J say?" Christina asked.

"He said he'd break his neck if he tries anything."

"So will we. I see he's still with Miss Bitch," Chantelle added.

"Yep, I guess that's how he wormed his way in. Melanie's sister and Jarrell are friends." Kieran told them.

"I hope she's not like her sister," Chantelle said raising her eyebrows.

Kieran sighed; Melanie was the least of her worries.

As Kieran expected, when she was alone, Darren approached her and asked, "Were you planning on telling me you are pregnant?"

"No." she replied curtly.

"Why not?"

"What has it got to do with you?" Kieran asked turning to face him.

"It could be mine." He was smirking.

"What makes you think that?" she asked narrowing her eyes at him. His arrogance really irritated her.

"I'm not stupid, you're showing, you have to be more than five months, we were still together."

"Clever you," Kieran said sarcastically.

"So, what are we going to do?" he asked seriously.

"We aren't doing anything. I'm having a baby with Joshua."

"And what if it isn't his?"

"It is,"

"I want to be there if it's mine."

"Are you deaf?"

"Why are you being so hostile?" he asked offended, "I'm serious, I don't want another man bringing up my baby."

"We're living together," Kieran reminded him as she stood up and poured a drink.

He's crazy if he thinks he's coming anywhere near my baby.

"Well then I'll take you to court," he said as he stood next to her.

"Yea, of course, you will. Grow up Darren," she told him before walking away.

He grabbed her arm. "It's time you started to take me seriously." he growled.

"Why? You're a joke and you don't scare me," she hissed pulling her arm away.

"I hope it isn't my baby. I wouldn't want it to have such a bitch for a mother," he spat back.

"I'd rather die than have your baby. I couldn't take having you around for the rest of my life," Kieran started to walk away from him.

Darren let rip obscenities at her.

"Is this how you plan to prove to the courts that you're mature enough to get custody of a baby?"

"I don't need to prove anything. They'll look at you and see that you're incapable of bringing up a child." He was being his usual petulant self. He would never change.

"Really, and what makes you think you're better than me?"

"Because you're shallow Kieran, always have been; all you care about is shopping and what's in fashion. You don't care about the real issues going on in life. How are you, of all people, going to take care of a baby? You'll probably freak out and end up giving it up because you are a selfish bitch and clueless about everything unless it involves shopping. That's the truth and that's why I had to leave. Go ahead, have your baby. If it's Joshua's, I wish him luck. He'll see how crap you are and leave too. He doesn't love you. He feels sorry for you. He just wanted a quick fuck. Unfortunately, you got pregnant, so he had to stick around; I'll tell you something, no sane man would ever want you to bring up his child. They wouldn't want the baby to be like you. I'd rather it died first."

Kieran looked at him gob smacked. She pushed past him and hurried up the stairs before anyone could stop her and locked herself in the bathroom, where she burst into tears. Half an hour later, she was still inside while Joshua and Chantelle tried to coax her out.

"When do you ever listen to that shithead? Why are you letting him bother you now?" Chantelle asked losing her patience.

"What if he's right? What if I'm a bad mother?" Kieran asked through the door.

"Kieran, you could never be a bad mother," Joshua reassured her.

"Am I shallow?"

"No," Joshua answered without missing a beat.

"He's just jealous that you've moved on. We know how much you care about this baby," Chantelle added.

"J?" Kieran called.

"Yea Ki?"

"If I'm a rubbish mum, are you going to leave me?" She hated how feeble she sounded.

"Don't be stupid. I'm doing this for the first time too, we can make mistakes together."

"I'm scared I'm going to disappoint you," she wasn't talking about her mothering skills anymore.

"You won't. I have faith in you. We all do. Will you open the door please?"

Kieran was silent for a while; she finally stood up and unlocked the door. Chantelle and Joshua hugged her.

"He said no sane man would want me to be the mother of their baby and if it was him he would rather it died first," she sobbed.

"He said what?" Joshua asked letting go of Kieran. He turned and walked down the stairs. Kieran tried to go after him; but Chantelle stopped her.

"Whatever Joshua does to him he deserves it," she told her.

Kieran sniffled and wiped her eyes. "My hormones are up and down today."

"I figured that," Chantelle teased as they walked down the stairs. Christina hurried over to Kieran and hugged her.

"Where's J?" Kieran asked her.

"He's in the garden talking to Darren."

Kieran walked out into the garden. Joshua and Darren appeared to be having a civil conversation. Kieran was unnerved as she walked over and took Joshua's hand.

"Are you okay?" Darren asked.

Kieran looked at him as if he had spoken a different language. "Excuse you?"

"I didn't mean to say all that stuff to you. I was angry and I wanted to hurt you," he explained.

"Are you on drugs?" It was a serious question but she could see Joshua biting his lip to stop himself from laughing.

Darren held his hands up in surrender "I'm sorry, okay. I didn't think you'd take it to heart. I thought you'd tell me where to go like you normally do." He had enough common sense to sound guilty. "I was out of line and I'm sorry. I just can't believe you're pregnant."

Kieran could practically see the wheels in his head turning, thinking, trying to make sense of the timings.

"Yea, well, it's none of your business, so you don't have to worry." Joshua said abruptly.

Darren ignored him. "I know you'd make a great mum. I was trying to piss you off, we used to be best friends Kieran; you know how I felt about you. All that stuff I said was to hurt you. Any child would be blessed to have you for a mum and I mean that," he said before walking off.

Kieran stared after him then looked at Joshua.

He shrugged. "I came over to have a go at him and he apologised,"

"I don't get him."

"I do. He misses you and probably wants you back. He sees that you're happy and just wanted to be spiteful."

"Talking from experience?" she asked smiling up at him.

"Yes, and I'm never going through it again." he whispered.

Kieran hugged him. She hated the thought of hurting him. She wouldn't be able to live with herself if the baby turned out to be Darren's.

In the early hours of the morning, Kieran awoke with a groan. She had been having pains in her back and her stomach most of the day, she didn't know what to make of them, But she wasn't concerned and put it down to her body changing. She couldn't panic every time she felt a strange twinge. The same couldn't be said for Joshua.

"You okay?" he asked in the darkness.

"Please stop fussing, I'm fine," she told him reaching out for his hand.

"You said you didn't feel well earlier."

"I still don't, but you don't need to worry."

"I just want to make sure you're comfortable." he kissed her forehead.

She groaned again, this time to herself. "It's just a stomach ache. I'll be okay."

"Are you sure?"

"Positive. Thank you."

"For what?"

"Being here."

"Anytime." he said before kissing her on the forehead again. Kieran grimaced in the darkness, every time he kissed her like that she was reminded of Rome. She began to wonder how he was doing and then stopped herself from going there. He was not in her life anymore. She had moved on and he probably had too. The thought made her feel sick and she resisted the urge to run to the bathroom. It would only make Joshua panic even more.

23 CHAPTER TWENTY-THREE

On the morning of Kieran's appointment for the amniocentesis results, she was nervous and had thrown up twice. She had never been more nervous or scared and sat in a tense silence as she waited in the waiting area. Chantelle and Christina sat on either side of her.

When her name flashed up on the electronic board she groaned. She was not sure if she could handle bad news.

"It will be okay." Chantelle said reassuringly.

Kieran didn't answer her; until they knew the results she could not be sure of anything. The doctor greeted them with warm smiles, clearly not understanding the severity of the situation or why the girls looked so on edge.

"I have your results," she told Kieran once she was settled, "first, there was nothing abnormal in your results, so the chance of Down's syndrome, or any other abnormality is very small," she started.

"That's great news," Kieran said smiling slightly. If the paternity results were bad at least something good had come out of it. The baby was healthy.

"In regards to the paternity results the chance that the baby is Mr. Simmons is ninety nine point nine percent positive."

Chantelle and Christina let out audible sighs of relief.

"Are you sure?" Kieran gasped.

"Positive," the doctor replied. Kieran thought she may have looked a little judgmental after seeing the girls reactions.

Tears filled her eyes and Kieran leaned into her friends as they hugged her. Overwhelmed with relief, she returned home feeling more relaxed than she had been in a long time. Finally she felt she could plan her future with Joshua.

Later that night, Kieran was relaxing in bed reading a book for new mothers. She was still having back pains but it hurt less when she was not moving around. When Joshua came home she could smell the alcohol on him as soon as he entered the room. He'd been on a boy's night out with Jarrell and some of their friends.

"I can't believe I'm having a baby," he said as he lay down next to her and rubbed her belly.

"Has it just hit home?" she asked looking at him with a smile.

"Yea, it's weird." he said yawning and closing his eyes.

"I know," she rubbed his head with affection. He had no idea how happy she was.

"Marry me?" he opened his eyes to look at her.

Kieran froze, she knew she looked horrified but didn't have time to rearrange the expression on her face.

Shit, shit shit!

"You said you couldn't trust me, but since we cleared the air, things have been so much better so..." his voice trailed off.

Kieran didn't look at him. She couldn't. The truth was she wasn't ready to get married. She loved Joshua, but she didn't know if she wanted to marry him. Not knowing if he was the baby's father served as an excuse, how was she going to get out of it this time?

"Well?" Joshua persisted.

"Um, I don't know what to say. I wasn't expecting this so soon," she said still avoiding his eyes.

"You could try, yes."

"I'm still not ready J."

"What do you mean you're not ready?" he demanded as he sat up to glare at her.

"I'm not ready for marriage and I don't want to talk to you about this when you're drunk."

"You lying bitch!" he shouted.

"Excuse me?" Kieran was stunned at his outburst.

He got off the bed and turned to face her. "You heard, I said you're a lying bitch. You don't want to marry me at all do you?"

"I'm not a bitch Joshua and as you're drunk, I'll let you get away with it; no I don't want to marry you now. I'm not ready for marriage and I'm still not sure I trust you enough."

"Are you fucking out of your mind?" he suddenly yelled.

"You'd better stop swearing at me," she warned as she got out of the bed and put on her dressing gown. What the hell was his problem?

"Or what?"

"Just stop it! What is wrong with you?"

Lily started to growl at him not appreciating his behaviour either.

"Shut the fuck up!" Joshua roared at her.

Lily whined once and flattened herself to the ground. Kieran narrowed her eyes suspiciously. His behaviour was unusual; it wasn't like him to be so angry and aggressive. Lily wasn't the only one who was scared. "What else have you been doing apart from drinking?" she walked over to him trying to get a good look at his face.

"None of your business." he hissed at her.

"Have you been smoking Joshua?" she asked folding her arms across her chest.

"Fuck off Kieran!" he shouted as he pushed past her into the bathroom and slammed the door.

Kieran followed him. "Were you and Jarrell smoking weed?" she asked through the door.

He didn't answer her. She was sure he had been. His behaviour brought back memories of how he acted when he did. He'd started at fifteen then stopped because it altered his mood. However, anytime he was under pressure, it was the first thing he turned to for temporary relief. "I asked you a question!" she banged her fists on the door.

"Who the fuck are you talking to?" he shouted as he wrenched the door open.

"You." she told him.

He stormed past her and back into the bedroom Kieran was right behind him, "I thought you gave that shit up years ago?"

"I did. I felt like some tonight," he said as he sat down on the bed.

"We have a baby coming and I'll be damned if you think you're going behave like this around our baby!" she ranted as she got back into bed.

"Do you hear yourself? Jesus Christ woman!" Joshua snapped.

"I don't like you when you smoke. You know what it does to you, so why do you do it?" she asked making an effort to lower her voice.

"Because I can. It's my life; you have no right to tell me what to do." he turned to look at her. His eyes dared her to tell him otherwise.

"You are the father of my baby. I have every right," she said glaring at him.

"Oh, so now you know it's mine you think that changes things? It doesn't mean shit!" he shouted.

Kieran's stomach lurched. *What did he say?*

"What doesn't mean shit?" she asked quietly, the confusion on her face genuine.

"The fact the baby is mine; it doesn't really change anything, does it?"

"What the fuck are you talking about?"

Joshua took a step towards her, Lily began growling again so Kieran picked her up.

"You think you're so smart don't you? I thought there was a chance it was his from the beginning; but you didn't mention it, so neither did I. I didn't think anything of it even when you kept going on about having the damn amniocentesis, and then you turned down my proposal and I knew you weren't telling me something. I researched it online and guess what I found out? You can have them done for paternity tests too," he said laughing, even though it wasn't funny. "And I read that the father has to give consent, and I sure as hell didn't sign anything, so what did you do fake my signature?" When Kieran didn't answer him, he shook his head in disbelief. "Unbelievable."

How did he find out?

"I went through your bag when you got home. You slipped up when you said you had to go the hospital but I didn't need to be there," he said answering her silent question. "Did you really think I wouldn't find out? You're not that clever," he said in a spiteful tone.

"You know why I didn't tell you, you would have left me," she said trying not to cry. The disappointment in his eyes was heart breaking. She knew he would never trust her again.

"No, Kieran, I wouldn't have. You underestimated me. I thought that was the real reason you didn't want to marry me; but this baby being mine means nothing to you, because you don't want to be with me anyway."

Lily's incessant growling was driving her crazy. She backed away from Joshua to see if this would calm her down, knowing she was only being protective.

"That's not true; I want to be with you J. I'm so happy this baby is yours. You have no idea how much it was killing me. I just can't marry you, not yet."

"Do you really want to be with me? Because it doesn't feel like it, ever since we got back together it's like every now and again your mind is elsewhere and I can't figure out what it is or who it is,"

Kieran was silent. She had definitely underestimated him. He had no idea how close to the truth he was.

"I'll ask you again, do you really want to be with me?"

Kieran stared at him. Her mind was running wild. She'd forgotten how well he knew her. She couldn't admit her true reasons for not wanting to marry him. "I was just worried about us being back together that's all, I want to be with you." She spoke softly and looked into his eyes.

He swore then kicked his trainers across the room. Kieran jumped and Lily barked and jumped out of Kieran's arms and over to where his trainers had landed.

"What the fucking hell are you doing?" she shouted as she followed Lily.

"Fuck off!" Joshua shouted at her.

Enraged, Kieran hurled one of his trainers at him. "Why don't you grow the fuck up?" she shrieked.

Before she could blink, he had grabbed her and pinned her up against the door. "Don't forget who I am and that I'm bigger than you," he warned.

"You're going to hit me?" Kieran challenged.

"That's not my style; but don't push me, because I can hurt you," he said with a menacing smile.

Kieran, in terror, slapped him. When Joshua raised his hand to hit her back, Lily was between their feet growling at him louder than ever.

Joshua lowered his hand, Lily was still growling at him.

Kieran stared at him in shock. For the first time in her life, he was a stranger to her. The Joshua she knew would never have done that to her.

"I'm going to bed; I think you should sleep on the sofa." she told him while trying to keep her voice steady. She was shaking but she didn't want him to know he had gotten to her.

"Kieran," he said quietly still rooted to the spot.

"What?" she snapped.

"I'm scared," he looked into her eyes; she had never seen him look so sad, so lost, so betrayed.

Her face and voice softened "Of what?" she asked. It was all her fault why he looked like that.

"Becoming a father. It hit me tonight. I can't believe how much I love the baby already, and when I realised it could've been different I got scared. I want us to be a family so bad, and I just don't want anyone to take you away from me."

It was already too late for that, she had never been his, he had lost her the moment she met Rome.

"That doesn't excuse your behaviour." she said getting angry again. He had almost hit her and no matter what she had done, she didn't deserve that.

"I know, but that's why I smoked," he admitted.

"I don't care right now Joshua."

"I'm sorry." he said sadly.

"Great," Kieran said handing him a pillow. He took it and walked out the room. It was only then Lily stopped growling. Kieran shut the door and locked it behind him.

Surprisingly, she soon fell asleep, until a sharp pain woke her the next morning. It felt like period pains, only worse. She frowned and rubbed her belly waiting for the pain to pass. The baby usually woke her up in the mornings with gentle kicks. On reflection, she hadn't felt it kick during the night either. Maybe it was still sleeping. She got out of bed and felt a tiny kick from inside her. She smiled relieved and rubbed her stomach.

Morning little one.

She walked into the living room. Joshua was nowhere to be seen. She must have really crashed out; she hadn't heard him leave. Kieran got dressed and took Lily for a quick walk. When she returned, they had breakfast and she got down to work. She had chosen to work from home as she had a bit of a temperature and wanted to take it easy. By noon, she took a break from work and went online to shop. She had found some great clothes sites for babies.

She was still on the computer when Joshua came in with flowers, Calla lilies – her favourite. Kieran looked at him and then back at the computer. It would take more than flowers for her to forgive him.

He cleared his throat, "Ki Ki."

"What?" she said not looking at him.

"I'm trying to say I'm sorry."

"Really?" she said her eyes glued to the computer screen.

"Babe, I didn't mean to scare you."

"I wasn't scared," she lied. She would never let him know he had that power over her.

"So why'd you lock the door?"

"You'd try to get in."

"I know you don't like me to smoke, but sometimes I have to."

"Is this your idea of an apology? What about "Kieran I'm sorry for not understanding that you're not ready to get married and I shouldn't have tried to hit you?"" she snapped looking up at him.

He scowled at her. "You have a nerve, don't you?"

"Excuse you?" Kieran asked raising her eyebrows at him.

"Are you forgetting the real argument here? You've been lying to me for months, and you did something behind my back when I asked you not to. You didn't give a shit how I felt, you did it anyway!" he shouted and hurled the flowers across the room.

Kieran was scared to move and scared to sit in front of him in case he went for her again. "I didn't know what else to do! You don't know how hard it's been keeping it from you. How could I tell you that I'd still been sleeping with him? You wouldn't have understood!"

Lily appeared and began growling at Joshua again. He looked

down at the dog and back at Kieran.

When he spoke his voice was a normal decibel "He was your boyfriend, as much as I might not like it, I would've understood. Maybe you shouldn't have taken so long to finish with him after we slept together?"

"What did you expect? I didn't trust you enough to believe we were going to start where we left off. You cheated on me. Why was I going to trust you with my heart again?"

"Well, I trusted you with mine while you were cheating on him," he told her.

"Oh please, it is not the same thing," Kieran said in a dismissive tone and reverted her attention back to the computer screen.

"It's worse." Kieran heard the hurt in his voice; she stayed silent. "Tell me something, if you hadn't gotten pregnant would we be here now?"

"I don't know." Kieran said. Even though she knew exactly what the answer was.

"You don't know?"

"What do you want me to say?" Kieran asked looking at him. "It happened so fast, I didn't have time to think about how I felt about us, I didn't think we'd get serious so fast,"

"And then you got pregnant and didn't have a choice? So why didn't u tell Darren?"

"I didn't want him involved, I wanted it to be your baby," she said quietly.

"Why?" he demanded.

"I love you," she said looking up at him.

Joshua narrowed his eyes at her. "If you loved me, you would have told me the truth, instead you had me believing the baby was mine for months. If I hadn't admitted I knew, you never would have told me. You talk about trust; how am I meant to trust you when I know you can hide stuff from me?"

She stood up to face him, "You have no idea what I went through. Yes, I know I was wrong for what I did; I didn't want to hurt you by telling you unless it was necessary."

"Unless the baby wasn't mine?" he questioned.

"Yes, Darren and I used protection. I knew it was only a small chance it could be his, but I had to make sure, otherwise it would come out eventually and it would be worse the longer I kept it from you. If I knew it was his, I would've told you straight away," she explained. "I am sorry,"

"Kieran, I'm sorry too."

She turned to move away from him and a sharp pain went through her. She gasped and rested her hand on the desk to steady herself.

"Are you okay?" Joshua asked frowning.

She winced as the ice cold burning pain shot down her back. "I'm fine. I'm going to have a bath."

He walked across the room to retrieve the flowers; he put them on her desk. "I'm going for a walk." he said quietly.

Kieran didn't answer him.

She wasn't sure how long she had been in the bath. She may even have fallen asleep for a while. The pain had startled her awake and now she was trying not to panic at the amount of pain surging through her body. She opened her eyes and looked down at her stomach, willing the pain to stop - then she saw it.

Oh dear God I'm bleeding! Please no, not my baby!

Trying not to fall apart completely she decided to get out of the bath. As she moved an unbearable burning sensation shot through her. What was going on? She should've known something wasn't right when she woke up with a temperature.

Hang in there little one, don't you go anywhere, Mummy is going to get help.

She waited for the wave of pain to pass then stood up. She drew in a sharp breath as the burning was replaced with stabbing pains in her back and the top of her thighs. Her legs gave way from the pain but she couldn't give up. She had to save her baby.

Come on move!

It took every ounce of strength to lift her leg. She winced and lifted her other leg to step out of the bath. Blood trickled down her legs leaving a red puddle on the floor. She clutched her stomach and steadied herself against the wall inching herself towards the door. She grabbed her towel and wrapped it around her. The burning sensation returned, along with the stabbing pain, they surged through her middle section and she groaned. Her pelvic area felt as if it was on fire.

Oh God why is this happening?! Don't panic…. just get to a phone…it will be fine, just get to a phone! Shit where did I leave my mobile?

Just as she opened the bathroom door, she heard a noise from the bedroom she hoped it was Joshua and not Lily.

"Joshua, help me!" she screamed.

He was in the bathroom in seconds and turned pale when he saw the red water in the tub and blood puddles on the floor. "Oh my God, Kieran."

"I can't walk it hurts too much!" she sobbed.

Joshua picked her up. Kieran screamed and cradled her stomach. "The baby, save the baby," she murmured, she couldn't talk, or keep her eyes open, all of a sudden she felt very sleepy.

He carried her into the bedroom and laid her on the bed. Joshua grabbed the phone and called the emergency services. The last thing Kieran heard was him giving them their address before everything went black.

Joshua cursed and shook Kieran. He shouted into the phone telling the operator what happened.

"Is she still breathing?" the operator asked.

"Yes but she won't wake up and there's so much blood."

"We'll be there shortly."

Joshua rested her head in his arms rocking her back and forth. "It'll be okay Kieran, it'll be okay," he told her trying not to cry and ignoring the blood that trickled down her legs.

After what seemed like hours, the doorbell rang. He hurried to the door and let the paramedics in. They followed him into the bedroom.

"What's her name?" one of them asked opening her eyes and checking her pupils.

"Kieran. Can you stop the bleeding?" Joshua asked through his tears. He couldn't avoid looking at the blood on the pastel green duvet cover. He watched as the paramedics checked for a pulse and other vital signs. It scared him to look at Kieran's lifeless body.

"We have to get her to the hospital now, She may have gone into premature labour." One of them said after a few minutes.

"What?" Joshua asked. He wasn't sure he had heard right.

Everything was confusing and blurry.

"She's lost a lot of blood; we won't know what's wrong for sure until we get her there," the other paramedic explained, as they lifted Kieran onto a stretcher, and strapped her in. Within minutes they had wheeled her out of the flat, down the stairs and into the ambulance.

Joshua was sobbing; he couldn't lose either of them. He tried to pull himself together as he climbed into the ambulance praying to all the different gods he could think of to save his family.

24 CHAPTER TWENTY-FOUR

For the first time in Joshua's life he was scared. He couldn't lose Kieran. He loved her too much.

It's going to be fine; we are going to be a family.

Everything they had been through couldn't have been for nothing. They both had to survive.

"How are you holding up J?" Chantelle asked sitting next him and interrupting his thoughts.

Both his and Kieran's family met him at the hospital including her friends; Joshua, however, just wanted to be left alone.

"I can't take this. I need to know what's going on," he mumbled standing up and pacing the room. He'd been doing that since he arrived.

"It'll be okay. You know she's a fighter," Christina told him.

"I can't lose her," he said turning to face them. Joshua looked away when he saw the pain in their eyes. They were as scared as he was.

Fuck this is bad.

"None of us can," Kieran's mum Denise said.

"I think she lost the baby." Joshua whispered, "There was so much blood; the baby couldn't have survived." he sat back down and held his head in his hands. He should've stayed at home; if he had been there she wouldn't have been in the bath for so long, he would have checked on her sooner, the argument hadn't helped either.

God there was so much blood in the water, the floor, the bed...

it was like a horror movie. Fuck! Are they going to survive?

"She'll be fine," Courtney patted his shoulder as if he could hear his thoughts.

Joshua couldn't hold back his tears and Chantelle leaned over and hugged him.

An hour later, the doctor came into the family room. It had been the longest two hours of Joshua's life. He stood up, his jaw set as if bracing himself for bad news.

"Kieran picked up a kidney infection." he informed them. "We don't know how long she had it, but it probably started as a bladder infection, it caused her to go into premature labour. She had been in labour for a few hours and obviously hadn't realised. Kieran gave birth to a little girl," he explained looking at each one of them.

His face was void of any emotion and Joshua couldn't read anything. He felt though, that they weren't out of the woods yet.

"How are they?" he asked barely breathing.

"Mother and baby are stable for the moment—"

"Thank God," Joshua let out a sob. Then asked, "Stable for the moment?"

"Yes, we had to operate to get the baby out as Kieran was too weak to deliver naturally. She's still asleep. The bad news is the baby had to be put on a ventilator. She's too weak to breathe by herself. Because of the infection, the chance of survival is low; as I said, she is stable right now. You'll be able to see her in about an hour. She's in the I.C.U. I'm sorry."

"Can I see Kieran?" Joshua asked. Everything would be better once he saw her.

"Yes, she isn't awake, but you can see her." Joshua followed the doctor down the corridor through two sets of double doors and into the room where Kieran was recovering. Her parents' followed.

He opened the door and he thought his heart would break seeing her lying motionless. Various tubes were attached to her body. Joshua brushed away the tears that fell from his eyes, sat down next to the bed and took Kieran's hand. Denise held her other hand. There was silence in the room apart from the machine that was monitoring Kieran's heart which bleeped every few seconds.

Joshua stared at the screen and watched the jumps as it registered her beating heart.

Please keep doing that don't even think about stopping, As long as you keep bleeping she's still here. We have a daughter who needs her. Our little girl is all alone. Kieran please wake up.

He brought her hand to his lips. "Ki Ki, we have a daughter," he said quietly. "I haven't seen her yet, but I know she's going to be beautiful. I'll wait for you to wake up so we can see her together. I'm so sorry for not being there and I swear to God if you get through this, I'm not going smoke again. I can't lose you Kieran, not again," he sobbed as he rested his head on the bed.

He heard Denise sniffling from the other side of the bed. Joshua felt Kieran's hand move in his and raised his head to look at her.

"Kieran?"

She groaned and opened her eyes. Joshua stared at her as she looked around the room smiling weakly at them. Joshua watched as her parents stared at her with a mixture of shock and pure relief.

They took turns hugging and kissing their daughter before leaving the room to get a nurse and let the others know she was awake.

Kieran knit her brows, as if trying to comprehend what was happening.

"Shh," Joshua told her as she tried to speak.

A nurse entered the room and did a few checks on Kieran; Joshua held her hand the whole time.

"It's okay Kiki." he told her swallowing the lump in his throat.

Kieran was frowning and Joshua knew she was trying to remember what had happened. Her eyes widened suddenly and her hands went to her stomach. "The baby?" she asked a frantic look in her eyes.

"We had a little girl," Joshua said quickly.

"Try not to talk too much, okay? I will bring you some water, sip it slowly," the nurse told Kieran before leaving the room.

"How is she? It's too early." she croaked.

"She's on a ventilator, she's stable." he explained and squeezed her hand.

"I want to see her," she said pulling the sheet off herself, the sudden movement made her wince.

"We can't see her yet; soon," he said pulling the sheet back over her.

"What have the doctors said?" Kieran asked avoiding his eyes as she lay back down. It was too early for the baby to be born. Way too early. She'd read enough to know that any birth before the seven month of pregnancy had little chance of survival. Kieran didn't want Joshua to know the severity of the situation, not yet, it would kill him.

"The doctors don't know for sure; they think she has a good chance," he lied. The doctors had practically told him to prepare himself, but he couldn't tell her the truth, not yet, it would kill her.

"I want to see her," she said again and tried to sit up then clutched her stomach.

"Babe, you can't get out of bed yet, at least not on your own. You're not well; you lost a lot of blood, you had surgery." Joshua told her as he forced her to lie back down.

"I want to see her," Kieran repeated.

"Okay, I'll speak to the doctor," he said standing up. He kissed her on the lips. "I'm so glad you're okay. I thought I was going lose you."

"I'm not ready to go anywhere just yet," she said, "my family needs me."

"I love you," he told her.

"I love you too," she replied.

Joshua left the room. Kieran's parents stayed with her while he tried to pull himself together. He sat down in the waiting room and held his head in his hands. He could not believe he had nearly lost the both of them. He felt a soft hand on his shoulder and looked up to see his parents and brother in front of him.

"We went to see the baby," Donna told him, she looked like she had been crying.

"How is she?" he asked. It didn't feel real to him that the baby was there. It hadn't meant to happen like this. He was so worried for both of them.

"She's tiny and pink." Jarrell said smiling

"She's beautiful and perfect," Patrick replied, his voice cracked a little and he cleared his throat. Joshua could tell he was trying to be strong.

He stood up and hugged his family. He allowed himself to cry for a few minutes before he pulled away and took a deep breath to compose himself.

"I need to find the doctor, Kieran is anxious to see her." he told them as he wiped his face.

"Just be prepared J, it's hard seeing her like that," his mum said tearfully.

He nodded. He knew it would be hard.

Later that night, Kieran had demanded to see her baby and would not take no for an answer Joshua helped her out of bed and into a wheelchair. He could see how much it hurt her to move, but she would not back down. They arrived at the intensive care unit and a nurse led them over to the clear plastic container where the tiniest baby Joshua had ever seen lay helpless..

Joshua hugged Kieran as she burst into tears. He too was crying, though he was quiet, he wanted to be strong for Kieran. He couldn't lose it for her sake.

After a few moments, Kieran pulled herself together and they just sat and watched their daughter. Joshua knew Kieran was dying to hold her and kiss her, and tell her everything was going to be okay. He wanted to do the same.

She had on a tiny nappy. Wispy tufts of curly black hair poked out a little pink hat. Her skin was almost translucent and held hardly any colour. Her little chest moved up and down rapidly as the machine breathed for her. Her lungs not well enough developed for her to breathe on her own. Her eyes were closed and tubes were in her nose and mouth. She was helpless, and there was nothing either of them could do to help her. Joshua felt a pain in his heart like he had never felt before. He didn't even have the words to explain it.

The little cubicle had two armholes; Kieran put her hand through and stroked her baby's tiny hand. It was pink, wrinkly and Joshua was sure, soft. He watched the tears roll down Kieran's cheeks. She didn't brush them away.

"What should we name her J?" she asked in a quiet voice.

"I don't know babe," Joshua whispered.

"I can't believe this is happening. Yesterday everything was perfect and now it's all gone wrong," Kieran sobbed.

"We're parents now babe, and no matter what, we have a

perfect daughter," he said hugging her.

"I want to name her," Kieran said through her sniffles.

"What?"

"Sienna Naomi Simmons," she said, her voice breaking into a whisper.

"It's perfect," Joshua replied as he kissed Kieran's forehead. He sat down next to the mother of his child, and the two of them watched helplessly as their daughter lay there fighting for her life.

25 CHAPTER TWENTY-FIVE

Two days later, Kieran was still in hospital under observation. She had been moved onto a maternity ward. She felt like she was being tortured every time a baby started crying. She had made sure the curtains stayed drawn around her bed so she couldn't see the joy on the faces of the women who got to hold their babies. She also knew they'd ask her questions and she didn't want to explain to the them that her baby probably wouldn't survive.

The doctors could neither confirm nor deny that it was the amniocentesis that caused the infection. Kieran blamed the test. She felt Joshua thought the same, but would not say it to her face. He was trying to be strong for the both of them; Kieran saw through his tough guy act. He was as scared as she was. Neither of them ever imagined they would lose the baby, now they were faced with that possibility. Kieran prayed for her daughter too, so that she could put it all behind her and start family life with Joshua.

She appreciated the support of her family and friends. Darren, too, visited. Kieran knew he was riddled with guilt because of what he had said. Chantelle's head appeared through the curtain disrupting her mental agony. Christina and Amelia followed her into the small space. Kieran smiled, happy to see them.

"How are you coping?" Chantelle asked giving her a hug.

Kieran shrugged. "I named her Sienna," she said in a sad voice.

"That's a really pretty name," Amelia told her as she sat down.

"I can't believe I'm going through this. You never think it's going to happen to you and when it does, you just wish it was happening to someone else; but nobody deserves this." Kieran said fighting back tears.

"How's Joshua handling it?" Christina asked.

"His heart is breaking. His little girl is probably not going to survive. He told me not to have the stupid amnio, but I went ahead and now my baby is going to die,"

"Kieran you don't know that," Chantelle said softly as she hugged her friend.

"Yes I do, she's not going to make it. Joshua knows it too. She's underdeveloped, and not strong enough to fight the infection. It was in my system too long. It's only a matter of time. Have you seen her yet?"

"Yea," Amelia said her voice breaking. "She's gorgeous."

"Can't tell who she looks like though," Christina added with tears in her eyes.

"Please don't cry," Kieran said before bursting into tears. This set them all off.

Chantelle was the first to calm down "Shit, we're sorry." she said taking a deep breath.

"We agreed not to cry, but seeing her, then seeing you well…" Christina tried to explain. She didn't need to finish her sentence. Kieran understood perfectly.

Just before her friends left, Joshua returned. "You okay?" he asked as he sat on the bed next to her.

Kieran rested her head on his shoulder and nodded.

"Okay, we're leaving; we'll be back tomorrow," Chantelle announced, motioning to Christina and Amelia.

"You don't have to," Joshua told them.

"It's fine, you two should be alone." Chantelle said. The three girls gathered their things and said their goodbyes.

Once they were alone, Kieran and Joshua sat in silence; neither of them knew what to say. There was nothing that could be said to make the situation better.

"Lily is fine. Jarrell says she misses you. You got loads of cards and flowers at home from the neighbors;" Joshua said breaking the silence first.

"I hate this," Kieran told him.

"I know Ki," he said stroking her hair.

Kieran closed her eyes. "Do you think it's my fault?" she asked not wanting to see the expression on his face.

Suddenly there was a murmur of voices outside the curtain. For whatever reason, Kieran's heart thudded and her stomach dropped.

Sienna's gone.

Her eyes met Joshua's. They wore the same expression on their faces; they knew it was bad news.

A doctor entered through the curtain with a solemn look. He removed his glasses from his face. Joshua squeezed Kieran's hand. She couldn't breathe. Bad news was written all over the doctor's face.

He took a deep breath and looked directly at them. "I'm sorry to have to tell you Sienna didn't make it."

After a pause, Joshua asked, "What happened?" They'd spent an hour with her not long ago.

Kieran let out a groan and Joshua tightened his hold on her.

"Her heart gave up. It just wasn't strong enough to keep going."

After another pause, with emotion in his voice Joshua said, "Thank you for everything doctor."

"You're welcome, I'm sorry again," he said before disappearing out through the curtain.

Even though Kieran was expecting it, she was crushed. Her mind was oddly blank as Joshua held her and cried into her hair. After a while, she stroked his face.

He kissed her hand. "Are you ready to see her?" he asked.

"Not yet."

"I knew she wasn't going to make it," he whispered.

"I'm so sorry J," she said dejected.

"Me too babe."

"I hate myself for having the amnio now. When I found out she was yours, I thought finally we were going to have a fairy tale ending; someone up there doesn't want us to have it so easy."

"We've been through enough," he said nodding.

"She's with her brother or sister now," Kieran said as tears streamed down her face.

"Third time lucky?" he said, realising Sienna was the second child they hadn't been able to keep.

She ignored his question and asked her own. "What do we do now?"

"We have to bury our daughter."

Kieran said nothing and Joshua held her close. She was aware it was all he could do to let her know he was there for her, and she wasn't going through it alone. She wasn't sure how much time passed before she spoke again. "I'm ready to see her now."

"Are you sure?" he asked looking at her.

Kieran nodded. "Are you?" she asked him. She wasn't sure if he was strong enough for this. She didn't know if she was either.

"I'll go and speak to the nurses."

They were led to a private room. It was cold and Kieran shivered as she sat down on a hard plastic chair and waited. She wondered how many people had sat in that room and said goodbye to someone they loved. How many people had said goodbye to their newborn baby?

A lump formed in her throat when the nurse walked in pushing a cot with a tiny bundle inside; Sienna wrapped in a pink blanket. She was not ready to say goodbye. She took a deep breath and shivered again. She felt Joshua's body trembling next to hers.

The nurse placed the cot near the window. "If you want to hold her you can. Call when you're ready for me to take her," she told them in a gentle tone.

Kieran nodded. Neither of them moved nor said a word for the next few minutes. Eventually, Kieran stood up. The few paces to the cot were the longest and hardest she had ever taken. Her body shook with every step. She held her breath as she took the first glance at her baby daughter. She was perfect, tiny, but perfect. Kieran's heart swelled. She loved her so much. What was she going do without her? How could she be gone? All the dreams Kieran had danced before her as she watched her baby – dressing her up in girly dresses, using pretty hair clips in her hair; hearing her laugh for the first time, seeing her smile, playing with Lily, taking her for walks, introducing her to everyone in the family, watching her grow from a tiny baby to a beautiful young woman.

I'm so sorry Sienna, Mummy's so sorry she did this to you.

Kieran eventually reached out and stroked her black curls then picked her up as the tears rolled down her face. It was the first time she was holding her baby. She felt a calmness flow through her body, as if Sienna was telling her it was okay, she would be alright and they didn't have to worry about her. She was as light as a feather in Kieran's arms, but there was a heaviness in her heart. She sat next to Joshua who was so still. Kieran looked at him. He was barely breathing.

"She's sleeping J, just think of her as sleeping," Kieran told him.

"Kieran I can't do this," he said standing up and backing towards the door.

"What?" Kieran asked tearing her eyes away from her daughter to look at him.

"I can't hold her and say bye."

"She's your daughter," Kieran said looking down at her baby. "She has your nose."

"No she isn't, I can't think of her as my daughter," he shook his head and began pacing.

"How can you say that?" Kieran gasped.

"She's dead Kieran and I don't know what to do with that information. I can't make sense of it. Looking at you holding her seems so natural, but she's dead. If I don't think of her as my daughter it might make it easier to deal with," he said as he stopped pacing and stared out of the window.

"Everything's about you, isn't it?" Kieran hissed at him.

"What?" he asked turning around to face her.

"You are so fucking selfish," she spat at him.

Joshua shook his head at her. "Kieran, don't do this now,"

"When would it be easier for you to hear?" She couldn't believe what he was saying. No matter what, she was still his daughter. She was still their daughter.

"I've never done this before. I don't know how to grieve, she doesn't feel like mine right now," he explained.

"Get out," Kieran told him in a quiet voice.

"Pardon?" he said stunned.

"If she doesn't feel like your daughter then get out. I'll say bye on my own."

"Don't be like that Ki. I'm just trying to explain that I don't know how to say bye. I don't know what I'm meant to do," he sat next to her and for the first time looked down at Sienna.

"Hold her," Kieran said handing her to him. He hesitated; his hands were shaking. "Babe, it's okay. Hold her," Kieran placed Sienna in his arms.

She watched Joshua as he looked at his daughter and cradled her to his chest. "She's the most beautiful thing I've ever seen," he whispered as the tears rolled down his face.

"I know."

"Why did she have to die? How are we meant to pretend she didn't exist? It's always going to feel like she's missing and that we can't find her."

Kieran kissed his shoulder as tears rolled down her face, too. She didn't have the answers to his questions. She had questions of her own that would never be answered. They sat with Sienna taking in their last moments with her, willing her back to life so that they could be a family.

"Sienna, Mummy and Daddy love you very much and we wish we could've gotten to know you better and that you could've stayed with us longer. We are always going to miss you and we are always going to love you, sleep well angel," Joshua whispered as he kissed his daughter on the head.

Kieran was choked to silence. She, too, kissed her baby on the head.

I love you little one.

Joshua stood up and put Sienna in the cot. He pressed the alarm for nurse. Within minutes she entered the room.

"You can take her now," Joshua said quietly.

"You can take a few minutes before going back to the ward," The nurse said smiling sympathetically at them before wheeling Sienna out of the room.

"I'm going to get a drink, do you want anything?" Joshua asked Kieran, she shook her head.

He was only gone a few minutes but when Joshua returned Kieran was pacing back and forth across the room.

"I want her back," she was mumbling the four words over and over with a wild look in her eyes. She wrung her hands together as she paced.

"I know Ki," he said. He had never wanted to comfort anyone as much as he wanted to comfort her at that moment.

"Get her back now. I haven't finished saying bye," she said.

Desperation showed in her eyes.

"Kieran she's gone."

"I can't live without my baby."

"We have to," he said trying to pull her close to him.

She pushed him away. "Get off me!"

"Don't do this to yourself Kieran, I know you are angry and scared."

Kieran felt as if she was having an out of body experience, as if she was in a dream. She was numb to the pain; at the same time, it was right there crushing every fibre of her being.

"Kieran please, let me hold you," he said holding his hands out to her.

She stared at him as if he were a stranger. "Bring her back," she mumbled. She felt as if her lungs were about to collapse. She couldn't breathe.

"She's gone," Joshua said looking helpless.

"Bring her back," she repeated.

"We already said goodbye," Joshua took a step towards her.

"J, bring her back," the tears spilled from her eyes as she stood with her hands clenched into fists at her side.

"I can't." Joshua told her in a firm tone.

"I'll do it myself then," she said turning and walking towards the door.

Joshua grabbed her arm and pulled her towards him. She struggled for a few minutes before pulling away from him and falling to the floor. Joshua sat next her and held her as she cried.

"She can't be dead!" she wailed into his chest.

He stroked her hair "It's okay," he whispered.

"Why our baby?" she asked almost breathless.

Joshua didn't answer. Kieran didn't want him to. Whatever he or anyone else said would never be a good enough reason. Kieran felt a pain like no other. It stamped on her heart, and lungs. Breathing was painful. A part of her was missing and she found it difficult to function. How was she supposed to live after losing her baby?

"This is all my fault. I wish I was dead." she sobbed.

"What?" Joshua asked releasing her. He stared at her.

"I want to die too!" she said in between her sobs.

Joshua looked at her, horrified "Kieran, don't ever let me hear you say that again."

She wasn't listening to him, she was staring at the space where the cot had been and a fresh wave of despair washed over her knocking the breath out of her body. "I want to be with my daughter and if the only way I can be with her is to be dead then I fucking want to be dead!" she screamed hysterically.

Joshua slapped her. Kieran held her tear stained face.

"You selfish bitch!" he said in anger, "You're not the only one who's lost a daughter you know. She's gone. We have to get over it and pick up the pieces. What do you think it would solve if you killed yourself?"

Kieran couldn't believe he was being so clinical about it. "It would make me feel better." She would give anything to take away the guilt and pain even if it meant death.

"And what about me?" Joshua asked.

"What about you?"

Joshua looked at her clearly hurt and sat down on the bed. "Kieran, I know you're not thinking clearly right now, but knowing that you want to give up hurts me more than you'll ever know, go ahead; kill yourself if that's what you really want."

"I thought I wanted you," she mumbled.

"What's that supposed to mean?" he asked looking into her eyes.

"Nothing," she said with a shrug.

"Well if you want to be on your own that much I'll go," he suggested.

Kieran didn't answer him.

He left and she didn't see him again until he picked her up the following day when she was discharged. Kieran could tell he had been smoking; she was too distressed to say anything to him. It was his way of dealing with his grief, just like lashing out at him had been hers, though she would never forgive him for leaving her. The nurse had found her curled up on the floor and had helped her back to her bed.

She cried the entire journey home. Images of mothers leaving with their babies haunted her and she felt jealous. She couldn't wrap her head around why they got to keep their babies and she didn't. It felt like it was all a dream. She hadn't even told her family and friends, she didn't want to say it out loud. It made it too real, too final. She was not pregnant anymore and she had no baby.

My poor Sienna.

"Can I get you anything to drink, eat?" Joshua asked her once they were home.

"I'll make some tea for us, thanks."

"Let—"

"It's okay, put my stuff in our room please," she interrupted him and walked slowly into the kitchen. It still hurt her to move, but she needed to keep busy otherwise her thoughts ran riot.

She filled the kettle with water, flicked it on and turned to get the milk from the fridge. Kieran stopped in her tracks when she saw the picture of the baby scan she had less than two months before. She stared at it. She had been so happy that day seeing her baby on the monitor; her pregnancy had finally felt real. She traced the shape with her fingers as the tears fell silently down her face. She removed the picture from the fridge, screwed it up into a ball and let it slip from her hand on to the floor.

Joshua was talking on the mobile with tears in his eyes when Kieran entered the living room. She couldn't watch him and she didn't want to listen to what he was saying. She set the tea down on the coffee table, went into the bedroom and called her mother.

"Where's Mummy?" she asked her little sister when she answered the phone.

"Is Sienna still in the hospital?" Charlie asked her.

Kieran's eyes caught sight of the baby's things stacked in a corner and her heart lurched. She couldn't bring herself to answer her sister's question.

"Can you get Mum please Charlie," she croaked as more tears rolled down her face. She lay down on her bed and closed her eyes. How was she going to tell her mum?

"Kieran what's going on? Charlie said you're crying," her mother spoke into the phone urgently.

"It's Sienna" she said quietly.

"What's happened?"

Kieran was silent, all she could do was cry.

"Kieran, what's happened?" her mum said again, she could hear the panic in her voice.

"She's gone mum."

"What do you mean? When?"

"Last night."

"Oh Kieran, why didn't you call me sooner? Where are you?" Denise asked her voice breaking.

"I didn't want to speak to anyone; I didn't want to say the words," Kieran sobbed.

She could hear her mother sniffling "Where's Joshua?"

"He's here, we are at home,"

"You two are too young to be going through this."

"Something or someone doesn't think so," Kieran said in a bitter voice.

"Have you spoken to Corey?"

"No, Mum, can you let everyone know please, I can't do it. I keep crying and it's hard for Joshua too."

"Yes, of course, I'm so sorry Kieran."

"I keep expecting to feel her kick or something, but she's gone. I have a house full of baby stuff and she's not here, it all has no meaning now."

"We'll be over soon love; okay?"

"Okay."

"Do you need anything?"

Kieran glanced at the pile of baby things in the corner, her stomach knotted. "No, thanks Mum."

"Go and talk to Joshua, you have to help each other through this."

"I know, but I want to shout at him all the time, I'm so angry."

"Don't push him away; you need each other now more than ever."

Kieran sighed and held her head in her hand. "I know."

"We'll be there soon. I love you Kieran."

"I love you too, Mum."

She found Joshua sitting and staring into space. She sat next to him. His was shaking. She rubbed his back and they sat in silence until the doorbell rang a while later.

"I'll get it," Kieran told him. She opened the door. Chantelle, Christina and Amelia stood outside. From their facial expressions; Kieran knew they'd heard the news.

"Your mum called." Chantelle explained in a hoarse voice.

"We are so sorry," Amelia sympathised.

"Is there anything we can do?" Christina asked following them into the living room.

"Not really, we have to decide when the funeral will be; until then there's nothing much for anyone to do." Kieran said sitting next to Joshua. He stood up, greeted the girls and then disappeared into the bedroom.

"Are you two okay?" Chantelle asked quietly.

Kieran shrugged. "I think he blames me, why would you want to be around someone you hate?" she asked.

"Joshua loves you." Christina told her.

Kieran said nothing.

Amelia frowned at her "This isn't your fault."

Kieran sighed, "It probably is, my one job was to protect her and I failed."

Amelia stood up and sat next to Kieran, she took her hand and squeezed it. "I know there's nothing we can say that's going to make it better but please don't blame yourself."

Kieran was silent. It was already too late.

26 CHAPTER TWENTY-SIX

The following days arranging Sienna's funeral. Joshua was withdrawn and increased his smoking habit. Kieran felt alone, though her family and friends were supportive; she needed Joshua. She was sat home alone with her torturous thoughts with Lily curled up next to her when Darren paid her an unexpected visit.

"Hi," he said, when she answered the door, "I saw Christina, and she told me what happened. I'm so sorry Kieran."

Kieran stepped aside so he could enter. Darren handed her a bouquet of flowers. "These are for you."

"Thanks."

"I didn't know what else to bring. I know you like sunflowers," he said awkwardly.

Kieran smiled. They were beautiful. Sunflowers were her second favourite next to lilies. She motioned for him to sit.

"I know this is a stupid question, but how are you?" he asked as he sat down opposite her.

"I don't know. I'm sort of on autopilot. It probably won't seem real until tomorrow."

"Why tomorrow?"

"Sienna's funeral," Kieran told him. Darren sighed. "It seems unfair doesn't it? She was a tiny baby and she deserved a shot at life."

"Yea, she did. It makes you wonder if there really is a God up there," Darren said looking up at the ceiling. "How's Joshua taking it?"

"All he does is smoke," Kieran said bitterly.

Darren raised his eyebrows. "Maybe that's how he's dealing with it."

"What about me? I can't smoke to deal with it. I need to talk to him, how can I talk to someone who's always high?"

"Where is he now?"

"Probably getting a draw," Kieran said holding back a sob.

Darren got up and hugged her. It went through Kieran's mind that it should have been Joshua holding her. As if hearing her, Joshua walked in. Kieran moved away from Darren guiltily.

"Don't stop on my account," he told them heading into the kitchen.

Kieran dried her eyes on her t-shirt. "We weren't doing anything, he was just comforting me," she explained.

"Whatever, it didn't take you long to be back in his arms considering you're meant to hate him so much," he said coming back into the room with an ashtray.

"She was crying," Darren explained. "I'm leaving now anyway."

"I'm not bothered, there's nothing to keep her with me now, so if she wants you back then fine," Joshua said with indifference and sat down.

"Joshua stop it," Kieran said glaring at him.

"Stop what? Isn't it true? You don't want to marry me. We don't have a baby anymore, so why are you still here?" he lit a joint, took a long drag and closed his eyes.

"We're not doing this now," she told him looking at Darren apologetically.

"What have we got to hide? Answer the question," Joshua said looking at her.

Kieran saw he was serious. "I'm here because I love you and you know that."

"Do I? So why won't you marry me?" he narrowed his eyes.

"For the love of God! Because I'm not ready, we've been through this!" she was exasperated.

"But you were ready to have my baby, which is the bigger commitment?"

Kieran caught Darren's eyes. "I'm going," he said standing up.

"Yea, fuck off," Joshua told him.

"I'd really like to come and say bye to Sienna tomorrow if that's okay?" he said to Kieran ignoring Joshua.

"Of course, it is. Call Chantelle for the details," Kieran said as she walked him to the door.

He stepped outside and then turned to face her. "Will you be okay?" he asked with a worried look.

"Yea, he gets like that when he smokes."

"Are you sure, he won't hurt you or anything will he?"

"Oh Darren get over yourself! He's not like you!" she snapped irritably before shutting the door in his face. She felt a tiny bit guilty but brushed it off.

"What the fuck was he doing here?" Joshua shouted as soon as she entered the room.

Kieran wondered if she had spoken too soon, he was behaving exactly like Darren. Now he was the crazy irrational one. "He came to show he cares like everyone else has been doing," she told him pinching the bridge of her nose, her head was pounding.

"Well, he isn't everyone else."

"Can you calm down? Every time you smoke that shit you get like this."

"Kieran did you fuck him?"

"I'm sorry?" Kieran asked shocked. Did she hear him right? He couldn't have said that to her, not after everything that had happened.

"You fucked him didn't you?" he was glaring at her.

"Just because you're hurting, don't think you can speak to me like that. I'm hurting too, and I need you to be here for me, not accuse me of shit that's in your head."

He put the joint down in the ashtray and looked her up and down. "Look at the way you're dressed, you're not exactly covered up are you?"

Kieran looked down at the T-shirt she wore. It belonged to Joshua and almost touched her knees. She hadn't even paid any attention to what she was wearing. It was the last thing on her mind.

"I don't have to listen to this. Think what you like, I'm going to bed," she snapped at him. She picked up her phone and marched into the bedroom.

Joshua jumped up and in a second was in front of her, "No you're not," he said blocking her way.

"Move Joshua," she told him.

He grabbed her arm, "If you're fucking him and I find out, I'll kill you!"

"Get off! You're hurting me!" she screamed at him. She could hear Lily barking frantically from the bedroom. Locked in and unable to get to her.

"You like it rough," Joshua said with a demonic smile.

Kieran was suddenly terrified. "J, I'm serious, get off me!" she shouted.

He let go of her.

Without another word she went into the bathroom slamming the door shut behind her. She took a deep breath and began to brush her teeth. She was livid and scared all at the same time. She thought about staying over at Corey's. Somewhere she felt safe. Lily suddenly appeared through the door that led to her bedroom, she jumped up happily when she saw Kieran.

Joshua was sitting in bed watching TV when Kieran entered the bedroom. She got in without a word. Lily jumped up on the bed next to her and curled up against Kieran's side. It was as if she sensed Kieran needed protecting. Joshua was unstable. Kieran had never seen him so angry, angry at her, angry at the world. He had shut her out and she didn't know how to help him because he wouldn't let her.

Sometime later, she woke up with a start. She heard noises and her heart pounded. She reached out to Joshua. He wasn't there. Kieran breathed a sigh of relief realising the noises were him. She got out of bed and found him crying on the sofa. She sat next to him and put her arms around him. "It's okay J."

"No, it isn't, I wanted to hurt you tonight."

"I know." It scared her how calm she was about it.

"But why? How can I want to hurt you? I love you so much and I just don't know what's going on in my head," he pounded his head with his fist in frustration.

"You're grieving, that's all," she soothed.

"You don't understand. When I smoke I feel like none of this is real. I don't have to deal with the fact that my baby is dead, or how she died; once the drugs wear off, it's ten times more real and

I want to lash out and hurt people."

Kieran knew he meant her. He wanted to lash out and hurt her. If only he knew how much she already hated herself.

"I think that's normal," she placated him.

"Hurting you isn't. I can't hurt you Kieran. I'd die before I lay a hand on you," he said looking into her eyes.

Karen saw a broken man before her. She saw parts of him in his eyes; the parts she loved were missing and she didn't know if she was strong enough to bring them back. He blamed her for Sienna's death, and that was the number one reason he took it out on her.

She squeezed his hands reassuringly. "We'll get through it, I promise," she whispered.

"I need you so much and I can feel myself pushing you away; I don't know how to stop," he stroked her face.

"Stop smoking," she pleaded with him.

"I can't! It's keeping me sane!" he roared.

Kieran jumped at the loudness of his voice. "It's driving you crazy J, it's not helping you. Let me help you."

"I don't know how to be strong for the both of us and I feel like I have to be," he told her.

"You don't have to be strong; no-one expects you to be either. The situation isn't going to change; you can't block it out. I know it hurts, but you have to go through the pain, the grieving process. It might be the only way to get you through it - to get us through it."

"I want our daughter back," he whispered.

"She's not coming back and we both have to deal with that."

"I don't know how," he said as tears rolled down his face.

"Neither do I, and drugs won't help you; it's only numbing the pain temporarily."

"And for those few hours, I am grateful," he said with a sigh.

"Okay, I'll grieve for the both of us. I'll be strong for the both of us. I'll do everything for the both of us!" She snapped and instantly felt guilty, so she took a deep breath and changed her tone "We have to bury our child tomorrow, let's get some sleep."

27 CHAPTER TWENTY-SEVEN

Kieran had been ready for an hour, and Joshua was not home; he was not answering his mobile either. By the time her parents arrived to pick them up, he still had not returned.

"Where's Joshua?"

"I don't know, Mum," Kieran said on the verge of tears as she looked out the window and saw the hearse with the tiny pink coffin. She couldn't believe her perfect baby was in there. She couldn't believe she had to bury her.

"Is he meeting us there?"

"I have more important things to worry about than Joshua and his selfishness today Dad. I don't know if he's even coming, he's decided he's too distressed and doesn't feel like burying his daughter." Kieran saw her parents exchange looks. "Yep, unreal isn't it? He's probably gone round to his druggie friends' house to get some more weed."

"I beg your pardon?" her mum asked raising her eyebrows.

"That's how he's been dealing with his grief Mum."

"That's how he's coping?" her dad repeated. "Maybe he should see a counsellor?"

"I don't know if we are going to survive this. I love him, but he's just not helping me or himself right now. I feel like I'd be better off on my own." she said to herself, more than to her parents.

"Don't make hasty decisions now. You have both gone through a traumatic time. Things are bound be a bit tense and strained," her mum hugged her.

Kieran sighed and said nothing, she allowed herself to cry for a few minutes and be comforted by her mother before they left for the church.

It was a cloudy miserable day. Kieran felt the fine drizzle on her face, as she stepped out the car. She looked up at the sky and thought back to when her mother used to tell her it rained because God was crying. Was God sad for what he was putting them through? How could Sienna's death be part of a greater plan? What sense did that make?

She walked toward the church where her parents were married, Kieran was christened, had her first communion and confirmation. And now she had to bury her daughter there too. The church was large, with a steeple. Old fashioned; beautiful. Colourful pictures of stories from the bible outlined in gold contrasted well with the white colour throughout the inside, right up to the high ceilings. Kieran had fallen in love with the church since she was a little girl. She would never look at it the same again.

"Where's Joshua?" Donna asked Kieran when she approached them outside the front of the church

"I don't know."

"Are you kidding me?" Jarrell asked.

"I wish I was, I don't know where he is." Kieran said trying to ignore the ache in her throat as she spoke.

Donna hugged her. "It's okay. We're all here, you're not alone," she reassured her Son's girlfriend.

Kieran couldn't meet her eyes. Had Joshua told her about the amnio? He was entitled to and she expected them to blame her. She had told her parents, though she was careful not to mention the paternity test. She couldn't bear to see the looks on their faces, she didn't want to hear their silent judgment.

Kieran had never felt more alone in her life. The ceremony lasted twenty minutes. There wasn't much to say for a life so short. After the priest prayed for Sienna's soul, they sung a hymn and the service came to an end. It went by in a blur for Kieran. Her eyes were locked on the tiny pink coffin in front of her for the duration. Sienna was dressed in the tiny pink dress she had bought for her just a few weeks earlier. It was huge for her, but Kieran felt it was only right that she be buried in it; it had been a particularly hard moment for Kieran when she'd had to dress her. But it was the last time she would ever have the chance, so no matter how hard it was for her she did it and she would cherish that moment forever. Sienna had looked beautiful in her dress.

They walked out into the cemetery to where Sienna Naomi Simmons was to be buried after just forty eight hours of life. Kieran looked for any sign of Joshua. She didn't realise until that moment how much she needed him. He was letting everyone down. She clung to her mother as the coffin was lowered into the ground. A sob caught in Kieran's throat. She couldn't breathe. She needed to sit down. Her knees buckled when strong hands steadied her.

"I'm sorry I left you for so long, I'm so sorry," Joshua whispered into her hair.

Kieran collapsed in his arms with relief. The anger she had felt earlier evaporated as he held her tightly.

They watched as their daughter was lowered into the ground, then Joshua let go of her and he and Jarrell shovelled dirt onto the coffin. Kieran watched wishing the hole in her heart could be filled just as easy. Sienna would always be missing. No words could express how much it hurt her.

She watched Joshua. Tears poured down his face as he shovelled more dirt into the hole in the ground. Kieran was sure he couldn't see what he was doing. She walked over to him, took the shovel from his hands and gave it to her dad. Joshua slumped to the ground and cried for the baby he was burying. Kieran knew that reality had finally kicked in and knocked him over. She crouched down beside him and held him as he heaved and struggled for breath.

"She's okay. She knows you love her. It doesn't matter that you were late. You were here when it mattered and that's what matters to me. I love you and I'm here for you no matter what," she told him.

"I'm sorry."

"I know and she knows."

"Will we be okay?" he asked standing up and pulling her up with him.

"We'll be fine," Kieran reassured him. She wasn't sure how

true that was. When her baby's coffin was one with the earth, everyone placed flowers on the small mound of dirt. Kieran and Joshua were the last to do so. Kieran had chosen sunflowers.

"Bye little one, you will always be in my heart," Kieran whispered and placed the flowers on the earth.

"Love you," Joshua added.

Kieran looked up at Joshua and was blinded by a slice of sun that had snuck from behind the clouds. In her moments of grief she hadn't noticed the clouds parting. The rain had stopped and the day promised to be beautiful. Kieran looked up into the blue sky; she wished Sienna could've seen how beautiful the world could be.

"Would you mind if I say hello to my friends?" she asked Joshua.

"No, course not. I'm gonna go speak to my parents."

"How about I meet you back at Mum's house? I'll go with the girls."

"Are you going to be alright?"

"I'll be fine."

He kissed her forehead and Kieran walked over to her friends who stood together by a dark blue Audi A3 she didn't recognise. They group hugged and she noticed Amelia was crying inconsolably. As a mother, Kieran knew she understood her pain first hand and better than the rest of her friends.

"You're so brave. I don't think I would've been able to get out of bed," Amelia said drying her eyes.

Kieran swallowed the lump in her throat and hugged her friend. "I almost didn't," she said honestly.

Her eyes caught sight of Courtney stepping out of the car. Her heart stopped when Rome suddenly appeared out of the driver's side. She stared at him, not knowing what to say as he made his way around the car and towards her. Kieran was frozen to the spot.

He stood in front of her and stroked her face "Hey," he whispered.

Kieran burst into tears. She felt familiar arms around her and for the first time that day she felt comforted. Rome stroked her hair as she cried into his chest. She was touched beyond words that he had turned up to pay his respects. She couldn't believe he was there. She'd missed him so much.

"I'm so sorry this happened to you Kieran, I'm so sorry I

wasn't there for you," he whispered.

Kieran couldn't speak. She revelled in the comfort of his arms. As she cried she tried to remember when she had last been carefree and relatively happy. When all she had to worry about was her relationship with Darren. Everything had been less complicated before she had gone to Greece, before she had met Rome.

Her life nosedived when she had met the man consoling her at that very moment. In the comfort of his arms, Kieran realised that it was him she had wanted to console her all along. It felt right, and she felt solace for the first time. How was that possible? How could she still want him more than Joshua after all that time? What did it mean that he was there? She couldn't believe she was even thinking about it when she'd just buried her child.

But it was a strange connection they had, an instant spark, some might say, like finding your perfect half, your soul mate. Kieran wasn't sure she believed in soul mates anymore. Finding that perfect person that you were meant to be with, share a life with and love unconditionally. A soul mate was someone you couldn't live without. In truth, people were not perfect, and sometimes it didn't matter what kind of connection you had with someone, sometimes life happened and that connection had to be broken. Sometimes people had to live without their soul mate, so she wasn't sure what the point was in it all.

She had known instantly that there was something between her and Rome. Were they meant to be together? Or was he the soul mate she had to live without?

God I can't deal with this now.

Whatever the hold was between them, it hadn't disappeared. Almost a year on and it was strong as ever. Just the sight of him brought back a rush of feelings that she thought she had put behind her. She hadn't felt more carefree than when she was with him, everything was fresh and new between them, there were no scars on their relationship, no resentment, no pain and that had been the difference between him and Joshua, and why she would have chosen Rome. It would have been easier to be with him, plus she knew what she felt for him was completely different to what she felt for Joshua.

Rome showing up was his way of reminding her of that, to let her know that he was still there. He knew now that the one thing keeping Kieran and Joshua together was no longer. She didn't need to feel obligated to stay with the father of her child. She couldn't do that to Joshua, he wouldn't survive if she left him, and she wouldn't do it to Sienna. She wouldn't rubbish her memory like that.

Kieran was too broken to even consider being with Rome, whether they were soul mates or not. She owed it to Joshua to fix the black hole that had become their relationship. Rome would always be a temptation to her the longer he stayed in her life. She'd already unintentionally ruined Joshua's life and was determined to fix it even if it meant being with him when her heart wasn't in it anymore. Sienna was her heart.

Rome's sudden reappearance created instant confusion in her mind. She took a deep breath, and looked up at him. Kieran felt the familiar sensation in her heart. She diverted her eyes. He was the catalyst that started the chain of events that led to where she was. If they were to be together she wasn't sure if she would ever let him forget that.

"I think you should go," she whispered.

"Are you okay?" he asked. He looked so worried, so concerned, that it made Kieran feel even worse for what she was about to do.

"It's not appropriate for you to be here." she said seriously as she stepped away from him.

"Kieran I'm here as your friend," he told her.

"We can't be friends, remember?" she reminded him. He'd wanted it that way and he'd been right.

"Kieran don't push me away," he moved towards her trying to close the distance between them.

She stepped further back. "I have to push you away. Please Rome, I'm not strong enough to be around you. I've done enough damage because of you." She raised her eyes to his face.

His jaw tightened as he processed what she was saying. "It doesn't have to be this way Kieran," he told her.

"It does, this never would have happened if we hadn't met, if you hadn't lied to me, and I know that's a really shitty thing for me to say to you."

"Babe I get it, honestly I do, but we can fix it now, we can do it properly, take it slow, be friends first, I just want to be here for you," he made it sound so easy.

"Joshua needs me." she said as the tears rolled down her face.

"What about you? Who do you need?" he reached out and took her hand. Kieran let him. She could feel her resolve breaking.

They both knew the answer to his question.

She was torn; she couldn't face giving him up again, but she couldn't bear to cause Joshua any more heartbreak and she couldn't split herself into two either. Rome would have to be the one who lived without her. What else could she do? She knew she would have to be honest with him; it was the only way he would walk away. It was the only way she could save him; otherwise she would ruin his life, like she had ruined Joshua's.

"I can't be with you knowing that part of me holds you accountable for this, I don't want to hurt you any more than I have and I will end up punishing you and you will take it out of guilt, it won't be healthy for either of us." She began crying again. Rome pulled her towards him and just held her as she cried. "I'm so sorry Rome," she sobbed.

"No, I'm sorry, for everything." he said sadly.

Kieran's heart exploded from the hurt that shadowed his eyes when she looked into them willing him to hear her thoughts. There was so much more she wanted to explain to him. She wanted him to know why it had to be that way; she couldn't; he would try to talk her out of her decision and she would let him, because she was selfish and only thought about herself. He deserved more than that. He deserved more than her.

"Please don't contact me either," she whispered. She could be strong as long as he stayed out of her life.

"Okay," he mumbled before kissing her forehead.

Kieran closed her eyes and inhaled his scent for the last time; He was wearing his trademark Armani Code cologne, her stomach hurt as those memories she had locked away for so long, came rushing back to her. She took a deep breath and stepped away from him before she could return his embrace. She wanted to, but she couldn't because she knew she wouldn't let him go. Her arms hung lifeless at her sides.

"If you ever change your mind, you know where I am," he whispered before releasing her.

"Goodbye Romeo," she said with a slight smile.

He stroked her face one last time, exhaled and then he was gone.

Kieran didn't watch him leave; she didn't think her heart could take much more. Blinded by her tears she turned to look for her friends. They were talking to her parents a distance away. She hadn't even realized they had left them alone. She guessed they felt she and Rome needed space, time to talk.

Now there was nothing left for them to say.

Lily met them at the door when they entered the flat. Kieran was relieved the day was over. It had been the hardest day of her life, and she looked forward to the future now. For Sienna she had to fix their relationship, otherwise her life meant nothing as far as Kieran was concerned.

"Oh, Lils, I'd better take you for a walk," Kieran said closing the door. Lily wagged her tail in agreement.

"I'll come with you." Joshua told her as he picked up the post, scanned it and put a stack of envelopes on the table. "More cards," he told her.

"You don't have to; I'm only taking her down the road."

"I want to," he said as he flopped down on the sofa.

"Okay, let me change first." She took off her jacket and walked into the bedroom, undressed and stood in front of the mirror. She stared at her scar from the caesarean, and ran her fingers over the stitches. It was still tender. It felt like a million years ago since she was in the hospital watching her daughter struggle for her life. She rubbed her stomach the way she had rubbed it when she was pregnant. She would give anything to be pregnant again, to feel a kick, a movement, even a contraction. Anything other than what she was feeling... nothing.

"J," she said as Joshua stood behind her.

"Yea, babe," he said kissing her neck and shoulders.

"I take you for granted and I want you to know I'm sorry," she said turning to face him.

"I do it too," he said kissing her on the lips.

Kieran kissed him back. He pulled her closer to him, and they stood holding each other. Each lost in their own thoughts. Kieran's heart ached for him. She had hurt him in the worst way possible, and she didn't know how she was going to live with seeing it on his face every day. Staying with him meant Sienna would always be with her. It wasn't the right reason to stay, but Joshua would be the constant reminder of what she had done; it was a punishment she deserved.

Kieran loved Joshua, that wasn't the problem. The problem was that something was missing when they got back together; it wasn't the same as it had been when they were younger, and she had been delusional to think it would be, especially since he broke her heart. She hadn't expected their reunion to last, the pregnancy changed everything. Regardless of what she felt about their relationship before Sienna, now she felt tied and bound to him forever. Maybe in time he'd forgive her. Maybe she could forgive herself if she sacrificed her happiness for his. She should do something for someone else for a change.

"Do you still have the engagement ring?" she asked then felt a strange feeling in the pit of her stomach. She couldn't tell what it was, nerves, excitement, anxiety, dread. She settled for all four. Her heart pounded loud in her ears.

He looked at her "Yea, why?" he asked with a slight smile.

Kieran's stomach twisted. She ignored it and took a deep breath. "If you were to ask me to marry you again, I just want you to know I'd say yes. I'd like a long engagement; and the smoking has to stop, but I'd say yes. I want us to work," she told him in one breath.

"Who said I was ever going to ask you again? You turned me down twice," he teased.

"I'm just saying," she said.

"So now you want to be my wife?"

"We've already shared so much, why shouldn't I be your wife? I've wanted to marry you since I was fourteen. I want us to be happy J. I want you to be happy; it just depends on whether you accept my conditions."

"I promise you, I won't mess up again," he said with sincerity.

"I hope that's true, we have so many issues to deal with, and it's going to be hard. I need for us to lay all our stuff on the table and deal with it. You can't be running off to get your next fix."

He grimaced at her words. "I'm not a crack head Kieran; it's just a bit of weed."

"This isn't just about the weed J. I need to know that you can deal with our problems without the weed. All it does is add to the fire. If we don't deal with our issues, we are not going to make it, and we can't fall apart now, otherwise we weren't that strong in the beginning and she was what was keeping us together."

Joshua kissed her forehead, "Kieran I promised you I would fix things. Do you really think Sienna was keeping us together?" he asked hurt.

"No." she lied, "That's what it will be like if we can't prove to ourselves otherwise."

"There's nothing to prove. I loved you before Sienna and I will love you after her."

"Sometimes love isn't enough." Kieran was irritated as to why it was so black and white for him, nothing was ever that straightforward.

"It is for me," he replied.

Kieran sighed. They'd hurt each other so much; there was always something to throw in each other's faces. She wished they hadn't made a mess of everything, they could've been so good together, and he could've been her soul mate. She refused to think of the other contender.

Lily barked at their feet reminding them she was still waiting. "I'll take her, you should be taking it easy," Joshua said as he let her go.

It entered Kieran's mind that he suggested taking her so he could smoke. He hardly ever walked her. She bit her lip. If they were going to be together she had to trust him. She couldn't be second guessing him every time he wasn't around her.

After Joshua left, Kieran headed to the bathroom while picturing Sienna's face in her mind. She did it every night before crying herself to sleep. She didn't want to forget her baby; she knew the more time went on; it was going to be harder to remember what she looked like from memory. There were pictures; of course, it wasn't the same.

Joshua returned to the bedroom when he heard Kieran close the bathroom door. He tiptoed over to the wardrobe and pulled out a little plastic parcel from his sports bag. Kieran's theory about his smoking was wrong; smoking didn't add to his issues at all, it freed him from them, and it freed him from the less than loving feelings he felt towards her.

Kieran's eyes flew open the following morning. She had the best night's sleep since Sienna died, and she knew it was because the worst was over. She rolled over and watched Joshua as he slept. She felt hopeful, positive. She wasn't sure if it was because she had buried her child the day before and the weight had been lifted, or if the ten hours sleep cleared her head.

The man that lay next to her had been her first love. Their relationship wasn't bad before the pregnancy and even during the pregnancy. Kieran was confident that once things got back to normal, so would they. Maybe she just had to look at it from Joshua's perspective. She knew from past experiences that if you expected something bad to happen, it usually did. What else did she expect if she thought that way?

Kieran felt an uncontrollable amount of affection for him at that moment and rubbed her nose against his.

He opened his eyes and smiled, "Morning."

"Why didn't you wake me when you got back last night?"

"I didn't want to disturb you," he said pulling her closer.

She wriggled away from him and got out of the bed.

"Where are you going?"

"To brush my teeth," she called over her shoulder.

"Kieran you don't have morning breath," he said with a yawn.

"Everyone has morning breath," she said closing the bathroom door.

After emptying her bladder, Kieran stood in front the mirror and started to brush her teeth. As she did, something caught her eye.

What the hell?

She looked down at her left hand and gasped when she saw the engagement ring on her finger, sparkling and bright, almost blinding her. A wave of nausea hit her, and she threw up in the sink. The ring blinked at her again. She moved her hand out of her vision.

Oh God I'm engaged.

She closed her eyes as the tears slid out and the truth sunk in; they were engaged. It felt wrong, forced, and unnatural and she couldn't figure out why. The feeling in the pit of her stomach was back and she realised it hadn't been excitement at all. It was fear and doubt and knowing that she did not want to spend the rest of her life with Joshua.

She let the water run to drown out her sniffles while she composed herself. She looked at the ring again. It felt heavy, like her heart. This was not the happy occasion it should have been. Kieran hadn't imagined it would feel so wrong. If she had, she never would have brought it up with him. A lot of her feelings she had ignored in the past; she could not ignore this, even if they made it to their wedding day she would not make it to the altar. But she couldn't change her mind; she had given him permission to do it.

What have I done? How did I get here?

Kieran quietened her mind and thought of a scenario. She'd wait until he was stronger and then break his heart. She couldn't hurt him right then. It was too soon after losing Sienna. Leaving would kill him, she couldn't do that. She was such a coward when it came to the truth. She sighed and smiled into the mirror. It didn't reach her eyes. Was she capable of keeping up the pretence? The door knocked and Kieran jumped. She turned the tap off and dried her face.

"Ki, are you okay?"

"Yea," she called back. Her voice sounded strange.

No, I'm not okay at all.

"You've been in there a while," he reminded her.

Kieran was silent. She closed her eyes, took a deep breath and smiled a smile she hoped looked genuine. She opened the door, put her arms around Joshua's neck and kissed him. "Yes," she whispered. It was the best she could do.

"I didn't ask you anything."

She held her hand up showing him the ring. He grinned. "Oh that," he said casually.

He was so happy; Kieran could see it all over his face. As if she hadn't tortured him enough, she was torturing him with the belief she wanted to marry him. She had believed it for a moment, but seeing the ring on her hand filled her with such dismay, and that should not be the reaction of someone who was excited to be engaged.

"I meant what I said though; I will only do this if you quit smoking."

"Okay."

Their exchange was unromantic, clinical; there was no passion, no romance. Love, yes, but it was consumed in guilt, anger, dishonesty, and betrayal.

"I don't think we should tell people just yet," she said avoiding his eyes.

"Why not?" he asked.

"It's too soon."

"Kieran, do you really want to marry me?" he asked looking into her eyes.

This was her way out. She should just tell him the truth before it got out of hand. She looked at him and then she saw it; a flash of Sienna, his nose, his mouth and chin they were all her. Kieran would lose that if she walked away from him. She needed to keep that with her, every day. She couldn't walk away.

"Of course, I want to marry you," she heard herself saying. The need to be close to her daughter overtook every logical part of her brain.

"So why don't you want people to know?"

"They won't understand, they will tell us we need to wait. It'll only be for a few months and when things are back to normal we will tell everyone. I promise." She was a better actress than she thought; he bought every word of it which made her feel even worse.

He hugged her tightly.

Kieran hadn't imagined this was how her engagement would be. Wasn't love and marriage unconditional? Accepting someone's flaws regardless; maybe it depended on what you were willing to accept. If she loved him unconditionally, his smoking wouldn't be such a big deal. She'd care enough to make him get help. She was not doing enough to help him. If he was drug-free, he'd realise they couldn't be together, and she'd lose him and Sienna. That could not happen. She couldn't lose her twice. He was never going to stop smoking, she knew that, and that was her get out of jail card. She could be with him but they would never get married.

"I'm so happy you're here Kieran. I will do anything to keep you. I really do love you," he told her.

"I love you too," she breathed as she started to cry.

28 CHAPTER TWENTY-EIGHT

Almost a month later, Kieran and Joshua were still trying to be there for each other. It made dealing with their grief a little easier, however the blame for what they were going through rested heavily on Kieran's shoulders, and it developed into more of a co-dependent non-physical relationship. The mental strain was taking its toll, but they clung to each other as they hung on to the past.

Joshua continued to smoke and Kieran pretended not to notice. At times he was approachable, while at other times he would explode. Kieran wasn't sure if his state was dependent on how much he smoked, or whether his system was becoming immune to the weed. He developed two personas and Kieran fell in with his moods and she too developed an alter ego.

He appeared approachable one evening when he returned home while she and Lily curled up watching TV.

"Hey," she said.

"Hey."

Kieran watched as he undressed, got into the bed and pulled her towards him. She raised her eyebrows. Their physical relationship had become redundant since Sienna died. One of them always pulled away when faced with the actual sexual act. It was as if they were scared to cross that line, because sex made babies and neither of them were ready for that. She lay still as Joshua kissed the back of her neck. Her heart accelerated. She was not sure how to respond and she asked the dumbest question when his hand moved up her night shirt.

"J, what are you doing?"

"Don't you want to?"

Kieran sighed. "Yes."

"But?" Joshua pressed.

Kieran turned to face him. "Things haven't been great between us, I'm surprised you want to," she said studying his face.

For a fleeting second he looked sad. "Kieran, I always want to. I'm trying here."

"I know. I'm curious to know what is different now."

"Forget it," he said rolling away.

Kieran counted to five then kissed his shoulder. "J, don't be silly."

"I'm not."

"Well, then look at me and let's talk about this."

He was silent for a few seconds then said, "I love you," he brushed her face with the back of his hand.

It was the first time he said those words in a long time. She kissed him, "I love you too." She wished they could go back to the way it was.

Joshua rolled on top of her. A part of her wanted it to be just about them, even if only for a little while. The other part of her didn't want him anywhere near her. Joshua had been two different people for so long; it was hard for Kieran not to do the same. There was always conflict between which Kieran she would allow herself to be depending on his mood.

She told the hostile Kieran to shut up, and allowed her arms to wrap around his neck. She crushed him closer to her, immersing herself in him so she didn't have time to think, or change her mind. She allowed the Joshua she knew and loved to comfort her. It seemed like he wanted the same thing. Their love making wouldn't fix their issues; for the moment however, Kieran felt close to him. Joshua opened up to her even if it was brief. It gave her hope that with more time they would get back to how they used to be.

The following day, Kieran had her third appointment at the hospital since the funeral. The visits brought back memories she was working hard to forget and she didn't feel up to it.

She looked across at Joshua who lay staring up at the ceiling.

"Are you okay?"

He looked at her and smiled. Kieran was touched. It was a genuine smile. "I'm good, you?" he said leaning over. She snuggled closer to him and he put his arm around her. It felt reassuring.

"I'm fine," she said and she meant it.

"No regrets?" he asked.

Kieran kissed his chest, "None."

"Good, I've missed you and I've missed us. I think last night was good for us, it made me remember how we were. I want us to get back to that," he said.

Kieran tried not to look shocked by what he said. It had been ages since they were on the same page. "Me too."

Joshua lifted her face and kissed her lips. Kieran felt a familiar sensation stir within her as she responded.

"What time is your hospital appointment?" he asked through the kisses.

"Twelve," Kieran mumbled. She wanted to forget about the hospital.

"Plenty of time," Joshua whispered as he pulled her on top of him.

"For what?" she asked with an innocent smile.

He stroked the hair away from her face. "I'm sorry for the way I've treated you and I will make it up to you. I promise."

"I deserved it," she said with a shrug and avoided his gaze.

"Don't say that Kieran. I'm meant to be here for you and make it easier and I haven't. I've been selfish and shitty and I'm sorry," he said with sincerity.

Kieran kissed his hand. She didn't know what to say; she stayed silent.

"So, ready for round two?" he asked with a grin.

Kieran smiled and nodded. It almost felt like they were back to how they used to be, back to how they should be.

After, as they got dressed, Joshua asked, "Hey want to go shopping later?"

"Sure," she mumbled.

"You okay?"

"I don't want to go to the hospital," she said as she tried to hold back the tears and sat on the bed.

He sat next to her and took her hand. "We don't have to if you can't face it today."

"I have to."

"I'm sure they'll understand." he said hugging her.

"I want to get it over and done with though."

"Then let's get it over and done with. I'll be there, don't worry," he said, "It'll be alright."

Later that day after they had been to the hospital and were sat having lunch, Joshua suddenly asked "When are we going to tell everyone we're officially engaged?"

Never! Kieran heard the reply in her head, but ignored it.

"I haven't really thought about it." she lied. She should've known he'd ask sooner rather than later.

"How about we tell them at your birthday dinner?"

"Birthday dinner?" Kieran wasn't particularly in the mood to celebrate anything, let alone her birthday.

"The one you're having tomorrow," he told her, a smile played on his lips.

"I'm not having a party," she said crossing her arms over her chest.

"It's not a birthday party. You would have had one if things were different, and it doesn't make you a bad person if you celebrate your birthday."

"Yea but—"

"No buts, I've planned a dinner for you, whether you like it or not," he said.

"What will people think?"

"I don't care what people think. I'm telling you it's okay."

"I don't know about this."

"Liar," he said and gave her a playful nudge.

Kieran didn't want people to think she was heartless. "Okay, I hope it's just our families and close friends."

He nodded.

They strolled around Nike Town when Kieran spotted a group of people surrounding her favourite footballer. She had helped arrange the event and had completely forgotten it was happening. Work had not been on her list of priorities of late. She had been working from home mainly a few hours a week. She hadn't been able to face the office, she didn't want to see the looks of pity on people's faces. She was tired of having everyone's pity, she just wanted things to go back to normal. She made her way towards the crowd of people, French fancy looked up and waved for her to go over. Kieran saw him lean over and whisper into the security guard's ear.

Kieran took Joshua's hand and walked towards him. The security guard let her through and French fancy kissed her on the cheek and shook Joshua's hand.

"Great turn out," he said as he signed an Arsenal shirt handed to him by a man in an Arsenal cap. Kieran smiled. She loved that even though he had left the club, the fans still showed him love.

"I know, I did tell you it would be a good idea," Kieran said looking around at the group of one hundred or so people who won a competition to sit in on a Q and A session with the star and get their memorabilia signed.

"Oui, merci beaucoup," he replied.

"Je vous en prie," Kieran said, surprised that she remembered what he taught her on his visits to the office.
He grinned, clearly impressed.

Kieran was further surprised when he suggested they go for coffee. "I won't keep you waiting long?" he said, dazzling her with his smile. Kieran grinned back stupidly at him before looking at Joshua.

"Sure," he said without hesitating.
Kieran laughed.
"Meet me back here in half an hour, oui?"
They agreed and Kieran quickly googled places in the area they could have a quiet drink. They took the short taxi ride to 'The Sports Café.'

Once seated and out of view from people calling his name, or asking for his autograph, they relaxed.

"I'm sorry to hear about Sienna," he said in a quiet voice.

Kieran looked away from him as tears filled her eyes.

"Thanks for the flowers, we appreciated them," Joshua said squeezing Kieran's hand.

"Janet told me," he explained.

Kieran nodded. If she spoke she would cry.

"I saw the pictures of the wedding. Very nice," Joshua said as he sipped his drink.

Kieran was thankful he had changed the subject. She remembered browsing through 'Hello' magazine. An entire section was dedicated to his wedding. "They were beautiful. I'm sorry we couldn't make it," she told him. The wedding had been a week after the funeral.

"Don't be silly," he said dismissing her apology.

"How is married life?" Kieran asked sipping her macchiato. She'd heard whispers that he had been spotted looking at houses in New York and wondered which avenue of his life would be taking him there.

She smiled shyly when she noticed he was staring at her. "What?" she blushed.

"I see you're engaged," he observed pointing to the ring.

"Oh yea, it's been about a month now," Kieran said twisting the ring on her finger. "We're having a long engagement," she told him before she could stop herself. "No-one knows so please don't say anything to Janet,"

"Your secret is safe with me," French fancy told her.

Kieran smiled, the relief clear on her face. She could feel Joshua's questioning gaze on her but she pretended not to notice.

29 CHAPTER TWENTY-NINE

Kieran spent a few hours with Chantelle, Christina and Amelia on her birthday. She wanted girl time, though they would be joining in the birthday celebrations at The Mango Rooms in the evening.

Everyone, including her friends had given her space to grieve since the funeral. She enjoyed catching up on what was going on in their lives. It gave her less time to think about her problems.

She was dressed by the time Joshua returned home. Kieran knew he was stoned as soon as he walked through the door. Anger surfaced, but she asked him in a calm tone. "Where have you been?"

"With my brother,"

"Did you forget we are meant to be at the restaurant for eight?"

"No, I didn't. I'm ready, let's go," he said dangling his car keys.

Kieran held out her hand. He gave her a blank look. "We are taking a taxi," She told him. She was surprised when he gave her the keys without a fuss.

Kieran apologised for their late arrival when they entered the restaurant. Joshua sauntered in behind her and waved at everyone.

"It's your birthday you are allowed to be late," Chantelle said. Her eyes flickered towards Joshua and back at Kieran who shook her head as discreetly as she could.

She brightened when she noticed presents in the middle of the table. "For me?" she teased "Wow! And champagne?" She went around the table and kissed everyone hello before sitting down.

Joshua sat down noisily rattling the glasses with his movement. He looked tired all of a sudden. The shadows under his eyes were testimony to his lack of sleep.

"J, you need to have an early night bro," Jarrell told him.

"I will go to sleep when I like," Joshua snapped at his brother.

Kieran saw her parents exchange glances. The birthday dinner may not have been such a good idea. She sipped some champagne and picked up a menu, hoping everyone followed suit. As long as he wasn't antagonised, he would be quiet.

At intervals, Joshua would leave the table and return minutes later smelling of weed. He didn't seem concerned about keeping up the pretence. Kieran was perturbed. The previous day had been good. They had turned a corner, hadn't they? Maybe it hurt him to pretend he could be with her after everything she'd done.

While they were waiting for desert, the lights dimmed and a cheesy version of 'Happy Birthday' played through the restaurant stereo system. Kieran looked around horrified hoping it wasn't for her. Her friends and family were all laughing at her expression, all except Joshua. A waiter appeared carrying a cake lit with candles. Kieran hid her face behind the drinks menu, as other guests in the restaurant turned to watch. Some sang along, but it was hard to hear over the noise her family and friends were making as they sung. Kieran was mortified. Laughing she blew out the candles and the lights returned to normal.

"Speech!" Janet cheered tapping her glass with a knife.

Her friends joined in, drawing even more attention to their table.

Kieran glared at them as their chants grew louder. "Okay, okay," she said to silence them, before they were removed from the restaurant. She stood up and held up her glass. The chanting stopped. "Thank you all for being here. It's been a hard month and if it wasn't for each of you, I would be at home drowning my sorrows, so thank you for a special birthday." She turned to Joshua. "Thank you J."

He stood up without looking at her.

Kieran jumped when his phone fell off his lap with a loud

clatter. He didn't seem to notice. Jarrell picked it up and placed it on the table while he gave his brother an anxious look.

"I have something to say," Joshua announced. Kieran looked at him and then at Jarrell who looked as horrified as she did. He was in no state to give a speech.

"J, do you think you should?" Jarrell asked him.

"Yes, shut up and let me talk!" Joshua snapped.

Kieran's heart pounded as she sat down. *Shit, shit, shit!*

"Thank you all for coming. I wanted Kieran to have a special birthday. I also want you all to know that I love her and always will. That is why I asked her to marry me. She said yes, so not only is this a birthday dinner, we are celebrating our engagement too." He raised his glass looking proud of himself.

Kieran was again mortified. She heard the silence. Why wasn't anyone talking? She could see in everyone's eyes that it wasn't the best time for them to be thinking about marriage. It was no secret that she and Joshua were not getting along. She looked at him standing with his glass raised; a puzzled look crossed his face.

"Sit down please, J," Kieran told him pulling his arm.

He yanked it away.

She felt everyone shift in their seats.

"So, have you set a date yet?" Donna asked looking from her son to Kieran in an attempt to ease the tension.

"We are having a long engagement," Kieran told her as she played with the menu. Why did he open his mouth? She didn't want to have this conversation.

"Oh, yes, a long engagement is one of her conditions," Joshua sneered.

"You know why," Kieran told him. "Will you sit down please?" she asked again.

He looked down at her hands. "You're not even wearing your ring!" he shouted.

Ten pairs of eyes flew to Kieran's hand.

"I didn't wear it because we agreed not to announce it yet," she explained

"You agreed. I didn't."

"So you went against my wishes?"

"Have you never gone against mine?" he challenged.

Kieran was silent.

"Marriage is a big step J. It's probably for the best if you take it slow. It's too soon. I don't think you two are ready," his dad cut in.

"We had a baby. I think taking it slow is a bit late now," he snapped.

"J, will you please sit down?" Kieran pleaded with him again.

This time he did as he was told then turned to her. "Why? Embarrassing you, am I? That's a joke. How can I embarrass you? I'm not the slut," he said coldly.

Kieran heard gasps around the table. She looked across at Jack, her brother-in-law, who looked uncomfortable in the middle of the friction; it was as if he was caught up in a car crash and couldn't leave the scene.

Her dad reached across her and grabbed Joshua by the collar of his shirt.

Kieran saw Joshua's family tense. "Dad, stop it!" she grabbed his arms and tried to prise them away from Joshua.

"He will not speak to you like that!" he snapped.

Kieran was conscious that if her dad threw a punch, Joshua's brother and dad would jump in. They would have to. She panicked and pulled a bit harder on her dad's arms. "Please Dad! Let him go!" she told him desperately.

He looked into her eyes and must have seen how scared she was. He conceded and sat down fuming.

Joshua slumped into his chair grinning. "Why are you all looking so disgusted with me? It's true."

"J, please don't do this," Kieran whispered tearfully.

"I'm not doing anything. You did it already. The real reason Kieran had that fucking test was because she wasn't sure who the father of the baby was, and now our daughter is dead. The doctor reckons he can't determine whether it was the amnio that caused the infection; we both know it was," he looked at Kieran with contempt and utter disgust.

"Is that true?" Denise asked stunned.

Kieran couldn't look at anyone. She nodded as the tears rolled down her face. How could he do this to her on her birthday? Did he hate her that much? She knew she deserved it; she couldn't even blame him. Why should he pretend to be over it?

Kieran felt a sob rising in her chest and forced it down. She wished she hadn't refused the counselling the hospital offered, because now it seemed like they needed help. How much more could she take?

Her sister was the first one to speak. "How could you not tell me?" she asked with a hurt expression.

Kieran looked at her and back down at her hands that rested in her lap. "How could I tell you?"

"We tell each other everything Kieran. I would've been there for you, you know that," Corey said, tears in her eyes. Jack put his arm around his wife. It was the first time he'd moved in minutes.

"I'm sorry. I didn't know what else to do. I didn't want everyone to be disappointed with me." She covered her face with her hands. The shame was too much to bear.

"Seems like you underestimated a lot of people, doesn't it?" Joshua said.

"You're really pushing your luck!" Corey snapped at him.

"It's okay," Kieran told her. She couldn't judge Joshua for his behaviour. She felt sorry for him. He wasn't the man she loved anymore. He was the man she had created.

"What's wrong Kieran?" he continued. She still didn't answer him. "Was the sex that good that you couldn't let him go?"

Chantelle opened her mouth to speak; Kieran's dad beat her to it. "Shut your face!" he roared.

Kieran winced.

Joshua gave him a smug smile, and for the first time Kieran felt a flash of hatred towards him then she felt guilty.

"Dad, leave it," she told her father. The situation was going from bad to worse. Kieran was conscious of the other guests staring and whispering. It had only been a few minutes since they had been singing to her.

It felt like hours ago to Kieran. Time was moving slowly to torment her.

"I'm just stating the facts. You can't hate me for it. I haven't done anything wrong. I was in the dark too!" Joshua explained looking at everyone. "What kind of person have you raised?" he asked her parents.

Kieran's friends gasped again.

Her mum and aunt exchanged looks. He had gone too far.

"Joshua, that's enough!" his mum told him in a stern tone. Kieran's dad stood up, his face a mask of fury, his hands balled into fists rigid at his side. He sucked his teeth before leaving the table.

Kieran knew if he hadn't left, he would've punched Joshua's lights out, and that would have led to a full scale brawl.

"It'll never be enough. She killed my daughter then as if she hasn't fucked me over enough, there are conditions I have to stick to before she'll marry me. You owe me!" he shouted while pointing at Kieran,

She looked at him shocked. "What?"

He expected her to marry him out of guilt? He did not love her. He had his own agenda. Chantelle was right. He was still manipulative.

"I love you Kieran, that's why I proposed. I thought after everything you would marry me. I would marry you now," he said starting to cry.

"Now is too soon. I need time. We need time. I said I would marry you," Kieran reminded him.

"With conditions. Why don't you admit that you don't want me? Your guilt is the only reason why we are together. We've grown apart Kieran. Our relationship is something we were holding onto for old time's sake; we are different people now. It will never be the way it was," he said holding his head in his hands.

Kieran knew she'd lost him. Her heart ached. Yes, it was guilt why she was still with him. She knew that, but for him to know, it must have been killing him. She was not ready to let him go though. That would mean letting go of Sienna. Kieran clung to that last bit of hope. "I want to try J. I love you and I want to marry you; just not like this. Not when you don't even know what you're doing. Marrying you like this is as good as me saying it's okay, and things are not okay," she explained as she took his hand. It was partly true, plus she wanted him to get better.

"I will get help Kieran I promise. Just don't leave me. Not now. I can't get through this without you," he sobbed.

She looked at him helplessly. She learned that night what he really thought of her. Kieran didn't blame him; she could never forgive him for exposing her secret like that though.

Regardless, he needed her and she needed him. As long as she felt responsible for what happened, she would stay in the relationship and be punished. That's what she deserved for killing her baby. It was her personal prison sentence and she would do her time.

30 CHAPTER THIRTY

Kieran felt slightly irritated when Janet's secretary told her she wanted to see her in the conference room. She was in the middle of a project and hated being interrupted when she was on a roll. She was surprised to see the manager of the New York office there also. After the pleasantries, Janet told her that the US office was rapidly expanding and though she employed the services of a contract publicist, she preferred a full-time in-house publicist dedicated to the company and their brand. She wanted to know whether Kieran would reconsider relocating there for a year.

Rome's words infiltrated her head, "Next time you get an opportunity like that, take it, no matter what."

Kieran heard herself say, "I'd love to," before she had even thought about it. Her aunt had gone to see her in her office after the meeting and had a heart-to-heart about her relationship with Joshua. She was glad Kieran had taken the offer, after witnessing the dinner fiasco first hand, she felt a break would be better for the both of them. Kieran agreed.

She drove home in a daze. She'd been singing Frank Sinatra's 'New York New York' in her head since she accepted the position. Kieran wanted to stop the car and shout it out to the world and do a little dance, too. She wouldn't even care if people thought she was crazy. Instead of testing her theory, she wondered how Joshua would take the news. He'd probably jump for joy given the way things were between them.

The previous two months had been nothing short of a

nightmare. There was no communication, no affection and most nights Joshua didn't sleep in their bed. He was too stoned to move from the sofa.

He refused to get help to stop smoking and chose to go cold turkey instead. For two days after her birthday fiasco he stuck to his word and didn't smoke. Unfortunately he put her through hell, screaming, crying and throwing things. On the third day, his rages towards her became too much for him; he conceded defeat and went back to smoking. It helped to control his emotions, control his hatred towards her.

It killed Kieran to look into his eyes and see that while he loved her, a part of him hated her; and that part grew stronger each day. How could he love and trust someone who lied to him, betrayed him and who he held responsible for the death of his child? He was better off without her.

Kieran knew he was counting on his habit pushing him out of her life. She'd refused to give in. Her need dominated her logic, until now. Would her leaving end things? Would he want them to try long distance? Would he think the space would do their relationship any good? Would he tell her she couldn't go? She wasn't sure whether those questions disturbed her or not. It was like she had come full circle.

Rome was right when he told her that if she ever got the opportunity again to do something she dreamed of; she should take it no matter what. She owed it to herself. She had to do it, otherwise she would always be wondering what if?

Kieran intended to start afresh, a nice clean break. She could cope on her own. She had to accept her daughter was gone. She and Joshua created her, so she would always be a part of them in spirit and in their hearts. Kieran had started to feel alive again, and she realised that she no longer needed to tie herself to Joshua. She was freeing herself. Her punishment was over. Everyone had suffered enough.

Losing a child made her grow up some; she learned a lot about herself, Kieran was stronger than she thought she was for one. She had also realised that while she was a good person, she couldn't deny she was selfish. Her decisions had hurt a lot of people. She hadn't thought about how they would affect everyone in her life, only how they would affect her. She paid for her selfish needs. The best thing was to remove herself from the situation. It was the only way she would be able to get to know and fix the bad parts of herself without anyone else's influence. Maybe then she could think about being in a relationship, when she could be sure that she wouldn't destroy anyone else's life.

Kieran sighed as she stopped at the traffic lights. A fire engine pulled up next to her. A couple of fire fighters looked at her and waved. Kieran chuckled and waved back. Seeing the fire engine wasn't the first sign she had from her past. She had been thinking about Rome ever since she found out about the job offer and had come close to dialling his number a few times, but stopped herself at the last minute.

She picked up her phone, scrolled to his number and almost jumped out of her skin when she heard a loud car horn. The lights had turned green. She chucked the phone on the passenger seat and pulled away. She took it as a sign not to call him. Maybe she just had to let him go. Mentally, she was in a healthier, stronger place than when she last saw him. She knew she had been unfair to blame him. She was hurting, and thought pushing him away would be the only way to save her relationship with Joshua. How wrong she had been. Her behaviour over Rome had been irrational and she would never forgive herself for being so stupid.

On reflection, she couldn't believe the way she behaved. There were worse things than a guy hiding something, or letting you down. Nothing she had been through could ever be as bad as having to bury her child.

She wondered what he was up to. It would be nice to hear his voice. Kieran still missed him. She still had feelings for him. She couldn't help but wonder what things would be like if they were together.

"Enough. Rome is the past, New York is my future," she dismissed him and brought her thoughts to the present. She began humming Frank Sinatra's song again as she thought how much she had to plan. First of all she needed somewhere to live. She wondered how much would it cost to rent a brownstone, she absolutely loved those houses. They were so... New York.

She parked behind Joshua's car and sat for a moment. She was in no rush to have the conversation with him. Her excitement dissipated and she bit her lower lip. This was going to crush him.

She heard hushed voices coming from the bathroom after she entered the flat and felt a sense of panic. Placing her bag down, she walked towards the door listening. The sound of running water and muffled voices was clear.

Kieran knocked on the door and asked, "What's going on?"

The voices stopped.

Jarrell opened the door a fraction. His face was pale and held a serious expression. Kieran could smell the weed as it wafted out of the door. "What's up?" he asked casually, contradicting the expression on his face.

"What's going on?" she asked again pushing the door. Jarrell held it in place. "Don't panic," he told her.

Her heart started to pound. "What's happened?" she pushed the door again. It didn't move, Jarrell held it in place.

Kieran wondered what he had done that he didn't want her to know.

"She's going to find out eventually. Maybe she'll talk some sense into you. You need to go to hospital," Jarrell said turning to face his brother.

Seeing his distraction, Kieran pushed the door hard. She stumbled forward and Jarrell stumbled backward. Her mouth fell open when she saw blood in the bath, on the floor and in the sink. It trailed out of the bathroom into the living room. Kieran hadn't even noticed when she walked in. There were bloodied towels and balled up tissues strewn on the floor and in the sink. Joshua sat on the closed toilet seat holding a blue towel to his leg that had turned purple from the blood.

"What the fuck happened?" She screamed suddenly terrified.

"We got jumped," Jarrell answered.

"What do you mean you got jumped? Where the hell were you?" she rushed over to Joshua. Blood covered the towel. It was obvious he couldn't walk. She grabbed his face and forced him to look at her. The shadows under his eyes were darker than normal.

He pushed her away. "It doesn't matter. I am fine. It will stop bleeding soon."

"Your leg has been bleeding for half an hour; you need stitches." Jarrell shouted in frustration.

Kieran looked at Jarrell. His clothes were torn in places and his lips swollen. He had a black and blue bruise under his eye and a cut on the right side of his head was prominent. Kieran's heart rose to her throat and she began to cry.

"What the hell happened?" she couldn't breathe properly and felt like she was going to faint. She leaned against the wall for support and took a few deep breaths.

"We went to pick up," Jarrell confessed his eyes looking away from hers.

There was silence for a few moments.

"And then what happened?"

"We were talking to the guys we get it from. They're friends of ours and then all of a sudden these other dickheads appeared, jumped us, and we couldn't do anything but defend ourselves. Luckily, there were more of us than them. Joshua got it the worst," Jarrell explained, rubbing his head as if he couldn't believe it.

"You are going to the hospital," she told Joshua. He looked at her shocked. No doubt he expected her to scream and shout at him. What was the point? There was nothing to say, it was inevitable that something bad would happen. The drug trade was volatile. He was in the wrong place at the wrong time and sometimes that's all it took.

"I'm not. They have to report knife wounds. I will have to tell the police what happened."

Kieran clutched her stomach as the realisation of his attack sunk in. He'd been stabbed, he could've died.

"You need stitches before you bleed to death," she pleaded.

She couldn't work out her tone. Kieran put it down to a mixture of everything, relief, fear, hope, anxiety, sadness. Here it was: the reason they must end their relationship. He wouldn't stop smoking if she stayed. The next time he went to get drugs, it could kill him. Kieran could not, and would not, live with that on her conscience.

"Jarrell, take your brother to the hospital," she said turning to face him.

"I'm not going," Joshua insisted.

Kieran looked at him then noticed an ashtray by his foot. He'd prefer to sit and smoke rather than go to the hospital. She realised that was another reason why he didn't want to go. The medics would ask him if he'd taken any drugs.

"You're going," Jarrell ignored him, pulled him up by his

waist and put one arm around his shoulder to support his weight. Joshua winced and allowed his brother to carry him out of the flat. He didn't say a word; neither did Kieran.

Kieran looked down at the bloodied floor and sighed; it was another mess she had to clean up.

An hour later, she finished cleaning then remembered her plans for dinner with her friends. She had called Christina to tell her the news and she told her under no circumstances was Kieran allowed to go then agreed at least they could holiday in New York, so she had her permission to leave. Kieran had laughed. She knew her oldest friend was happy for her, and knew, that Chantelle and Amelia would be, too. Kieran wished she could take them with her. She didn't know how she was going to survive without her friends.

Chantelle made the calls. Christina and Amelia agreed that a dinner celebration was in order and now Kieran had to cancel. She picked up her phone and called her friend.

"Chan, we have to take a rain check on dinner,"

"Why? Did he go mad?" Chantelle asked.

"He got stabbed."

Chantelle's brief silence told Kieran she was processing what she just heard. "What?"

Kieran sighed and reiterated the scenario. Her eyes caught sight of Joshua's cigarettes on the kitchen counter. She took one out of the packet, turned the cooker on, lit it and took a drag. She hadn't smoked since she found out she was pregnant. Kieran hadn't even craved one, until then.

"Why are you so calm? Is he okay?"

"I don't know. Maybe I'm in shock. I freaked out at first. I don't think I'm that surprised. I was expecting something to happen eventually."

"You can't be around that shit. What happens if they follow him home next time?" Chantelle asked her.

Kieran exhaled; she didn't want to think about that. "He's at the hospital; Jarrell had to drag him there."

"Are you still going to New York?"

"More than ever. I can't do this anymore and neither can he."

"I don't get why he has to be that way."

"I killed his daughter Chan."

"Stop saying that. No one knows if it was from the amnio. He knows you loved her and he knows you are hurting just as much as he is, so he needs to get over it. You lied. Bad things happened, that's life," she said tersely.

"I don't blame him for hating me. I would be the same."

"You wouldn't hurt him like this."

"I already have," Kieran muttered.

Chantelle was silent. Kieran knew she couldn't think of comeback argument.

"Dinner tomorrow, no excuses," Chantelle told her.

"Definitely. I'm telling him tonight."

"Good luck."

"Thanks, I need it. "

At two in the morning Kieran heard Jarrell and Joshua come through the front door. She got out of bed and met them in the front room Joshua was on crutches. One leg of his jeans was cut off and Kieran saw a large square bandage that covered the wound on his thigh. With his leg cleaned up, it didn't look so horrific.

Joshua avoided her eyes as Jarrell helped him to sit down and then sat next to him.

Kieran perched on the arm of the sofa. "What did they say?"

"I got twelve stitches. The police came, we told them we were randomly jumped, end of," Joshua snapped at her.

Jarrell looked at Kieran. "I think you two should talk," he told them.

"We both know it's over, there's nothing left to say," Joshua said still not looking at her.

"Really J? You'd just walk away now and not even talk about it first?" she asked him.

He took in the expression on her face and softened. "No," he said quietly.

"I'll be round in the morning," Jarrell announced as he stood up. They touched fists.

Kieran followed him to the front door. "I'm going to end it with him Jarrell," she said. The words sounded as if she was asking permission.

"I think you should. He's fucked up," Jarrell said anger filling his voice.

Kieran stared at him. "I've always liked you Kieran, but what you've done to my brother is unforgiveable. I understand why you did it, you were scared of losing him and you underestimated how much he loved you. No matter what, he would have stuck by you and the fact that you doubted him enough to lie and betray him, proves that you don't know him."

"I know, I know it's my fault and I know I'm making it worse, so I'm ending it and I'm moving to New York," she looked at him to see his reaction.

He looked surprised then nodded. "Space would do you two good. A lot has happened and there's a lot you need to get over including each other."

"Will he be okay? Breaking up is one thing, leaving the country is a different story."

"Don't flatter yourself Kieran. He knows he's better off without you. He'll be happy as long as you're happy. He would do anything for you, even if he hated himself for it," Jarrell said.

Kieran looked into Jarrell's eyes. He'd figured out more than she thought. No wonder he'd been strange with her as of late. She'd messed everything up.

"I'm sorry,"

"Don't feel bad, you can't ruin his life any more than you already have, unless you stay with him. He knows it too, he's just not brave enough to tell you," he said snidely.

Tears welled up in Kieran's eyes. He'd obviously been holding back what he really felt for his brother's sake; now he knew that she was leaving and ending the relationship, he had no reason to remain pleasant with her.

"I didn't mean to hurt him Jarrell. You don't understand why I doubted him."

"He told me about the abortion." Jarrell said coldly, "Poor you. Unlike you Kieran, people grow up. J was an idiot when he cheated on you. He knew that. When you came back into his life, he said that he wasn't going to mess up this time and that no matter what; as long as you were honest with each other you could face anything. He was ready to settle down. You were the one for him and you shit on him this time. Maybe this is his karma for what he did to you all those years ago. It makes me wonder if Sienna dying wasn't your karma for what you did to J. Maybe you didn't deserve to have that baby just like you don't deserve my brother," he spat.

Kieran slapped him. Whether she was responsible or not, he was not allowed to speak to her that way.

"You deserved that Jarrell," Joshua said from behind them.

Kieran turned. She wondered how much he had heard.

"She deserves to hear what I think," Jarrell said calmly.

"No, she does not, this is between me and Kieran and I won't have you speaking to her like that about Sienna. She was our daughter and we didn't deserve to lose her," Joshua looked at his brother and Kieran saw a moment of understanding pass between them and Jarrell backed down.

"I'm sorry Kieran," he mumbled.

He wasn't but she nodded. Jarrell turned, walked to his car, climbed in and drove off.

Joshua turned and limped back into the house and to their bedroom and lay down.

Kieran followed and lay next to him. "Thank you for sticking up for me," she said.

Joshua turned his head and looked at her, "Don't be stupid Kieran; he had no right to say that to you."

"He was right though. I didn't deserve her, not when I disregarded her life by having the test in the first place. I knew the risks," she said looking away from him.

"I know why you had to do it so I don't completely blame you for it, but part of me does," he admitted.

"I know that and I know that's why you've been smoking," she told him.

He took her hand. "I still love you Kieran."

"I love you too, but this can't go on – we can't go on."

"I know. I tried. I really did try. I want you to know that," he said fighting back the tears.

"I do. I don't blame you for hating me. I blame you for not walking away before it got to this. I know why you didn't and I know why I didn't. We didn't want to hurt each other, for Sienna; but we are hurting each other the longer we pretend this is working," she said sitting up.

He sat up, too. She moved closer to him. "I tried to end it so many times; it was just so hard getting the words out. I didn't want to see the look on your face when I told you I couldn't be with you anymore," he said as he put his arm around her.

She rested her head on his shoulder. "I'm so sorry for lying to you. You have to understand that I never wanted to lie to you. I was scared that you would leave and I buried my head in the sand for ages hoping it would go away, hoping something else would prove it was your baby. I wasn't even as excited as I should have been, because it was always in the back of my mind. I was tempted to wait until the baby was born. I knew it would be ten times worse, so I had the test. Now I wish I had waited. I would've taken anything you threw at me gladly if it meant Sienna was still here," Kieran said starting to cry.

Joshua held her closer to him, "That's the thing that gets me. After she turned out to be mine it still went wrong. As much as it hurts me, it makes me question whether we are meant to be together. I don't see why this would happen to us if we were. Don't cry Ki, it will be okay,"

"It won't. I've ruined your life," she sobbed.

"No, you haven't. You gave me a daughter and I won't ever forget that."

Kieran was silent. Why was he now being honest with her? Why hadn't they had that conversation a month ago? Maybe his accident made him realise enough was enough. "Will you ever forgive me though? I can't forgive myself," she said drying her eyes and looking at him.

"Kieran, of course I forgive you. That's why I'm still here trying. Everyone is allowed to make mistakes. The problem is, I can't forget the consequences of that mistake and that's why we can't be together. I have punished you enough and if we don't end this now, I will punish you forever and you will take it out of guilt. I can't do that to you any longer," he said kissing her forehead.

Rome flashed through her mind.

Kieran froze. His theory was familiar to her When it came down to it, she and Joshua were in the same boat; punishing the person they wanted to be with the most. They just wanted to be with different people – not that Joshua knew that.

This was a sign; she had to get out the country. She couldn't think about the men in her life anymore. She had to think about herself, and this time it was for a good reason.

"J, I'm leaving," she announced.

"Leaving where?"

"The country. I got a job offer in New York." She studied her nails not wanting to see whatever expression was on his face, because it would haunt her forever.

"Kieran, that's great."

He sounded genuinely pleased and she looked up to confirm what she heard in his tone.

"Really?"

"Yes, really. You deserve good things. You are not a bad person Kieran everyone knows that. You just got caught up in trying not to hurt people, Darren, me, yourself. I think it would do you good to live by yourself for a while and figure out what it is you want."

"I don't know what I want," she admitted.

"But you will find out in New York. It'll be great for you Ki." His voice dropped a few octaves. Kieran heard the sadness. "I will miss you." he added.

The familiar lump rose in her throat and there was no stopping the emotion she felt for him. She would miss him too, more than he would ever know.

"I'm sorry J," she apologised and started to cry again.

Joshua took her face in his hands, and kissed her. She kissed him back. "Just promise me one thing," he said, his eyes stared deep into hers.

"What?" she croaked. She closed her eyes and stroked the back of his neck with the tips of her fingers. She inhaled his scent. He always smelt like cocoa butter, she would miss that about him. It had been her comfort on many nights, just the smell of him.

"Make sure you are happy. Do not settle for anything less than one hundred percent happiness, Kieran," he said with a serious look.

She opened her eyes. "Why would you say that? I was happy with you when it was good," she told him.

He kissed her again. Softer this time, as if he was slowly weaning himself off her.

"You were about ninety percent happy. I knew somehow that I wasn't going to keep you for long. I think that's why I proposed so quickly. I knew it was only a matter of time. There's a whole wide world out there waiting for you, eventually you would have outgrown me. I think in some ways you already have," he told her still holding her face close to his.

Kieran kissed him on the nose, "Don't be stupid Joshua. We have shared big parts of our lives together. We are connected forever. I could never outgrow you, you always made me happy and I love you," she said defensively.

He laughed quietly. "I know you love me. You're just not in love with me and there's a difference."

Kieran stared dumfounded at him. It clicked in her head that had been the problem between them. It was like a cog in her brain turned into place. That was why sometimes it felt wrong. She would always love him and he would always have a part of her heart, but she was not in love with him. "How did I not figure that out sooner?" she asked him.

"Because like me, you wanted it to be true, you wanted to be in love with me because of our history. I guess I had my head in the sand, too. I knew it wasn't the same as it had been. I felt like you were running from something, or someone. I never had you completely then when you got pregnant and wanted to keep the baby and be with me, I put those thoughts to the back of my head," he explained.

Kieran was quiet. The worst part was he had no idea about Rome, or Kieran's feelings towards him. Another reason she had caused Joshua to suffer.

"I don't deserve a happy ending. I don't deserve to be able to start again. It's not fair that you get stuck here with the memories."

"God you are stubborn! You deserve this. You were never meant to settle down and have kids so young. You never wanted that for yourself, it was your dream to go off and see the world. Here's your chance, and as much as I will miss hearing your voice, seeing you, touching you and loving you every day, I'm telling you to grab it with both hands. If you want to owe me anything Kieran, promise me you will be happy. Do not settle for anything less."

She wasn't sure which one of them moved first; soon they were kissing, fast and urgent, passionately, as if they knew time was limited for them. He pulled away from her breathless and stunned by the intensity of the goodbye that was lingering between them. Kieran felt the wetness of tears on her cheeks. She couldn't tell if they were his or hers. She threw her arms around him sobbing.

"I promise you I will be happy," she vowed, "never forget how much I love you J, promise me that."

He nodded in agreement. If he spoke, his voice would break and he didn't want her to see him cry. In truth, he didn't know how he was going to live without her; he would though, because he knew they could never again be happy together.

They never said anything else after that. It had all been said. They lay in each other's arms for what would be their last night together.

31 CHAPTER THIRTY-ONE

Joshua officially moved out a week later. It had been an emotional and draining goodbye. Kieran seriously thought of stopping him. She tried to find a solution to their problem, as she heard him and Jarrell loading his belongings into the car while she sat in the bedroom. It was painful to watch. She knew though that it wasn't about what solutions she could find. Joshua didn't want to be with her anymore. It hurt her to know that she had tainted his love for her enough that he couldn't be with her without turning to drugs. Plus, he was right, she was not in love with him, she would be settling at ninety percent happy and she had promised him she wouldn't do that. So Kieran let him go. Deep down, she knew it was for the best.

Two hours after Joshua left, Kieran was still on the kitchen floor crying. She took a deep breath and got up. Her whole body was numb. She hobbled into the bedroom. Lily had snuck onto the bed and was fast asleep, she knew she wasn't allowed. Kieran was about to pick her up and put her on the floor, but she felt so miserable she curled up next to her and cried herself to sleep.

The following day, she sat at the computer flat hunting in Manhattan and couldn't believe the cost for some of them. Luckily, the company would be paying the rent, which made her happy and gave her one less thing to stress about.

As Kieran was moving to a new city, her main priority was her safety and she left the brownstone dream behind. Now she wanted an apartment with a concierge. She had three weeks before she flew out and was stuck on which one to choose out of three. She went back and forth looking at the virtual tours of different places. Her mobile rang, distracting her from property hunting and she looked down at the screen and smiled.

"Bonjour!" she said cheerfully.

"Ah, bonjour," French Fancy's deep husky voice replied.

"Ca va?" Kieran asked giggling. It was ridiculous he still had that effect on her.

"I'm well, thank you. How are you?" he asked switching to English. Kieran was relieved. She only knew a few phrases in French, and she had used two of them in the space of ten seconds.

"Not bad thanks, just apartment hunting."

"Ah, New York, Janet told me you would be leaving." Kieran was sure he sounded happy.

"Yes, so I won't be working with you anymore" Kieran said sadly.

"Well, it's true we won't be working together in London."

"I don't understand," Kieran said frowning.

"I'm moving to New York, too."

"What?" Kieran exclaimed before she could stop herself.

He laughed.

God even his laugh is sexy.

"New York Bulls want me to do some coaching over there, they've given me a year's contract and I've always wanted to live in New York," he explained.

"Oh my God, so we will both be in New York," Kieran's excitement was evident in her tone and she flushed.

Calm down. Gosh! Obvious much.

"Yes, so I am calling to tell you to give me a call when you get there. I am leaving next week and it'd be great to have someone to, umm, hang out with. My wife is going to stay here for a while longer."

"Of course, I'm not too thrilled about being over there by myself either, so I'm glad I will have some company."

"We can be tourists together," he joked.

Kieran laughed. Her friends were going to be so jealous when she told them.

"Where will you be staying?" Kieran asked clicking on another website link.

"They have found me an apartment in the West Village."

"Oh fancy," Kieran teased.

He chuckled. "I know. Where will you be staying?"

Kieran launched into her selection dilemma. Like a good friend, he listened and offered advice which she was grateful for.

She continued to ponder until a week before she was due to leave then chose a two bedroom condominium on the twenty fifth floor of a building, which came complete with a doorman on the upper east side of Manhattan. Kieran was excited when she made the decision and emailed the HR department to get the ball rolling. She couldn't believe one of her dreams was coming true.

She had been up late the night before packing and left work after lunch to go home to continue. She got easily distracted by other things and her flat was in chaos. So far, she managed to pack one suitcase of clothes, and there was still a wardrobe and a half left. She had yet to pack CD's and DVDs, the latter she wasn't sure if they would work in the states. She had arranged for Lily to go with her as she couldn't bear the thought of leaving her behind. She had taken her for all her vaccinations and she would travel in a special compartment on the plane. Everything else would be placed in storage. The new flat was furnished, though she would need crockery, cutlery, bed linen and some appliances, and new clothes were always needed.

In an attempt to get motivated, Kieran listened to her favourite India Arie CD, lay on the couch and grinned as she imagined her first shopping trip to the department stores. The sound of the doorbell interrupted her and she groggily looked at her watch. It was eight in the evening. She had fallen asleep for four hours. She was more tired than she thought. Her eyes scanned the room.

So much for packing! She thought as she headed to the door.

"Who is it?"

"I'm sorry I didn't realise you had other friends," came Christina's sarcasm through the door. Chantelle's laughter followed.

Kieran opened the door. Christina's mouth fell open. "Is it that bad? You look like hell," she said looking at Kieran's wrinkled clothes and her hair which was literally all over the place.

"It's a good thing you have friends like us," Chantelle joked.

Kieran closed the door and followed them into the front room. "We've come to help you pack," Chantelle told her.

"I still have a week." Kieran told them. She wasn't worried.

"No, you have five days, you're spending one night with your family and one night with us," Christina reminded her sitting down on the sofa, she turned on the TV.

"I have plenty of time. I don't even have that much more to do," she said shrugging.

Kieran saw their eyes scan the room and back at her like she was seeing something different to them.

"We are starting now, and here is something to help us," Chantelle pulled a bottle of wine out of her bag.

"You are a genius," Kieran told her as she went to find glasses and a bottle opener.

"Have you got boxes yet?" Christina asked an hour later when they were almost finished with the bottle and hadn't started packing.

"I have a few," Kieran said. *More like two.*

"How are you going to live by yourself if you can't get organised?" Christina asked, her face serious.

Kieran looked at Chantelle and saw her roll her eyes. Kieran tried not to laugh. She should have been expecting the lecture from her friend. "I am organised," she protested.

"So, what have you packed? Have you sorted out what you're taking? Have you sorted out what you are throwing away or putting in storage?" Christina questioned.

Kieran hadn't thought that far and tried to think on her feet. Noticing her hesitation Christina gave her a smug look.

"Okay, okay, let's pack," Kieran said laughing. She didn't see what the big deal was. She didn't have that much left to do.

They ended up driving around North London for hours, looking for all-night shops that had empty boxes before returning to Kieran's house to pack. She was relieved her friends had forced her to get her act together and were there to help, otherwise she would still be packing while her flight left without her on board.

"Kieran never again," Christina groaned at seven the following morning.

"I didn't know it would be that bad," Kieran said and yawned.

"Now your stuff is ready to be shipped. That's one less thing to worry about," Chantelle told her.

Kieran nodded and closed her eyes. She was going to have fun unpacking it at the other end - alone. A chorus of 'All by myself' rang in her ears. She groaned. She could think of nothing worse. For the first time Kieran wondered whether she was ready for the next chapter of her life.

On the morning of her flight, Kieran woke up earlier than usual. She had a serious hangover and regretted all the cocktails she had drunk the night before. She remembered having a great time with her friends, but didn't remember how she had gotten home.

She remembered feeling unsettled when Joshua hadn't been waiting up for her. Kieran still wasn't used to him not being there. She missed him and knew she must have eventually cried herself to sleep like she had done most nights, not just for Joshua; for Sienna as well.

She picked up a stack of baby clothes and placed them between her clothes in a suitcase. Kieran couldn't bear to give them away, or put them in storage. They were going with her. No one asked her what she did with them and she was glad. They would not understand her taking the memories with her when they were so painful.

She mentally went through her to do list for the day. Her dad was picking her up at one p.m. so she had plenty of time - in theory. Her flat was almost bare, just her bed, sofas and electrical appliances remained; everything else had been moved to storage or shipped. Her dad would meet the removal men the following afternoon to take the rest of her things to the storage unit.

After showering, Kieran packed her hand luggage and the remaining clothes in her suitcase. She heard the doorbell as she was washing the breakfast dishes. She took off her rubber gloves and answered the door to see Joshua standing there. Kieran's heart skipped a beat.

"Hey Ki," he said with a beaming smile.

Kieran threw her arms around him and hugged him tight. "I've come to wish you luck and say, bye," he told her. His face was pressed against her hair. She stepped back and surveyed how he looked. She was happy with what she saw.

"You're looking good J," she told him.

"So are you," he replied stroking her face.

"Going to work?" she asked.

"It's my weekend off, I wasn't sure what time you were leaving and didn't want to miss you," he explained looking into her eyes.

"Would you like to come in?" she asked, hesitantly. She wasn't sure if it would be uncomfortable for him.

"I'm not stopping. I just came to give you this," he told her bending toward the wall. He handed her a small bamboo plant in a vase, "It's for luck and happiness, although I know you won't need it. You'll be fine."

Kieran took it from him, touched by the gesture. "You didn't have to do that. Thanks J."

He kissed her on the cheek. "No problem," he took a step back. "I guess this is it then?" he brushed the side of her face with the back of his hand.

"Yep, I guess," Kieran said forcing the lump down her throat. She hated goodbyes and couldn't believe she had so many to do that day.

"Be happy Kieran, remember you promised," he reminded her.

She nodded as she fought back the tears.

He dropped his hand, turned and walked down the stairs to his car. "Take care," he said waving at her.

She nodded as the tears blinded him out of focus. She heard the car door shut and the engine start.

"Love you," she whispered as she waved at him, he looked at her one last time, waved and then he was gone.

"I'm not ready to say bye to you!" Kieran wailed a few hours later, as she walked her friends to the door for the last time.

"Kieran, we will see you next month," Chantelle said laughing and dabbing the corner of her eyes.

"When was the last time we went a month without seeing each other?" Kieran reminded her.

Christina and Amelia sniffled and the four of them group hugged, this time they found it hard letting each other go.

"I can't do this!" Kieran sobbed.

"Kieran, stop it! We said we weren't going to say goodbye,"

Amelia snapped.

"Seriously, you girls have been my rocks, more than my friends. You are my sisters, and I don't know how I'm going to survive one day without you being down the road from me. Thank you for understanding me when I didn't understand myself and thank you for always being there, I don't think I would've gotten through the last few years without you. I love you and I'm going to miss you so much."

"Gay," Christina mumbled before bursting into tears. They all embraced each other again as they cried. Saying goodbye was harder than any of them thought it would be.

Chantelle pulled away first. "I can't watch you leave, so I'm going," she said.

Kieran's lip trembled; she held in the tears.

This is it now, it's really happening.

"Yea, it's time," Christina mumbled.

"Don't let me down. Make sure you guys are on a plane in a month," she threatened trying to lighten the mood.

"Don't worry, we will be there," Christina said. They hugged again.

"Call us when you land," Amelia said as she walked down the stairs hand in hand with Christina.

Kieran nodded. The pain was worse than when she'd said bye to Joshua. Saying bye to her friends was like losing her limbs. They had always been so entwined in each other's lives it was going to be a big adjustment. Kieran stood and watched them leave, her heart breaking. She wished more than anything she could take them with her.

"Love you," her friends called as they walked up the street.

Kieran couldn't get the words out. She waved until she couldn't see them anymore and then went inside where she cried like a baby.

While waiting for her family, she had a sudden urge to call Rome. She had to explain to him how sorry she was. She felt that he was one part of her life that hadn't been resolved. She scrolled to his number and pressed the call button. Her hands were shaking and her heart was pounding. What was she going to say to him? What if he was rude to her? She'd deserve it...

"The number you have dialled has not been recognised," the recording of a woman's curt voice told her.

Kieran kissed her teeth and threw the phone onto the sofa next to her. What did she expect? She told him not to contact her so if he changed his number, he wouldn't be telling her about it. She sighed. It was a part of her life that would have to stay unresolved—unless she begged Courtney for his new number?

No, maybe it's just better left this way.

32 CHAPTER THIRTY-TWO

After her dad practically carried her to departures, while Corey stood rolling her eyes at her, Kieran said an emotional goodbye to her family.

It was hard watching them walk away from her and in the end she forced herself through the departure gate while they had stood and waved. She couldn't believe she was going to be so far away from them.

She thought back to when she had broken the news to her mother and Corey. She had been trying to drop hints to them for days, but always ended up chickening out. When she couldn't take it anymore she had blurted it out without warning, in the middle of a coffee shop.

"…I'm moving to New York."

Corey had almost choked on her coffee "What?" she asked frowning.

"I got a new job, so I'm moving…. to New York." Kieran knew her sister had her heard her the first time, Corey was staring at her in shock.

Kieran glanced at her mother who was unusually quiet, she hadn't even burst into tears which would have been her usual reaction, she wondered if her mum already knew.

Denise smiled as if hearing her daughter's thoughts. "Janet mentioned it to me before she spoke to you, she wanted to know how I felt about it first."

Corey gasped. "You knew about this?"

"Yes, and I think it's great," Denise told her daughters.

Corey looked at her mother like she was the biggest traitor in the world. "I can't believe this! She's talking about moving halfway across the world!" she said loudly.

"New York is eight hours away, it's hardly halfway across the world." Kieran grinned at her sister, trying to lighten the mood. It didn't work.

Corey's eyes filled with tears. "So you're going to up and leave just like that?" her voice cracked and Kieran suddenly felt bad for teasing her, she took her sister's hand.

"I just need to get out of here Corey, I can't put my life back together when there's so many bad memories here."

Corey pulled her hand away. "If you had told us what was going on in the first place you wouldn't be in this mess."

Kieran exchanged a pleading look with her mum.

"Just be happy for your sister and understand this is what she needs right now,"

"I am happy for her, I just don't think running from your problems is the way forward,"

Kieran noticed she certainly didn't look happy. "If I had gone to New York the first time none of this would have happened, I just think it's for the best." she said quietly.

"I agree," Denise said leaning over and hugging her.

Corey stared at them like they were crazy. "What does dad have to say about all this, surely he thinks the same as me?"

"Actually he thinks it's a good idea too," Denise smiled.

"He does?" Kieran asked raising her eyebrows.

Corey huffed from beside her. "Seriously?"

"Your dad is thrilled for you, he saw how bad things were on your birthday and he hated that he couldn't do anything to help, he just wants you to be happy." Denise said, this time it was her voice that broke.

"Don't," Kieran warned her.

"What about the twins?" Corey asked suddenly.

Kieran bit her lip to stop herself from laughing.

Denise rolled her eyes "They're twelve, they don't get a say."

"So I'm meant to just be okay with it?" Corey asked looking at the two of them.

"Yes," they answered in unison.

"I'm going to New York," Kieran said firmly. She had made up her mind.

Corey suddenly burst into tears. "You can't leave us!" she sobbed.

Kieran threw her arms around her sister. "You can visit me whenever you like, and I will try and visit as much as I can, please don't cry Corey,"

"It will be okay Corey, we will all miss her but your sister has to find her happiness, and right now it's not here," Denise said reaching out to squeeze her eldest daughter's hand.

Corey sniffled and wiped her face. "If this is really what you want you know I will support you, I just don't want you to think you have to do this, you could be happy again if you stayed."

"I do have to do it, but not to get away from my problems, it's something I've dreamt about my whole life, I can't not go," Kieran said before taking a sip of her now cold coffee.

"Anyway it's only for a year, it will fly by in no time." Denise said smiling at the both of them.

Corey looked at her mother and then at Kieran. The sisters exchanged a knowing look. Kieran could tell Corey knew there was every possibility her little sister would fall in love with the city and not want to return home. They couldn't tell their mother that though, not yet.

"I'll be back before you know it," Kieran said smiling.

Corey burst into tears again which had set them all off.

Their conversation felt like a lifetime ago and Kieran couldn't believe the day had come round so quickly; she was really leaving.

By the time she boarded the plane, she was tired of crying, though fresh tears fell at the thought of flying alone. She gripped the armrests of the chair as the plane started speeding down the runway.

She wanted to tell the pilot to turn the plane around. She'd changed her mind and wanted to go back home where it was comfortable, familiar and safe. What was she thinking? How could she survive by herself in New York?

I'm so not ready for this.

Kieran felt sick to the pit of her stomach at the horrible mistake she had made, she was seconds away from either screaming, or bursting into more tears then Rome entered her head. She held her breath and counted to ten before she deciphered the meaning. Was it a reminder, or was she upset that she didn't fix things?

She began to hyperventilate. The man next to her shifted in his seat. Kieran didn't look at him. She shook her head and exhaled trying to calm herself down. She told herself it was normal to be anxious and that there was no point freaking out. The other passengers were going to think she was insane and have her locked up when they landed if she was not careful. That would not be a good start to her new amazing life.

She took another deep breath. "I can do this," she said over and over. It was the only way she could stop herself from screaming out that she wanted to go back.

Her mantra didn't work. Halfway through the flight, Kieran started to think of excuses that would get her back home. She knew 'I've changed my mind' wasn't going to cut it. Maybe she could stay a week and then go home? She could even go check out the office, meet her new colleagues, she'd explain to them she'd made a mistake, they'd understand. They'd have to.

She had two hours to go before landing, so she decided to watch a movie to quiet her mind. Sleep eluded her and the panic about living in New York made the panic of flying tenfold.

When the plane started its descent Kieran looked out of the window The sun was setting in the West. Though the scenery was beautiful; masses of land surrounded by dark blue waters, Kieran had not imagined that landing in New York would look like that. Where were all the buildings?

The plane turned and the sun blinded her. After a few seconds, it turned out of the path of the sun, her eyes refocused and she gasped. Was that the famous jagged Manhattan sky line she could see in this distance? The sun cast its rays of golden light on one side of the buildings, so the city looked like half of it had been dipped in gold and the other side was covered in semi darkness. The side of the buildings facing the sun were a deep orange from the suns reflection, and they lit up the dark blue backdrop of the sky behind them.

Lights in buildings had started to come on and she could faintly see what she assumed were the headlights of the cars in the grid like streets.

It didn't look real at all. She must have been dreaming. Was she really flying over the city she'd wanted to visit her whole life? Her stomach flipped. Was it dread or excitement?

Kieran sat up and strained to see what else she could see. Her mouth fell open as she saw how beautiful the city looked at sunset, she had seen a lot of sunsets in her time; this one was magical, almost as if it was welcoming her.

"We have started our descent into New York City, you may be able to see many of the famous buildings of the New York sky line in the distance to the left including The Empire State building, the Chrysler building, the New York times building and the Bank of America tower, the four tallest buildings in New York. The Rockefeller Centre is also down there in Manhattan," the pilot announced over the tannoy.

Kieran heard other passengers exclaiming; she craned her neck to see if she could spot the statue of liberty; she had no idea where to look. She was going to make sure she visited all these places. She was a tourist even if she was going to live there.

Oh. My. God!

Her eyes caught sight of what could only be the Empire State building in the distance. Its height was amazing compared to the other buildings surrounding it. The excitement well and truly took hold of her and she realised how remarkable an island it could be for her. It was a little metropolis, and she fell in love with it before her feet had even touched the ground. A few minutes passed and Kieran still had her head glued to the window in awe.

"Good evening ladies and gentleman," the air hostess said. "We will be landing in New York City at La Guardia airport in approximately seven minutes, at seven fifteen. The temperature is a pleasant twenty degrees, so it will be a warm evening. We hope you enjoyed your flight and hope you will be flying with us again soon. Cabin crew prepare for landing," she said cheerfully.

Kieran gave a little squeal, or so she thought. She realised how loud it was when the man next to her shifted uncomfortably in his seat, and looked up from the magazine he was reading to frown at her.

Kieran grinned at him and he leaned as far away from her as he could, considering the space between them. Kieran laughed and turned back to the window. She was too excited to care.

She was not going home. She had so much exploring to do and so many adventures to go on. This was her personal island of dreams and possibilities. She would meet many people, make lots of friends and experience new things. Kieran would have the time of her life there and she couldn't wait for it all to start. The island was her home now and she couldn't turn her back on it yet.

Wow! This is where I live now!

The plane continued to descend and Kieran felt the shaking of the plane as its wheels came out ready for landing. She was ready for landing too, landing into her new life. Her new world.

There was no doubt in her mind that at times it would be hard. She would get homesick and she would miss her family and her friends terribly, but one thing she was certain of, she owed it to herself and she owed it to the people she left behind, especially her daughter, to be happy.

She thought about her bamboo plant as she stared out of the window at the city that never slept, the city that was waiting for her.

Joshua knew she wouldn't regret it once she got there. He knew her better than she knew herself. He knew that she settled with him for the wrong reasons and it almost ruined their lives. If he could stop her from doing anything like that again he would, and for everything she put him through, she had to stick to her promise.

The bamboo plant was her reminder; she would look at it every day and remember what she had been through and what she lost. Now she could look forward. She had been on a life changing journey and though she had regrets, that journey had led her to her dream. It led her to New York. Somehow Kieran knew she would be happy there, and to think she had nearly missed out on the city twice. She almost destroyed her life and she didn't want that for herself. Kieran wanted to be happy, that was all she was looking for; in her relationships and in her career.

As the wheels touched the concrete of New York City, Kieran felt real tears of joy roll down her face and it hit her then what she had been missing. She felt like she'd almost caught up with the happiness that had eluded her for so long, the chase was nearly over.

And so, as she undid her seatbelt and prepared to step off the plane and into her new life, Kieran made a deal with herself. Never again would she settle for anything less than what she wanted; anything less than what she deserved and just like she promised, anything less than one hundred percent happiness.

The End....For now...

ABOUT THE AUTHOR

Laurene Bobb-Semple was born in London, England where she continues to live and work full time.

She enjoys retail therapy, cocktails, travelling and, of course, reading and writing romantic fiction. Chasing Happy is the first in the 'Chasing Happy' trilogy.

If you are already missing **Rome** please visit www.laurenebobbsemple.com and sign up to my mailing list, you will receive a free copy of my eBook, 'Rome in a Day' where you'll relive the moment he and Kieran meet, from his point of view.

Enjoy and thanks for reading!

Printed in Great Britain
by Amazon.co.uk, Ltd.,
Marston Gate.